THE INSIDER THREAT

Also by Brad Taylor

One Rough Man
All Necessary Force
Enemy of Mine
The Widow's Strike
The Polaris Protocol
Days of Rage
No Fortunate Son

SHORT WORKS
The Callsign
Gut Instinct
Black Flag
The Dig
The Recruit

THE INSIDER
THREAT

BRAD TAYLOR

A Pike Logan Thriller

DUTTON
—• est. 1852 •—

DUTTON
— est. 1852 —

An imprint of Penguin Random House LLC
375 Hudson Street
New York, New York 10014

Copyright © 2015 by Brad Taylor
Penguin supports copyright. Copyright fuels creativity, encourages diverse voices, promotes free speech, and creates a vibrant culture. Thank you for buying an authorized edition of this book and for complying with copyright laws by not reproducing, scanning, or distributing any part of it in any form without permission. You are supporting writers and allowing Penguin to continue to publish books for every reader.

DUTTON—EST. 1852 (Stylized) and DUTTON are registered trademarks
of Penguin Random House LLC.

LIBRARY OF CONGRESS CATALOGING-IN-PUBLICATION DATA
Taylor, Brad, 1965–
The insider threat : a Pike Logan thriller / Brad Taylor.
pages ; cm
ISBN 978-0-525-95490-3 (hardcover)—ISBN 978-0-698-19085-6 (ebook)
I. Title.
PS3620.A9353I57 2015
813'.6—dc23
2015009129

Printed in the United States of America
1 3 5 7 9 10 8 6 4 2

Set in Sabon Lt Std
Designed by Leonard Telesca

To Jodie and Allan, for always being there, no matter what.

IS are animals. They're not human. They have a bloodlust the like of which I've never seen—it's as if they enjoy killing. They revel in cutting heads off—it's like their trademark.

—Kurdish refugee Ekram Ahmet, on witnessing atrocities in the town of Kobani after the Islamic State rampaged through it

You think you're safe where you are, in America or Britain. You think you are safe, you are not safe. We are coming for you.

—Florida resident Moner Mohammad Abu-Salha, the first United States suicide bomber, in a videotaped speech before his death in Syria

I say to America that the Islamic caliphate has been established . . . and we will raise the flag of Allah in the White House.

—Abu Mosa, spokesman for the Islamic State

1

Jacob Driscoll watched the four men, fascinated that they showed no resistance whatsoever. Completely resigned to their fate. A fly landed on the forehead of the nearest one—the one he was to kill—and the captive let it crawl about, tasting his sweat.

Jacob listened to the spokesman continue to rail in Arabic, a small crowd gathered in the square, outnumbered two to one by the gunmen. He didn't understand the language but could guess at what was being said.

These men are traitors. This is the fate that befalls all who oppose the Kalipha. *Stand with us, or suffer the same.*

Far from cheering, the small grouping of people looked cowed, as if they wanted to be anywhere but there. Well, that wasn't exactly true. They'd rather be on the outside watching than on their bellies with their necks stretched out.

The spokesman droned on, building toward a grand spectacle, his black tunic covered in dust, the AK-47 swinging about with his body language, and Jacob knew it was coming close. Execution time. His first.

In the seven months he'd been inside the cult of death known as the Islamic State, he'd witnessed many, many executions, acting as a gunman on the periphery, but he'd never done one on his own.

Not that he minded killing. It hadn't bothered him in the past, but the action had always been at the barrel of a gun, and he wondered how this would feel. In a detached, almost scientific way, he wondered if it would be different from carving the carcasses of the rabbits he'd killed in his youth. When he'd literally had to hunt for survival.

He looked at his partners, seeing Hussein fidgeting, the nervous tics growing more pronounced. He wasn't built for this cauldron, and Jacob thought it ironic that Hussein was the one who had recruited them. Convinced them to come to this faraway land.

Not that they had many alternatives after fleeing the cesspool of "rehabilitation" they'd been placed within. Killing the guard had ensured that.

Carlos and Devon, now known as Yousef and Talib, showed no such hesitation. They had embraced the cult of death completely, changing their names and fervently soaking up the Salafist ideology like a cactus in the rain. They were on board one hundred and ten percent, considering this day a sacred one.

Jacob played the role, but he'd long since lost belief in religion. Any religion. He'd had that whipped out of him by the pious Christian guards in the white house.

No, it wasn't the religion. It was the power. In this land, from Mosul to Raqqa, all that mattered was the courage of the battle-axe, and he'd found a skill that he didn't realize he possessed. He knew he would die here, but it caused no angst. In truth, he had died long ago. All that remained was for him to slip the coils of his mortal frame. The difference was a cause. He wouldn't end up as a page-two news story, caught stealing hubcaps and gunned down in the street. And neither would the men he had brought.

Hussein may have recruited him, and the other two may have changed their names, diving headlong into the myth of the Islamic State, but he was the leader of their small group. Just as he had been inside.

With that mantle came a responsibility.

A man in black, completely covered from head to toe, like something out of a *Star Wars* movie, began walking his way. Jacob inwardly grimaced.

His name was Abu Yabba Dabba Do, or some other unpronounceable Arabic crap, but Jacob called him Ringo. As in the Beatles. An Islamic fighter from England, he and others like him considered themselves above Jacob and his band because they were of Arabic descent. Ringo was Yemeni. Jacob was a mutt.

"So, Jacob, are you ready for your first kill?"

He drew out the name *Jacob*, showing his disdain for the Biblical reference and the fact that Jacob refused to take an Arabic one.

Jacob said, "It isn't my first, you shit."

Ringo smirked and said, "Death with a gun is not killing. You'll see. This is absolute control. Absolute. As Mohammad dictated. But your little band of Lost Boys wouldn't know about that."

He was being tested, which was what he expected. Ringo had beheaded many men, and had developed a cult following on Twitter and other social media, but he was an ass. A small man who gained importance after the fact. After the fighting was done, using his knife and a camera to become famous. At his core, Jacob knew Ringo felt a challenge from him and his friends.

Four tightly knit brothers, forged by a fire outside the Islamic State, with—except for Hussein—no attachment to any Arabic or Islamic heritage, they were an anomaly. True foreign fighters in a foreign land. They called themselves the Lost Boys because of the iconic '80s movie, but the analogy was apt. They lived in a world of the shadows.

And they killed better than most.

Jacob said, "Ringo, step away."

That was all.

And Ringo did.

Ringo had seen the punishment the Lost Boys had endured. With two blond Caucasians, one African American, and Hussein, the one who had recruited them, their arrival had been anything but welcoming. Convinced they were spies or, at best, journalists, the emir had subjected them to inhuman conditions and cruelty. And they had thrived.

Because of the white house.

Ringo said, "You are not the future. *We* are the future. *Kafir.*"

Jacob looked up, catching Ringo's pompous eyes with the dead ones he possessed, and said, "The future is dictated by the man who isn't afraid to die. Is that you?"

Ringo said, "I am not afraid. I have proved that multiple times."

"Do you wish to die today? Without fear?"

Jacob knew his reputation from Mosul preceded him. Knew that

Ringo hated the fact that he was a blond-headed, blue-eyed American, with no ancestral ties to the coming caliphate, but he also knew that Ringo couldn't get past the stories that had grown into legends.

Ringo snarled and said, "We'll see, Lost Boy. We'll see."

And walked away.

The man on the square finished his speech, which was like every other one, and not unlike speeches given by the blowhard preachers Jacob had heard every night in the reform school. There was a flourish at the end, then a knife placed in his hand.

He looked at the four men prostrate in front of him, and felt the hatred.

They were snitches. People who'd sold out the clan for money, giving information to the enemy for targeted air strikes and intelligence on how the Islamic State functioned. Jacob would have had qualms about killing someone for eating pork or not wearing a head wrap, but he had none for traitors.

They were the ones who had caused the pain in his past. Had caused the trips to the white house.

He looked at his man, a Kurd. Strange that such a person had been able to penetrate so deeply, given the fight against the Peshmerga, but he had. And he'd given massive information about the Islamic State to the Americans. Now he would die.

But the fly on his forehead would live.

He swished the man's face and saw it buzz away. Then leaned down, wrapping his hand into the hair, pulling it up.

As he had as a child, when the next "new" father had come into the room, stinking of whiskey and taking off his belt, he let his humanity float away, flying on a cloud. Gone.

He became a man of stone.

He looked down the line, seeing the ubiquitous cameraman recording the killing, then Carlos and Devon eagerly snatching up their own heads and looking to him for guidance. He waited on Hussein.

He caught the tears on Hussein's cheeks and wondered if the man would go through with it. He saw Ringo advancing and shouted, "Hussein!"

His friend looked at him and Jacob said, "For the white house. Do it for the white house."

Hussein rapidly nodded, then pulled up the head.

Jacob turned to his own man, seeing his eyes rolling back, feeling the shaking in his body, the bright orange smock soaked in sweat.

The first swipe brought a gout of blood. He reached bone, and began sawing.

2

Omar al-Khatami watched the tape without a shred of revulsion, technically looking for the propaganda value. His media specialist described how he had enhanced the image, optimizing it for YouTube, and said, "This will show the Americans what happens to their spies, and prevent others from following in their steps."

Omar said, "Yes. Post it tonight. End with the heads on the bodies."

The door opened and the emir of northern Syria entered.

Mildly surprised, Omar exchanged greetings and said, "Adnan, I thought you weren't returning for two days. What is happening with the oil?"

Adnan smiled and said, "It's coming along. We only have the wells pumping at a quarter of capacity because of a lack of technical skill, but we have found men to change that. Soon, we will double our output and our revenues. As long as you don't lose the fields."

Omar said, "No chance of that."

"Good, because I have some news. The caliph has bestowed a great honor on you. He has promoted you to the emir of external operations."

The mention of the leader of the Islamic State brought a pause. Confused, Omar said, "External operations? I am the military commander here. I still have work to do. Aleppo to take. Damascus to burn."

"The caliph has heard of your Lost Boys, and he thinks it is time to use them."

"Then do so, but don't pull me from my men. They fight because of me. The time is growing short for victory. This will be a setback we can't afford, given the American attacks."

Adnan scowled and said, "The caliph believes in you. And your American cell. He chose you."

"Why? We have many men who could do this. You, for instance."

"Because of your skill, for one. And because you are Chechen. You have traveled in Europe. You know the contacts. You can build the attack he desires."

"These Lost Boys are untested. I'm unsure of their commitment."

Adnan looked at the computer screen, the video paused with four men slicing and cutting. "Is this not them?"

"Yes."

"They show commitment here."

"It could be simple fear. Hussein, the Jordanian, cried throughout."

"And the others?"

Omar grudgingly admitted they showed no qualms, but said, "The leader of these so-called Lost Boys hasn't even taken a proper name. He still goes by Jacob."

"But you tested him, yes?"

Omar nodded. Adnan said, "The name is why we want them. They will all revert back to their true names. They are gems buried in the sand. Four Americans with no ties to America. No families, no Facebook, no Twitter. They are unknown. Unlike the others who brag to their friends back home, nobody knows they exist. No authorities are fervently tracking their moves. True?"

"Yes. We instructed them on methods of recruitment, but they have shown no interest."

"Good. Keep it that way. Their mission will be the greatest recruitment drive we have ever seen."

The media specialist fidgeted, getting Adnan's attention. He said, "Emir, they are on this video. The one we're going to post for the world to see."

"Don't. Broadcast the stills of the verdict, but keep the executioners out."

Omar said, "We lose the impact with our own people. They need to see. They need to fear."

"Then let our men see it, but obscure the faces, and do not put it on social media. The Americans must be protected, and those *kafirs* in the United States have ways of determining the tiniest things."

Omar nodded. "It will be done. What about me?"

Adnan looked at him with a question, and he said, "When do you wish me to start, and what will the target be?"

"Targets. Plural. Every attack attempted by that windbag Zawahiri and his diseased al Qaida has resulted in failure because the *kafirs* managed to hear about it before execution. We have to assume the same will happen here, so we will plan two attacks. One for them to chase, and one for you to execute."

Omar went through the ramifications in his mind. Having fought in Grozny against a barbaric Russian army, he recognized the wisdom. He said, "Just preparation for the false flag attack?"

"No, no. A real attack. One that you will plan from start to finish. You pick the target and the method. The only parameter is that it must be outside of the caliphate. Outside the borders here. If it succeeds, so much the better, but its primary mission is to protect your American cell. Obviously, don't tell the other team about that. Let them think they are the chosen ones."

Omar absorbed the words, glancing away and nodding, thinking through the possibilities. He said, "And the real target?"

Adnan smiled and said, "The real one will destroy the heart of the *kafirs*."

3

Waiting on the president to finish, eyes glued to a television, Colonel Hale sat with the rest of the Oversight Council, watching him getting raked over the coals in the White House James S. Brady Press Briefing Room. Kurt heard a little exasperation escape President Warren, a sign of the pressure he was under. Kurt felt for the president, but was glad it wasn't him on the stage. The conversation would have been much less civil.

"Kathy, I don't know how to make it any more plain. None of the men in the picture are either American or working for United States intelligence. They are not in any capacity agents of the United States. Clearly, those barbarians will kill anyone just to prove a point. And that point is fear."

The hands in the pressroom rose again and President Warren said, "Thank you," then walked off, hearing a chorus of shouted questions. Sitting in the Old Executive Office Building next door to the White House, Kurt knew it would be a good ten minutes before he arrived for their meeting.

He looked around the room. Only half of the thirteen members of the Council were present, the other half most likely getting castigated right now in the Oval Office over the scourge of the Islamic State.

Kurt knew how President Warren felt: impotent.

For nearly a decade he'd been hunting terrorists with a unique counterterrorist organization that had unparalleled success; yet despite its efforts, a greater threat had appeared. Not only appeared but had thrived like the spread of Ebola in a ward of children. And his unit could do nothing about it.

The thought made him sick, driving home the fact that the application of military force would never be decisive in this fight. The roots were too deep, and the siren call too sweet. No matter how many terrorists he prevented from individually killing, there was a pervading ability for ideology to transcend logical thought, spreading like a cancer through whole societies he would have otherwise thought normal, civilized humans.

Because of it, the Islamic State had become the most powerful terrorist organization on the face of the earth.

Encompassing broad swaths of terrain across Syria and Iraq, the group possessed a brutality unheard-of in the modern world. But it was not unlike the history of the past. The Islamic State cowed its opponents with an unparalleled ability to instill fear, using new social media grafted on twelfth-century barbarism to depict beheadings, crucifixions, torture, and mass executions, and in so doing recruiting waves of others to continue the killing.

As much as Kurt would have liked to take the war to them, that wasn't his job. The current fight was for overt conventional and special operations—something he had done long ago, but had given up for the secret war. A war he had thought he was winning. Now he wasn't so sure.

He was the commander of a Taskforce created after 9/11, designed to operate in the shadows outside of the established intelligence or defense architecture. In short, to operate outside of the law. The entire experiment had been an enormous risk—but deemed necessary due to the threat. They worked without legislative oversight, and routinely flouted the Constitution to protect US national interests—read: US lives—and, while Kurt had his qualms about creating such an organization, he'd agreed to head it up because the menace had been grave.

Now, after nearly a decade of work, he wondered if it had been worth it. The threat had grown beyond grave, and they'd created an organization that could prove absolutely cancerous to US liberties. And for what? To see the rise of the most powerful terrorist organization in history ripping through the Middle East like Genghis Khan?

The light flashed above the SCIF secure door, and President Warren entered, followed by Kerry Bostwick, the director of the CIA, Alexander Palmer, the national security adviser, and the secretary of state, Jonathan Billings.

They took their seats, and without preamble, a staffer brought up a digital photo showing four bodies lying facedown, dressed in orange, each with a grisly head positioned above the shoulder blades.

President Warren said, "Everyone here?"

Kurt said, "Everyone except for the vice president."

The Oversight Council was the sole body that approved Taskforce actions. With the exception of Easton Beau Clute, the chair of the senate select committee on intelligence, all were either civilians or in the executive branch. The president had wanted no part of politics interfering with the decidedly explosive operations the Taskforce conducted, and had made the decision to exclude the legislative branch.

Clute had been read on because of a past operation involving his son and daughter. While serving in the military, both had been taken hostage and faced certain death. They'd been saved from slaughter by the Taskforce. Because of it, Kurt had no doubt about his loyalty.

President Warren said, "Kerry, give them the damage."

The D/CIA said, "We have managed to introduce three assets into the architecture of the Islamic State. Their crypts are BOBCAT, LEOPARD, and COUGAR. The third from the end in the picture was BOBCAT, and he was the only one reporting."

Kurt thought, *Holy Shit. He* was *ours.*

"BOBCAT was a Kurd we'd recruited in Sulaymaniyah a long time ago, back when we were still in Iraq and still fighting against the Ba'athists and al Qaida. We activated him seven months ago, and he agreed to penetrate into Syria. We knew it was a risk, because he was a Kurd, but there have been several reports about Kurdish recruits, so much so that the Kurdistan administration is beginning to fear a second front, inside its territory. He made it in and began reporting, surprising the hell out of us. I mean, he was *really* reporting. Quality stuff. He was very good, and our biggest fear was that he'd be caught by a Kurdish PKK, YPG, or some other Peshmerga unit and skinned alive as a traitor. We never saw this coming."

The secretary of defense said, "And the others? Are they in the picture as well?"

"No. We don't know who they are. Probably poor saps just caught in the wrong place at the wrong time, or on the outside, reporting for one of the Gulf States or a rival militia. They aren't ours."

Kurt said, "You mentioned 'quality stuff.' What was he reporting?"

"You know our greatest fear is that a bunch of radicalized citizens come home or go to Europe to wreak havoc. With the FBI in the United States and the CIA's liaison with European allies, we have a pretty tight handle on who's gone overseas. Or at least we thought we did. Ninety-nine percent are 'citizens' of a country but are one step removed from the Middle East. Like the English rapper who beheaded James Foley. He's a British citizen officially, but he's of Egyptian descent and his father was extradited to the United States for the African embassy bombings in '98. Which is to say, he had a background of terrorism to begin with.

"BOBCAT popped our comfortable bubble on our view of the threat. Six weeks ago he reported on a group called the 'Lost Boys.' He didn't know what they were, only that they existed. It was included with a ton of other reporting from him. Four days ago, he sent an in-extremis message saying they were United States citizens, and they were 'Americans.' That was all. We don't know what he meant, but we think it indicates that they're *not* of Arabic descent. They're pure, dyed-in-the-wool all-Americans. And they might be coming home."

His words settled in the room like a foul stench and President Warren said, "So, the question is, what do we do about it?"

Secretary of State Billings opened his mouth, and, after the words spilled out, Kurt wondered if he'd forgotten every single Taskforce mission he'd ever been involved with. Or maybe he was just stupid. But then again, Kurt had grown a little biased against the man.

"Can't the Taskforce get in there? Maybe send them to Damascus to start looking for these guys?"

Kurt waited for someone to describe how stupid that was, then realized it was on his shoulders. He said, "Sir, we are not a green-machine combat force. We operate within the fabric of sovereign nations, taking the fight to the terrorists who use the infrastructure of those nations either wittingly or unwittingly. Clandestinely."

"Yeah? So what? Wasn't Pike's team in Damascus a few years ago?"

Kurt ground his teeth, looking at the president. Warren simply nodded at him to continue, but with a little bit of a glare, meaning, *Don't embarrass him.*

"Okay, the 'so what' is that, for one, ISIS isn't in Damascus. President Assad still owns that terrain. Even if we could get a team in—which we can't now—it would do no good. Secondly, the damn country is a war zone. I don't know if you've been watching the news, but we're pummeling the shit out of them from the air. The Taskforce operates using plausible covers in otherwise unsuspecting countries. I can't send a team of supposed agricultural engineers into Syria and expect that cover to last more than five minutes. There *are* no NGO gringos operating in the countryside. There's no way to penetrate ISIS with the Taskforce. I mean, are you dumb enough to think they could drive into Raqqa, the heart of the Islamic State, wearing mirrored shades and hauling genetically altered wheat seeds and not expect them to end up on their own video?"

He saw President Warren scowl at the last statement and turned his own glare on the man who'd asked the question.

Billings snapped his head up at the harsh words, glancing toward President Warren for support. He wasn't getting any. He said, "What about your vaunted walking disaster? Pike Logan? We pulled him back in against my vote, but maybe we can use him here. Surely he could do something. I thought he was Captain America."

Kurt knew he was being baited. Pike was the best team leader he had, with a supernatural ability to solve problems. Which is to say he killed terrorists with an unbridled skill. He was also a trouble magnet—both on the enemy side and on the side of the Taskforce, causing massive headaches when he went off the reservation, using his own intuition instead of listening to the very council that was supposed to authorize his actions. Because of it, he'd been fired twice, and brought back into the fold each time due to his abilities. At the end of the day, no one could argue with success.

Kurt knew Billings was sick of being on the Oversight Council. Tired of the risk of being exposed for operating outside the law, leaving his long tenure in public service in tatters on the front page of the *Washington Post*. He was a career diplomat, and the very notion of the Taskforce assaulted his sensibilities. He didn't like authorizing missions for a normal team, but was petrified of Pike. In his mind, Logan was a loose cannon who was going to cause the downfall of all of them. Pike's past successes mattered little. Secretly, Kurt believed Billings would rather have a terrorist attack occur than sit on the Council for one second longer.

As much as he wanted to, Kurt didn't need to get in a fight right now. He chose the better—and honest—answer.

He said, "Yeah, I'm with you. If anyone could do it, it would be Pike's team. Unfortunately, he's engaged right now in Africa. As a matter of fact, trying to shut off some Islamic State funding from a corrupt Saudi citizen."

4

I felt a fingernail stroking my back, right between my shoulder blades, then a whisper. "Wake up, sleepyhead. I have to go. Before one of those early birds comes and knocks on the door."

Meaning, *Before someone finds out I'm here.*

We'd been out very late the night before developing a pattern of life on our target, who wasn't what one would call a pious Muslim, and I figured everyone from the mission was still asleep. The target wouldn't be doing anything until at least noon.

I rolled over, leaning on an elbow. "Jennifer, I don't think we're fooling anyone anymore."

She said, "Pike, appearances matter. I know they know, but there's no reason for the team leader to throw it in their faces. I think Knuckles tolerates it, but only because we make an effort to not let it show during operations."

Knuckles was my second in command, a Navy SEAL who, strangely enough, was a stickler for the military prohibition on fraternization within the chain of command. I think it had something to do with a bad experience in the close quarters of a ship with a male supervisor. Or maybe he was just a stickler. Either way, unfortunately for him, neither Jennifer nor I were in the military, and it was my company. My team. But she had a point.

"So you want to scuttle out of here doing a walk of shame to keep up the appearances of 'don't ask, don't tell'?"

Before she could answer, I heard the door to our room fly open. Like a high schooler hiding from her mother, Jennifer threw the covers over her head. I bunched up the thick bedspread to hide her form, tossed a pillow over her pile of clothes, then turned to rip into the idiotic maid who'd entered.

Instead, I saw Knuckles standing in my room.

He said, "Retro's finally cracked into the backbone server for the hotel. We've got Panda's computer, and he's making plans."

I scowled and said, "What the hell are you doing? Don't you know how to knock? How'd you get in here?"

He held up a keycard and said, "I just told you Retro got into the server. We can make a key for any room in the hotel."

"So you figured you needed one for *my* room?"

He smiled and said, "I figured you'd be asleep and didn't want to bang on the door."

"I *was* asleep. Asshole."

"You want to dress and come up? Or stay in bed?"

I was already out and throwing on my clothes. He turned back to the hallway leading to the door, disappearing from view. I heard the door open, then, "Oh, Jennifer, you can come too. We won't say anything about you wearing the same clothes as last night."

Shit. The door closed and she poked her head out. "Well, that's pretty embarrassing."

I said, "Tell me about it. Getting caught skulking around like kids is more embarrassing than getting snagged red-handed."

She kicked over the pillow, grabbed her clothes, and went into the bathroom, saying, "I'm using your toothbrush."

I started shoving things into my pockets and unplugging my phone from the charger, saying, "I guess that makes it official."

I was putting on my shoes when she came back out fully clothed, brushing her hair. She said, "It wasn't before?"

The words caught me off guard, because I was just making a joke. Jennifer and I had definitely become partners in more ways than just our business, but we'd never verbalized it. I'd made one statement in the heat of the moment on our last mission, then we'd just sort of dropped it. I was a shit show when it came to such things, and she knew it. She was patient, but I wasn't sure how long that would last.

I said, "Well . . . yeah . . . I mean . . . I was just . . ."

She hit me in the chest with a towel and said, "Oh, please. Spare me. Should I go up?"

Relieved, I stood and held out my arm to the door. "Yeah. Get it over with. You show any weakness with these guys, and they'll start ribbing us forever."

We got in the elevator and I noticed her clothes, stained from our mission last night and wrinkled from lying on the floor of my room. She looked like she'd slept in them. I said, "You're really going to wear what you had on last night?"

She snapped her head to me and said, "I was. . . . Should I go change?"

The car stopped and I said, "Too late. Welcome to the lion's den."

I stepped out and she said, "I'm not going in if you think they're going to laugh at me."

"Come on. They know better than to laugh at the managing partner of Grolier Recovery Services. You can fire them."

Jennifer and I were the owners of GRS, ostensibly a firm that specialized in archeological research. We worked for private entities, universities, and others to help facilitate excavations around the world. Since most archeological digs were in areas that were borderline Wild West—like Nairobi, Kenya, where we were now—I handled the security side of things, something that fit my military background. Jennifer, with her anthropology degree and insatiable appetite for annoying anyone within earshot about ancient history, had the hard part of acting like we really were a legitimate archeological firm.

In truth, the whole thing was a shell company that cloaked a top secret counterterrorism unit called the Taskforce. Back in the day, when I was on active duty, I had been a team leader in the unit. Now, I was a civilian co-owner of a cover organization and a team leader yet again. It had been a rocky road, starting with recruiting Jennifer—a pure civilian and a female to boot—getting her read on, trained up, and admitted to the unit, and had ended with me convincing the commander, Colonel Kurt Hale, to let my company start operating not as a support asset, but as an actual team.

On the surface, for anyone looking at the pure black and white, the demands were insane. *Let a female Operator into the Taskforce? Let a civilian company start running missions? No way.* But there's much more to special operations than what can be tallied on a sheet.

Jennifer had passed selection with flying colors, and had put away a few bad guys with her innate skill alone before even attempting that trial, and I . . . well, I was fucking Pike Logan.

Enough said.

That might be a little bigheaded, especially given some of the mistakes I'd made in my past, when I'd slipped into the abyss and lost my way. But that was history now, and at the end of the day, even with the stains, I was the most successful team leader the Taskforce had ever used. Just ask all the people walking around today because I had been there to prevent their death. You couldn't, of course, because they didn't know I existed.

The Taskforce command and I had been going back and forth, with me running things off the books and the Oversight Council wetting their pants because of my actions, but finally Kurt had said I was officially in charge. Which gave some members of the Council fits, but since I'd personally saved the lives of Oversight Council family members on my last mission, those idiots were shut down.

Kurt had told me not to screw it up, then sent me to Africa to chase a fat Saudi with bags under his eyes that made him look like a panda bear.

5

I knocked on the door of our makeshift tactical operations center, a suite at the InterContinental Hotel in Nairobi, feeling foolish that Knuckles had waltzed right into my room while I had forgotten to get a key to my own TOC.

I waited for the door to open, knowing someone was eyeing me through the peephole. It took forever, making me wonder if they were screwing with us. Brett finally turned the knob, saying, "Retro's in back, working the computer. Someone's on it right now, but it ain't Panda."

A short African American built like a fireplug of solid muscle, he moved aside and I said, "Did you need to get a box to see out the door?"

I walked in and waited on a reaction to Jennifer. All he said was, "Hey, Jenn. Good work last night."

That was it.

Whew.

She gave off her brilliant megawatt smile and said, "Thanks."

I started back to the bedroom and heard Brett say, "Yeah, it was a long night, huh?"

Good work? Long night? I slid my eyes his way, but he was innocently standing by the door. No grin or anything else to indicate a double entendre.

I went to the back bedroom, where Retro had set up all of our computer network stuff, and saw him staring at a screen, Knuckles standing over his shoulder.

I said, "What's up?"

"Retro's accessed Panda's computer through the hotel Wi-Fi. He's covertly turned on the laptop camera and we can see who's typing, and it's not him. It's the security chief."

"And? Why do we care?"

"He's setting up a visit from an escort. You know, because Panda's forty-two wives aren't enough. Real pious."

A thought hit me. I said, "Hey Retro, if you can see what he's typing, can't you just rip through the computer? Image the hard drive and end this mission right now?"

"Already did. This laptop isn't the one we want. I'm willing to bet that one is air-gapped from the Internet. We still need to locate it and physically access it."

Ali Salim al-Naggar—aka Panda—was a wealthy Saudi businessman with strong indicators he was providing money to Salafist jihadist groups. One of many around the world defying their government—or, in some instances, operating with its tacit approval—to fund extremists. In this case, we believed he was using his business connections as a clearinghouse to funnel money to the Islamic State—otherwise known as ISIS, ISIL, or Da'esh in the shifting sands of Arabic naming conventions—the rampaging lunatics running amok and beheading everything in their path in Syria and Iraq.

This mission was strictly intelligence collection. Ordinarily, we would physically remove the terrorist from the playing field, but in this case, Panda was a well-known businessman with ties to the royal family. There was no way to remove him covertly. Unlike the assholes we usually chased, his disappearance would cause an unacceptable investigative effort, so we decided to simply gather irrefutable evidence of his wrongdoing, then feed it into the system.

Our relationship with the kingdom went from hot to cold, depending on the political vagaries of the day, but the Saudis were scared spitless about the Islamic State, and worried about the growth of jihadist insurgents in their own country. There wouldn't be a lot of tolerance and love once we boxed up Panda's transgressions. Which is where the laptop came in.

So far, we'd been stymied because his penthouse was always manned, and nobody had been allowed past the door, including the daily maid service.

I said, "Why do we care about his sex habits? It's not going to help us. Going in when he's with her is the worst time because his security force will be on edge for the duration she's there."

Brett said, "That's true. We can't get in *behind* the escort, but if we can control the escort herself, maybe she could do it."

They were all looking at me and I could tell they'd already come up with some half-baked plan. Had already talked it out. I said, "Okay, spill it. You want to pay off an escort to attack his computer? No way. I'm not trusting some prostitute to do it."

Retro said, "He's not requesting some skinny local. He wants a white girl. A very expensive white girl. Over a thousand dollars for the night."

"What difference does that make?"

They all looked at each other, gathering their courage, then Knuckles threw it out. "We have a white girl."

It took a moment for his words to register. *Jennifer?* I said, "No fucking way. You have lost your mind."

Brett saw me winding up and said, "Wait, Pike, wait. Just listen. This'll work. She goes in as the escort; we go in as security. We'll be there the entire time."

Retro kicked in, "Yeah, come on. You've been saying all along that Jennifer offers the team something because she's a female, and this is it."

I said, "Acting like a whore? Really? That's what you thought I meant?"

Jennifer interrupted, "Hey, you've got a short memory. You threw me out on the streets in Prague as a streetwalker. Remember?"

Everyone quit talking and looked at her. I said, "That was just an act to get a reaction from organized crime. I wasn't sending you in with a man. No way."

Retro said, "She won't be with him. . . ." He started to continue, but dribbled off at my glare.

She said, "I'm willing to listen. What's the plan?"

I said, "Jennifer, no way. If you think I'm—"

She cut me off with a raised hand, something I would never have tolerated from the men. She said, "What's the plan, Knuckles? I'm sure you've thought this through."

He looked at her, then at me. He waited a beat then said, "Well, first we interdict the real escort. Then, Brett, Pike, and I go with you as security. You get in the bedroom with the guy and swipe him with ABS. When he's in the bathroom shitting his guts out, you clone the computer."

She nodded, thinking, then said, "How quickly does ABS work? I don't want to fend him off while I'm waiting."

Knuckles grimaced and said, "Trust me, it works within seconds."

I heard the discussion and realized the plan might actually succeed. In fact, it most likely *would* succeed. ABS was a chemical compound applied to the skin in the form of ChapStick, lipstick, or other ingenious methods. It was absorbed into the bloodstream and caused massive, explosive gastric distress. Being knuckle-draggers, we couldn't pronounce its complicated chemical formula and called it ABS—for Atomic Blow-Shits. We'd used it on a past operation, and Knuckles had accidentally gotten it on himself as well as the target, and had suffered the consequences.

He said, "It's fast, but if you get it on yourself the mission's over. Then you'll both be fighting for the toilet."

I said, "But we don't even know where the computer's located. What if it's not in the bedroom?"

"Then we call it a wash and she leaves. Panda will be in no condition to do anything either way. The only risk is that Jennifer's potentially out of play for future operations."

I said, "You're good with this?"

"Well, yeah. It's just a mission, and Retro's right. Unless that guy's asking for a male, I'm the only one who can do it. You'd do the same if he was gay, right?"

Not on your life.

"Uhh . . ."

Brett cut in, saying, "She's already proven she can sneak in and out of hotel rooms at night. She's a natural."

I whipped my head to him, catching a smirk, which wound me up.

He said, "Whoa, why are you getting pissed? She's climbed walls as slick as marble to access rooms all over the globe. That's all I meant."

I glared, seeing all of them trying mightily to stop from grinning. Even Knuckles. Jennifer said, "Yeah, Pike. *You're* the one that's always making me climb and break in somewhere. Let's do it."

She started walking to the door and I felt the shame of her being the butt of a joke she wasn't even getting. I was disappointed in the team's lack of respect.

I gave them a death stare, then caught up to her with the team trailing behind. I stopped her, wanting them to admit they were secretly giving her a slight. "That's *not* what Brett meant."

She rolled her eyes and said, "Pike, I know exactly what he was saying. I just didn't think it required a response. They're juvenile boys playing juvenile games. Just like you do. But it's the first time they've ever made fun of me to my face. Progress."

And it dawned on me she was right. It wasn't a lack of respect. It was the opposite. They felt comfortable enough with her on the team to actually start ribbing her. Just like the guys on the team did with one another. As I had done when I'd entered the room with Brett.

She continued, glancing from man to man. "But they'll be a Taskforce team tonight. Wired for the mission. Right?"

Knuckles smiled. "You better believe it."

6

Under his breath, I heard Knuckles say, "Holy shit." I turned and saw Jennifer coming out of the bathroom of the cheap hotel room we'd rented to prepare for the mission. She looked stunning. I mean, I might be biased, but she was breathtaking. I wondered if it was just me, but I saw that Brett was slack-jawed. Mesmerized.

She caught the looks and said, "What? Is this not what a high-end escort would wear? Should I look sluttier or something?"

Nobody said anything, and she said, "Hey, what's the problem?"

Knuckles finally managed to find his mouth. "Man alive, Jennifer, you clean up nice."

"What's that supposed to mean?"

"Nothing . . . It's just that you're always wearing jeans or something. Hair in a ponytail. No makeup. I've never seen . . . I mean, you never . . ."

"So my natural state is ugly?"

He started stumbling over his words, and I saw her smile.

She's going to have no trouble with Panda.

We'd spent the better part of the day getting ready for our little adventure, going to the Westgate mall in Nairobi, the same one those assholes from al-Shabaab had assaulted in 2013, slaughtering over seventy people. The men had spent all of thirty minutes buying cheap suits. Jennifer, on the other hand, went hog wild. She was allowed to shop on the Taskforce dime, and she'd spared no expense, buying a black cocktail dress with a modest décolletage, jewelry, makeup, a mani-pedi, a high-end wig, and some sort of ridiculously expensive high heels called

Jimmy Choos. I had no idea how she knew what to purchase, because she routinely wore nothing but work clothes for the business, but apparently, it was in the female DNA.

Now that she was wearing the outfit, complete with elbow-length black gloves to protect her hands from the ABS, it made our suits look like sweatpants.

She said to me, "You sure Retro's stopped the real escort? It's going to be embarrassing if we both show up."

Knuckles said, "Yeah, he confirmed while you were in the bathroom. He spoofed Panda's IP and canceled the appointment. Taskforce had to pay the cancellation fee, which I'm sure will cause some issues after we get back when the bean counters see what it's for. I told him he was the one claiming the receipt on his travel voucher."

She smiled and said, "Okay, then. Let's get it done."

I said, "Final backbrief. We get to the door and do what?"

Brett said, "I knock and talk to the head of security, telling him we have to be in the suite while she's there."

"And when he says no?"

"I insist."

"But not too hard. Act like you're doing your job, but don't turn it off. Jennifer?"

"When it gets heated, I say I'm good going in alone."

"Knuckles?"

"I interject that we're staying right outside. Then hand her a phone, telling her to call if there's trouble."

Before I could ask, Jennifer said, "I go in and place the phone on the nearest available desk or table."

I wanted the phone in her hand when she entered, so she could set it down with the small clutch she held, without having to pull it out, which would look awkward. The "phone" itself was a digital camera with multiple fish-eye lenses that would give us a view of what was going on inside.

I said, "Then, you do your siren dance and go into the bedroom. Wait until he closes the door, which he will, then wipe him with the ABS. When it takes effect, slave the computer. I promise it'll be sitting somewhere close to where he sleeps."

She nodded and said, "If there's trouble?"

I held up a keycard. "We're coming in, courtesy of Retro. Keep on comms with your earpiece. You call, and we're in. Backup, just start shouting. Retro's got the security laptop slaved, so he'll hear it even if we don't."

She held up the thumb drive with the software Retro had built. "How long will this thing take?"

"Retro says five minutes. It's got a search algorithm imbedded in it, so it won't be imaging a bunch of porn, but depending on how much data he has, it might be longer. It'll flash green when it's done."

"What if it takes a lot longer?"

"He'll be shitting for hours. You'll be fine."

She squinted at me and I smiled. "Hey, we don't pay you just to be eye candy."

She said nothing, but I was sure I'd hear about that comment later. I went around the team and said, "Any more questions? We good?"

Nobody said anything, and I looked at Jennifer. "On your command."

A devious little grin slipped out, and she said, "Showtime."

7

Brett pulled the car into the drop-off lane at the InterContinental Hotel, and Jennifer saw the doorman looking quizzically inside the town car, then gawking full-on at her. Brett jumped out from the driver's seat and engaged him.

She felt Pike nudge her and heard, "You good? Ready?"

She smiled, and it wasn't false confidence. "You just be ready to get in if this goes sideways."

He gave her a reassuring grin and said, "I hear *buffalo*, and I'm breaking the door down."

Buffalo was the code word Jennifer would use if she needed help, chosen because the likelihood of it being used accidentally was nonexistent, but she could slip it into a conversation without the other party knowing. It would be completely her call, and they would do nothing unless they heard it.

Knuckles said, "Time to act the part."

They passed through the lobby and reached the elevator, Brett pressing the penthouse level. The car began to move and Jennifer leaned back. Behind her, Knuckles practically knocked her into the wall, exclaiming, "Watch what you're doing!"

She stutter-stepped in her Jimmy Choos, slapping her hand into the rail, glaring at him. He said, "You've got the damn ABS on your zipper. No way do I want that on me again."

They'd created a layered approach to applying the compound, starting with the zipper on her dress. If he didn't use that, she had condoms laced with the stuff and a final chance with a lipstick tube holding a piece of red plastic that looked exactly like it should, but was coated with the chemical like poison from a dart frog.

Pike said, "Okay, okay. Knuckles is a little sensitive to the effects. Shitting your pants will do that. Break out the camera for test."

Brett pulled out what looked like a Samsung Galaxy S5 and turned it on. Pike said, "Retro, you getting feed?"

"Yep. Seeing all like intended. Jennifer, where'd all your hair go?"

She was wearing a black wig with a bob cut that ended just below her ears. Pike said, "Truthfully, I was wondering the same thing."

Jennifer said, "Female secret."

The elevator stopped and Pike said, "Game on. No mistakes. We get in and out clean."

Knuckles said, "All you, babe."

Pike said, "Six on security. Two outside and four in. We go hot, remember the numbers. Take them all out."

Jennifer took a breath. He saw it and said, "Hey, it won't come to that. Just making sure for worst case."

She said, "You guys had better be there if I call."

Brett said, "You know it."

She looked at him, saw the determination on his face, and became calm. They might make fun of her, and even have qualms about a female being on the team, but she knew that all such issues were gone now. On the X, all that mattered *was* the team. And she was one of them.

Worst case, she also had an ace in her back pocket.

Pike.

An inhuman wrecking machine that would break open the earth itself to protect her.

The elevator's doors opened, and they saw two security goons outside Panda's suite. They got within five feet of the entrance before both men held up their hands. One was Caucasian, and when he spoke, they heard a strong Eastern European accent.

"Please stop."

They did.

"I must search her."

Pike said, "Yes. We understand. We've done this before."

He did so, working professionally, patting the length of her body and massaging her breasts and groin, but taking no pleasure from it. He turned and nodded to his partner, who swiped the door.

As planned, Brett took the lead. The European stopped him and said, "Only her."

Brett said, "No way. That's not how it works. We go in with her."

"Not here. You stay outside."

"We can't do that. She's our commodity. We protect that. It's why we're paid."

The European repeated, "Not here. Your company knows that. No harm will come to her. It's why I'm here as well."

Jennifer said, "It's okay. I'm willing to go in alone. He's a repeat customer."

Brett looked disgusted, then Knuckles said, "Take this. If there's a problem."

And the phone was passed.

Pike said, "We stay out here. Right here."

The European said, "If you want to do that, I must search you."

She entered the suite, hearing Pike say, "Fine. We don't have any weapons."

The room was large, even by penthouse standards, with a full-length dining table, a sectional sofa, and a gigantic wide-screen TV tuned to an American sitcom. To the left was a bedroom, and deeper in she could see a small hallway leading to what was presumably the master suite. And her target.

Three men were on the couch, and a fourth met her at the door. She recognized him as the chief of security from the night before, a large Arab with a neatly groomed beard wearing a suit.

He said, "Leave your things out here."

That was easy. She put the phone down but kept her small clutch. He said, "Remove your jewelry."

"What?"

"No jewelry in the room. I'm sorry."

She nodded and removed her earrings, a bracelet, and her necklace, setting them next to the phone. He said, "Your Bluetooth as well."

Uh-oh. "Why? That can't hurt anyone. I use it to talk to my security."

"You don't need security. Please. Remove it."

She debated, then did as he asked. He said, "Thank you. Your purse as well."

No way. Deal breaker.

She opened it, saying, "This is for the client." Inside were a bottle of lubricant, a tube of lipstick, and several condoms. Hidden in the lining was the thumb drive.

He poked his finger around the inside, pressing the lining and causing her to hold her breath. He nodded. "Is okay. Follow me."

She felt the eyes of the other three men on her as she walked to the main bedroom, the large Arab leading the way. He stopped and knocked on the door, saying something in Arabic. There was a muffled reply, and he opened the door.

She entered, seeing Panda lying on the bed in a bathrobe, the front open, exposing his erection, large folds of flab dripping onto the bedspread. About as disgusting a sight as she could imagine.

He looked her up and down and said, "Beautiful as always."

She scanned the room and saw a laptop on the desk by the bed. *Bingo.* She heard the door close behind her, then felt movement, startling her. The large Arab had remained in the room.

Panda saw her reaction and said, "Don't worry. He only watches."

8

I saw Jennifer enter the room, feeling a little like a pimp. Disgusted with myself. As the door closed I almost wished Panda *had* been gay. Then I would have sent in Knuckles without any qualms. Hippie hair and pretty-boy face—he'd be perfect.

As we backed away from the door, Knuckles saw my grin slip out. We moved a respectful distance down the hall away from the two security men and Knuckles asked, "What's funny?"

I said, "Nothing. Just thinking about the mission."

Our earpieces came alive. "Pike, this is Retro. Camera's in place, but they made her remove her earpiece."

I glanced at Knuckles. "Why?"

"She had to remove all of her jewelry. Probably just a security precaution."

Retro knew what I was going to ask next. "Don't worry. I'm getting good audio from the laptop in the den. I can hear well enough."

"Even when she's in the bedroom? With a closed door?"

"Well, no. Not if she's not shouting."

Knuckles saw my face and said, "Don't even think it. She made the call to go in. She could have aborted. Let her play it out."

Retro came back on. "Uhh . . . Pike, the head of security went in with her and he hasn't come back out."

I took one step toward the door, and Knuckles grabbed my arm. "Don't. She can handle herself. Don't let your emotions get in the way here. She's just a teammate. Let her solve the problem."

What he really meant was *I told you this fraternization would become an issue*. Did I want to go in because a teammate was in trouble, or because it was Jennifer? I tried but honestly couldn't separate the two. I locked eyes with him and he slowly shook his head. I knew if I went in, he would question my judgment forever. Just like I was questioning it right now.

I keyed my Bluetooth and said, "Retro, roger. Keep eyes on."

Jennifer turned back around to the fat Panda and said, "I'd rather he didn't stay. This isn't a show. It's all about pleasing you and you alone."

Panda scowled and said, "He stays. I pay you well enough to do anything I want. In fact, when we're done, you can pleasure him as a reward."

Great. Well, he's about to leave, you fat little Jabba the Hutt.

She turned on the megawatt smile and said, "Okay," then motioned to the security chief. "Can you give me a hand with my dress?"

She kept her eyes on Panda, watching his own widen as the dress slipped over her shoulders. She said, "You must wear protection, you know?"

He said, "No, no. I paid extra. I'm not unclean."

The dress pooled at her feet and she saw his breathing increase. She twirled around, wearing nothing but her bra and panties, still dressed in her Jimmy Choos, and said, "You want this, you wear protection."

He said, "I don't have any."

She saw his lust and knew she held the cards.

"I have one," she said.

She pulled out the poison-laced condom packet and tossed it to him on the bed, wondering how long the ABS took to work and beginning to believe the security chief had missed getting it on him.

Panda gave what he thought was a sultry smile and said, "You want me to wear it, you put it on."

You have got to be kidding.

She winked at him, hiding the desperation building like a freight train picking up speed, and said, "I'm going to freshen up. You be ready when I get back."

She started to move to the bathroom when the security chief doubled over, holding his stomach. He stood up and looked physically tortured, gritting his teeth so hard she thought she could hear the grind. He shouted something in Arabic and raced out of the room.

Panda said, "Looks like you got your wish. Something he ate."

She flashed the megawatt and sauntered into the bathroom, feeling his eyes boring into her bottom. She closed the door and sat on the toilet, breathing heavily.

She waited for an eternity, fearing she would hear him call, ordering her to apply the condom. *Just get it over with. How bad can it be? You still have on your gloves. They're sterile.*

She gathered her courage and stood up just as Panda came flying into the bathroom, robe trailing behind and limp penis flopping under his flabby belly, successfully encased in a condom.

He screamed, "Get out, get out!"

And she did, closing the door behind her. She heard an explosion of gas, and what sounded like someone pouring muddy water into the toilet, then a moan.

She grinned, racing to her clutch. She dumped the contents, tore open the lining, and pulled out Retro's thumb drive. She leapt across the bed, jammed it into the port, and powered up the computer. According to Retro, passwords and other security were irrelevant. If it started blinking red, it was working.

The computer beeped and blinked, a small hourglass turning in circles on the screen forever, and she wondered if it had some protection against their exploit.

Come on, come on.

The thumb drive light blinked red, a rapid strobe. She smiled, and the door behind her burst open.

She whirled around, seeing the three remaining security personnel. One shouted at her in Arabic, another ran to the bathroom. The third charged, a tall African with long, ropy braids.

She screamed, "Buffalo! Buffalo, buffalo, buffalo!"

The African reached her and she raised her fists. She struck him once in the head and he bodily threw her across the room, slamming her into the wall. She fell to her hands and knees next to the contents of her clutch. She snatched up the lipstick tube and stood.

She kicked off her heels, ripped off the lid, and jabbed it forward, waving it back and forth like a knife. The man laughed at her and said something to his partner. The first man returned from the bathroom and rattled off something in Arabic. Their faces grew grim, and they advanced on her.

Keep them off of you. Seconds. Only need seconds.

The African darted forward, and she slashed his face with the lipstick. He batted her hand away, the lipstick tube flying across the room, and he slapped her cheek with a glancing blow. She tucked her head and tried to knee his groin. The second man reached her and both began punching.

She drove through them, holding her hands against her head for protection, trying to reach the door. The African grabbed her around the waist and threw her onto the bed. The other two dove on top of her. She shrieked the code word over and over, and for the first time felt genuine fear.

Two things happened that restored her courage. One, the man on top of her explosively shit his pants. And two, she heard her name shouted.

From her personal wrecking machine.

9

I paced in a tight circle, waiting on either Jennifer to call or Retro to tell me she was coming back out. Neither happened.

Knuckles said, "Easy, slayer. No news is good news."

"I know. I know. But this is killing me."

Retro came on the earpiece. "Security chief just came running out holding his stomach."

Knuckles smiled. "See. Told you. Let her go."

The words brought great relief. Somehow Jennifer had managed to separate the two, and was driving on with the mission.

I paced about for another five minutes, then heard Retro say, "One of the three remaining went to check on the security chief. The other two are getting antsy. Standing up and pacing. Staring at the door. They don't have the courage to go in yet, but it's building."

I looked at Knuckles and said, "Get ready. Which one do you want?"

"I'll take the Arab."

Brett said, "I'll take the white boy. Kick some cracker ass."

I said, "Okay. This goes bad and I'll jump in to help either one of you that's losing."

Retro said, "He just came back out. He's shouting in Arabic. They're moving to the door."

Knuckles understood the same thing I did. He said, "It just went bad."

I flicked my eyes to the men outside and said, "Get to it."

Brett and Knuckles started walking toward them, me falling in behind. They glanced our way and Knuckles said, "Hey, we got a question about the timeline here. We got some boozing to do. How long does your boss take?"

The Caucasian smiled and said, "He's quick. Trust me. Even with the Viagra, he can't last more than thirty minutes. Your girl will be making easy money."

Through the earpiece, Retro said, "They're in. . . . Buffalo, buffalo, buffalo. She's calling buffalo."

I said, "Execute." And unleashed a little bit of hell.

Brett darted inside the reach of his target and drove his knee into the man's groin before he could react. The European doubled over and Brett grabbed his hair and redirected his knee to the man's face. He collapsed.

Knuckles' man saw the movement and had a split second more time to react. His brain realized a threat, but his reaction time was nowhere near what was necessary. Knuckles came in full bore, forgoing any submission holds for total destruction.

The man snarled and snapped out with a jab. Way too late to do any good. Knuckles blocked the ineffectual blow and slammed his fists forward like a pile driver, one, two, three, four, snapping the target's head back so hard it hit the wall and left a dent. I saw him slide to the floor, his face a bloody mess.

Doesn't have the callsign Knuckles *for nothing.*

I moved to the door and said, "Get their weapons. Give me an up. Hurry."

I held the keycard from Retro, ready to swipe. They ripped through the clothing and pulled out two SIG 226 pistols. They nodded and I said, "No killing unless necessary. We can still get out clean."

I swiped the card and nothing happened. I swiped again. Nothing.

Retro said, "She's screaming. Get your ass in there. She's in trouble."

I said, "You fuck! The card isn't working."

Brett went back to a body and started ripping through pockets. I felt the fear grow, my imagination running wild. He found a card and tossed it to me. I swiped, and the door light went green. We flowed in.

I entered on the run and saw the size of the room, a bedroom on the right. I said, "Brett, hit the bathroom with the security chief. Knuckles on me."

We ran to the back bedroom, exploding in and seeing Jennifer on the bed wearing nothing but a black lace bra and panties, three men on top of her.

I lost my mind.

I reached the first man before he realized I was there. I snatched him by the collar and the groin, hoisted him in the air over my head with rage alone, and threw him directly into the mirror on the wall, shattering it. I turned to the next man and saw Knuckles applying a submission hold, the man screaming in pain, bent over with his arm in the air, his wrist locked up. I took a hop, gaining speed, and kicked him in the face as violently as I could. His head snapped back, a spray of blood blooming.

Knuckles dropped him, looking at me in shock. The mirror man was rolling around on the floor, and I returned to him. Giving out a little rage.

He held his hands up, woozy from the impact with the wall, and I whipped my leg, catching him just behind the ear and laying him out. I whirled to the final man and saw that Jennifer had wriggled out and was now standing on the side of the bed, breathing heavily.

The man rolled onto the floor, holding his stomach, groaning. Then I noticed the odor. The man farted, his bowels letting loose a wet sound. Jennifer said, "He's no threat."

Knuckles said, "What the hell was that? Why didn't you just shoot my guy? Easier than beating him to death."

I said, "Hey, like you said, she's a teammate. You fuck with my team, you get my heat."

He shook his head and said, "Uh-huh. Yeah. Right."

I turned to Jennifer. "You okay?"

Brett entered the room, weapon at the ready. He nodded at me.

Jennifer said, "Yeah, yeah. I'm good."

Brett sized up the situation and lowered his weapon, saying, "Oh, you're better than good. All sweaty and wearing lace. Pike's not going to sleep tonight."

I snapped my head to him, not believing what had come out of his mouth. He said, "What? Are you blind? Am I wrong?"

Knuckles gingerly picked up her dress and said, "No, you're definitely not wrong."

He handed it to her and said, "I'm not touching the zipper. No offense."

Brett moved to the laptop and said, "I got green. We have it."

Jennifer wriggled into her dress, using her gloves on the zipper, and I said, "Let's get the hell out of here."

We started to the door, with Jennifer still rummaging around the room. I said, "Jenn, get a move on. What are you doing?"

She looked up at me, in between one body with significant damage and another rolling around on the floor voiding his bowels, the odor almost overpowering.

She said, "I'm not leaving my Jimmy Choos."

10

Kurt stopped his Oversight Council briefing at Kerry Bostwick's outburst, not wanting to believe what the director of the CIA had just said.

The room went quiet, and Kurt's triumphant update on the successful mission in Nairobi crashed against the very data that Pike had obtained. On the screen was a graphic uncut video of the beheading of the CIA source known as BOBCAT, found on the Saudi facilitator's computer, but that wasn't what had the room shocked.

President Warren said, "You're telling me that the man holding the knife is LEOPARD?"

"Yes. I believe it is."

"But their faces are blurred out. How can you be sure?"

"Before LEOPARD was inserted, he bought a shirt for the rock band AC/DC. It said 'Back in Black,' just like the one that man is wearing. He thought it was funny. And LEOPARD had a tribal art tattoo on his forearm. Just like that man."

Kurt thought, *That's not good.*

President Warren said, "So a source who was recruited, trained, and vetted by the CIA was inserted into Syria and never reported. Instead, he ends up beheading the one CIA source that *was* reporting? BOBCAT?"

Kerry swallowed and said, "It appears so. And that's not the worst. He's an American citizen."

The room broke into a buzz, cut short by President Warren waving his hand for silence. He said, "Lose the crypt. You're not protecting a source anymore. Tell us the story."

Kerry took a deep breath and said, "We had no penetration of ISIS. No way to determine what was going on inside the organization. At the same time we were scouring the Middle East and finding BOBCAT and COUGAR, someone came up with the idea of inserting an American. I mean, we've had plenty of US citizens go over and join the fight, so we decided to cloak an asset in that mantle. We conducted research and found LEOPARD in Florida. His real name is Ali Jaafar Hussein, and he's basically a hood. His father is Jordanian and his mother is a crack addict. The father left the family when Hussein was only four, going back to Jordan, then his mother went to jail. He's been in and out of foster homes and reform schools ever since. He was perfect. No familial ties and he had handed us leverage in the form of some charges he was facing for shoplifting. We offered to get them dropped and he accepted."

Jonathan Billings, the secretary of state, said, "And you thought this was a good idea?"

Kerry bristled. "It *was* a good idea. Actually, a *great* idea. Intelligence work is never perfect. We couldn't predict this."

"Couldn't predict it? You sprung a guy from jail and expected him to become James Bond? Really?"

Kerry said, "We knew the risk of him fleeing once he was in Turkey, and we were comfortable with that. Worst case, we figured he'd just disappear, but best case, he reported, and that far outweighed turning free a small-time hood in Europe. We never expected him to join the fight. He had no jihadist background. He knows more about Christianity than Islam. We conducted a thorough background on him. He was vetted. He had not a shred of anti-American sentiment."

"Or he hid it well, playing you much better than you played him. Did you hear what was said before he started carving?"

"Yes."

The secretary of defense said, "I didn't catch it. What was it?"

Kurt pulled out a transcript from a folder and said, "The man known as LEOPARD appears to hesitate, and the man on the right says, "For the White House. Do it for the White House."

Kerry said nothing, knowing the evidence was damning. President Warren said, "Is he the leak? The reason that BOBCAT was exposed?"

"No. The two were completely separate. LEOPARD had no knowledge of BOBCAT. None."

"Well, with that statement, we have to assume he's doing the killing because of the US government. And so is the man who spoke on the right. Any idea about him?"

Kurt said, "All we know is he's Caucasian. He's not an Arab."

Billings said, "And that he hates the United States. Great. The CIA just trained a terrorist to come back home and blow up the White House."

Kerry said, "LEOPARD won't get one foot into the United States. As soon as I leave here, his passport information will be out to every government in the region."

President Warren said, "Okay, okay, this isn't Taskforce business. We'll deal with the fallout later. Kerry, get ready for a blistering from the intelligence committees."

Easton Beau Clute, the chair of the Senate Select Committee on Intelligence, said, "Yeah. I'll do what I can, but it's not going to be pretty."

President Warren said, "Continue, Kurt. You were saying something about ISIS oil?"

"Yes, sir. We have enough evidence on Panda to convince anyone in the royal family that he's doing things antithetical to their interests. We pass it to the Saudis and he's a goner. Unfortunately, Panda wasn't just a financial facilitator. He was in Nairobi coordinating for actual expertise. Manpower for ISIS in the form of technical experts in the oil industry."

"He was smuggling men?"

"Yes. ISIS has captured several oil fields in both Syria and Iraq, but they don't have the expertise to make them operate at full capacity, so they're losing money. They already sell the oil at a steep discount on the black market, and they need the income to maintain their hold on the terrain."

"So we stopped that as well?"

"Yes and no. We have a name on the far end. A guy in ISIS called

Adnan al-Tayyib. We think he's some finance minister and the man co-ordinating for the technical skill. Panda's going to be gone, but not soon enough. He's arranged for the passage of five Nigerian Muslims who worked the oil fields near Lagos. They're set to travel in three days, and the Saudis won't do anything to Panda until he returns to the kingdom. They aren't going to arrest him in Kenya. Which means the men are going to make it into Syria."

"So what do you recommend?"

"Take them off the board. All five. We can't remove Panda because of the repercussions it will cause, but these guys are nobodies."

"How can you do that? We've never executed a problem set that large."

"Pike's working the issue now. All he needs is the authority."

11

Jacob heard Ringo's familiar voice and thought, *Great. They had to bring that asshole here as well?*

"Looky here. The little Lost Boys. They must need you to carry my luggage on this mission."

Hussein gave a weak smile. Carlos and Devon hooted, as if it were the funniest joke in the world, not even understanding that they were the butt of it. Jacob said nothing.

Ringo sidled up to Jacob and said, "Do you really think they're going to use a 'Jacob' on this mission? This is the Islamic State. The caliphate."

Jacob bit back his words, remembering the warning the Chechen had given. Not so much the words, but the way they were delivered. Omar was not a man to trifle with. Unlike Ringo.

But not here. Not now.

After the killing of the snitches, the Lost Boys had been pulled out and loaded on a truck, Ringo laughing at their fate. They'd driven for hours in a convoy of four trucks, out of Raqqa and into the desert. Jacob knew they were heading east. Toward Iraq.

They'd passed the town of al-Mayadin and had veered south, the rest of the convoy heading to al-Qa'im and the Iraq border.

Now on their own, the dust and wind growing tiresome in the bed of the Toyota HiLux, Jacob had recognized the terrain. They were going back to the training camp where they'd learned to fight. Where they'd also had to prove their fealty to the Islamic State. He questioned if it was more punishment or more training. They still had their weapons, so he was hopeful it was the latter.

He saw Hussein trembling against the cab, and began to wonder about the man. On some makeshift parole for good behavior, Hussein had been freed from the school and the punishment of the white house, and had—according to him—traveled to Syria, then spent six weeks in the embrace of the Islamic State. When he'd come home, he'd visited Jacob, Devon, and Carlos, still inside. He'd told wonderful stories about Syria and life in the Islamic State. He'd begged them to return with him, and looking back, Jacob wondered if he just didn't want to go alone. If he had been afraid to go alone.

Jacob had listened, and had liked the idea. After Hussein's visit, he'd researched the Islamic State, and seen what they were. Carlos and Devon had begun watching YouTube videos, consumed by the violence and the absolute law of the sword. In short order they'd converted to Islam, reading everything they found on jihadist websites, falling head-long into the siren call of the biggest gang on the planet. Forget about the Crips and Bloods. The Islamic State was taking the concept and making it span the globe. And they were doing it for a greater purpose than just money or drugs.

The kicker for Jacob had been the total control over his own destiny. He knew life would be brutal, and possibly short, but it would be his choice. No more dealing with authority. No more trips to the white house. When he died it would be on his terms, for a cause. Not for some sadistic guard's pleasure.

Jacob had faked the interest in Islam well enough, and all three decided to make the trek. They'd set a plan in motion for escape.

The reform school was, at its base, a prison, but it was privately run by a supposedly Christian institution, and as such, it fell outside of any federal oversight. A contract money mill that served the state as a dumping ground for malcontents who weren't worthy of flooding the real prison system, it wasn't very secure. Fear of the guards kept everyone in line, the white brick building in the center of the courtyard a daily reminder of the beatings and molestation administered for any breach of protocol.

When that fear ceased to exist, though, it was easy enough to escape. Especially if, like Jacob, you were willing to kill to do so. He only wished the hated captain of the guards was on duty the night they had fled. He would have enjoyed beating him to death with the pipe-legs he'd pulled from the dormitory bunk bed. As it was, he had to settle for a lesser guard. One who'd been somewhat kind, and had never taken him to the white house.

As he slammed the pipe into his head over and over, the skull splitting open and the brain matter staining the concrete floor, he reflected on how the smallest bit of scheduling had defined the guard's fate. And the fact that the guard had done nothing to stop the others from using the white house.

They'd fled into the woods and met Hussein, waiting with a pickup. He'd taken them to an abandoned hovel in the slums of Miami, and they'd waited for the door to be kicked in. It had not. The closest thing had been their names and faces spread across the news for a day and a half. After that, they were forgotten, at least by the slavering twenty-four-hour cable channels.

Even so, they lived like hermits, not daring to venture out except for the one risk they needed to attempt to leave: applying for passports. A scary prospect, they'd ventured to three separate post offices and made the applications, the bored postal employees dutifully taking their information for a trip to the Cayman Islands.

They'd lived in the dark, eating junk food delivered by Hussein, for four weeks. Miraculously, the passports had arrived without the police delivering them in a SWAT van, and they'd purchased tickets to Turkey, fleeing with nothing but the clothes on their backs.

Hussein had said that IS was paying for the flights, and Jacob had believed him, but now, due to Hussein's behavior, he was having doubts. The three of them from the school had flown together, connecting through JFK in New York. Hussein had flown separately, going through Dulles airport in Washington, DC. He'd stated at the time that he'd already purchased his ticket, and it seemed to make sense, as they linked up just fine in Istanbul, but watching Hussein tremble gave Jacob questions.

He said, "Hussein, you all right?"

"Yes. Just tired."

"Tired? Or scared?"

Hussein huddled against the wind and said, "A little of both."

"Why is it different to you now? Syria seems exactly what the news reports said it would be. What's changed from when you were here before?"

Hussein said, "Nothing. I don't know."

"Did you come here before? Did you really travel here?"

Hussein's eyes slid to the desert for a moment, then came back. He started to say something, then thought better of it. He said, "Yes, of course. How do you think I got the money to pay your way here?"

"Hussein, I don't know, but we're tighter than the Islamic State. We lived through the white house. There is nothing stronger than our brotherhood."

Hussein said, "The Islamic State sent me. That's what happened."

Jacob said, "Okay. Okay. But if you want to run, I'll help you. We'll stay."

Jacob glanced at the pair in the back of the pickup, the wind preventing them from hearing. He said, "Carlos and Devon have found a home. A reason to exist. And so have I, but I haven't forgotten what you did for me inside."

Hussein said, "I can't run. I wouldn't make it back to Turkey. Have you seen what they do to anyone who turns their back on them? They'll torture me. Kill me."

Jacob looked out at the setting sun, the red rays scorching the desert sand. He said, "We're all going to die sometime. Better to do it on our feet."

Hussein put his head into his hands and began to weep.

12

They'd continued on the dirt road, seemingly driving straight into the desert, until Jacob could see the training camp in the distance. A collection of tents and crumbling buildings, it was some type of abandoned industrial facility. Maybe for oil. Maybe for something else. It reminded Jacob of a scene out of *The Road Warrior*. Whatever it was, the compound provided the necessary infrastructure to house up to two hundred men, and ample buildings to learn the art of urban fighting.

The lone HiLux drove straight through the center, Jacob seeing armed men dressed in black scurrying about and hearing shouted commands filling the air. But the triumphant black flags of the Islamic State were nowhere to be found. When Jacob had first arrived on the battle-field, it was all the rage to wave them about for Internet videos and pure intimidation. Now they were hidden. An indication of the fear the leadership felt from American surveillance, and the devastating air strikes that followed.

None of the men gave them a second glance. They drove past the collection of tents used as a barracks to house the fighters, an area that Jacob knew well, and continued on to a two-story concrete building on the outskirts of the compound. A much more hospitable residence than the tents, it was where the instructors stayed. And where the Lost Boys' motivation had been tested.

Jacob tightened his grip on his AK-47, feeling his pulse increase. The driver, a thin Arab with a sharp nose and a spotty, mangelike beard, stopped the truck and waved them forward.

They jumped out of the back, following him single file inside the building. They were led to the second floor, walking down a hallway of broken brick and buckled windows. The Arab stopped outside the one room with a functioning door and knocked. Something was shouted in Arabic, and he opened it.

Jacob saw a dilapidated couch, two metal chairs, and a desk. Behind it was an imposing man with a ginger beard and a face made of cracked granite. Creases like veins running through stone and faded blue eyes that had seen more than enough to eradicate any notion of mercy.

He said, "I am Omar al-Khatami."

Jacob heard the name and wondered what was going on. Omar had been his upper-echelon commander in the fight for Mosul. A Chechen with a myth of invincibility surrounding him like a black shroud because of his battlefield prowess and his unrelenting cruelty. Something learned long before the Islamic State, in the bloodbath known as Grozny.

"Take a seat. We have some things to discuss."

The Lost Boys looked at one another for support and he barked, "Sit down. Now."

They did so without further encouragement, cramming themselves into the broken couch.

He went face-to-face, searing them with the absolute power he held over their fate. He settled on Jacob last.

"Jacob, yes?"

"Yes, sir."

"You came to us from the United States, swearing *bay'ah* to the caliphate. To the Islamic State, yet you still bear the name of the infidel. Why?"

Jacob saw the heat coming from the Chechen's eyes, and met it with his own. "That's the name I was given at birth. It's my identity. It is who I am."

"Most, when they embrace the true path, also embrace Allah. Dropping the false trappings of the hedonistic West. Yet you do not. It causes questions."

Jacob felt the fear drop away, his soul moving again into the netherworld, just as it had when he'd sliced the traitor's neck. And every time he had crossed the threshold of the white house. He retreated to a numb place where pain existed but didn't control him.

He looked the Chechen in the eye and said, "My commitment isn't held in my name. It's held in my actions."

He waited on the outburst. Waited to be led to the Islamic State version of the white house. He was surprised.

Omar glared at him for a brief pause, then laughed and said, "Yes, yes, I guess that's true. You were a lion in Mosul. Can you be such a lion when there are no bullets shooting at you? Can you show the same commitment?"

Jacob said, "Of course. Just tell us what you want. We'll execute."

"What I want is for you to martyr yourself."

The words hung in the air, Hussein hearing them and beginning to hitch his breathing, Carlos and Devon entranced, wide eyes staring at the Chechen.

"Can you do that? Or is your name an indication of your commitment?"

"My commitment was shown in the creation of the caliphate. In the fight for Mosul."

He maintained his eye contact with the Chechen, no longer caring about his fate, and said, "There was only one Iraqi army unit in Mosul that fought. While the other Iraqis ran away, and the Islamic State claimed victory, I ensured that success. I killed them all."

The Islamic State succeeded by terrorizing its enemies, using brutality to beat them into submission before a fight, which is exactly what happened in Mosul when the Iraqi army fled. All but one element. They apparently didn't get the word that their buddies were running through fields in half-dressed civilian clothes and getting gunned down by giddy Islamic State fighters driving in SUVs.

So they fought.

Jacob and the other Lost Boys were merely cannon fodder in the battle, as his element was composed of new recruits, and had no real martial skill. When their leader had been killed, the discipline broke down and the recruits began to retreat. Jacob had rallied them, fighting like a demon, and had actually routed the Iraqi element force on force, using will alone.

Afterward, he'd mopped up the survivors, shooting them in the back as they lay in a ditch pretending to be dead, or running down dark alleys, camouflaged pants under hastily stolen civilian shirts.

Omar considered his words and said, "Yes. I have heard." He stood up. "I've done the same thing in Dagestan, fighting the Russians. It gives me a soft spot for you, but I promise, it will disappear at the slightest indication you or your men are considering leaving. You're in it now. Forever."

Jacob nodded and said, "Remember, we volunteered to come here. We have nowhere to go now. The Islamic State is our home."

"You'll be leaving your home soon. Going back to the West, where you'll conduct an attack that will leave you etched into the history of the caliphate."

"What is the target?"

"All in good time. You have some *shahid* training first, along with other selected instructions. First, some rules. One: Never, ever use any social media. Stay out of pictures being taken, and never tell anyone here you are on a mission. Nobody is to know. Two: There will be others arriving. They are on a mission as well, but they know nothing of yours. Do not let them know you are doing something different. Let them believe you are with them."

The Lost Boys nodded and Omar said, "Fine. Get settled. You stay here, with the leadership. Your instruction will begin tomorrow."

They'd awoken the following morning, conducting prayers and wondering when they'd start learning the art of the suicide bomber, when Ringo had shown up with a band of about twenty men. All of Arabic descent, some from the West, like Ringo, but most from countries in the Gulf States, they filtered past bringing in their makeshift luggage and weapons. The same man who had driven the Lost Boys directed them to their rooms.

Jacob watched them disappear. Jordanians, Tunisians, Algerians, and others, all younger than twenty-five. By this time, he'd learned to distinguish nationality by dress.

Ringo saw Jacob following the men with his eyes and said, "That's right. Those are the chosen ones. Like me. The only Lost Boy helping out this mission will be Hussein. A true member of the Islamic State. Not some American surfer-boy imposter."

Hussein snapped his head to Ringo and said, "What? I'm American too."

"Yes, I know." He gave his little arrogant smile and said, "If it were up to me, I'd leave you behind just because of your company, but your father's Jordanian. Something that's apparently going to be useful."

Jacob said, "He can't go with you. He's with us. We need him."

"For what? Cleaning our weapons? Cooking our food?"

Jacob saw his friend looking at him, Hussein's eyes betraying panic at the words, realizing he was lost. Jacob said, "For . . . for the mission."

Ringo laughed, and slapped Hussein's back, saying, "Exactly right. The mission. The one you won't be a part of."

Jacob felt Hussein's gaze on him, begging for help. It was all Jacob could do to physically restrain himself from killing Ringo outright.

13

Brett called, saying he was in position, but he was unclear how long he could remain. I looked at Knuckles, wearing a knit hat and a dreadlock wig, with his face, neck, and hands blacked out. I knew what he was thinking. *If Brett is having trouble just standing around, how the hell am I going to last five seconds?*

I keyed my radio and said, "What's the issue?"

"Nothing big. The area's just really rough, and the cockroaches are coming out now that the sun's down."

I winked at Knuckles and said, "Want me to send in your partner?"

"Hell no. I'd rather get beaten to death than be caught next to him in that ridiculous outfit. He looks like Dan Aykroyd on the train in *Trading Places*."

Knuckles rolled his eyes. I studied him, and he *did* look a little like Aykroyd's character. Didn't matter. He wasn't going to talk to anyone, and the whole idea was to prevent a random shanty-dweller from doing a double take at a white man wandering around the Kibera slums. It sounded stupid, but during the Rhodesian War a Special Forces unit called the Selous Scouts—arguably one of the best the modern world has ever seen—had done this very thing, infiltrating terrorist strong-holds wearing greasepaint that made them look like the terrorists themselves.

We'd sent all of our data taken from Panda back to the Taskforce for analysis and learned that he was attempting to help the barbarians of ISIL increase their oil production, not with funds but with actual expertise. I'd recommended taking them off the board, and that had caused some consternation within the Oversight Council. Especially when I told them how I wanted to do it.

Retro came on. "Panda's in position. Looks like the meeting's a go."

I said, "You clean? No issues?"

"No. We're outside the ring of security, and Jennifer looks nothing like she did."

We'd scrubbed everything associated with Panda from our entry earlier, and due to his huge electronic tether, could now follow his every move with Taskforce assets. Right after Jennifer's little escapade in his room, we'd been forced to relocate to another hotel in the city center and stay as far away from Panda as possible, focusing on the five Nigerians. I'd come up with the plan to neutralize them, then Panda had initiated a meeting with the group's leader.

I'd halted our operations, going back to the Taskforce and asking for a modification of the course of action. Asking to interdict the leader of the Nigerians after the meeting instead of my original plan. Simply removing all five would have been easiest, but we would lose valuable intelligence against the Islamic State. We might get information from the Saudis after they interrogated Panda, but it wasn't a given, and even if we did, the information would always be suspect.

The last time we'd wholeheartedly trusted our Arab counterparts had been in late 2009, when Jordan had fed us an asset from inside al Qaida, who supposedly had a location to Osama bin Laden. The CIA had met him at a forward operating base in Afghanistan to debrief, eager to learn what he knew and never questioning his motivations for turning against his AQ masters. They completely relied on his vetting from Jordanian intelligence.

He had other plans.

He turned out to be a triple agent on a suicide mission. He exited his vehicle inside the perimeter of the base and detonated his vest, causing the largest single loss of CIA personnel in history.

I preferred a little ground truth to secondhand KSA intelligence, and had convinced the Taskforce to let me give it a try after this meeting. Panda might be a bigwig Saudi, preventing us from putting the screws to him, but the Nigerian was a nobody, and interrogating him could provide quality information. The problem was that only Retro remained clean. Everyone else on the team had been involved with the extraction of Jennifer.

We'd mulled over options, and Jennifer had convinced me that she was good to go also, since she'd had on a wig and fancy clothes when they'd met, and Panda had spent most of the time in the toilet. Today, she was back to being a dirty blonde, with her hair let down and covering her face, and had dressed blandly, with a set of glasses to further alter her appearance.

Retro's call was letting me know they weren't close to being burned. I clicked over to the command net, calling Lieutenant Colonel Blaine Alexander, currently staged in a warehouse four miles away with the support team.

"Showboat, this is Pike. Conditions are set. Do we have execute authority?"

It wasn't his official callsign, but the only time Blaine ever showed up for an operation was to control the endgame, so I liked poking him in the eye. In effect, he got all the glory without slogging through the work, something I always kidded him about.

"Pike, Showboat. Standby for Omega."

The Taskforce called every stage of an operation a different Greek letter, starting with Alpha for the introduction of forces. Omega—the last letter—meant we were at an endgame. Ordinarily, we received Omega from the Oversight Council prior to an operation and that was it. We executed how we saw fit, then told them the results. In this case, I had Omega for my plan of removing the five, but given the size of the target, the fact that we'd just executed a separate Omega operation against Panda on Kenyan soil, and the curveball I'd thrown about taking the leader for interrogation, the Council had grown skittish. For the first time, they held execute authority in DC with Kurt. Which was cutting things a little close, to say the least.

Brett called. "Trigger. The men are headed to dinner. The leader's on the move."

We'd watched the group for three days, and they were extremely clannish. Everything they did, they did together, which had been the genesis of my plan. Right up until we'd gotten the intercept about a meeting.

On the team net I said, "Leader's broken from the group?"

"Yep. He's headed north. They're headed east."

North was to the Adams Arcade shopping area on Ngong Road, and to the coffee shop where Panda was sitting. *Phase one's a go.*

I said, "Fall back. Meet us at the linkup. Dan Aykroyd here's got the package ready."

I put the van in gear, seeing Knuckles grimace. I called Blaine and said, "Do we have Omega for the leader? He's on the move, and Panda is set."

"Pike, they want to wait until after the meeting before giving you Omega on him. You report the situation, and then they'll decide."

"Damn it, Blaine, you know we can't run an operation like that. I need execute authority before, so I can deal with any contingencies."

"Then you don't have it. Execute the original plan and let him go."

Shit.

I said, "Okay, okay. I'll send a SITREP when I have it."

We continued south, and the area began to get seedy as we approached the infamous Kibera slums. Thankfully, the Nigerians were staying in a decrepit building on the outskirts and not in the shanty-towns of the slum proper. If they had been, there was no way we could execute my plan. Kibera was a no-man's-land of gangs, glue-sniffing youth, and splintered lives wreaking desperation.

Comprised of a rat-warren maze of houses built out of plastic, scrounged wood, and tin cans, Kibera was one of the largest slums in the world, jam-packed with an incredibly dense population that had nothing better to do than sit around and stare at whoever was around. Probing it would have been a nonstarter. Luckily, the Nigerians' safe house was in a courtyard of broken concrete structures just north. It prevented us from driving right up, but at least we could infiltrate it on foot.

I saw a penlight flash and pulled over. Knuckles slid open the door, and Brett entered the van. He saw Knuckles and laughed, shaking his head. "You sure you don't want me to do this on my own? I've done it plenty of times in the past."

Brett was an old-school ground branch operative from the CIA, and had conducted some seriously hairy singleton operations in his career, but there was no reason to do that here. I wanted one Operator pulling security while another penetrated the house.

I said, "He's going."

"Okay, but he's also carrying the dope. We get held up, and I'm leaving him behind, dumbass disguise and all."

Knuckles scowled, not liking the mission at all. He held up a bag of what looked like balloons filled with brown sand, about thirty of them, each a half inch across. He said, "That's not the plan. You carry the dope. I break inside."

And that was the operation, in a nutshell. We were going to plant black tar heroin, ready for distribution, inside the shack the Nigerians were using, then alert the police. They'd be locked up indefinitely after the arrest, and no longer available to help the Islamic State. It seemed like a pretty simple plan to me, but man alive, trying to sell that to the Oversight Council was damn near impossible. I mean, it wasn't like we weren't walking outside the law anyway. You'd have thought I'd demanded to start selling heroin on the streets of DC to fund our own activities.

Eventually, since there weren't a lot of options and it solved the problem neatly, Kurt had convinced the Council, and Blaine had flown over, illegally smuggling in heroin so that we could illegally plant it then illegally frame the Nigerians. Neat. At least, I thought it was. Blaine, on the other hand, was decidedly piqued when I'd met him in the storage facility.

He'd said, "You know how hard it was to get this? And how much trouble you've caused?"

I said, "Don't blame me. Blame the Islamic State."

14

Knuckles held out the bag and Brett said, "Why me?"

"Because you can run like a cheetah. I get caught, and I'm doing some serious explaining as it is with this paint on me. You get caught, and it's because you wanted to."

He was right in that assessment. Brett was somewhat of a freak of nature on foot, running faster than anyone I'd ever met. I said, "Look at it this way, if you did this as a singleton, you'd be carrying it anyway."

He took the bag and our earpieces squelched. "Pike, Retro. Panda and the Nigerian have made linkup. Meeting ongoing, and he's already passed some sort of package across."

All right. Intel.

I said, "Sounds good. Keep us abreast of what's happening. Drop team is on the way."

I turned to the two cat burglars and said, "Get lost. You need to be in and out before the meeting breaks up. I need you for phase two."

Brett slid the door open, saying, "See you on the back side."

They disappeared into the darkness and I began readying the kit necessary for the takedown. Tasers, drugs, and flex ties.

I called Blaine, saying, "Meeting's ongoing. We've got a lock-on to the target, as briefed. What's the status with Omega?"

"What's the status with the product?"

"Being executed now."

He said, "Stand by."

I sat in the van, listening to the cooling engine tick in the darkness, waiting. Resisting the urge to contact Retro or Knuckles to see what was going on. I saw two men coming down the street, barely visible and blending into the shadows. They stopped outside the van, whispering to each other.

Great. Just what I need. Someone looking for some hubcaps.

I leaned forward from the back, keeping to the shadows, and flashed the lights. They jumped like a firecracker had gone off behind them and scurried away, making me smile.

I waited another seven minutes, growing antsy. Finally, the command net came alive. "Pike, Showboat. You got Omega with a caveat."

"Roger. What's the caveat?"

"Everything has to be perfect. You have the target and can get him without drama."

"That's always a rule."

"Pike, don't push my buttons. This isn't my first rodeo with you. Straight from the Oversight Council—if it smells even a little bad, you let him go to get wrapped up with everyone else."

"Okay. Roger all. You set with the Nairobi cops?"

"That was a little too quick. You understand the intent?"

I heard the team radio squawk.

I said, "Sir, I got it. Gotta go. Team's calling."

I clicked off without waiting on him to reply and said, "Last calling station, this is Pike."

"Pike, Retro. Meeting's breaking up."

"Already?"

"Yep. Leader's standing up."

Shit. "Does he have the package?"

"Yeah. It was one of those padded envelopes. He opened it. I saw an old-school flip phone and a notebook."

"Keep eyes on. . . . Break, break, Knuckles, this is Pike. Status."

"We haven't gone in yet. Got some squatters drinking chang'aa."

Chang'aa was an ungodly home brew that was about fifty percent alcohol and fifty percent formaldehyde, battery acid, jet fuel, or some other liquid. I said, "How long have you been watching?"

Knuckles said, "Since we got here. They're blitzed, but conscious. Wait, one just fell over."

"Ignore them. Get in. They're too stoned to remember anything."

"It would make more sense to just sit them out. A few more minutes, and they'll both be sleeping."

"I don't have that time. Panda's meeting's breaking up."

Brett came on. "If they intervene? What's the ROE?"

"Prevent them from seeing Knuckles enter. Period. Just get in, now. The leader's about to move and I can't execute without you two."

In a calm monotone I heard, "Roger all."

By all accounts, I should have aborted the second phase, letting the leader go. The situation had already exceeded Blaine's intent, but luckily, his idea of "perfect" and mine were two different things. I wanted the leader.

Jennifer came on. "Pike, Koko. Leader's shaking hands. What's the call?"

Koko was Jennifer's callsign. Something she'd earned on a mission in Indonesia by annoying Knuckles with repeated stories about a talking gorilla.

I said, "We have Omega. No change to the plan. You guys lock the back door."

She said, "I monitored last transmission. You have an assault element?"

"Not yet, but I will."

I heard nothing for a moment, then a long-drawn-out "Roger that. . . ."

The problem with the two-phased operation was that I had to use the same team for both. I had planned it for a staggered execution, but now it had become simultaneous. Retro and Jennifer would do nothing but prevent the guy from escaping. Brett would drive the van, and Knuckles and I would do a rolling interdiction. But that was all dependent on having Brett and Knuckles. I couldn't very well drive the van *and* assault.

Brett came on, breathing heavily, "Inbound, inbound, fire up the van. We're dragging an anchor."

I leapt into the driver's seat, saying, "Where are you?"

All I heard was, "Coming out right where we entered."

Which was about a half mile down the road. I started driving, saying, "What's up?"

"Gang territory. Chang'aa brewery."

"Knuckles?"

He came on, sounding like he was breathing into a paper bag. "Can't talk."

I saw movement ahead, and recognized Brett in the headlights. I stomped the gas, reaching him just as Knuckles broke out of the close confines of the buildings. Brett jerked open the sliding door, and both spilled inside. I looked to my right and saw a pack of shouting youths waving sticks and running up the alley.

Brett slammed the door shut and shouted, "Go, go, go!"

I did, hearing something slam into the back of the van. I went about a quarter mile, circling back toward Ngong Road, then stopped. I turned around and said, "What the hell did you two chuckleheads do?"

Knuckles sat up, his dreadlock wig askew and his paint starting to run. He said, "I ought to kick your ass for making me wear this."

I said, "Tell me you didn't compromise the operation."

Brett said, "No. That went fine. Drugs are in place. In fact, everything went fine right up until we were walking back through the neighborhood. A couple of thugs stopped us, demanding to know what we were doing in their AO. Apparently, there's been some gang fighting between the various chang'aa brewers over turf. We just had the bad fortune to stumble into it."

"And?"

Brett grinned. "And everything was going perfectly, right up until they shoved Knuckles. It was too dark to tell he was a cracker white boy, but his dreadlocks slipped. They saw that just fine."

Knuckles said, "Tell him the rest, you shit."

"What?"

Knuckles looked at me and said, "He took off running. Leaving me behind."

Brett held up his hands, saying, "Just following orders. You said no fighting that would spike."

I laughed and said, "All right, all right. Shake it off. Phase two is a go. We've got Omega and the leader's on the move. Brett, take the wheel. Knuckles, get ready."

Brett and I switched positions, and Knuckles growled, "I oughtta use the damn Taser on him."

I called Retro and Jennifer. "Koko, Retro, this is Pike. Assault element secure. Moving your way."

Retro said, "Pike, we've got an issue. The target is being tailed by one of Panda's security. The black guy from inside the hotel that Koko swiped with ABS."

15

I heard the transmission and cursed. We were now moving out of what even *I* would call perfect conditions.

"Why? What happened? What did the target do to spike security?"

"Nothing. I think Panda's actually providing him protection without him knowing."

"Is he moving on the projected route?"

"Yeah, but we can't take him in view of the security."

We had planned on assaulting the target just south of Adams Arcade. There was a road that ran east to west on the southern edge, acting as a border between the security of the mall and a flea market called Toi. Unlike Adams Arcade, Toi was a maze of vendors jam-packed together in makeshift huts, and was a local favorite for buying secondhand clothing. Most of the stalls would be closed at this hour, but not all.

I looked at the map and said, "Okay, we're bumping the kill zone one road to the south. See Kinangop? See where it curves? He hits that and he'll trail it back to Kangethe and home. Hopefully."

I looked at Brett. "Start moving. Stage on Joseph Kangethe Road where Kinangop dead-ends into it."

Jennifer came on. "He just broke out of Adams Arcade. He's into the Toi Market, and security's still following. What about him?"

We had maybe three minutes.

She repeated, "What about the security following him?"

"Retro interdicts him. He's the only one that's clean. Retro, can you penetrate inside Toi?"

"Yeah. I can get in. I'll stick out, but that's not the problem. I take out the security and everybody's going to see."

I said, "Retro, don't take him out. Just stop him. Is he well dressed?"

"Yeah, he's in a suit."

"Okay, act like you're lost. Act like a tourist. Stop him as a nice-looking Kenyan and ask for directions. We only need seconds. Get a gap between him and the target."

Jennifer said, "And me?"

Brett stopped the van, saying, "We're here."

I said, "All elements, we're staged. Koko, penetrate into Toi with Retro. Split when he moves to the security man. Same profile. Prevent the target from running back the way he came."

I didn't want to do that, because a single white female walking around out here was like dropping bloody chunks of meat into shark-infested water. I heard nothing for a moment, then Jennifer said, "Pike, target's spotted security. He's getting skittish."

"Okay, okay, stay on him. Nothing's changed."

"He's speed-walking now. I say again, he's moving fast through the stalls. He's headed west, not south."

My first thought was *Abort.*

I looked at the map, seeing my plan of action was way off. I said, "He'll hit Suna Road, then go south. This is it. Retro, interdict security. Jennifer, stick with him. Brett, get up there. Get to the intersection of Suna and Kinangop."

He goosed the engine and we went flying past our projected kill zone. Knuckles said, "We're not going to make it in time. He'll be through the intersection before we get there."

"Nothing I can do about possibles. We'll deal with the situation when we get there." I keyed the radio. "Jennifer, Retro, status?"

Jennifer said, "I lost him in the stalls. He's headed straight west."

From Retro, I heard mumbled conversation. He couldn't talk, and had keyed the mike to let me know he was executing.

Brett raced up Kinangop, luckily the only car on the road, the weak headlights from the van providing barely enough illumination for the speed we were going.

Jennifer called, "I'm on Suna. I see him. He's running south now. And I mean running."

Retro came on. "Security's broken contact. He got sick of me, and he's moving west."

Blaine's orders flicked through my head. *The drugs are set. I should really let him go.*

I saw the intersection of Suma and Kinangop just as Jennifer called, saying, "He's going east now. He's on your road, but I've got an issue. Some youths are following me. Closing on me. No idea of their intentions."

What else can happen? Where's my luck?

"Retro, get to Koko, now. Break, break, Koko, we're ten seconds out. Keep moving south. Call if you need help."

She said nothing, but I could feel her wrath at my words. Knuckles said, "Pike, maybe we should . . ."

Before he could finish his sentence, something flashed in front of our headlights like a bad horror-movie strobe effect. There one second, gone the next. I strained my eyes outside the window, and finally saw my vaunted luck. It was a tall African, waving his arms to get us to stop.

The leader.

You're kidding me. About time.

"Brett, see if we can help that man out."

He grinned and pulled over. Our target ran to the passenger window, shouting something in broken English. Knuckles slid open the side door and stepped out. The Nigerian glanced toward him, saw his wig and running black face paint. He drew back, confused and alarmed. I followed Knuckles and the man backed away, preparing to sprint. Knuckles hit him with the Taser, dropping him like a sack of dirt.

We heaved him into the back of the van, Knuckles keeping the juice going while I stabilized him. Knuckles slammed the door shut and Brett called the dismounted team. "Retro, Koko, status."

Retro said, "I got her. I'm with her, but the thugs are still following. They're blocking our ability to get back into Toi. You want me to escalate?"

Meaning, *Can I draw my weapon?*

I said, "Negative. Let's see if we can't get you out clean."

Brett hit the gas while I flex-tied the leader, his head rolling left and right. I pulled out the manila envelope from under his shirt, a flip phone and notebook spilling to the floor of the van. *Jackpot.* Knuckles readied a syringe and the target began flopping up and down, like a fish trying to get back into the water. I used my weight to hold him down and Knuckles hit him with the sedative. He thrashed a bit more, then his eyes rolled back into his head.

Brett slammed through the intersection, ripping right hard enough to fling us into the side. He said, "I got them, I got them."

I leaned forward and saw Retro walking quickly with Jennifer, holding her hand like they were a couple. Behind them was a pack of men following like wolves pacing a wounded deer. Lost tourists they planned on fleecing as soon as the hapless couple cleared the area of Toi and entered the outskirts of the slum.

Retro said, "Is that you to my front?"

"Yeah, we're going to roll right up. Get to us and get in. If they start running with you, we'll handle it."

Brett pulled abreast, the headlights on the group thirty meters away. Jennifer broke into a sprint, with Retro right behind her. The thugs were surprised for a split second, then began to give chase, two starting to catch up.

Jennifer dove inside, followed by Retro. The door slammed shut and we were gone, hearing nothing but a couple of fists banging the quarter panel.

Brett swerved onto the main road in front of the mall, and I got smacked in the shoulder by Jennifer.

"Call if I'm in trouble? *Call if I'm in trouble?* Really? That's *why* I called."

I said, "Hey, I knew Retro had your back."

Knuckles said, "Don't blame me; I tried to get him to help."

I said, "What? In the hotel you said I was on the verge of compromising the mission because I thought Jennifer might be in trouble. Now I'm at fault for letting her work it out?"

She muttered something and I turned to Brett, telling him to get rolling toward the support crew in the storage garage. I started to call Blaine, then paused, saying, "Everyone listen. No matter what Blaine asks, this went perfectly, okay?"

Knuckles said, "Why?"

Jennifer squinted and said, "What are you hiding?"

All innocent I said, "Nothing. Just tell Blaine it went like clockwork. Trust me, that would be for the best."

16

Sitting at the long makeshift table, Jacob caught the Chechen and another man studying him. He ignored them, waiting on Ringo's team to arrive for dinner. In truth, he was growing tired of the constant blanket of Islamic State minions watching his every move, and tired of the so-called instruction they'd received.

Expecting to learn the art of the suicide bomber, they'd done nothing of the sort. The mornings were spent working with the tools of the *shahid*, but it was nothing like Jacob had been expecting, like from the movies, with detonators and ticking red numbers. They mostly worked with chemicals. Learning how to break a cylinder of glass inside a plastic container. Then how to break the next one. Beyond that, they learned to hide and remove small wooden dowels inside the shell of a smartphone, then hook them to plastic tubing before inserting them into sleeves of clay.

They were tested endlessly and told their very lives depended on the training, but the "chemicals" they used were nothing more than colored water, and the wooden dowels made little sense. It grew boring.

The afternoons were spent studying the Catholic faith, including all of the strange trappings of that religion. Scripts, ceremonies, and arcane trivia that meant little beyond reminding him of the hated reform school he'd fled.

Having had to absorb the multitude of Islamic strictures inherent in the Islamic State had been bad enough, but something he could tolerate because it was all forgotten on the battlefield. But he was disgusted at being forced to learn about Christianity and Catholicism. He'd had enough of that beaten into him at the school, in what he felt was an incredible show of hypocrisy. They preached tolerance and love on Sundays, forcing the boys to listen to one itinerate preacher after another, then tortured him and his friends the other six days of the week. In his mind, Christianity was nothing but a cloak for abuse, and, if the world were just, he'd take every one of those hypocritical preachers with him in a blaze of glory.

There was no such duplicitousness within the Islamic State. They proclaimed up front what would occur for any infractions, and adhered to that creed with brutal efficiency. While he didn't really care for all the Islamic diatribes, he found symmetry in his existence here. A life worth living, even if it meant death.

Next to him, Carlos rubbed his chin, now shorn of its patchy, juvenile beard, and said, "Rumor has it we're leaving soon. That we've done all we can here."

Devon said, "We haven't done anything. Where is all the training like Mohamed Atta got? All we've done is break some glass and learn about an infidel religion."

Jacob inwardly smiled at the statement, amazed at how deeply his two companions had embraced the propaganda. Wanting so badly to belong, to feel a sense of inclusion and purpose, they'd absorbed the myth of the Islamic State like gauze on a gunshot wound, the blood soaking through and permanently staining whatever remained.

Jacob saw Ringo's team enter and waved to Hussein. Watching him walk over, he recognized that the same hadn't happened to his other friend. If anything, Hussein's wound was too great, the blood of the Islamic State overwhelming his defenses. Instead of absorbing, Hussein was fighting it, and he was losing. He looked haggard. Scared.

He's not going to make it.

Hussein fist-bumped Carlos and Devon, then sat down. Devon said, "What do you hear? Yousef says we're leaving soon."

Jacob scowled and said, "What were you told about our names? You *forget* the Muslim one. Use our given names."

Chagrined, Devon snuck a glance at the Chechen, hoping he hadn't heard. He whispered, "Carlos. Carlos says we're leaving."

Hussein said, "I don't know about you guys, but I am. I'm leaving tomorrow."

Jacob said, "So are we. Maybe not tomorrow, but soon."

Carlos said, "How do you know?"

"They had us shave. There's a reason for that. They want us to look American, and they want it now."

Devon said, "I hope so, but we don't even know what we're doing. We haven't learned anything."

Jacob said, "Maybe it's like *The Karate Kid*. Wax on, wax off. Maybe we've learned something without even knowing. Or maybe there's more training that can't be done here. Even Mohamed Atta had to learn to fly, and he couldn't do that in a cave."

Carlos smiled and, like a kid discussing college applications, said, "I sure hope so. Hussein, what are you doing? Did they tell you?"

Hussein nodded, his head bobbing over and over, as if he were trying to convince himself that what was occurring was real. Jacob thought he might start crying. He said, "Yes. We're going to Jordan. It's why they told me to keep my mustache. They want me to look like a local. Ringo's in charge, and he's taking the team to Ma'an, in the south. I'm going to Amman. To meet my father."

"What is the target?"

"I don't know, but my father works at a hotel. A fancy one."

17

Watching the Lost Boys eat, Adnan al-Tayyib said, "My friend, I gave you permission to train and lead our external operations, not break them up as you see fit. You had two tasks to accomplish, and I didn't give you the authority to use one of the untainted Americans for the false flag attack."

Omar said, "You told me my mission, then said it was up to me to ensure success. I didn't realize there were restrictions. The boy Hussein is weak, and his name is Muslim. I considered him a threat for the primary mission. His heritage alone will raise eyes, even with an American passport. Don't listen when governments say they don't profile. They do. On the other hand, he's Jordanian, and his father still lives in Amman. He's perfect for the false flag."

"Don't make it a habit of such decisions without consulting me."

Omar said, "I won't. I'm sorry if I seemed to usurp your authority, but because of Hussein I no longer think of the second attack as a deception. It may prove more instrumental than the primary operation."

Adnan turned to him and saw he wasn't fabricating a story to cover his disobedience. "You truly believe this?"

"Yes, especially since we control all of the assets. The city of Ma'an is ripe with recruits. Ever since the Jordanian pilot's death they have been hounded by the authorities for their religious convictions. All they require is a catalyst, and we can give them that. It will provide a second front for the crusaders to fight. One in the backyard of Jordan, their favorite *takfir* ally. I'm more confident of it than the primary attack."

Adnan said, "Come. Let's not talk here, among the men."

They left the ramshackle two-story building, the clatter of dishes and eating utensils fading behind them, the desert air rapidly cooling from the day's heat.

They walked in silence, Omar patiently waiting on his emir to start the conversation. They crossed the compound, little dust devils swirling in the gathering gloom, formed by the wind of the temperature inversion.

Reaching the front stoop of a one-story brick building one hundred meters away, Omar finally decided to break the silence.

"I hope our accommodations are to your liking."

Adnan opened the door, saying, "They're fine. Come in."

Omar followed, waiting on the man to speak yet again. When Adnan remained mute, he broke the silence one more time but stayed away from the mission, not wanting to antagonize his emir. "How did your recruit of the oil field technicians go? Is all well with that endeavor?"

Adnan adjusted several pillows and took a seat on the floor. He said, "Sit."

Omar did. Adnan said, "The recruiting went fine. They're flying into Turkey as we speak. When they get here, they'll contact me, and I'll put them to work."

"How?"

Adnan pulled out two Thuraya satellite cell phones. "On this. Both are clean, and the other one is for you."

Omar said, "You know how I feel about phones. Especially satellite ones. It's how Dzhokhar Dudayev was killed in Chechnya. It's how the crusaders kill everyone since they're too afraid to fight man-to-man."

"I know, but sometimes we take risks. In this case, minimal. These phones have never been used. Once I get my recruits, I'll throw this one away. Once you get the material for the explosives, you can throw that one away."

Omar studied the phone, then said, "Okay. This once. Who will be calling?"

"A man named Rashid al-Jaza'iri. He's giving us the explosives."

"Al-Jaza'iri? As in 'the Algerian'?"

"Yes."

"The French intelligence officer? From Jabhat al-Nusra?"

Adnan took a date from a bowl, popped it into his mouth, and said, "Yes."

Omar said, "Adnan, I don't think you know the history between us. He won't help the Islamic State. He and I have had some issues."

Adnan laughed and said, "Issues? From what I hear, he would like nothing more than to skin you alive. But he's dealing with me. He doesn't know about you, and I intend to keep it that way."

"Why would he help? We broke from al Qaida, and when we did, we slaughtered al-Nusra in Aleppo. I know. I did the killing. I came close to beheading Rashid myself, but he got away, running through our checkpoints dressed as a woman in a niqab. They're nothing but pompous asses putting out tapes, but they've sworn vengeance. Tell me we haven't put the success of the attack in their hands."

"They *are* pompous, spouting proclamations from hiding, but they also have much greater expertise in making improvised explosives. Expertise they intended to use to attack the crusaders, but were prevented. They now want to give that expertise to us, courtesy of the United States."

"What do you mean?"

"Remember the initiation of the crusader air strikes after we threatened Irbil? When they bombed individual tanks and empty buildings all night in a great show of force?"

"Yes."

"Remember the Western press hysteria about the 'Khorasan group'? How they were an al Qaida offshoot and were on the verge of a spectacular attack, so they bombed them as well?"

"Yes, yes. What's the point?"

"Those stories were true. The Khorasan group has been perfecting nonmetallic methods of explosives to be used in bringing down a multitude of aircraft in an attack that would span the globe. Methods which can defeat almost all detection capabilities, but the air strikes wiped out most of the participants. But not the expertise. The explosives research was completed, and the attack was being planned. As always, the devil was in the delivery, not the device. The crusaders drove al-Nusra to us. I reached out, and they agreed to pass the explosives. We will use them for our attack, courtesy of the Algerian."

"So the man who's been teaching them all of those strange things knows the weapon system? It's like nothing I've ever seen. Is he Jabhat al-Nusra as well?"

"Yes."

Omar stood, tossing the phone on a pillow and saying, "If you think the Algerian will help me—help us—you're wrong. He's using this as a means to attack. As a way to get inside."

"Omar, I was Jabhat al-Nusra before I joined the Islamic State. Even that arrogant British fighter you've chosen for the Jordanian mission was al-Nusra before. I still have contacts there, and so does he." He smiled. "Contacts that don't want to kill me. If I am the intermediary, they'll do as they say. They want to harm the crusaders much, much more than they do us."

"Maybe you. I doubt the fire has left their belly for me."

Adnan picked up the phone and handed it back. "It's already done. They're delivering the explosives to Albania. A man in that country— who has no knowledge of you—is the contact. He thinks he's dealing with me. You answer that phone and don't tell him otherwise."

Omar took the phone, shaking his head. "You just said Rashid would call."

"Rashid delivered the explosives to the contact. The contact is calling you."

Omar sat in silence for a moment, then said, "I'm sending my men to Jordan tomorrow. They will succeed. The Lost Boys are going to Istanbul. I have the tour schedule for the Americans, and can interdict them. I can control all of that, but without your explosives, I can do nothing. I control nothing for that mission. And yet you tell me to succeed."

"You *will* succeed. *We* will succeed. Who stands in our way? The Syrians? The Americans? The Iranians? They all fight each other, handing us the caliphate."

"The Iranians are no problem. Their fighting in Iraq helps us forge the true Islamic world. The undecided despise them, and fear the Shia militias enough to succumb to us. The Americans are a different story. They know nothing of Islam and blunder around like a drunken dog, but they should not be underestimated."

Adnan waved his hand. "What have they done but help us? They struck some tanks and killed the Khorasan group, giving us the means to attack."

Omar opened the door, saying, "Maybe. But remember, I didn't succeed in Mosul because I underestimated the enemy."

Adnan laughed and said, "Don't build yourself up into something you're not. The Islamic State won in Mosul. Our message won. Not you."

Omar felt his face grow red. He came close to a rebuttal, but nodded and slammed the door, walking swiftly away. It wasn't until he was across the compound, about to reenter the training wing and inform the Lost Boys of their trip, before a buzz penetrated through his anger.

The same faint noise he had heard multiple times.

Drone.

He stopped and scanned the sky, hoping to see the aircraft break the light of the stars. He saw nothing. He strained his ears to locate the noise, still staring hard. He caught a flash, then a sputtering of light streaking toward the emir's residence.

Hellfire missile.

He dove to the ground, and the missile sliced through a window, looking deceptively small, like a bottle rocket spouting sparks. The earth split open, lighting up the night sky, the building torn from the inside out, masonry falling like devil's rain.

Men began spilling from the teaching residence, shouting and pointing. He stood up, screaming at them for silence, trying to determine if the floating death still circled.

He could not.

He felt a lump in his pocket and realized he still held the phone. He ripped it out of his pocket and hurled it across the compound, then began running.

18

Sitting behind the Resolute Desk in the Oval Office, President Warren said, "So we hit something big? More than just a facilitator for the oil fields?"

Kerry Bostwick, the director of the CIA, said, "It appears so. The number the Taskforce found led us to an abandoned industrial facility. Flying just inside the Iraqi border, Rivet Joint picked up the phone signature—a lucky break for us—and a Reaper UAV delivered the surgical strike. We hit exactly what we aimed for, then the chatter lit up across the board."

Because the lead came from the Taskforce, the meeting was restricted to what was colloquially called the "principles committee" of the Oversight Council. Five of the thirteen members had an overwhelming presence because of their past experiences and power, and President Warren had taken to bringing them together for discussions before engaging the entire Council. Sitting in the office were the secretary of defense, the secretary of state, the national security adviser, the director of the CIA, and the president himself. Off to the left, in earshot, but not part of the official debate, sat Kurt Hale.

President Warren said, "What else was there?"

"A lot of personnel on the ground, but we couldn't determine their status. This area hasn't been on our intelligence picture before."

President Warren said, "Why didn't we just line it up into the queue for a package of air strikes? Smoke that place to the ground?"

Kerry looked at the secretary of defense, then back to the president.

"Sir, it might be a training camp, but it might also be a place where refugees have fled. We just don't know. The only thing we had was the SIGINT of the Thuraya phone."

The SECDEF spoke up. "Sir, I agree with the surgical strike. You don't want a bunch of women and kids on the news tomorrow. We just don't have eyes on the ground to determine what's real."

Jonathan Billings, the secretary of state, said, "Because of that bastard Hussein. Could BOBCAT have told us?"

Kerry bristled and said, "You want to get into the blame game, I'll start with State's ignoring Iraq five years ago."

President Warren cut him off. "Enough. There's no reason to rehash what-ifs. Only what-nows. So, what now?"

"We've got Rivet Joint trying to suck every bit of communications from the site, and have it blanketed with UAVs, but they're not getting a whole lot. There's no GSM cell coverage in that area, only satellite, and we're not getting any radio traffic. The UAVs are seeing movement, but no black flags or technical vehicles. Just people."

"But wouldn't they do that if we hit them? Hide, I mean? Haven't they done that everywhere else?"

"Yes, they have, but that's not enough to blow it all up. An absence of evidence of ISIL isn't evidence of ISIL. We did strike a convoy north of the compound that made the mistake of trying to shoot down our drone. We had positive ID of a hostile force in that case. In the compound, all we had was a cellular signal and a bunch of movement."

"So, I ask again, what now?"

Kerry said, "Well, the SIGINT from across the entire area of operations—outside of the target—has pretty much confirmed that we killed the emir of northern Syria, Adnan al-Tayyib. We thought he was just facilitating the oil field workers, but it turns out, he was much, much bigger. The Islamic State leadership is segmented into four operational areas, and we just killed one. It's a pretty good day for the red, white, and blue."

President Warren's face turned sour at the bravado. He said, "How do we capitalize on that? Can the Taskforce do anything?"

Kerry turned to Kurt Hale and he said, "I've got Pike's team finishing up cover duties in Nigeria. Doing the basic covering of their tracks. The Omega package and support team redeployed without any issues, and are on standby. I've also got Johnny's team prepping for deployment to Turkey, just in case. He's not ready to go yet, but I can flex Pike in a day or two. The problem is we don't have anything to go on. There's no thread, and we still can't penetrate into Syria. The Islamic State itself is a granite wall. They need to come to a different playing field."

President Warren tapped the desk with a finger, then said, "Isn't that what these Lost Boys are planning? Leaving Syria and coming to the West? Jesus, we're just sitting here waiting to get punched."

Kerry saw his frustration and said, "Sometimes you just wait it out. Let them make a mistake and give us the break. Forcing the issue leads to missed opportunities."

President Warren took that in, then, in a slow, measured tone, said, "I don't want the 'break' to be a bunch of dead bodies from some assholes holding American passports. Tracking them down after the fact plays well in the press, but preventing the attack is what matters."

The room became quiet. After the silence grew uncomfortable, Kerry said, "Sir, I understand. I don't think I was clear. Usually, we'll get something from the chatter. Someone will break operational security and ask for guidance or permission for something, now that the chain of command is in disarray. The Lost Boys are a threat, but they won't solve the problem of the Islamic State. We killed a very big fish, and now we're looking for a specific name."

"Who?"

"A Chechen. Omar al-Khatami. Adnan obviously lived in the shadows, since we didn't know his importance. He had the ear of the senior leadership, but Omar is the reason they've succeeded as much as they have. He's an absolute killer, and a strategic genius who learned his talent fighting the Russians. Killing Adnan might cause spiritual and leadership issues, but he had no skill in the fight. Omar is the sword he wielded, and we've been trying to find him for a long time."

"So this targeting might lead us to him?"

"Yes. With any luck."

"And that would be a good thing?"

"Yes. He's the military commander who took all the terrain in Iraq. The man who swept through Mosul on his way to Irbil before we initiated air strikes. Adnan may have been the emir, but Omar is the real target. We get him, and we knock them back on their heels."

"So you think he's more important than the reporting of these American 'Lost Boys'?"

"Oh yeah. Much more. The Lost Boys are just stray voltage at this point. We don't even know if they're real."

Kerry closed his briefing book. "The only way I'd lose sleep over them is if I heard Omar al-Khatami was in charge of their targets."

19

Feeling completely out of place, Ali Jaafar Hussein waited for his father in the lobby of the five-star Grand Hyatt hotel. He felt the stares of the hotel staff and knew they weren't misguided. He didn't belong here. He only hoped his father wouldn't throw him out. If that happened, if he had to report failure, he was sure he'd be beheaded by Omar. Even here in Jordan.

The trip out of Syria had been surreal, starting with the bombing of the VIP residence at the camp. The regular fighters had fled their tents in a convoy of Toyota pickup trucks, driving off into the darkness and leaving the men in the two-story building behind. Omar wouldn't allow his team to do the same. He'd forced everyone out of the building, marching them on foot into the desert, where they'd curled up into balls to ward off the nighttime chill. They saw air strikes in the distance, to the north, and Omar had said, "Idiots. They made themselves a target."

When dawn broke, and no further missiles had come down, he'd allowed them to return to the camp. Barking in sharp, clipped sentences, he'd instructed them to pack their belongings and load up the remaining Toyota HiLuxes.

Hussein brought his meager possessions downstairs, but didn't know which vehicle to board, Ringo's team or the Lost Boys'. He was slated for Jordan with Ringo, but Ringo was driving to al Qa'im, a town on the Iraqi border, and then south, through the desert, to slip across Jordan's border to Ma'an. Hussein was supposed to use his American passport to fly from Istanbul.

He looked for Omar and saw him across the compound, digging in the dirt for something. Omar bent over, picked up an object, then came walking back. Hussein saw a phone in his hand.

Omar said, "What are you waiting for?"

"Which truck should I use? The one going to Jordan, or yours?"

"Mine." He turned and shouted into the building. "Come on. Time to go."

The men gathered around and he said, "We're leaving sooner than I wished, but the Americans have clearly found this place. They won't shoot individual trucks without positive proof of the Islamic State, so don't give them any."

Ringo said, "How did they locate us? How did they know where the emir was staying?"

Omar held out his hand, showing the Thuraya phone Adnan had given him. "Through one of these."

Ringo shuffled his feet, wanting to say something else, and Omar said, "Load up. The Jordan team in the last two trucks. The Lost Boys in the lead truck."

Everyone began moving except Jacob. Omar said, "Load the truck."

Jacob said, "Why did you retrieve the phone if the Americans are tracking it? We'll get killed on the move. You say don't give them a reason to attack, and yet you're holding the reason."

Hussein saw Omar start to boil over, but Jacob stood his ground, unperturbed at any potential outcome, his eyes devoid of life, pale blue like the meat stamp on a haunch of rump steak. Amazingly, Hussein watched Omar back down.

He said, "The attack last night was from a drone. It was surgical, directed to that one building. They could have used a flight of aircraft and obliterated this place. They did not. If they were going after this phone, it would have been struck last night, and I'm glad it wasn't. It is our contact for the explosives for your mission. A necessary risk."

Hussein waited, feeling the greasy sweat of fear begin to sprout, praying that Jacob wouldn't push it any further. He was sure Omar's patience was at an end.

After a moment, Jacob climbed into the back, settling next to him.

Omar nodded, then moved to Ringo's vehicle. "We didn't get the chance to adequately prepare, but you know your mission. Find the contact in Ma'an. He is ready for his phase. When you do, call me on this."

He held out the phone and read off a number, Ringo copying it down.

He said, "You only call me, understand?"

"Yes. Who else would I call?"

Omar slitted his eyes and said, "The al-Nusra front. Do you still have contacts there?"

Ringo nodded, then contradicted the action with his words. "I did, but I don't talk to them anymore. Only on Twitter and that sort of thing. We share stories."

Omar snatched Ringo's chin with his right hand and said, "Do you feel allegiance to them?"

"No, sir, no. I'm the Islamic State now."

Omar let him go and said, "No more. I hear you're talking to them, and I'll cut your heart out."

Ringo bobbed his head up and down, over and over, like a child.

Omar continued. "Hussein will be arriving in Jordan in two days. He'll provide access. You do the killing. I want at least a hundred. If you can make it to the convention center, you should get three times that. Videotape everything. If you can behead some, all the better. Once the news hits, the contact will turn the city of Ma'an into a river of blood for the Hashemite kingdom. He'll start the second front. But it rests on you."

Hussein saw Ringo's eyes slide to him, and he looked away. Ringo said, "I don't like our mission relying on a Lost Boy. He's a weakling."

Ringo said it loud enough for Hussein to hear, and he felt shame. Before Omar could respond, Jacob stood up, his hollow eyes on Ringo. He jumped over the side of the truck and walked to the man in a measured pace. Ringo was a few inches taller than Jacob, but the size difference mattered little. Jacob leaned into his face. No anger. No fear. Nothing but potential violence, like an axe hanging in a shed.

Jacob said, "Ringo, you complain that I haven't learned the ways of

Islam, but I have. I and my brother against my cousin. I and my cousin against the world."

Omar stepped in between them, his face inches from Jacob's. "Do not test me, Lost Boy. Get. In. The. Truck."

His face expressionless, Jacob backed up, then turned to the HiLux, saying, "Ringo, my tribe, my war. Remember that."

Hussein could feel the tension in the air like static before a storm. The only one who was immune was Jacob. He'd sat down in the bed across from Hussein, and had smiled. A wicked, twisted thing. Hussein had grinned weakly in return, and they'd set out, a single truck making the long trek to the Turkish border, losing sight of the dust cloud made by Ringo's caravan headed east.

After hours of bouncing in the back, they passed through Raqqa without stopping. Jacob said, "Looks like there's no going back now."

Carlos and Devon grinned and fist-bumped. Hussein said nothing, studying Jacob. Seeing the change that had occurred in his friend, like a virus that had invaded his soul and taken whatever humanity he had left.

20

Jacob had always been crazy, even on the inside of the boys' school, but he'd had a limit. You could push him only so far before he'd react, but even then, he'd cause just enough damage to solve the problem. Now those limits were gone. Destroyed in the cauldron of the Islamic State. What remained was anybody's guess.

Hussein knew Jacob would never be a Muslim. He was nothing like Carlos and Devon, two men who lacked both the intelligence and the self-esteem to even understand the cause they were being used to serve. Embracing the charnel house as a womb, they projected onto others the pain they'd felt their entire lives, for the first time harnessing a power they'd never had by holding a blade in their fist. A blade that was not only sanctioned but encouraged.

Jacob was different. And had grown more distinct in the time they'd been inside Syria. He was like a pit bull that had been trained in a gladitorial arena, punished again and again, then released into the wild. Free to run among the other dogs, but holding a killer instinct that none of the others possessed.

Hussein remembered cutting the head off of the other Kurd. Remembered the revulsion and the absolute fear. Remembered the man's life force leaving his body as his limbs vibrated in their binds, the tapping of his legs as he cut, the image seared into his conscious like a physical branding, never allowing him to sleep again.

But what he remembered most of all was Jacob yelling at him. Jacob ordering him to do it for the white house. Jacob's eyes boring into him.

A visage completely devoid of emotion or empathy. A man who had crossed over. It scared him beyond belief, and he no longer knew if his greatest sin was killing the Kurd or turning Jacob loose.

The truck bounced along, traveling ever north, and Jacob scooted over to him, leaning in close. He said, "You can leave once you get to Jordan. You know that, right?"

Hussein said, "I won't do that. I know my duty."

"Bullshit. You aren't cut out for this. Get to Jordan and get out. Anyone says anything about hunting you, and I'll deal with them."

Hussein studied his friend, seeing the same compassion from after the white house, when he'd been thrown back into the barracks. After the atrocities. Seeing the man who had helped him survive those days. Conflicted, he said, "Ringo told me what will happen if I flee. They'll kill my father."

"Why does that matter? That asshole left you when you were four. You don't even know him. He's getting what he deserves. You wouldn't even be in this mess if he'd hung around."

Hussein looked into Jacob's dead eyes and wished he had the same pitiless mind-set. He did not.

"I know. I know in my heart, but I don't know if I can do it."

Jacob laughed and said, "You were always soft. Even inside."

Hussein had a wild fantasy flit through his head, a solution to all of their problems. He said, "My mission is easy. All I have to do is get a door open, away from the security of the hotel."

"So killing a hundred people is worth the life of your father? A guy you've never known?"

Hussein drew in, tucking his head like a turtle, wanting to get away from what his simple opening of a door would accomplish. He said, "What about you? You're going to be a *shahid*. Kill yourself. You want to go out like that?"

Jacob got that distant look on his face and said, "I'll follow this a little bit further." He glanced at Hussein and said, "They made us study the Catholic faith. Remember when we used to talk about jamming broomsticks up the asses of those preachers? The same way the guards did to us? It looks like I might get that chance."

Hussein said, "Our school wasn't Catholic."

"Fucking close enough."

Hussein thought about telling Jacob his terrible secret. Fantasized about recruiting Jacob, then turning himself in at the Jordanian border, explaining how he had to ditch all of the communication methods he'd been given for survival—instead of the truth that he'd simply crumbled under outright fear.

They'd be pleased he'd survived, and would want to know what was being planned, and he could tell them. About Jordan, anyway. He had no idea what the rest of the Lost Boys were up to. But he could tell them he had a much stronger man on the inside. Jacob.

The thoughts flitted through his head, and he realized he could not. He was trapped between the loyalty Jacob required and the insanity of the Islamic State.

If he broached the *hows* and *whys* of his trip to Syria, laying bare his recruitment as a snitch, he would feel the wrath of Jacob. And he'd seen how his friend treated traitors.

He said, "Maybe we should both flee. Maybe you could meet me in Jordan."

Jacob said, "Maybe so."

But Hussein knew it wouldn't happen. Saw the divide growing ever larger between them. Hussein was still clinging to his self-preservation. Still trying to find a way out of the maze of death he'd created.

Jacob was embracing it.

21

For the first time in his career as commander of the Taskforce, Kurt Hale sat to the side as Kerry Bostwick, the director of the CIA, took a pounding. While he would have enjoyed the respite, he couldn't help but feel sorry for the man, along with a hefty dose of skepticism as to why he was even in the room. Ali Jaafar Hussein, aka LEOPARD, was turning into a disaster, but it wasn't a Taskforce problem. This was a mess for the congressional intelligence oversight committees, not for the principals of the Oversight Council.

President Warren shook his head in disgust. "How in the hell did he get from Syria to Jordan?"

Kerry said, "He flew. Some podunk airline from Oğuzeli Airport in southern Turkey."

The secretary of defense said, "How did that happen? I thought you were going to spread his name all over the place."

Kerry said, "I did, I did. The point was to keep him from coming home. The no-fly list is for people traveling to or from the United States. I can't help it if a two-bit commuter airline still using paper tickets let him go."

Billings, the secretary of state, asked, "How did he get through immigration? If you told our allies his name?"

Kerry rubbed his eyes and said, "Once again, that was to prevent him from attempting to come home. To conduct an attack here. Getting out of Turkey from that airport required only a stamp because he has an American passport. I doubt his name was even run. Getting into

Jordan required a visa, which he bought at the airport. He was let into the country, but our liaison alerted me, just as I asked. If he'd have tried to board an aircraft to the United States, he would have been stopped."

President Warren said, "Why didn't they detain him in Jordan?"

"Because I was afraid of the repercussions. They alerted me, and I thanked them. I couldn't tell them he was a rogue agent, and I certainly didn't want them interrogating him. After what happened in Afghanistan with the Jordanian triple agent, if Hussein had said one word about being a US asset, then about beheading someone in Syria, it would be on the world stage. The Jordanians would leak it sure as shit, and we don't need those complications."

President Warren said, "So what now?"

Cynically, Kurt wondered if the conversation had been scripted between the president and Kerry. Then realized why he was in the room, even if everyone else didn't.

Kerry said, "Now we go get him."

Billings said, "Inside Jordan?"

"Yes. He never reported, but he has information. He can give that up willingly or unwillingly, but he's going to give it up."

The SECDEF said, "If you're going to roll him up in Jordan, why not just do it at the border?"

Billings said, "He's already through the border, so getting him in Jordan is ridiculous anyway."

"No, it's not," said Kerry, "We have an anchor. We know where his father works in Amman. That's the only reason he could be in Jordan."

The SECDEF said, "Then why not just have the Jordanians go get him?"

"The same reasons I said before. I want a clandestine hit. A Taskforce hit. I don't want anyone even knowing he exists. I can't do that with CIA assets. We're too close to Jordanian liaison for an operation like this. Too many equities in play. I stand by my earlier words, but the fact is that we need to maintain our relationship with the Jordanians. They *are* a staunch ally, and we need their help in the fight. I want to separate this. Keep it clean."

Kurt heard the words, remaining silent, but already calculating the operational parameters. President Warren said, "Kurt?"

He leaned forward and said, "I can do that. It's pretty much a textbook operation, and Amman is an easy place to work. We've been there many times. As long as you guys are comfortable with me targeting a US citizen, I'm okay with it. It's a gray line, though. I don't want to hear any yelling after it's done."

President Warren looked around the room, then said, "He cut off a man's head with a butcher knife. I don't think that'll be an issue."

Kerry said, "You mentioned a team in Istanbul. I was thinking you could redeploy them tonight or tomorrow. Get them on the ground and start working. I'll give you all the intelligence you need."

Kurt nodded, thinking, then said, "Yeah, that would be quickest, but I'd like to keep them in Turkey. Their cover is working a natural gas pipeline contract, and that doesn't translate easily to Jordan. I break them free, and I can't get them back into Turkey. We might need to pull that trigger later."

"So you're saying you can't do it?"

"No. I'm saying that Jordan has other unique cover opportunities. It's full of old stuff, all over the country. I already have an established UNESCO world heritage site cover there, and I want to use it."

Like he was spitting out spoiled milk, Billings said, "You mean Pike."

Kurt smiled and said, "Yes, that's exactly what I'm saying."

"Why him? I thought he was tied up in Nairobi. Surely there's someone else."

"There are a lot of archeological sites in Jordan. It's perfect for his team's cover. Get him and Jennifer in there, and they'll have free rein."

"Free rein to cause an international incident."

Kurt bristled, and President Warren interrupted. "Enough. We make the Omega call, Kurt decides the operational parameters. So, is it Omega here?"

Kerry said, "Yes, for me. I think it would be best. The quicker we get Hussein under controlled interrogation, the longer we'll have to determine the inside threats from the Islamic State."

The president went around the room, and the Oversight Council raised their hands one by one, with Billings being the only dissenting vote.

President Warren said, "Looks like you've got your Omega. Get Pike moving."

22

After waiting much longer than he thought he would, Ali Hussein began to believe his father had decided to ignore him, which brought a sliver of fear. Ringo and his team were supposed to arrive from Ma'an tomorrow, and if he couldn't deliver, he was sure he'd be discarded, his throat cut, left to bleed out in an unnamed village in the desert.

He glanced around the cavernous lobby of the Grand Hyatt, seeing a woman at the reception desk stealing furtive glances his way. Soon enough, one of the security guards manning the metal detectors at the door would ask him his business, then ask him to leave.

He stood up, thinking he'd go to the restroom just to quell the heat of the glares, when he saw a man coming across the lobby. He stared, trying to remember, peeling back layers of vague recollections from a lifetime ago. Trying to reconcile the person walking with a wrinkled, yellowed photo of his father taken fifteen years earlier. The only one he'd ever seen.

He thought it might be him. When the man looked him dead in the eye, he knew it was. He waited, shifting from foot to foot and running through in his head what he had come to call "The Speech."

As he got closer, Hussein saw he was well groomed and immaculately dressed, with a pair of crossed gold keys on his lapel.

He's the concierge. He never mentioned that in our emails.

Before they'd fled into the desert from the training camp in Syria, Omar had located his father and had had Hussein initiate contact.

They'd emailed back and forth twice, but beyond Omar knowing that he worked at the Grand Hyatt—because that was the email address Omar had found—he'd never mentioned being a concierge. Which was both good and bad. Good in that it meant that his father had worked his way up from the bottom, and was valued by the hotel management, but bad precisely because he would hold his reputation before anything else.

The stranger stopped in front of him, and Hussein was at a loss for what to do. He tried a smile, which came out as a grimace, and his father said, "Ali." The stranger stared at Hussein for a moment, overcome by emotion. He said the name over and over again, as if to convince himself it was real. "Ali, Ali, Ali, I never thought I would see you again."

Then his father embraced him.

Hussein was shocked. He plumbed the depths of his memory, trying to remember anyone showing him true affection. He could not. Even the love he'd experienced with women had all been paid, either in dollars or drugs. He was unsure what to do, his arms in the air looking for a place to go.

His father drew back, holding both of Hussein's shoulders at arm's length. Hussein actually saw a tear in his eye. Unable to come up with anything else, Hussein said, "Hello, Father."

Which caused another round of embracing. The entire episode was confusing to Hussein. He'd expected to cajole or beg, knowing that his father wanted nothing to do with him. After all, if he did, why did he leave so long ago? He had so many questions.

His father said, "Come, come," leading him to a table in the foyer, away from the front door. "Sit, sit."

Hussein did so. His father said, "How did you come here? How is your mother?"

"She's in jail. Drugs. I haven't seen her almost as long as you."

The smile faded from his father's face. "I'm sorry to hear that. I truly am."

Hussein had a planned speech. A quick way to get what he wanted, the same act he'd used to get through most of his life. A plausible lie wrapped in a pit of treachery. What came out surprised him.

"Why did you leave us? Why did you leave *me*?"

His father glanced out the window, staring but not seeing the street beyond. Reflecting. He said, "I always intended to come back. I never wanted to leave. I was on a visa when I met your mother. She became pregnant, and I began to apply for citizenship. Then she became hooked on drugs."

His eyes teared up again, and Hussein felt his conviction falter. His mission began to dissolve. His father continued, "I was a taxi driver. I made no money, and she began to burn through it all. I tried to get her out, but failed. Then, the terrorist attack in New York happened. The World Trade Center fell, and everything changed. She was arrested one more time, and my visa was revoked. They said I was involved in her crimes, then accused me of planning attacks against America. They threatened me with jail, and I saw the news about the detention centers in Cuba. They couldn't prove anything, but I was so scared. They just deported me as a nondesirable. There was nothing I could do. I didn't fight it."

He began to cry, and Hussein rubbed his arm, reeling with the truth that obliterated all of his pent-up loathing. "It's all right, Father. It's okay."

His father looked up and said, "I am ashamed that it is you who had to find me, but I'm proud at the same time. You are what I would like to be. You look good."

Hussein laughed and said, "No, I don't."

"That's true. You don't, but you look good to me."

They sat in silence for a moment, his father drinking in the visit and Hussein conflicted about why he'd come. Eventually, his father said, "So, what can I do for you?"

Snapped out of his thoughts, Hussein gave his speech. "I'm only here for a month. I traveled a great distance to see you, and I've used up all of my funds. I have a place in east Amman. It's paid for, but I need work to live. I need a job."

His father said, "Nonsense. You'll come live with me. Leave that place behind."

Which was the complete opposite of what Hussein had expected. He thought about it. Freedom, tantalizingly close. Then he remembered Omar. Remembered that Omar knew where his father worked. Knew everything, including how to punish.

There was no easy way out.

"No, no. I want to make my way. I want to work. I want to establish myself. Let me do this my way. All I ask of you is a job."

His father leaned back and said, "I wish I could do that. I can give you my home, but I can't give you a job. You are probably too young to remember, but terrorists blew up this hotel in 2005. I was working, and it was horrible. Since then, they've become very, very strict about hires. Background checks and everything else."

"I'll do anything. Clean rooms, maintenance, whatever. I'm not looking for a cush job. Just one that lets me survive." *And gives me a key to a door away from the security.*

He banished that thought as something to deal with later. When he could analyze where he was.

His father said, "It's not the position. Everyone gets the same scrutiny."

"But I'm an American citizen with a well-respected father. Right? Surely that counts."

His father reflected for a moment, then said, "There's an opening in the kitchen. It's a cleaning position. You'll have to spend your time scrubbing ovens and hauling trash out of the building, but I think I can get through the red tape because of the unique circumstances."

Hussein said, "I'll take it."

His father patted his arm and said, "Let me get the applications. Help you fill them out."

He left to gather the paperwork, and Hussein wondered again at his father's love. Wondered if he had it in him to use that love to kill.

23

Rashid al-Jaza'iri said, "Play the tape again."

The man to his front clicked the digital button on the computer, and the conversation came out anew. A voice discussing a meeting, and another voice agreeing. The second man on the recording was the one that intrigued him.

He said, "That isn't Adnan."

"I know. We believe that Adnan was killed in a crusader air strike. Everyone is talking about it. Much like happened to us."

The man speaking was an emir of Jabhat al-Nusra, and the one who had bankrolled, sheltered, and championed the Khorasan group. He had a direct line to the heart of al Qaida, and wasn't someone to trifle with. Even so, Rashid—known as the Algerian—understood the respect he commanded. As Rashid was one of the few remaining Khorasan members, and a man who'd served faithfully in both Afghanistan and Syria, Jabhat al-Nusra listened to what he had to say. He'd fought valiantly on all fronts, but that wasn't what made him special. Like many before him, he'd come from a European state, but unlike them, he brought with him some specific skills.

He'd defected from French intelligence, the highest-ranking man in any country to ever do so. He'd served in the belly of the beast of the DGSE—Directorate General of External Security—learning the dark arts, and then had decided to use those skills in the fight for Allah. He hadn't been instructed in the ways of tradecraft and treachery at some camp serviced by camels. He'd been trained by the best, in a first-world country, and everyone knew it.

A fact he could now use, even as he was talking to an emir in Jabhat al-Nusra.

"So, this new man is the go-between to get the explosives we developed? He's the new contact?"

"Apparently so."

Rashid hit the play button again, just to be sure. When the conversation ended, he said, "What, exactly, is the Islamic State planning?"

"We don't know. Only that it will be big. After our members were martyred, Adnan reached out, saying that he had an attack against the West, and could succeed."

"Yes, yes. I know all of that. I'm the one that agreed. When it was Adnan."

At a loss, the emir settled for "It's still Adnan. The mission was already put in motion, with some Amriki that are without scrutiny. Completely clean. This man is the one who is leading them."

"Amriki. Americans. It sounds tempting, but I'm not so sure." He said it offhand, hiding his true feelings. Hiding his hatred. He needed to be convincing.

"Adnan called them the Lost Boys. They are undetectable. In fact, one is in Jordan right this minute. He's planning an attack there, with some of our members."

That picked up Rashid's interest. "What members?"

"Remember al-Britani? The one who relishes being in the propaganda? Delivering justice?"

"Yes. I do. I used to lead him. He's not that impressive. He fought when he had to, but spent more time in front of the camera after the fact. He has half the world chasing him because of it."

The emir said, "Not this time. He's in Jordan right now, and he has one of the Lost Boys with him. They're planning a synchronized attack with the man you just heard. A significant blow that we can claim with the Islamic State. It will be our joining. Showing the world that our fight from the past is done."

"Really? And why wasn't I told about this?"

Rashid saw the pique in the emir's face, and knew to back off. If only to get what he wanted.

"Because you were with the Khorasan group. Tasked with the very attacks they are conducting. Yet you failed."

Rashid heard the words and felt the sting. He wanted to lash out, but he was too close. Too close to getting his hands on the man who had humiliated him.

Two years before, in response to al Qaida siding with Jabhat al-Nusra over a question of legitimacy, the Islamic State had declared them an enemy, slaughtering al-Nusra as easily as the regime's soldiers in a vicious bloodletting that rivaled the civil war itself. Al-Nusra should have mopped up the Islamic State in short order. Would have beheaded all of them for their treachery, as they had the better men and skill, except for one soldier: Omar al-Khatami. The Chechen. Fighting for the Islamic State, he had proven to hold a battlefield prowess like none other—even the Syrian army—and had laid waste to huge swaths of al-Nusra terrain. The culminating point for Rashid was a battle in a village outside of Aleppo.

Terrain cut off, no supplies coming in, men beheaded or shot on sight, al-Nusra had collapsed, and Rashid had fled, escaping dressed as a woman, his face hidden by a niqab veil, his body cloaked in black. He'd been stopped at a checkpoint, and had known he was dead. The only question was how slow it would be.

Omar had interrogated him, searing his voice into Rashid's brain. Omar had punctuated each statement with the blade of a knife, then, inexplicably, had left the room without killing him.

Lying in a pool of spit and blood, Rashid had feigned weakness, lulling his captors. When he'd seen a fleeting opportunity, he'd seized it. Using his skills and a healthy dose of luck, Rashid had slaughtered the guards holding him with a steel spring torn from a mattress, fleeing into the dark still dressed as a woman.

A shameful woman.

The rage that memory brought could never be calculated, and now he had the means to deliver retribution.

If only he worked this right.

He said, "Okay. Let's give him the contact in Albania, but tell him the meeting is twenty-four hours later. Tell him we've had issues."

"Why?"

"I want to vet him. I want to be sure he's who he says he is. I know Adnan, but I don't know this man. I'm going to Albania personally."

The emir smiled and said, "That's not necessary."

"It is to me. I'm going. And I'm taking my men with me. I need support assets. I need passports and clean money. Credit cards and cash."

The emir considered him, seeing the conviction, and said, "The fight is here. Now. If they succeed, they succeed. If they don't, nothing has been harmed. Let them continue."

Rashid nodded and said, "I have the skill to blend into the population. The intelligence training to evade the crusader net. I want to help him, and this is the best way."

The emir pursed his lips and sat back. "You feel this is necessary for success?"

Rashid smiled, saying, "Yes."

But he failed to articulate what he meant by *success*.

24

I felt the heat start to rise inside the car and wondered why the hell I'd decided to control the operation. I could have put Knuckles in charge and been inside with Jennifer.

Dumbass.

Truthfully, after the last operation, I wasn't looking forward to another follow-and-catch mission. I wanted some high adventure, not the boring slog of building a pattern of life, then a single takedown. Yeah, the final endgame had been a little fun, but the damn buildup was murder. But apparently, this guy was somewhat important, made more unique because he was American.

Kurt had called, redirecting us just as we were headed to Hyrax Hill in Kenya, the famed cradle of civilization discovered by the Leakeys back in the 1920s, and the reason we had supposedly come to the country. Which aggravated the hell out of Jennifer.

She could live with the guns and blood, but she did so primarily because we always got to do some digging around old pottery shards to maintain our cover—although I secretly believed she was beginning to like the Jason Bourne stuff. This time, her expected trip was cut short.

We were redirected to Jordan under some flimsy excuse of checking out the deterioration of Umm el-Jimal, some Byzantine relic full of archaic bricks. Ostensibly we were under contract for UNESCO, the UN organization charged with preserving culturally significant sites around the world. Before Jennifer got to drag me to that place, though, she had to build a pattern of life on our target, and this one had some peculiarities.

Kurt had given us a complete data dump, and the history of this guy really made me wonder what the hell we were doing in the grand ol' US of A. The target was an asset recruited, trained, and inserted into Syria by the CIA only to end up killing other CIA assets. Made me shake my head. The second head-scratcher was why we were chosen for the mission. When we were used, it was precisely to evade the prying eyes of the host nation, which sort of defeated the whole "coalition of the willing" thing. But then again, given the sensitivities with Jordanian politics, I could at least buy that.

Anyway, it was going to be an in and out. The detail we'd gotten from the CIA was spot-on, with potential locations, current photographs, and biodata. We'd deployed with Omega authority in hand and had found the guy yesterday right where they said he'd be—at his father's hotel—and now we were doing the necessary boring work of developing his habits so we could pick a kill zone.

Easy stuff. Except for the heat in my car.

My earpiece crackled and I heard, "Trigger. Got Hipster. He's headed out. This time with a uniform in hand."

Looks like he got the job.

His name was Hussein, but we didn't use that on the radio. He had a wispy mustache thing, and was skinny, wearing tight jeans and looking like some twentysomething that frequented Brooklyn coffee shops arguing sections of Proust, which is where Retro had come up with the code name "Hipster."

From what we could tell, he'd been interviewing for a position inside the hotel. I guess trying to build a new life for himself. I hated to crush that aspiration, but it was my job. Okay, I didn't at all. Seeing an asshole cut off someone's head does that to me.

I said, "Roger. Loose follow. Just confirm the same route and residence."

Amman, Jordan, is a unique city in that the entire place is split right down the middle, with the haves and have-nots clearly separated, much like all of the small towns you read about in old stories of America, with a "right side of the tracks" and a "wrong side of the tracks." In this case, the entire section of west Amman was the right side, with high-end shopping, expensive cars, leafy parks, and spas. The east was the wrong side, with claustrophobically close stone buildings, dripping pipes, and refugee camps from the spillover of wars from the formation of Israel to the invasion of Iraq and the current Syrian fight.

The Grand Hyatt hotel, where Hussein's father worked, was right in the center, and from it, Hussein had routinely walked the four kilometers home, winding his way through the narrow streets until he reached the famed Citadel, an old Roman ruin in the heart of the city. From there, he entered the packed confines of the east, leaving the glow of west Amman behind and slinking his way past the cloistered buildings, scattered clotheslines, and open markets to a concrete apartment complex of the kind that was ubiquitous in east Amman. Really, the same type of thing you saw all over the Middle East.

Parked within view of the hotel entrance, I saw the target exit with a smile on his face, and I wondered how long he'd hold it.

I said, "I got him. Retro, he's on the same track. You ready?"

"Roger."

From there it was a boring leapfrog, with me manipulating teams. Something I could have done in my sleep. The only hard part had been following his route on day one, since it appeared that every street in Jordan had multiple names, depending on who was doing the talking or who had made the street sign. We'd created our own surveillance maps, with our own codes for the major arteries, so everyone was on the same sheet of music, and if he followed his pattern we'd be set on that piece of the puzzle. What I really wanted to know was where he actually stayed at night. We had the building, but we might want to take him down right in his room, and so, after triggering, Jennifer got the job of rushing ahead to pick him up at the endgame while everyone else continued to confirm his route.

Jennifer and I had scoped out the area beforehand and had found a coffee shop that afforded her a view of his apartment complex. While east Amman was rustic, to say the least, the city had tourists traveling all over, with many wanting to see the old-world charms of the east, so she would blend in just fine. Actually, better than fine. She'd gone in for tea earlier, just to check it out, and they'd fawned all over her, amazed that a Westerner would want to see them.

Of course, true to form, she'd had her head covered in a scarf, learned enough Arabic to say hello, and had done research to be able tell the servers the history of the area. She was perfect that way. I'm sure if I'd gone in, they would have spit in my cup, mainly because I would have ordered a beer.

The apartment building had two entrances, and her sole function today was to see which door he used, then trigger Brett to penetrate so he could get atmospherics inside. Possible stairwells, mailboxes, or anything else we could use to neck down the location of his apartment. Building a pattern of life was like LEGO blocks. One brick at a time. Since there was no rush on this, and we had a handle on him, I would take all the time necessary to get it perfect.

I got all the calls saying he was continuing on his route, plotting each one on my computer for historical reference and growing bored. Wishing we had a more interesting target.

I realized I hadn't heard from Jennifer after her jump from the hotel to the coffee shop. I broke squelch. "Koko, Koko, this is Pike. Status?"

I heard nothing.

I sat up, now more alert. Not concerned, but anticipating.

I got a call from Retro, "Hipster is one block out. I'm off. Koko, you set?"

Nothing.

I waited, then came on again, "Koko, I'm about to call an abort and redirect to your location with all assets. Answer if you're on the net."

She did.

"Pike, Pike, standby."

What the hell? I broke in again, something I hated doing as surveillance chief. In my mind, the more the SC talked, the more screwed up he was. The *team* should be running the show, as had happened up until this point.

"Koko, the target is a block out. Are you set or not?"

"No. I'm not set. Pike, there's someone in the coffee shop. I can't get in without compromise."

Now things were getting downright strange.

"What do you mean? Someone in the coffee shop how? Someone you know?"

Which would be impossible.

"Yes. She's dressed like an Arab, but I recognize her. She's focused on our target building. She's conducting surveillance."

The words ran through my head, but even after review they made no sense.

I said, "*She* who?"

"Shoshana. Shoshana is operating on our target set."

25

Hussein bounded up the steps to his apartment, running through all of the things he needed to do before his first day of work tomorrow. He wanted to make a good first impression, showing the hotel he was his father's son. Forgetting, for the moment, the reason he'd really come.

He opened the door to his small two-room apartment, and that purpose came crashing back, slamming into his conscious brain like a wave tossing him onto the rocks.

Ringo was sitting at his makeshift kitchen table, typing on a laptop.

Hussein kicked the door closed, then stood silently.

Ringo said, "Lost Boy. You're home. And I see you have a uniform. So we are ready. Good little man."

Hussein said, "How did you get in here?"

Ringo's condescending grin leaked out, and he said, "Did you think Omar would let you loose on your own? I'm on the lease documents. I only had to pick up a key."

Dumbly, Hussein remained at the door. Ringo said, "Come inside. Cook me some food. I saw you've been shopping, and I'm hungry. It was a long trip."

Hussein thought about his past, then his future. He remembered his father's touch, and realized he could get out right now. Kill Ringo and flee.

Ringo saw the slice of emotion on his face and stood up, pulling out a thick knife with a blackened blade. Menacing.

He said, "I'm staying here, with you, Lost Boy. Unless you have a problem with that."

Hussein said, "No, no. Of course not. Where are the others? The team? I don't have room for them all."

"Don't worry about them. They're here, and they're ready. We're all waiting on you. Did you meet your father? Get the key?"

Hussein circled around him, entering the small kitchen area. He said, "Yes. Yes, I did. But I don't start work until tomorrow."

"That's no problem. We aren't attacking for forty-eight hours. You'll have a full day of work to figure things out. Just don't give any indication of what's going to happen."

Now within view of the laptop's computer screen, Hussein saw Ringo was on Twitter, going back and forth with direct messaging. The sight provided something to knock Ringo back and gain the initiative.

He said, "Why are you on Twitter? Why are you still using social media after we were told not to?"

Ringo abruptly sat down, putting the knife on the table and closing the web browser, his fear of disobeying the Chechen clearly evident. He said, "I'm not. All I did was check my Twitter feed."

"No, that's not all you did. I saw the feed. I saw the direct message app. Who were you talking to?"

"None of your damn business. I'm in charge here." He picked up the knife, tapped the table with the blade, then used it to point at Hussein. He said, "You need to remember that."

Hussein leaned into a doorjamb and crossed his arms. "I understand my place. I don't understand what the Islamic State is planning. What is it?"

"You don't need to know. You open the door, and we'll do the rest."

"I *want* to know. My father told me what happened at this hotel in 2005. Are you going to repeat that?"

Ringo scoffed and said, "Hell no. I'm no *shahid*. My life is worth much, much more."

Hussein took that in, wondering what else it could be. He said, "I need to understand so I can help. I'm working in a vacuum."

Ringo said, "The plan is mine. You just provide the entrance. Can you do that?"

"Yes. I can now. My father gave me a job."

"Dumbass. Hope he stays away from work in two days."

The words reminded Hussein of the threat that would affect some-one other than himself. A thought that gave him an unfamiliar sense of apprehension.

He said, "Ringo, you can't kill my father. He's the concierge. Make sure the men know. There will be plenty of other people to make a statement. My father is just a worker. Understand?"

Ringo said, "Don't tell me who I can and can't martyr. The mission is all that matters here, and we'll be moving fast. He gets in the way, he's dead."

Hussein shuffled his feet, wanting to push the issue but afraid of the repercussions. Ringo saw the doubt and realized Hussein could cause the failure of the entire undertaking. He said, "Look, okay, I'll tell the team to leave him alone."

Hussein smiled with relief and Ringo said, "What can they use to identify him?"

"He's the concierge. He'll have two badges of crossed keys on each lapel. Big gold things. You can't miss them."

Ringo slowly nodded, then said, "All right, Lost Boy, we'll keep your father out of this, but if you fail to deliver, if we can't get in, I'll person-ally hunt him down and kill him. Do you understand?"

Hussein rapidly jerked his head up and down.

Ringo said, "Where's the door? How do we get in?"

"I work at Thirty-Two North, a fancy restaurant on the lobby level. It has a kitchen in the back that also facilitates two other restaurants. One of my duties is taking out the trash. There's a loading dock there with the Dumpsters. It's in the back of the hotel, in between it and the convention center. Away from all security."

"No metal detectors or guards?"

"No. You get in and you'll be facing some secondary cooks, maybe a waiter or two, but no security. There's a camera, but I'm assuming you don't care about that."

"No, I don't. And the waiters or cooks can be the first to die. So you have a key to this door? You can get in?"

"Not yet. The door has an electronic entry. They say I'll have a badge by tomorrow, my first day."

"You can bring that to me."

"No. I can't. I need it to get into work."

Ringo ignored that and said, "Can we park next to the door and get in?"

Hussein thought, then said, "I don't believe so. They have barriers to prevent someone from parking a car bomb. You'll have to stop outside of the perimeter and walk up. The only way to drive is to go through security. Is that a problem?" He hoped it was. Prayed it would prevent the attack. He'd done what he could, and if the kitchen door wouldn't work, it wasn't his fault.

Ringo said, "I won't know without seeing it. Take me there. Can we walk from here?"

Hussein nodded, saying, "Unless you brought one of your trucks, I walk everywhere I go."

26

I slammed my car into drive and entered the nuthouse known as Amman traffic, heading east to the Citadel and yelling into my earpiece.

"Knuckles, status?"

"Still staged to pick up Koko. Dropped her off and found a place to spell."

"So no visual on the target?"

"Nope. I'm a block away."

I tried Brett, using his callsign on the radio. "Blood, you have visual of Hipster?"

"Negative, negative. I was waiting on Koko's trigger to go in. I never saw him. You want me to go in now?"

Shit.

"No, no, we're in no rush. We'll just repeat tomorrow, and I don't want to burn you. Break, break, Koko, how sure are you it's Shoshana?"

"Positive. I mean one hundred percent."

"What the hell is she doing here?"

It was a rhetorical question, and Jennifer knew it, not even bothering to respond. *Shoshana. Just what I fucking need.*

She was an Israeli assassin who worked for Mossad. She belonged to a hit team called Samson that had grown out of the fabled Wrath of God missions against Black September during the 1970s. She was very, very good at her job, and if she was there, somebody was going to die. There was no way it was a coincidence. If she was sitting in the exact same coffee shop we'd chosen, she'd picked it for same reasons we had. She was looking at the same building we were. I just prayed she wasn't looking at the same target.

Shoshana and I had originally bumped heads on another mission in Istanbul, crossing paths much like this one, only I hadn't known her then and had come close to killing her, believing she was the enemy. I'm glad I didn't, because she ended up saving a lot of lives.

I cleared the road around the Citadel and said, "All elements, all elements, listen up. Box the apartment. Put a net on it and let me know if the target leaves. Keep an eye out for the rest of the Samson team. I know they're here, and odds are they've already seen you."

I got a roger from all elements but Jennifer. She said, "You want me to disengage or keep eyes on Shoshana?"

"Keep eyes on. I'm three minutes out."

"What are you going to do?"

"I'm going to brace her ass."

Knuckles said, "I want to be there. This is going to be fun."

I didn't reply, but I had to admit, he was right. This mission had just gotten interesting, and I couldn't help but feel a little adrenaline rush at the fact Shoshana was here. I genuinely liked her, and was looking forward to burning her little operation. If I had half a brain, I'd be afraid of what she'd do, because she was positively lethal. But I had an ace up my sleeve: She was sweet on me.

I jammed my Land Rover up onto a curb in a small alley and jumped out, pretty sure that there wouldn't be any tow trucks coming. I jogged toward the coffee shop, saying, "I'm thirty seconds out. Jennifer, location?"

"At the corner on the hill. The one to the south."

I knew where she meant. It was the same corner we'd used on our reconnaissance earlier. I held up short in an alley full of trash and running, slimy water. "I'm here."

"Where?"

"About to pop out. Alley to your west."

I kept walking and saw Jennifer turn the corner. She jogged up to me and said, "It's her, Pike. I'm sure. Maybe we should let her leave instead of interfering with whatever operation she's doing."

Meaning, she might go nuts. I didn't think she would, but with Shoshana, you never knew. She was impossible to predict, working on a gut instinct that sometimes bordered on clairvoyance. Actually, I hadn't told anyone, because it sounded nuts, but I believed she *was* clairvoyant. There had been times in the past when she seemed to be able to read my thoughts, scaring me.

I grabbed Jennifer's hand, dragging her with me, saying, "She just busted up our operation. Turnabout's fair play."

"What if she reacts?"

We reached the road for the apartment complex and the coffee shop, and I saw Shoshana, sitting by herself on the outside patio. She was dressed like a local, wearing a hijab and drinking tea, but it was her. I'd done enough operations side by side with her that I could sniff her out even if she was wearing a Darth Vader costume. I have to admit, seeing her brought a little nostalgia.

I said, "Come on. She won't go nuts. She's smitten with me. You jealous?"

Jennifer jerked her hand out of mine and said, "Have you lost your mind? She's a cold-blooded killer. And she's a lesbian. You *know* that."

Which was true, but didn't alter the facts. Our relationship was a little complicated, but it *was* a relationship. I said, "I know. But she's still smitten with me. Or maybe it's you."

Jennifer glared at me. I started walking down the hill and she pulled my sleeve. She said, "I think you're smitten with *her*, and it's clouding your judgment."

The comment took me aback. I stopped and turned to her. I knew she hadn't said it out of jealousy. Jennifer was *way* beyond that. She instinctively knew that I'd follow her into hell just to smell the sulfur if she asked. Truth be told, we'd already been through the fire, and she understood me more than anyone else on Earth. More than myself at times. Like now. Maybe she had a point. Maybe I was forgetting Shoshana's less-than-stellar edges.

I looked at her, seeing nothing but concern. I said, "Okay, I won't do anything stupid. Let's just see what she's about."

She squinted at me and I said, "I promise. No antics, but we can't let her walk, and there's no way we can follow her if she's working with a Samson team."

She shook her head to let me know she thought it was a mistake, but said, "Okay. Okay."

I turned and strode down the hill, reaching the small rope that marked the deck of the outside patio. I stepped over it and got within ten feet of her table before Shoshana shifted, sensing my approach. She looked up and I saw her eyes widen. She showed no other outward sign, maintaining her nonchalant tea-drinking attitude.

I sat down at her table, then looked at Jennifer standing behind me. I said, "See. Told you."

Shoshana shook her head, a bemused grin on her face. "Nephilim Logan. I suppose this is some prophecy coming to life."

Shoshana had always had a strange attraction to my given name, thinking it meant something more than the hippie purpose my parents chose in giving it to me.

She said, "Should I draw my weapon?"

"Do you have one?"

She laughed and said, "No. Actually I don't."

"Where's Aaron? The rest of your team?"

"Aaron's around. In fact, he's listening to you right now."

She glanced to the ground, and I realized she had in an earpiece. She said, "No problems. Don't break position."

She paused, then said, "Yes, you heard right. Believe it or not, I'm sitting with Pike and Jennifer. I don't know why. I'll call in a second."

She looked at Jennifer and said, "Might as well have a seat. As Pike would say, this has turned into a circus."

Jennifer did so, and Shoshana said, "You're looking good. I have to say I missed you."

Only it wasn't to me.

I said, "Don't start that shit. You can't push my buttons like that anymore. Not after Brazil."

She laughed, a genuine thing, and said, "Okay, I missed you too."

She picked up her small glass of tea. Saying nothing. Waiting on me.

I said, "What are you doing here? I mean, we're here to look at some

UNESCO heritage sites, check on their deterioration, that sort of thing. You know, for my company. We were walking around this little enclave, and holy shit, Jennifer saw you."

She said, "You guys want something to drink?"

"No. I want to know what you're doing in the same damn coffee shop I was going to plant Jennifer in."

She looked at Jennifer and said, "So, this *heritage* site is probably inside that apartment building across the street."

She is *on our target set.* But maybe the apartment complex was just a jihadist hotbed. It could still be coincidence.

I said, "Yeah, it is, and you're becoming like Uncle Kracker at a Kenny Chesney concert."

She scrunched up her eyebrows. "What does this mean?"

"It means people are paying to see me in concert and you keep popping up in the middle of it."

Jennifer rolled her eyes, realizing my clever response was lost on an Israeli. She said, "It means we're on a mission here as well, and we're wondering if you're chasing the same guy. Like last time."

"So you are Uncle Kracker?"

I said, "No, damn it, I'm Kenny Chesney. . . . Never mind. What are you doing here? What is Mossad doing here?"

"I'm no longer in government service. Aaron retired, and we're on our own."

"It's just you and him?"

"Yes."

"So you're a gun for hire now? Who are you working for?"

She said, "It's complicated."

Of course.

My earpiece came alive. "Pike, Pike, trigger. Target just left the apartment complex. He's walking with an unknown."

Shoshana's eyes narrowed, but she couldn't have heard the call. I followed her gaze. She was looking at Hussein and the unknown, walking up the street and retracing the route Hussein had taken earlier.

She *was* tracking our target.

Her eyes still on them, she stood, saying, "I have to go."

I grabbed her wrist, drawing a flash of anger, a deep well that I had seen in action before. Jennifer clamped her hand on my arm and said, "Let it go, Pike."

I looked into Shoshana's eyes and saw she was begging me to not push the issue. Begging for me to back down. But I also saw she was willing to push it to the limit, and I'd seen what that entailed. I released her, saying, "You've only got two. We can help here. Let's work together."

She threw some money on the table and said, "Like old times?"

"Yes. But we get the target. He comes with us."

She said, "He's not going anywhere but into a pine box."

At those words, I stood, saying, "I don't know how you got on this target, or who's pulling your strings, but I can't let you kill an American. Friends or no friends."

She whipped her head to me and said, "American? What are you talking about?"

27

Omar al-Khatami stared into the mirror, the steam from the hot water fogging the glass. A stranger stared back.

His hair now cut short into stubble, he'd finished the transformation by shaving his beard. The first time he'd done so in . . . in . . . he couldn't even remember. The only thing that remained were the eyes. Something that could pose a problem. Even he saw it, staring into the hotel mirror. He'd never be mistaken as a church group leader, no matter what he did. His eyes had seen too much, and had filled up with the death, like a blood bucket in a slaughterhouse. The carnage of his past now leaked out no matter what he looked like.

He pulled a towel from the rack and blotted his face, putting the thought aside. It was something to worry about later. First, he had to get the instruments of destruction from Albania, and he wondered if he was walking into a trap.

The contact call had gone fine. He'd answered with the correct responses, even as he feared using the traitorous satellite phone. He'd been given a clean email address, and he'd demanded that the phone be used only for emergencies, and the man on the other end had agreed. There was nothing outward that gave Omar pause. The man hadn't said anything wrong, but he'd sounded tinny, as if he were talking through a pipe. Or talking through some technology that was recording what Omar said.

Maybe I'm paranoid. But it wasn't the first time, and wouldn't be the last. Especially given the email.

Omar had received the message tonight on his new account. He'd been told it would simply be a test to ensure they could talk. He was just to reply, letting them know he'd gotten it, but the email had more than innocuous test words. It said the meeting in Albania had been bumped twenty-four hours. A change that raised the hair on his neck. The excuse given was some problem with the Albanians, which very well might be true, but the delay made him wary for reasons more than just his skin.

The mission had a myriad of different links, all which, if broken, would guarantee failure, but the biggest one was the elimination of the church group. It was the most important element, and he needed to be there for that. Needed to control the event and make sure the killing achieved its objectives. Death alone was nothing. They needed to assume the identities of the boys they killed, and he wasn't sure the Lost Boys could do that on their own. He had no doubt they'd slaughter on command, but wasn't convinced they had the vision to understand the delicate nature of the task.

He scrubbed his face with the towel and tossed it aside, thinking.

Jacob knows. Jacob can do it. But he has no real identity with the Islamic State. And the other Lost Boys are children looking for a home.

It was a problem he'd seen over and over while trying to build a true Islamic army. Foreign fighters flocked to the Islamic State, but most for the wrong reasons. They professed allegiance, but not for the true love of Islam. Instead of Islam drawing them in, it was their own sorry existence in whatever country they came from pushing them out, like a mother bird getting rid of a weakling. Unlike the true visionaries of Afghanistan, Chechnya, and Iraq, these men came without devotion to Islam. They came with a void to fill, and used Islam to satisfy the emptiness. They came to become something they were not.

It worked well on the battlegrounds of Iraq, where cannon fodder was needed, but was not something he trusted here, where the attack was built on the intelligence and commitment of the men. In this, he understood the slow fight of al Qaida. Understood the reasons of the Khorasan group, even as he fought them on the plains of Syria. He also recognized his own limitations.

Omar wasn't the man for this mission. His skill was the seizure of terrain. The overt crushing of towns, cities, and provinces. He'd proven that first in Dagestan, then in Mosul. He wasn't Mohamed Atta, and wished fervently for such an iron commitment from the Lost Boys. That man understood this type of mission. When Atta looked out of the window of American Airlines flight 11, seeing the New York skyline, he *knew* what it meant to be a martyr, unlike the foreign fighters Omar sent into battle.

Those men, like the Brit he'd sent to Jordan, were at most losers looking to kill just to prove their worth. Cutting off heads on camera as if that made him worthy. Omar had heard Jacob call him Ringo, and, while he should have put a stop to it, he'd actually thought it funny.

Jacob was a different animal. Omar wasn't sure what drove him forward, but he was made of the same steel as Mohamed Atta. And he'd proved it on the border crossing into Turkey.

They'd driven through the desert only at night, the Lost Boys in the back and him at the wheel. During the day, they'd hidden in enclaves held by sympathizers of the Islamic State. Or at least people who were afraid of feeling the Islamic State's wrath.

The black flags of the State were harder to find now because of the unrelenting air strikes, but at least he knew they wouldn't kill a solitary vehicle. He kept going, feeling the press of time.

They reached the border of Turkey at a sympathetic crossing. One that had been reliably used as a veritable fountain of men flocked to their cause. There, Omar had learned that the state of play had shifted.

Before, Turkey had allowed anyone willing to fight the hated regime of Bashar al-Assad free passage, no matter their allegiance or group. Had allowed anyone who wanted to kill into the cauldron, but during the time Omar had been fighting in Iraq, something had changed. Now the passage was blocked.

He'd rolled into the checkpoint, moving slowly, seeing the barrels burning and the men standing around with AK-47s. One held out his hand. He stopped.

The man said, "Who are you and where are you going?"

As he had in the past, he held out the bribe and said, "Who I am is of no concern. I'm going where I'm going." The man took the money, then looked in the back. Omar sensed something was amiss. He could see it in the attitude of the men manning the checkpoint.

The sentry, his face completely covered in a keffiyeh, had said, "Show me identification. Are you a Kurd? PKK?"

Omar had breathed a silent relief. They were more concerned with the Kurdistan Workers' Party flowing through here fighting the Islamic State than any attempt at catching him. As strange as it was, they cared more about the slow insurgency in their own country than the raging bonfire just south of the border. Something he could use.

"No. I'm not PKK. Or YPG. Or anything Kurdish. I'm Chechen, and I'm just trying to get home."

The man's eyes had hardened, and the rifle brought to bear. "Chechen how? What have you been doing in Syria?"

Omar realized too late the man cared about more than just Turkish interests. The crusaders had managed to actually get something done. Had managed to make the Turks look for the danger in their midst. And now he was in trouble.

He looked at the men around the fire barrel, all alert and pointing weapons. Not yet hostile, but he could sense the potential violence from them.

28

Omar had thought about running the man over and fleeing, turning back into the heart of Syria, when Jacob had shouted from the bed of the truck.

"What the fuck is going on? Can we not pass? Get me the hell out of this place."

The man with the weapon snapped up at the words and, in halting English, said, "Who are you?"

"Braden Smith. American journalist. Trying to get the fuck out of this hellhole. I made the mistake of coming here, and barely escaped with my life. Let us through. I'll pay you. Just let us through. I'm done with this shit."

The man had paused, then said, "Who is back there with you?"

"My camera crew."

While Omar sat still, the man had walked to the back of the pickup, seeing nothing. He said, "Where are the cameras?"

Jacob had leaned out of the bed and shouted, "They were taken from us! Right before they threatened to cut our heads off! Jesus Christ. We're American citizens. Let us through!"

Omar had seen the emotion on his face, and was amazed. He really *was* a reporter in that moment.

The man had said, "Okay, okay. No problem. Follow me. We need to record your passports."

"Why?"

"It's a new rule. Blame America. They want to track people like you.

We record your passports with a phone, and you get to leave. Unless there's a reason you don't want to."

"No, no. I'm fine with that. What about my driver?"

"He must remain."

"He saved our lives. He wants to leave as well."

"He can't."

"He *can*."

"No, he can't. Get out."

At that moment, Omar had known the mission was done. If they couldn't even cross out of Syria, they had no chance of penetrating Rome.

Jacob had lightly jumped down and said, "Where do we go?"

The man had pointed to a small shack made of scrounged plywood and tin. "There. We'll take your information, then you walk."

Jacob said, "Fine. Devon, Carlos, get out."

Both men jumped down, looking confused, but saying nothing. Jacob said, "How can we get our truck through?"

"You can't. You need a pass, and there's no way to get one from south of the border."

"But you have them in that building?"

Now relaxed, the man laughed and said, "Yes, but your man isn't getting one. If you want to spend the night here, I suppose you can."

Omar had sat with the engine ticking, wondering what he was going to do. Jacob had walked to his window and said, "I'll be back in a minute. Get ready to drive."

Omar said, "They can't take a recording of your passport. That can't get into the system."

Jacob had looked at him with his flat eyes and said, "They won't."

Nothing else.

Omar had watched him walk away, the other Lost Boys in tow. They'd entered the shack, and he'd focused intently on the light spilling out from the seams in the wood, trying to ascertain what was happening, but seeing nothing but shadows dance back and forth. Four minutes later the door had opened, and the group had emerged.

The men at the fire barrel had glanced their way, curious, but not concerned. The other Lost Boys had jumped in the back, and Jacob had approached his window.

"I'm riding shotgun. Here's your pass."

For the first time, Omar had seen the blood on his shirt.

They'd gone through the checkpoint without issue, then driven the remainder of the way to Istanbul in silence. Omar wanted to ask what had occurred, but decided it was better not to. Not out of fear, but because he already knew.

Now he had to decide if Jacob's commitment was enough to execute in his absence. Jacob had done so once before, but could he succeed outside of Syria, when his life wasn't in play?

He left the small room of the TAV Hotel, a cheap, postmodern building attached to the Istanbul airport, all metal and pressed wood, with the rooms so close it looked more like military barracks than a place for business travelers.

He went down to the lounge—really more of a cafeteria, with harsh fluorescent lights overhead and cheap metal chairs—and saw Jacob sitting with Devon and Carlos.

He sat across from them, seeing Jacob drinking a beer. He frowned and said, "I got an email today. It's not good news."

"What?"

"The linkup with the supplier has been delayed. I must wait for a day, which means I cannot be there for the substitution."

Jacob said, "Why is that a problem?"

Omar pointed at the beer bottle and said, "Because I won't be there to make sure you do it right."

Devon and Carlos looked concerned. Jacob showed nothing but confidence. He said, "The target hasn't changed? A church group from Florida?"

"Yes, that's the target."

"And the ultimate target? Is it the same? Or are you just tricking us?"

Omar felt the vibration of hatred, and decided to press.

"Why are you here?"

"What does that mean?"

Omar looked at Devon and Carlos and said, "Leave us. Now."

They did, scurrying away like children scolded by a parent. Omar watched them go and said, "I know why they fight. I know what motivates them, but not what motivates you."

"Why does that matter?"

Omar settled back and said, "Because I can't trust them to wear a suicide vest correctly. I need someone to ensure they do so. Someone like you, but I don't know what motivates you. I don't believe you care about the Islamic State."

"I do what I do for my own reasons. Why does it matter? I'll get you what you want. I'm willing. That should be enough."

"Why should I trust you?"

Jacob leaned forward, getting his face inches away. Omar felt the heat of his anger and knew he was dealing with something beyond a wish to see Allah. Something stronger.

Jacob said, "You trust me because you see in me what you see in yourself."

Omar reached forward slowly, placing his hand on Jacob's neck. Not squeezing, but showing the threat. He said, "Don't test me, boy. I trust believers. And you are not one."

Jacob stretched his neck out, looking to the ceiling and giving Omar full ability to harm him. He said, "Not a believer in what? Life? Or my death?"

Taken aback, Omar said, "You think I will spare you?"

Jacob turned his flat eyes on Omar and said, "Yes. My death matters little to me. But it means a great deal to you, and therein lies my strength."

Omar pulled his hand away, a ghost of a smile on his face.

He said, "You will do."

29

Jennifer was sitting on the edge of the couch like she was balancing on a spring-loaded booby trap. She watched Shoshana pace the room, I guess waiting on her to explode and try to kill us both. I knew she wouldn't, as much as she might want to.

After a bit of a verbal debate at the coffee shop, she'd reluctantly agreed that my men were on the target, and maybe she didn't know everything that was happening. Which was par for the course for me as well. We'd gone back to the InterContinental Hotel, where she and Aaron were staying, and now we were waiting for him to show up.

She said, "They'd better not lose his ass."

I said, "That depends on the definition of *his*, I suppose."

At the coffee shop, she'd refused to tell me what was going on, or who her target was, but she had at least stopped her operation. I understood that, because I would expect the same silence from my men. Her team leader, Aaron, would be the only one with the authority to spill the beans. If he would even do it.

Shoshana turned from the window, no longer wearing her Arab garb, and now regretting her decision, stomping back and forth with her quick pace.

She was fairly tall, about five nine, with a tomboyish body made of muscle. No breasts, no ass, and hair cut short—you had to look at her twice to see if she was female. When you did, you saw a face like a porcelain doll, seemingly full of innocence; she looked fragile and weak while being anything but. There was no way you would fear her, right up until she put a blade to your throat. She wasn't conventionally pretty, but she *was* attractive. At least to me, but that may be because I envied her skills.

I heard the lock of the hotel door *snick* and Aaron Bergman entered, looking at me with as much interest as if he'd found a bowl of fruit delivered to his room. He had always been cool under pressure, but this was a bit much. I'd expected at least a little reaction.

I stood and said, "Hey, Aaron. Looks like you're playing Uncle Kracker again."

That finally brought some confusion. He said, "What?"

Seeing I was going the smart-ass route, Jennifer stood up, giving me a palm and saying, "Pike, stop that. Sit down."

I did and Shoshana's eyes shot open. She said, "What button do you push to get that? I want it."

Jennifer ignored her and said, "Sorry for interfering with your operation. I don't want to dance around, which is what Pike will do."

I said, "Jennifer . . ."

She held her hand up again, which was really, really embarrassing. I remained quiet. To me, Shoshana said, "Okay, what's up with her? How does she do that? I would have used it in the coffee shop."

Aaron removed his coat without a word, draping it over a chair. He sat down and said, "Shoshana, save it. You brought them here. If you wanted to fight, you would have."

He turned to me and said, "So, to what do I owe your incredible presence, Nephilim?"

I leaned forward and stuck out my hand, saying, "I didn't mean to wreck what you were doing."

He shook it and said, "You never mean to. But you always do."

I laughed and said, "Not this time. I think we can help each other out."

"Last time we 'helped each other,' one of my men was killed."

My face grew hard, I said, "Right after your actions caused the death of one of mine."

He said, "Okay, fair enough. Let's hear it."

I leaned back into the couch and said, "Unfortunately, I'm not cleared to talk to you unless I know who you're working for. Shoshana said you're no longer with Mossad."

"It's complicated."

"So she said. How complicated? Counter to me?"

He smiled and said, "Well, if you mean I'm going to compete against you for a contract to protect some archeological dig, no."

Meaning, I was as full of shit as he was. He still had no idea who I worked for, but also knew if the web was run back, it ended at the United States government. Which was at least something. I didn't know if he was working for a Russian oligarch.

I said, "That's not what I mean, and you know it. I'll cut the crap. We're here on a target, and you guys are chasing the same target. Well, at least the same target set. I want to know why."

He said, "I left Mossad. Too much bureaucracy to get anything done. Too many small-time operations and too much focus on overt war. Hamas, the Gaza Strip, and Hezbollah consume them. It took away from what I want to do, which is to remove terrorists." He glanced at Shoshana and said, "She agreed to help. We have our own business."

I knew that Aaron loved Shoshana, even as he knew that love would never be returned. At least physically. She cared greatly for him, and it didn't surprise me that when he'd decided to leave, she'd followed. They were a team, in more ways than simply operations.

I said, "So? Who do you work for now?"

He looked at Shoshana and she glanced at me. She turned back to him and nodded, surprising me.

He said, "Can I trust you?"

I squinted at the insult and said, "Of course."

"Who do *you* work for?"

Taken aback, I said my cover statement. "I work for myself. Grolier Recovery Services. Jennifer and I both do."

He gave a sour smile and said, "See what I mean?"

I shuffled my feet, looking at Jennifer. She nodded at me. I paused a moment, then said, "Okay, look, I work for the United States government. Is that what you want?"

He smiled and said, "Yes. Thank you for the trust. I work for an oil magnate in Indonesia."

My mouth fell open and I heard Shoshana laugh.

I felt a split second of fear, then relief. He was kidding.

He said, "Pike, I work for Israel. I'm no longer in the government, but I still work for Israeli interests."

"What does that mean?"

"It means there are times where my skills are necessary, but my government cannot intervene. Like here. Do you know anything about the attempt to kill the Hamas chief, Khalid Mishal, in 1997?"

"Yeah. A little. You guys poisoned him and got caught. Here in Amman."

Aaraon grimaced and said, "Blunt, but fairly close. Nobody could point to us, but the king of Jordan brought so much pressure to bear we caved and admitted to it, flying in an antidote. Either way, it was a huge embarrassment and a diplomatic mess. So much so that Mossad is afraid of working in Jordan, but such work is needed. Someone must fill the gap, and we can't upset the Jordanian government. They are a reluctant ally."

He paused a moment, then said, "I expect this is the same reason you are here."

I considered his words, trying to determine what to say. Reflecting on what he already knew. This game was borderline stupid, since everyone in the arena suspected what you were doing, but they really didn't *know*. You stating it was the only way to confirm. And, while that confirmation might look simplistic and like a forgone conclusion, it wasn't. Half the time the story ended up being some jerk working for USAID trying to get laid by acting like a secret agent. Or some asshole with four years inside Special Forces inflating his résumé, convincing everyone he was on the inside, spilling James Bond stories for the fanboys. The real truth nobody knew unless *you* told them.

I tossed the ball into the middle, ignoring whom we both worked for and focusing on the target. "Aaron, I'm here for a man. Like you. My target is an American who's working for the Islamic State. We want him back, and we're going to get him. From what little Shoshana has said,

I'm assuming he's not your target. I want to know what you're going to do, and why."

Aaron smiled. "Our work is complementary. I'm operating against the Islamic State as well. You know Steven Sotloff?"

"The American journalist? The one those assholes beheaded?"

"Yes. We're tracking his killer. He's here, in Amman. He's a British foreign fighter that goes by the nom de guerre al-Britani. He was walking with your target today. Shoshana has a date with him."

I looked at her, seeing the same determination from past operations. The same willingness to kill anyone who crossed Israeli interests. She had a personal history with the Munich Olympic massacre in 1972, where her grandfather had been killed, and now brought that wrath to anyone who would attack the State of Israel. Which begged the question, *Why here?*

I said, "What does Sotloff have to do with Israel?"

"It was kept fairly close, but he was a dual citizen. He had ties to Israel. He was one of us. But because he wasn't *officially* one of us, Mossad has stepped away."

I nodded, now understanding. "But not stepped completely away."

He smiled. "No. Not completely. They've hired a bumbling crew to help out."

"And the man who was walking with our target is your target?"

"Yes."

"You hit him and get away, you make a statement for Israel. You screw up, and you and Shoshana are hung out to dry. Am I right?"

"Pretty much."

"Well, today's your lucky day. I think I can keep your bumbling crew from getting caught. Shoshana agreed to meet with us here, but my team kept eyes on your target. You help me with my target, and I'll get you yours."

He leaned back and smiled. I saw the relief on his face, and realized he was operating under extreme pressure, not the least because of the size of his team. He said, "You can do this?"

"Yes. I can. It'll have to be two separate hits, but we can make it work."

Jennifer said, "Pike, we don't have sanction for that."

I said, "Jennifer, he cut off an American head. Nobody's going to deny us Omega. Anyway, it won't be Omega. Aaron here will execute."

Shoshana said, "How can we trust you? How do we know you won't just run when you've got your man?"

I said, "Really? That hurts. You can't trust me?"

"No. We can't. That British fuck is going to die, and if you trick us into helping you and fail to follow through, you'll pay a price. Understand?"

The comment brought a smile from both Aaron and me. He said, "I guess your goodwill with her is gone."

Understanding that at least *he* trusted me, and liking the change of position, where I could torque Shoshana a little bit for a change, I said, "Well, she's a pain in the ass anyway. Put her on ice and let's get this done. I've got the manpower."

I glanced at Shoshana, mightily trying not to let the smugness seep through.

I waited on the outburst, and instead, Shoshana was nothing but calm. She said, "Aaron, he might be right. All you guys can get his target, then we use his men to get ours."

I raised my eyebrows, confused at her passive response. She sat down next to Jennifer and rubbed her thigh, moving ever closer to her crotch. She said, "Us women will stay here, in our place. In our room."

My jaw dropped of its own volition, and I leapt up. Jennifer slapped Shoshana's arm away, then put her hand to her forehead, rubbing it like she had a migraine.

Shoshana saw my reaction and grinned. I realized too late that I'd just failed in my play, and *I* was the one burned.

30

Hussein's father kissed him on the cheek and waved him away, a large smile splitting his face. Hussein returned the joy with a grin of his own, twirling his newly issued badge and bouncing out the front door of the opulent Grand Hyatt hotel, his first day of work completed. Truthfully, his first day in more ways than one.

Hussein had never held a job for more than a couple of months, always quitting or getting fired, the sole purpose having been to gather enough money for a few nights of blissful sedation. Never solely for the pleasure of the job itself.

Today had been different. Today, he had been respected. Valued. And in turn he'd worked harder than he ever had, for the first time not wanting to let anyone down.

He barely noticed the people he went past as he pulled off his apron and folded it in his hands. Walking in the shadow of the Citadel, he placed the cloth reverently in his backpack, then laid his badge on top of it. The sight of his newly earned credentials brought him crashing back to earth, the badge reminding him why he was really in Jordan. What his real work would entail.

He sat heavily on a stone park bench and squeezed his eyes shut. *There has to be a way out of this. Something to prevent the killing.*

He cursed the CIA for bringing him into this cauldron. Cursed his mother for never having told him about his father. He could have avoided the boys' school. He would never have met Jacob, and the CIA would never have come calling. He could have had the life he'd dreamed about late at night, after his visits to the white house. When the pain ceased to control his mind.

He rubbed his face, staring at the ground, struggling for a solution.

He could tell Ringo that they hadn't given him a key. That he hadn't been entrusted with a badge. *But Ringo will only tell you to force someone to open the door. Failure isn't an excuse.*

He could disappear, taking the badge with him. Move in with his father and hide. *But Ringo will still execute the mission, and he'll kill father in the process.*

Maybe he should go to the US embassy. Throw himself at the damn CIA and tell them everything. Turn himself in. *But you killed a man. You carved his head off. And you brought in Jacob. You recruited and turned loose the Lost Boys.*

How could he tell them that? They'd torture him in a secret prison for the rest of his life. And Ringo would still kill his father.

The flopping of the Kurd he'd slaughtered flashed in his mind. The body bucking underneath him, the knife handle becoming slippery in his hands from the fountain of blood.

He curled up on the bench and began to cry.

"He's doing what?"

"Crying. Shoshana said he's sitting on a bench bawling his head off."

What the hell?

We'd tracked Hussein since leaving work, and he'd taken the same path he had since we'd started chasing him. Humans are naturally creatures of habit, and Hussein was no different. I had half the team waiting on him at the end of a narrow alley, a route he always took when heading back to his apartment, a trash-strewn footpath not unlike the one I'd met Jennifer in earlier. They would block his escape. Shoshana, having the ability to blend in better than anyone on my team, had been given the mission for a loose follow. The other half of the team was with me. The endgame for the traitorous bastard.

"Crying about what? Did something happen?"

Jennifer, who'd acted as the trigger for the surveillance but was now in my vehicle, said, "Not that I saw. He was smiling and almost skipping when he left the hotel."

"Well, maybe we ought to just pull up to him and throw him in the van while he's still blubbering."

Aaron spoke into his phone, then said, "Too many people around."

"That was a joke. We stick with the plan."

Aaron smiled. "Good. I won't have to tell you what Shoshana actually said."

I grimaced and said, "What, did that little empath decide he's a nice guy now?"

Shoshana marched to her own drummer, relying on some primordial instinct she could sense in front of her instead of reams of paper handed to her from some intel analyst. And more often than not, she was proven right. Seeing Hussein cry may have altered her calculus.

"No, no. She could care less about him if it leads to our target. She wants al-Britani planted in the ground. Your man means nothing to her."

Then again, like a vampire craving a feeding, she was also a little bloodthirsty.

Aaron looked at me, phone to his ear. He nodded and said, "Hipster's moving. Same line of march as predicted."

Hussein wiped his eyes, the last of the hitches subsiding, and wearily stood. He trudged forward, his emotional state as raw as skin scraped on concrete. He mindlessly continued moving, blotting out the persistent image of the Kurd. Blotting out all thoughts of where his path was leading even as he continued walking it.

There was one solution left.

He could kill himself.

It would be nothing less than he deserved, and would free him from all of the pain. But that murdering sociopath Ringo would *still* kill his father.

For the first time in his pointless existence, he cared about something other than his own skin, and if killing himself would solve the problem, he would have gladly done so.

But it would not.

He continued walking robotically, head down, lost in his despair. He turned into the shortcut alley next to his apartment, barely two arms wide, knowing his fortune was upon him, but not realizing the route it would take.

Kicking cans and plodding forward, he didn't hear the van block the entrance he'd just used. Didn't hear the footsteps behind him. Didn't even register anyone was in the alley with him until he felt a caress on his shoulder. He turned, seeing a woman wearing a hijab. Her eyes were cold steel, looking into his soul and seeing the damage he'd wrought. He stumbled back a step, confused, trying to assimilate how she knew, when a man appeared behind her. A big man, with a wicked scar tracking through his razor stubble and hard eyes expressing the same knowledge. No mercy. No sympathy for his plight.

And he was holding a gun.

31

Omar leaned into the window as the aircraft crested the mountains, the low clouds finally breaking to show the valley below. They began to lower into the bowl and Omar saw the concrete of Tirana spilling out, threading into the fingers and ridges in the distance. The international airport grew larger and larger, and he recognized a string of old Soviet fighters on the tarmac, rusting and stoic. Proud defenders of a system that no longer existed.

His plane hit the runway fairly roughly, jarring open two overhead bins far past their service prime on the Alitalia 737. The pilot applied the brakes, the engines reversing with a whine, and Omar wondered if they were going to drive off the edge. He began squeezing his armrest, exposing his anxiety as he stared out the window at the land racing by.

Truth be told, he didn't like flying. Actually hated the idea, but it might have been because the only aircraft he'd ever been on were ones that allowed goats in the aisles. Flights where the passengers clapped at the landing, amazed they were alive.

As they did now.

Omar didn't join them, but he wanted to. They taxied to the terminal, and his thoughts turned to his bigger worry: getting into Albania.

He had no idea how strict the immigration process was, or even if his cursory Internet search would be proven true. Unlike the Lost Boys, he had no United States citizenship to hide behind. His passport was Russian, albeit with a Schengen visa.

Created for the travel of citizens within twenty-six countries in

Europe—the so-called Schengen zone—it allowed them to cross borders hassle-free. Albania was not a member, but in the strange world of international diplomacy, they recognized the visa for entry into the country. At least the Internet said they did.

He hoped it was true, as this city had been chosen for a reason.

A majority Muslim country, Albania had been part of the mammoth Soviet Union, and, like all countries behind the Iron Curtain, had banished religion when the communist overlords secured control. After the wall fell, and the country gained independence, the Islamic faith once again flourished, and, like just about anywhere with a sizable Muslim population, sympathizers could be found.

Unlike other countries, with security services clamping down on the immigrant population, Albania had yet to draw the eye of the crusaders, making it a good location for the transfer of weaponry.

Omar remained seated until the flow of people allowed him to exit the plane. He followed the passengers to a waiting bus, then entered the immigration hall and got in line, one of the few times when his queue, as a visitor, had been shorter than the one for citizens. He presented his passport, hiding the trepidation as he had many times before. After a brief exchange, where he explained he was seeing friends, his passport was stamped and he was through.

He hadn't even had to provide a hotel or show any other proof of his intentions, which gave him comfort that Albania had been the right choice.

Twenty minutes later, in a cab where he'd given up trying to understand the driver's limited English, he entered the city center. Surrounded on all sides by concrete buildings with a depressing utilitarian bent, it reminded him of Grozny. Well, at least before Grozny had been leveled by the Russians.

The driver pulled over at a traffic circle and pointed across the street, muttering something unintelligible. Above a store selling luggage he saw the small sign of his hotel. He paid the fare and made his way across the street.

The hotel was a ten-room threadbare affair with a faint, musty odor, complete with actual metal keys and a communal bathroom at the end

of the hall. He cared not a whit about comfort, only that it was inconspicuous. He paid in cash, thanked the clerk, and climbed the narrow
stairs to his room.

He dropped his bag on the floor, then sat on the bed studying a tourist map of Tirana he'd found at an airport kiosk. He memorized his location, then found the restaurant where he was to meet his men. It looked
a short walk away, maybe ten minutes, in an area called the Block.

Twenty minutes later he was standing on a narrow street called Pashko
Vasa, trying to locate an address and having no luck. It had seemed
easy on the map, but the buildings were all jammed together with no
obvious numbering on the doors or windows.

He could at least read the corner signs. He knew he was on the correct street, and he thought he was at the right location, because his instructions had told him to stop at an Alpet petrol station.

Which was to his front.

He did a slow circle, eyeing the buildings, then heard his name called.
He glanced up and saw someone waving from a second-floor window.
He recognized Anzor, his friend, then saw the name painted below the
window, feeling like a fool. The restaurant was on the second floor,
above other businesses.

No wonder you couldn't find it.

He waved back, then jogged across the street to a stairwell below,
seeing a small sign proclaiming, CHEERS FOR BEERS. He followed footsteps painted on the tile, going up one flight and entering the restaurant,
an expansive open area clad in warm wood, with two full-length bars
lined with beer taps.

The room was empty at this early hour, with only the bartender
washing glasses. The far wall had large windows, all swung open to the
street below. Anzor and two other men were sitting at a high-top table
in the corner, near the windows.

Omar nodded at the bartender, then walked to the table, the men
standing and smiling. In Russian, Anzor said, "We were wondering if
the famous Omar had lost his navigation skills."

Omar hugged him, then the other two, pointing at the table, where three pints of beer rested. He said, "Where I come from, that would get you lashed at the very least."

Anzor laughed and said, "Not from what I remember in South Ossetia."

In 2008, Russia invaded the country of Georgia, ostensibly to support the breakaway independence of the province of South Ossetia, a Russian supporter. Still in Chechnya at the time, Omar had seen the water begin to boil before the invasion. He'd traveled into Georgia through the Pankisi Gorge, joining a paramilitary unit. He'd fought the Russians in a short, sharp war, at one point risking his own life to attack a prisoner convoy of captured paramilitaries destined for a torturous death. In so doing, he'd saved the three men in the room.

It had nothing to do with Georgian politics. He simply hated the Russians.

Omar laughed and sat down, saying, "Georgia was a long time ago. And a world away from where I am now."

Anzor said, "I know. We hear the stories about the famous Chechen taking over Iraq, and we laugh about how we knew him when he was but a foot soldier. But we never heard anything about taking over Albania. Why are you here?"

Omar said, "I should ask the same of you."

Anzor glanced at the two other men and said, "We have business here. Not all of us yearned to fight forever."

Omar knew not to press, understanding the "business" was illicit, either human trafficking or drugs—neither of which mattered to him.

He said, "Does this business have the ability to procure arms? Do you require protection?"

Anzor glanced at his two friends for confirmation. One nodded. He said, "Yes, Davit can provide the necessary things. Understand, sometimes the police are more trouble than the criminals. Protection is required, if you want to survive."

Omar smiled, "Of course. As always."

The one who'd nodded, Davit, said, "How much protection? What are you doing here?"

"I'm here simply for a business transaction, but I'm not at all sure about the integrity of the meeting. It was supposed to occur tomorrow, but the man coordinating the transaction was killed in a crusader air strike. Now the meeting has been postponed to the following day by people I have never met. It makes me skittish. All I want is the same thing you do for your business. Protection while I'm there."

Omar saw all three visibly relax. He said, "What? Did you think I was enlisting your help for something offensive?"

Anzor laughed and pointed to the third man. "Levan thought you were planning an attack and wanted our help."

Omar looked at him, and Levan raised his hands. "You have to admit, with your reputation, it would cross my mind."

Anzor said, "We're businessmen now, and we can't get entangled in your politics. We were chased out of the Pankisi because every intelligence organization in the world was hunting men like you. Nobody looks at us here in Albania, but an attack based from this area would change that. It would definitely hurt our business."

Omar said, "Are you not Muslim? Do you not feel a duty to help your fellow Ummah? Do you not remember the Pankisi?"

Anzor said, "Yes. And we do our part, contributing money to charities that help the cause. In your world, your religion trumps everything. In mine, it's business. We are opposite sides of the same coin. The Ummah needs your sword, but the edge is kept sharp with money. My money."

Omar nodded slowly, then said, "It's just protection for a transaction. I promise. All I need is for you to prevent something from happening that will interfere."

Davit said, "We haven't forgotten what you did for us. We all bear the scars. That's why we answered your call. It's just . . ."

Omar waved a hand, telling him without speaking he didn't care about the debt. He opened his knapsack, pulling out his map. He pointed to a huge expanse of green south of the city center and said, "Do you know this area?"

Anzor said, "Yes, of course. It's Tirana Park." He smiled and said, "We've conducted business there as well."

"Do you know the amphitheater?"

Anzor nodded. Omar said, "That's the meeting site. Can it be protected?"

"Yes. It will be hard, but it's not impossible. There are many ways to escape from that area, and I've had to use most at one time or another."

Omar grinned. "Your business doesn't sound that different from mine."

Anzor laughed, bumping Omar's knapsack at the table and causing a book to slip halfway out. Davit saw the black-and-yellow cover, then read the title.

Catholicism for Dummies.

He said, "What on earth is that?"

The other two men focused on it, their brows furrowed in confusion.

Omar shoved the book back into his bag and said, "Knowing the enemy. Nothing more."

He stood, slinging the bag over his shoulder. He saw their faces and said, "My business is none of your concern. That ends with protecting my meeting. The same way I protected your lives in Georgia."

32

I jammed the barrel of my Glock in Hussein's face, seeing his mouth open in surprise, then clench into a grimace of pain as Shoshana torqued his arm behind his back. She swiped his legs from under him and slammed him face-first into the pavement, then cinched his arms together with plastic flex ties and put a knee into his back, leaning forward and using her weight.

She looked up at me expectantly. I have to admit, I was impressed. I'd told her that she had the responsibility for the takedown, but it was only to put her on edge for her slights against me earlier. Give her a little worry about screwing up. I figured I'd be doing the slam dance either way, and was looking forward to it, but I hadn't even gotten the chance before she sprang into action.

I glanced down the far end of the alley, seeing Retro and Brett with eyes out toward the street, pistols held low, but ready. Brett gave me a thumbs-up and I leaned down into Hussein's ear and said, "Welcome home, shithead."

I yanked him to his feet, expecting to see fear and waiting on him to try to fight, giving me the authority to lump him up some before turning him over to the support team. Instead, I saw wonderment.

"You're American!"

It wasn't a question. I grabbed his flex ties, whirled him around toward our waiting van, and said, "What nationality I am is of no concern to you, I promise. What I'm going to do to you, if you resist, is a whole different world you should be worried about."

I began driving him forward, causing him to stumble in the debris of the alley. I kept him up by forcefully hoisting his arms in the air. He yelped and said, "No, no, I mean, I was trying to find you. Trying to make contact!"

We reached the van and I shoved him through the door, saying, "Shut the fuck up, you murdering little toad."

He sank into a ball, tucking his head into his chest. I leapt into the back, Shoshana following and closing the door. I put my knee into his chest and said into my earpiece, "Hipster secure. Meet us on our street, away from the target building. You lead to the support team. Any trouble, you provide blocker and deal with it."

I heard Knuckles say, "Roger all. Moving."

I looked at Jennifer. "Dope him."

Aaron put the van in drive and we began rolling. Jennifer withdrew a syringe, flicking the air bubbles out of it like a doctor on TV. Hussein saw the move and began to squirm. He said, "Wait, wait. Don't drug me. I have to talk to you. I have to tell you what's going on. They're going to kill my father. Please, you have to stop them."

I leaned into him and put my thumb against the base of his ear, smashing a tangle of nerves for compliance. His jaw snapped wide in silent pain and his eyes rolled back. I looked at Jennifer and said, "Hit him."

She leaned forward and he rasped, "Attack. They're going to attack."

I pulled my thumb back and waved Jennifer off. She sat on her heels, expectantly holding the needle. I said, "What was that?"

From the front, Aaron said, "Got the lead van. Five minutes out."

Breathing heavily, sweat rolling off of his head, Hussein said, "The Islamic State. The ones you sent me against. They're here. They're going to attack tomorrow, and they expect me to help."

I said, "That's great. You can tell us all about it under interrogation."

I nodded to Jennifer and he screeched, "No, no! They expect me to show up right now. If I don't, they'll know something's wrong. They'll think I double-crossed them. There's no telling what they'll do then. My information will be useless."

He sagged and said, "They'll kill my father."

I leaned back at the words, knowing if I chose to believe them, I was taking a detour off the reservation, where I would be forced to disobey the orders I'd been given. A choice I didn't want to make, given my past history. And past punishment. I looked at Jennifer for an answer. She slowly shook her head, telling me she couldn't parse the truth. I turned to Shoshana and raised an eyebrow, letting her know I wanted her opinion. Her instinct.

Her eyes narrowed, understanding that what she said was going to change the entire course of the operation, but not believing that I trusted her. Not believing I would want the answer she gave. I bored right back. She turned away and studied Hussein. He flopped his head back and forth between us, wondering what the hell was going on. She raised her head and locked eyes with me.

And nodded.

Still watching her, I keyed my radio. "Knuckles, Knuckles, pull over, we're going back. Stage at the back side of the alley, where I plucked the target."

Shoshana gave me a grim smile and I heard, "What the hell are you talking about? Did you drop your weapon?"

I said, "No time to talk. I need to coordinate with Showboat, and he's not going to be happy."

33

What the fuck do you mean you're going back? You have Jackpot. Mission success. We're not deployed here to do exploratory surgery. No Alpha mission. We have Omega for Hussein, and you've achieved that. Get your ass back here with the precious cargo."

Blaine Alexander was yelling so loud into the microphone it caused me to flinch. I said, "Sir, listen to me. I'm not making this up. Remember all the chatter about an Islamic State external operation? Remember that? I think it's here, and we're in the middle of it. Right now. Hussein says the target is the Grand Hyatt hotel. A Mumbai-style attack where they run around killing the hell out of everything that moves."

In 2008 a Pakistani terrorist group called Lashkar-e-Taiba had invaded Mumbai, India, and set about slaughtering civilians in shooting attacks lasting four days in multiple hotels.

"Pike, I don't want to hear this. I don't want a repeat of Ireland. Just get the PC back here. That's what we get paid for. We get a mission, we accomplish the mission. If there's something here, we'll interrogate, then deal with it after the appropriate consultation with higher."

I gritted my teeth. "Sir, we get *paid* to protect lives. Period. Let me flesh this out. Hussein is just the entry guy. He doesn't know exactly what they're going to do. Hell, they might have already planted bombs inside. We need to find that out, and he's no help. If it's nothing, it's nothing. I still have PC, but he's going to be worthless in an hour. They'll consider him compromised. We don't have time for a sit-down interrogation."

I heard nothing, but, having seen it many times before, I knew what was happening. Blaine was running his hands through his thick hair, pulling at the roots in frustration. Finally, he came back on.

"So you can maintain control of PC and still get the information?"

Now I paused, trying to coax an appropriate answer. I glanced back into the van, seeing Knuckles and Jennifer rigging up a scared Hussein with an audio microphone that would transmit to our van.

"Yes. I'll have enough coercive control to guarantee physical rendition."

"What does that mean?"

I blew the air out of my cheeks and said, "Sir, I have to let him go back into the apartment, but I'm telling you, he's on our side now. He's worried about his father, and seems to be in over his head. He wants to resolve this as much as we do. He's not going to run."

He only heard one thing. "You're going to let him out of your control?"

"Yes. I have to. I *have* to. Sir, come on. You mentioned Ireland, but you forget the end state of that operation. We saved everyone. *Everyone.* Because of your call. Do the same thing here."

Which was a little bit of a stretch, but not much. He'd made a hard call that had saved the husband of the governor of Texas, but then had balked at saving the one hostage that mattered to me. I'd had to take matters into my own hands then, and I didn't want to here. The personal stakes then had been much higher, and if he told me to back off here, I would. People might die, but they would be faceless strangers.

The thought came unbidden to my mind, and I was a little shocked at it. I never would have considered walking away from a threat like this in the past, and wondered if I wasn't becoming part of the bureaucracy. Or maybe I'd been slapped down enough times that I was afraid of the repercussions, like a puppy spanked for something it doesn't understand.

Crusty old warriors in the Army tell a story that there are plenty of soldiers who would jump on a grenade in a valiant act of heroism in battle, but very few who would sacrifice their careers for what they knew was right. And I was disturbed to learn I was now falling out of that very few.

Take away what a man values most, and he'll heel. They'd taken my ability to operate within the Taskforce once before, and it had scared me to the core of my being. I didn't like the thought, but I knew I'd comply. My actions in Nigeria had been pushing the edge, but I'd had the authority and known I could spin the results, no matter the outcome. Here, I'd be disobeying a direct order.

Blaine said, "How sure are you of the information? How do you know he's not stringing you for release?"

I looked at Shoshana, wanting to believe, because I wasn't sure at all. She caught my eye and knew the stakes in play. She'd heard my end of the conversation. She studied me for a moment, then nodded her head again. Telling me she knew it was true. And, after what I'd seen from her in the past, I believed it.

"Sir, I have a trained interrogator here who says it's accurate."

"Trained interrogator? Who?"

Shit. I'd failed to mention the Mossad participation in our mission planning earlier, knowing he'd blow a gasket. Of course, I'd duly reported the busted surveillance and the presence of the ex-Samson team, but only as it pertained to that specific mission. I'd conveniently left out that I was going to use them today, figuring I could cover it with them chasing their target and me chasing mine, whereupon we had to deconflict the battle space and coordinate for operational reasons. Nothing official. They just happened to be here.

It seems contradictory, since I was unwilling to continue without official Taskforce sanction from Blaine, but I've always had a healthy talent for stretching the orders I'm given. Before, that extended to outright disobedience if I deemed it necessary, but no longer. I wondered if that trait would continue shrinking like a balloon letting out air, until I was nothing more than a robot rigidly executing actions dictated by a plan that no longer applied.

I fumbled for a bit, grasping for an answer, and Showboat put two and two together. He knew Shoshana's skills, and he'd always been smart. We'd just done too many operations together. He said, "Are the Israelis with you? Is that who's doing the interrogating? Shoshana?"

I'd wanted to control the release of that information, but the cat was out of the bag now. I said, "Sir . . . al-Britani is their target. I'm not using them. . . . More like an intersection of events."

I heard nothing for a moment, but saw Shoshana grinning from ear to ear. I scowled at her, and she puckered her lips in an air kiss, which didn't help.

I heard, "Okay, Pike. We'll deal with your little subterfuge later. What's your course of action? How is letting him out going to do anything?"

Whew. "All I'm trying to do at this stage is keep their plan in motion. Apparently the ringleader is staying with him. Keeping him in check. Hussein's not fully trusted and doesn't even know where the rest of the terrorists are located. First call is to just get him home on time. From there, Hussein will learn what he can, then meet us at a predetermined location. We'll get a debrief and go from there."

I heard silence on the line for a moment, then, "He's meeting the ringleader?"

"Yes. That's the guy who doesn't trust him."

"Can he get him to dinner or something? Do they eat out?"

His words sank in and my first thought was, *Holy Shit. He can't be serious.* The adrenaline started to rise as my mind began creating a plan of its own volition. But before jumping that hurdle, I needed to make sure we were thinking the same thing.

"Sir, we have no Omega for a second takedown."

"If what you say is true, this falls into in-extremis authority. I have the ability to make the call. Do you have the ability to execute?"

"Yes, yes. I can execute. Same template. Same location. We'll just stage exactly like we did. If he can't get him down, then we'll follow through with what I said earlier. Get Jordanian liaison involved through CIA after a debrief. Let them clean up the mess."

I got another moment of silence and slammed my fist into my thigh, wishing I hadn't said those words. Jennifer gave me a quizzical look and I just shook my head at her, but I knew what was going to come out of Blaine's mouth next.

And sure enough, it did. "Maybe we should just do that anyway. Go with your plan. I'll go through the Taskforce to get the CIA operational, they can talk to the Jords, and we let them handle the assault. We go away with our guy, they get theirs."

"Sir, no, no. Way too many links in the chain. Getting them on alert with extra security for the Grand Hyatt is one thing, but spurring them into conducting a tactical hit is something else entirely. They'll never action the target without the corresponding credible intelligence, and we don't have it without giving them Hussein, which is the damn reason I'm here in the first place. To keep them from knowing about Hussein."

And Shoshana will kill me if I let her target escape into the hands of the Jordanians. Of course, I left that unsaid.

I could almost hear the hair being pulled out by the roots three miles away. I heard, "Okay, Pike. My call. Let Hussein go inside, and I'll start prepping the battlefield for the fallout. I'll start working the liaison services, get them oriented on the hotel. You snag the leader and we'll have the intelligence that we can provide the Jords, but we're going to let them handle the attack. You fucking bring me Hipster. You got that?"

I said, "Roger all, sir. Thanks."

34

Hussein felt the transmitter in the small of his back like a hot coal. Something he desperately wanted to rip out and throw away. The line to the miniature microphone traced under his arm, and he felt it against his skin, rubbing back and forth as he walked, making him wonder if it could be seen through his shirt. Reminding him at every step of what would happen if it was discovered.

He saw the end of the alley, feeling a cold drip of sweat run down his back. He wasn't cut out for this. He should have told the CIA from the beginning that he could never do something like this. Even as a child, he was the one who always crumbled.

Only one short year ago, Devon had made a fake ID for him, Jacob having said he looked the oldest because of his wispy mustache. Jacob had sent him into a store to buy beer, and Hussein had walked woodenly through the door, mumbling all of the data on the ID over and over to set it in his mind. At the counter, with the cashier staring intently first at him, then the false driver's license, he'd panicked. When the man had asked for his address, he'd raced out of the store, leaving the beer and the ID behind.

Jacob had laughed about it, but Hussein knew his weakness. And this time he wasn't buying alcohol. There would be no door to race out of.

Remember your father. This is the way out.

Hussein had never been religious, and in fact hadn't ever once prayed as far as he could remember, but he was convinced getting jerked into the back of that van was a message. Divine intervention from Allah, or

Yahweh, or something else. Walking stoically down the alley, he prayed for the first time. To a God belonging to no religion. Or all religions. He didn't care, as long as his prayer was heard.

He exited the alley, glanced furtively left and right, begging for a vehicle to allow him one more second of delay. The street was empty. He started to cross and heard his name shouted. He looked up and saw Ringo leaning on the concrete balcony outside their little apartment.

"We good?"

Hussein nodded, and Ringo said, "Come on up. I want to see."

Ringo disappeared inside, and Hussein jogged across the street, just one more young man in a sea of them on the east bank of Amman.

Hussein took the stairs one at a time, almost stutter-stepping, with each leg stopping on an individual step. He reached the apartment and knocked, then remembered he lived there. He put his hand on the knob and the door was yanked open, Ringo standing inside.

"Well? Did you get the access badge?"

Hussein dug through his knapsack and pulled it out. A long lanyard with a plastic card at the end, it was electronically mated to a receiver in the door of the kitchen. Ringo snatched the badge out of his hand, saying, "Perfect." He studied it, then said, "You don't take good driver's license photos, do you? You look like you're going to throw up in this one."

Hussein smiled weakly and said, "They don't care what you look like. Only that you match the picture."

Ringo tossed the badge onto their small table and moved into the kitchen, pulling out a microwave snack from the cabinet. Hussein saw what he was about to do and began to panic, just as he had in the grocery store a year ago.

"Ringo, I thought we'd go out to eat tonight. One last meal. Back to that place we ate at last night."

Ringo popped the microwave dish into the oven and said, "You thought wrong. The last thing we need to do tonight is be on the street." He waved a spoon and said, "With your luck, we'll get arrested for jaywalking."

Hussein stuttered, his mind spinning for an excuse to leave the building. He spit out, "I found something you should see. At the hotel. We can eat at the restaurant on the way."

"What?"

"A camera. I mean, I think it's a camera. I wanted you to see it just in case."

"Why in bloody hell would I care about a camera? I have half the world chasing me for my executions of the infidels. One more won't matter."

"Okay, okay. I . . . just thought you'd want to see it."

Hussein gave up trying to get Ringo to leave, focusing now on the secondary plan he'd been given, trying to glean any information he could. Getting away from Ringo to rejoin the predator in the van was a problem he didn't want to contemplate just yet.

One step at a time.

He asked, "When are you going to attack?"

"I'll call."

"I think I should know."

"Get used to disappointment."

Hussein laid his pack on the chair, his back to Ringo, pretending to dig through it. As nonchalant as he could, he said, "Are the men ready?"

"Yes. More than ready. And the cell in Ma'an is watching the news. As soon as we make the broadcast, they execute, spreading the fire in Jordan. A double blow."

"Where are our men staying? Is it around here? Do you have to drive them, or will they walk?"

"You mean to the hotel? Of course we're driving. Do you think we can walk with our weapons in our hands? Why all the questions?"

Hussein turned around and said, "No reason. I just think I should know. I'm part of this too."

Ringo stopped his fork halfway to his mouth, squinting. "Why are you sweating so much?"

Hussein wiped his forehead and said, "It's hot in here."

Ringo stood. "Not that hot. Why haven't you mentioned your dad? Yesterday that was all you cared about. Today, all you care about is how I'm doing the mission."

Hussein's lip quivered, but he said nothing.

Ringo advanced on him. "Did you tell your father something about the mission? Did you warn him?"

Hussein started backing up, holding his hands in the air. "No, no. Of course not. Ringo, I didn't say anything to my father."

Ringo grabbed both of his shoulders and shook him violently. "Tell me the truth. Tell me what you did."

"Nothing. I swear, I've done nothing. I got the badge like I promised. That's all."

Ringo pulled out his knife, the dull black of the steel contrasting with the shiny edge of the blade. Hussein panicked, jerking out of Ringo's grasp and tearing his shirt down the front.

The tiny microphone flopped out, a traitorous piece of metal attached to a black wire.

Time stood still for a brief second, Hussein panting, unaware, and Ringo staring.

Ringo said, "What the *fuck* is that?"

Hussein looked down and felt his world crumble. He stumbled back and said, "My iPod. It's for my iPod!"

Ringo jammed him against the wall and brought the knife forward. "You fucking *liar!*"

He brought his face within inches of Hussein's and said, "Know this, Lost Boy: Your father is dead."

He jammed the knife deep into Hussein's chest, and Hussein screamed. Ringo brought the blade up again and Hussein sagged against the wall. He began laughing, a crazy hitch that echoed off the cinderblocks.

Hussein said, "Kill me. Do it. Send me home."

When Ringo hesitated, Hussein grabbed the back of his head with both hands, feeling a strength he had never known. He said, "They're coming for you. They're going to slaughter you. They're on the way."

Ringo's eyes went wide and he threw Hussein aside. He fell to the floor, his blood pumping freely from the puncture in his chest. Ringo ran to the table and slammed his laptop closed, then dialed a phone. Hussein shouted, "Ringo, look at me."

Cell to his ear, Ringo did.

"You've taken the lives of many people, and now you will pay." Hussein coughed and sagged, then regained his strength. "I know who will extract that payment. I've met her. She's a Jew. And she's a greater killer than you. She's going to carve you up like all the men you murdered."

Hussein saw the fear in Ringo's eyes and felt victory.

He had won.

He lay back onto the floor, his life force draining, and thought of his father. He prayed that the predator in the van wasn't tricking him like so many others had in his life. Prayed that this one time, someone would honor what he said.

He heard Ringo shouting into the phone in Arabic, then saw him run to the balcony, laptop case flapping against his back. He heard distant footsteps on the stairs outside.

He closed his eyes, dreaming of his mother and father, lovingly together, in a world that didn't exist.

35

Jennifer heard the British terrorist say, "Why are you sweating so much?"

Then, the scrape of the chair.

She glanced at Pike, but he was already moving, prepping his weapon and talking on the net to the other van.

"Knuckles, kit up. Things are going south."

"We going in hard?"

"No. Same plan. The Brit is getting antsy and I just want to close the distance. All weapons concealed. Stage on the third floor. Brett leads, Retro takes the rear."

The conversation continued in the room, accusations of Hussein having betrayed the plan to his father filling the air. Pike slid open the door, telling Jennifer, "Let me know when to enter, but don't pull the trigger too soon. Worst case, we assault and Hipster could have handled it."

He nodded at Aaron, and they both stepped out, linking up with the men from the other van. Jennifer watched them jog across the street and enter the apartment building.

They were gone no more than five seconds when the sound of scuffling filled the van. Panting, breathing, a fabric tear, then the words that would alter Hussein's destiny.

"What the *fuck* is that?"

Jennifer knew the worst had happened.

He's burned.

"Pike, Pike, this is Koko. Execute. I say again, execute."

No questions came her way. All she heard was "Roger." She knew the team was now moving as quickly as possible, completely trusting her call.

She saw Shoshana reflexively squeezing her fists open and closed, her eyes rigidly fixed on the speaker.

She heard Hussein scream, then, "Kill me. Do it. Send me home."

She felt as if she'd been punched. *We did this. We sent him to his death.* She shouted into the radio, "Go, go, go! He's killing Hussein!"

She heard a body hit the floor and thought they were too late. She put her head into her hands, ignoring the noise until she heard. "I've met her. She's a Jew. And she's a greater killer than you. She's going to carve you up like all the men you murdered."

She looked at Shoshana, seeing her visage change into that of a dark angel, her knuckles white as she squeezed her fists.

Arabic filled the van and Shoshana stiffened. She looked out the windshield and said, "He's leaving by the balcony. He's running."

Jennifer leaned forward and saw a figure leap from the third-floor balcony to the one on the apartment complex next door. She heard a racket in the room from the microphone, then Pike on the radio. "We're in. Hussein's been stabbed. He's alive, but bleeding out. Room is clear."

The sound echoed through the speaker in the van, Pike's voice picked up by the microphone on Hussein. She said, "Pike, al-Britani jumped to the north building. He's in the wind."

Shoshana said, "He was telling the team they were attacking today. Now."

Jennifer snapped her head to Shoshana, and she said, "I speak Arabic. That's what he was yelling, probably into a cell phone."

Jennifer heard shouted instructions, the rustling of cloth, then Hussein.

"I'm sorry. I'm so sorry."

Someone said, "Shh. You're going to be okay. Lie still."

Hussein: "It's because of the white house. I never wanted to go there. Nobody wanted to go there. They did this. Ask Jacob. He'll tell you about the white house."

Jennifer cut in, "Pike, Pike, al-Britani is attacking now. He's on the run to attack. Shoshana heard him tell the team before he fled."

She heard Pike go robotically calm, and knew they were in deep trouble. The worse the situation, the more relaxed Pike's voice became, and he sounded like he was ordering pizza now. No yelling. No stumbling over words or hasty statements.

"Roger all. We need to stabilize Hussein, then get him out of here. I'm leaving Brett and Knuckles. Aaron, Retro and I will be at your van shortly. Get a fix on his last known location, determine the avenues of egress and come up with a search plan. I'll contact Showboat for an update and get him synchronized with Jordanian liaison services."

Shoshana said, "There he is, up the street!"

Jennifer leaned forward and saw a figure running north. A laptop case bouncing against his back, he skipped through the smattering of people, knocking aside those who weren't quick enough to move out of the way.

Shoshana slid into the driver's seat, fired up the engine, put the van in drive, and punched out of the alley, turning the wheel and going fast enough to make the tires squeal in protest.

Flung to the side, Jennifer grabbed the passenger seat for support, shouting, "What are you doing?"

Shoshana tossed her an indigenous hijab, saying, "Put that on. Cover your hair. Nobody will look twice at us."

Jennifer climbed into the passenger seat and said, "We should have waited on Pike. On Aaron."

Shoshana faced her, and Jennifer saw the dark angel again. The killer she'd seen once before, in Germany. Right before she'd slit a man's throat. She said, "He's not going to escape his destiny."

Exiting the building, still talking to Lieutenant Colonel Alexander, I saw only one van in the alley. Empty.

What the hell?

"Sir, I have to get back on the team net. I've got a developing situation. Keep me abreast of the Jords. I don't want a gunfight to go bad."

"Gunfight? You're out of it. Let the Jords handle it."

"I will, I will."

At least I hope I will.

I manipulated my smartphone, getting back on the team internal. "Koko, Koko, this is Pike. What's your status?"

"We've got al-Britani in sight. We're tracking him. He's running north, about a half mile from you. He just went east, deeper into the neighborhood."

"Damn it, Koko, I told you to sit tight. Showboat's spinning up the CIA. This neighborhood is going to be locked down in about thirty minutes with Jordanian security. He's not going anywhere. Our job is done."

"You need to tell that to Shoshana. She's driving."

I turned to Aaron. "Call Shoshana. Pull her off before she does something stupid."

He began dialing and Brett came on.

"Pike, Hussein's KIA."

"What?"

"He bled out. The knife wound must have nicked an artery. Nothing I could do."

I closed my eyes and took a breath. For all practical purposes, I'd killed him. By all accounts, he deserved it, but on this operation he was my asset. My responsibility. And I couldn't shake the feeling that he'd really wanted to help.

Something to think about later. As I had many times in the past, I compartmentalized the damage and continued the mission.

"All right. Sanitize the body and sterilize the room. Get anything related to him, then leave it for the Jords to sort out. Get down here ASAP."

"What's going on?"

"Shoshana's on the warpath."

36

Jennifer heard Shoshana say, "I got it, Aaron. I'll just track him then feed his location to you. I won't do anything rash."

There was silence. Shoshana said, "Aaron? Aaron, you still there?" Then, "Who is this?"

Jennifer saw Shoshana's face grow rigid. She said, "Pike, don't tell me what to do. The mission takes priority."

Pike said something and Shoshana glanced Jennifer's way, saying, "I won't get her killed."

Jennifer could hear Pike's voice from across the cab of the van, shouting into the phone. Shoshana hung up on him, tossing the cell in the back. She said, "Your little lover boy seems to have a soft spot for you."

Jennifer glanced at the phone and could only imagine the rage Pike was experiencing now. She said, "It's not just me. He has a soft spot for anyone on his team, especially when unnecessary risk is taken."

Shoshana smirked and said, "Oh no. It's you. He reeks of it, so much so he's willing to put the mission behind your safety."

Jennifer thought of past operations when she'd come within a hair-breadth of dying, all on Pike's orders. Then of Aaron. How he reacted to Shoshana. "He's no different from your team leader."

Shoshana scoffed, saying, "There's a big difference. Aaron doesn't control me." She gazed out the windshield, then sat upright. "That fucking Pike. I lost the target while talking to him. Where is he?"

Jennifer leaned forward, as if getting closer to the windshield would help. They'd entered a street lined with vendors selling fruits, vegetables, and other things, the going slow. She caught a glimpse of the laptop bag and said, "He's no longer running. He's just up ahead. See the rainbow awning? Look left. He's pretending to shop."

Shoshana did and said, "He's close to the hive. He's thinking of the operation. He's making a plan before he meets the team."

She pulled into an alley and put the vehicle in park. "Time to go. Keep your head covered. Walk steadily and don't make eye contact."

"No. We go nowhere. We've necked down the location enough for the Jordanians. They'll handle it."

Her radio came alive with an exasperated Pike. "Koko, Koko, status?"

She said, "I'm here. We think we're within a block radius of the terrorist team. The Brit is still on the move, but he's no longer running."

Pike said, "I've got your location on my phone. Sit tight. No action. Keep eyes on, and we'll relay location to the Jords."

Jennifer looked at Shoshana and said, "Roger all. Sounds good to me."

"Jennifer, don't let that nutcase Shoshana do something. She wants a scalp, but we've gone beyond that. Our mission is done. She gets caught, and it might unravel us. She won't listen to Aaron. She might to you."

Trying to talk without giving anything away to Shoshana, Jennifer said, "Okay. But if *they* attempt to execute, and I'm still here, what do you want me to do?"

"Take her down."

Shoshana opened the vehicle door and said, "Come on. We're going to lose him."

In one fluid motion, Jennifer dropped the phone and withdrew her Glock 30, the long tube of the suppressor making it unwieldy in the close confines of the van. She pointed it in a two-handed grip and said, "We wait. As Aaron ordered."

Shoshana's face grew dark. She slammed the door closed and said, "You fucking Americans. It's all about the orders. Never about the true mission."

Jennifer said, "Shoshana, just sit back. Trust me, it makes me sick to do this to you. We have equities in play."

Shoshana said, "That terrorist you're letting go cut the head off a man. Of many men. You're happy with him in a Jordanian prison? Do you know who else was in a Jordanian prison? Abu Musab al-Zarqawi. The fucking spawn of the Islamic State. The man who cut the head off of Daniel Pearl and murdered more American soldiers than anyone else."

Jennifer said nothing, watching the dark angel appear. For the first time, she felt real fear, knowing that Shoshana was going to push. Force her to shoot. And she knew she couldn't. She wasn't so sure about Shoshana.

Without warning, Shoshana lashed out, slapping one hand on the weapon and whipping an elbow at Jennifer's head. Instead of fighting for control of the pistol, as Shoshana expected, Jennifer dropped the Glock, ducked her head forward, and wrapped up Shoshana's arms.

The fight was short but brutal. Shoshana landed two well-placed elbows against Jennifer's head, wanting to strike, to maim, something that was the anchor of Krav Maga. Jennifer was all about control, and this she did.

She launched her legs against the footwell and drove Shoshana into the back of the van. They hit together, and Jennifer wrapped up her thighs with her legs, then scrambled for an arm bar that would rip out Shoshana's shoulder socket. Shoshana went berserk, raining down blows on Jennifer's head with her free arm until Jennifer saw stars and started to black out. She fought through the pain, ignoring the punches and methodically working her position just as Pike had taught her.

She saw the opening, felt an elbow tear into her scalp, slamming her head into the floor of the van . . . and then she had the bar. She twisted her body, hunching her hips and bringing Shoshana forward, into her deadly embrace, and she felt the joint lock set deep. Perfectly positioned.

Shoshana slammed a fist into Jennifer's skull one more time, and she stretched out, dragging the arm with her, stressing the socket to the point of irreversible damage. Shoshana screamed, slapping the back of Jennifer's thigh.

Jennifer let up slightly, breathing heavily. She blew bloody snot from her nose and said, "We go nowhere."

37

Knowing she was trapped, Shoshana went rigid and let out a keening wail, sounding like a wounded animal, then went limp, sagging into the floor of the van and giving Jennifer complete control.

She closed her eyes and said, "You're letting him get away. You're going to allow that murderer to go free. Why did you care about catching the American so much, but not al-Britani? Why do you fight me?"

Maintaining her position, not relaxing at all, Jennifer saw an actual tear in Shoshana's eye. She said, "Why do you strive so hard to butcher like them?"

Shoshana wiped her eye with her free arm, no longer fighting. She said, "Because they're evil. They aren't human. They tossed aside all humanity when they embraced the ideology, then set about killing. I'm no more like them than a hog farmer is. Yes, I butcher, but like the farmer, it's for a greater good. We're both killing a beast, but the hog is a much greater sacrifice."

Jennifer felt her hands slipping in Shoshana's sweat. She regained her hold and said, "You can't kill them all."

Shoshana scoffed. "You are so naïve. I hate that philosophy. Of course I can't kill them all. When a policeman arrests a rapist, do you say, *You can't arrest them all*? I can only kill the ones I can reach, and I'll gladly do so, just like the policeman."

Jennifer let that settle, then said, "Tell me the truth: Would you have killed me? To get to him?"

Shoshana looked at the ceiling of the van for a moment. She said,

"No. No, I wouldn't. I couldn't." She gave a bitter laugh and said, "It's a weakness, I suppose."

"Weakness how?"

Shoshana waited a beat, then said, "You call me a butcher, but some in the Mossad would say differently. I was 'discarded' to the Samson team because I refused to take out a Palestinian. He wasn't a terrorist, and our information was wrong."

Now genuinely interested, having had moments of doubt while working with the Taskforce, Jennifer said, "If I let you up, are you going to fight?"

Shoshana turned her head in surprise. She said, "No."

Jennifer released her. Shoshana sat up, rubbing her shoulder.

Staring intently at her, Jennifer asked, "How did you know? How were you so positive the intelligence was wrong?"

"I'm honestly not sure. I just *feel* it. I can tell. On that mission I . . . I slept with him." She looked to see a reaction from Jennifer. When none appeared, she said, "It was a honeypot operation. He was designated a target, and I allowed him to go free."

"How, though? How did you *know*?"

Jennifer felt her weird, penetrating gaze for a moment, then Shoshana said, "You're afraid. Afraid of harming someone innocent."

Jennifer hesitantly nodded and Shoshana said, "I just do. I saw that Hussein had blackness in him, but it wasn't of his choosing. I saw he was telling the truth. I see *you* for what you are. You and Pike. I know he thinks I'm some crazy assassin, but I don't kill what doesn't need to be destroyed." She faced Jennifer. "And al-Britani needs to be destroyed. Don't listen to your boss a thousand miles away. Listen to your heart."

Jennifer said, "It's not that simple. There are rules. Complications with the operation."

"It *is* that simple. *You* make it complicated. This man beheaded at least four people. Cut off their heads with a knife. It doesn't get any simpler than that. Our world is gray, but this is black and white."

"What if your intelligence is wrong?"

Shoshana smiled. "I don't need to sleep with this one. I felt it as soon as he appeared on the balcony. I *know*." She became agitated, saying,

"He kills without any remorse, and he's going to kill again. Right now. We can stop it. The Jordanians won't have this place under control before they're gone."

Jennifer felt her conviction wavering. Shoshana pressed, "Did you see what was on his back? A laptop. There could be enormous information in that thing."

Shoshana's eyes were boring into her, and she thought, *Jesus. She's reading me right now.*

Shoshana scrambled to the front of the van and began surveying the street, saying, "We've wasted five minutes beating each other up. Maybe he's still here."

Jennifer said, "Shoshana, no. We wait on Aaron and Pike."

"He's still there! He's meeting with someone. He's talking to another man."

Jennifer crowded forward and saw al-Britani in close conversation with a young man wearing a faded nylon jacket, stabbing his hand in the air to punctuate a statement. The man clapped al-Britani on the shoulder, and they turned to walk down the street.

Shoshana said, "Let's find the bed-down. Just locate them. Then we can decide, but sitting here is letting them get away."

Jennifer decided to punt. She keyed her radio. "Pike, this is Koko. What's your status?"

"Loaded up now. We're about four minutes out."

Jennifer relayed the information, and Shoshana said, "Four minutes is an eternity."

Jennifer felt the pressure like never before, now understanding what Pike went through on operations. The Lost Boys video popped into her head. The grisly, obscene killings. She watched the back of al-Britani walking away, glimpses growing smaller as he faded between people in the crowd.

She felt Shoshana's hand on her arm. She turned, and saw pain etched in Shoshana's face. A physical thing, making her wonder what had happened in the past.

"Please. Don't let him get away. *Please.*"

She realized that Shoshana was waiting on her decision. *Because I voluntarily released her. She promised she wouldn't fight. And she could. She could leave right now.*

Teetering on the brink, Shoshana's words pushed Jennifer over the lethal edge of a decision. The fact that Shoshana valued her promise over the incredible desire to deliver justice to al-Britani meant more to Jennifer than anything she had said before. It was enough.

Jennifer said, "Okay, but no killing. Location only, right?"

Like a time-lapse video, Jennifer watched the dark angel blossom, spreading throughout Shoshana's body. She pulled a suppressor out of a bag and screwed it onto an old 9mm Browning Hi-Power. She lifted her shirt, exposing a belly holster. She stowed the weapon and opened the door.

Alarmed, wondering if she'd made a mistake, Jennifer said, "Shoshana? No killing."

The dark angel stepped out, her earlier promise met. She said, "That'll all depend on him."

38

We were closing in on the location of the van when I saw it start to move again. Or at least, I saw the ping on Jennifer's phone move. I called.

"Koko, what's your status?"

I got nothing.

"Koko, Koko, status? Acknowledge."

I heard the dumbest damn thing imaginable. "Pike, the target has linked up with someone and has started to move. We couldn't maintain eyes on from the van. We're on foot, and tracking."

What. The. Fuck.

Aaron was driving our van, with the team in the back. I knew I couldn't go all ballistic in front of him, but I sure as shit wanted to. I went the team-leader measured-response route.

"Koko, stand down. I say again, stand down. Showboat says the Jords will be rolling in fifteen. We've done our work."

"Pike, these guys are going to attack before that time. They're going to evade the net. Let us find the bed-down. Get a physical grid location so the Jordanians don't have to search the neighborhood."

I forgot about the cool, calm team-leader route. "Damn it, listen to me! Stand the fuck down! Now! If Shoshana wants to wreck things, then get the fuck out of the blast radius. You read me?"

She didn't respond. I looked at Aaron and said, "This is your damn fault! It's just like Brazil all over again. Shoshana's some kind of witch doctor. Jennifer never does this shit, but every time she's with Shoshana she goes off the reservation."

Aaron turned into an alley, and I saw the van. Empty. He said, "Pike, trust me, I feel your pain. I've had to live with it since she was assigned to me. Shoshana's a handful, but if she's working the problem, there's a reason."

"Yeah. She wants to cut al-Britani's head off. And she's going to put Jennifer in the line of fire in the process. Bloodthirsty little bitch doesn't care who she hurts."

Aaron put the van in park and said, "You are wrong. Shoshana is special in more ways than one. She wouldn't do this if she didn't think it necessary."

I slapped the dash and said, "Bullshit. She'd sell her mother if it meant a kill."

"No. No, she wouldn't. You don't see it, but Jennifer does."

Head covered in a hijab and sunglasses on her face, Jennifer walked slightly behind Shoshana, letting her take the lead. Shoshana tracked the target expertly, stopping and perusing at the markets without ever losing sight. Shoshana was dressed like a local, but Jennifer was wearing cargo pants and a loose-fitting cotton shirt. Man clothes. She felt the stares and wondered if she was going to burn the operation.

She said, "Shoshana, I don't look Arab."

Shoshana took her hand and handed her a melon, as if they were shopping. She said, "I'm your guide. Westerners come here all the time. Your hijab shows respect. You think everyone is staring, but they're not. You blend in just fine."

They continued their little shopping tour, about fifty meters back from the target. As she watched him walking with his friend, she could see him talking at a frenetic pace. He was wired and on edge, waving his arms around and slapping the friend on the back. But not running anymore.

They stopped at each stand for a moment, but didn't do any real shopping, making Jennifer wonder what they were doing. Al-Britani had just found a microphone on a man he perceived as a traitor, and had to know he was set up. Had to understand that someone was chasing him, but, after escaping the building a mile away and ordering the attack, he was now stalling.

Why?

Al-Britani talked to a merchant, and suddenly Jennifer understood. It was an act. They were making sure people saw them. Making sure the store vendors knew who they were. They were creating a reality for the future investigation.

And she realized it wasn't a suicide attack.

He thinks he's going to get away. And the time he's wasting will be his undoing.

She looked at her watch and saw they had less than seven minutes before the deadline Pike had given. The Jordanians would be here soon. And he'd be caught.

But there was no Jordanian security on the street. No activity at all.

Where are they?

Pike's call from earlier had said they'd be here, locking down the block. In between his shouting, he'd led her to believe it would be some sort of Katrina hurricane response, the area flooded with police. But that wasn't happening.

She wondered if he knew more than her. Wondered if ignoring him was the right course of action, for reasons greater than the tongue-lashing she knew she'd get. She could handle Pike. He was full of bluster, but he understood operational success, and had done the same thing she was doing on multiple occasions. She was convinced she was right, and she was sure Pike would agree—after the operation. The only thing she was unsure of was Shoshana.

The two men turned left into an alley and Shoshana cursed.

"No way to follow them there. No reason for us to be in that alley. They'll look back as soon as we enter."

Jennifer pulled out her smartphone and said, "Let's figure out where they could be going."

"What, with Google Earth? Won't work. Too many unmarked alleys. They'll be gone. Google Earth doesn't have the resolution."

Jennifer smiled. "Yeah, I agree. But I'm not using Google Earth. I can see the depth of a pothole with this phone."

In the last ten years, US reconnaissance satellites had gotten exponentially better, gaining the ability of resolution down to the centimeter, a feat that bordered on science fiction. In the Cold War, the older generation of satellites were called Talent Keyhole, and treated as the crown jewels of US intelligence collection. With the ever-increasing technological capability, the old satellites were overshadowed, and this brought a decision that was about as astronomically bad as the new satellites were good.

The US government, having the new capability, decided to profit on the old. After all, the aging satellites were still up in space, and still working. Why just let them fly around if they weren't going to be used? Like a man looking at his outdated car in the yard and thinking of a quick buck, the US sold the Talent Keyhole constellation. To Google. And now terrorists all over the world leveraged the Cold War architecture to plan their attacks, using nothing more than a computer with a web browser.

But Google Earth couldn't see into the rat maze of alleys. That required the next generation. And Jennifer had it.

She manipulated the security settings on her phone, working through the laborious, multilayered process of access, and finally achieved the feed she needed. She swiped the satellite app to the left, accessing the GPS feature of her phone and marking her location. She copied the grid, then swiped right, bringing back the satellite feed. She pasted the grid, then waited as the small processor in her phone went into overdrive, trying to compute the massive instructions it had been given.

The screen slowly resolved, and she was looking at an overhead view that appeared to have been taken from a balloon hovering just above the rooftops. It wasn't real-time—the image had been taken four days ago—but it was certainly good enough to plan a surveillance route.

Shoshana saw the image form and said, "That is amazing."

Jennifer realized she was showing a classified capability to someone uncleared, and tilted the phone away. Shoshana scowled, and Jennifer said, "Sorry. It's NOFORN."

"What the hell does that mean?"

"The capability is top secret. NOFORN. 'No foreigners' can see it."

Shoshana just looked at her, deadpan.

Sheepishly, Jennifer tilted the phone back and said, "Yeah, I guess that's stupid. Don't tell Pike."

Shoshana studied the photo, saying, "That alley goes for a ways. Pull it right."

Jennifer did. She said, "Go left."

The screen moved and Shoshana said, "Stop. Right there."

Jennifer looked at the screen and said, "Yeah. No other exit out of the alley."

"We can parallel them and intersect at that point. Let's go."

"What if they stop before? What if the bed-down is in this alley? We'll miss them."

"We neck it down enough to help. We'll miss them regardless. We can't go into the alley behind them. This either plays out, or it doesn't."

Jennifer nodded, and Shoshana smiled. "It's going to play out, trust me. I've done these hunts many times. You ready?"

"Ready for what?"

"Ready for what destiny is bringing."

"What are you talking about? All we're doing is finding the bed-down. Right?"

Shoshana rubbed her waist, feeling the gun, and said, "Right. But destiny has a way of altering plans."

39

Ringo walked down the alley, thinking about the door to the hotel. He had the badge, but he wasn't sure how to use it. He assumed there was an access panel outside, and all he had to do was place the badge against it, but what if there was a code? What if he waved the badge and the screen blinked, telling him to start typing? They wouldn't get in, and the plan would fail.

The man he'd met, a *shahid* trained by Omar, held no such fear. All he wanted to do was get into the fight. He didn't care one way or the other if his actions accomplished anything. He knew he was going to die, and that thought permeated everything. He wasn't going to wear a bomb, but he was going to die. He could do so shooting outside of the hotel at random strangers, or inside the hotel, killing members of the Gulf States at a conference designed to deal with the very organization to which he belonged.

The man was a simpleton. A robotic killer. He had none of the responsibility that Ringo held. The planned attack had to have maximum impact, and strangers killed on the street wouldn't do it. But the men in the hotel conference center would.

The Gulf Cooperation Council was meeting in Jordan to discuss a plan to counter the Islamic State. Composed only of members of Sunni-controlled countries, such as Saudi Arabia and the United Arab Emirates, they were trying to find a path for eradicating the scourge even as some in their population actively supported it. By holding the conference in the Grand Hyatt hotel, they had become the perfect target.

Ringo and the *shahid* turned the corner, moving down a small, trash-strewn connector alley no wider than a hallway. They broke out onto a larger thoroughfare right next to an outdoor café—patrons sipping espresso or tea and paying them no mind. Ringo studied the surroundings for a moment, seeing nothing out of the ordinary. The rhythms of the street were natural, but he couldn't assume it would remain that way. He had no idea how far out his pursuers would toss the net, but was fairly sure, since nobody had chased him from the apartment, that he was secure for the time being. But that time was fleeting. They needed to attack. Now.

He had no illusions about what was occurring in the apartment he'd fled. It was probably full of CIA spies and Jordanian Special Forces. All trying to piece together the plan of attack.

Praise be to Allah I never trusted Hussein.

They didn't know who Ringo was, but they probably knew the target. They would be increasing security. Eventually. He had the magic key, away from the security of the main entrances, and was positive he wouldn't need to fight to get in. Even so, the increase of firepower could cut their mission short. He needed to beat their decision cycle, and he thought he could. Jordan authorities wouldn't want to interrupt the meetings. The last thing they would do was tell the GCC that the Islamic State might be attacking and shut them down, and that was only if they knew—which wasn't a given. If it was a United States operation against him, using Hussein, the morass of stovepipes would be much slower filtering the information.

He did wonder if the badge would work. It was a choke point over which he had no control. At the end of the day, he *was* walking out of this mission alive. Period. He had a team who would die, but he would not. He told himself he had a greater calling than the *shahid*, and even believed it. He wasn't going to martyr himself, and if the badge didn't work, the mission was done.

He turned left, moving down the lane, flowing in between the pedestrians milling about. He passed a small table, the farthest one out from the café, dismissing the two women engrossed in conversation.

He jogged across the street with his partner, entering one of the ubiquitous concrete hostel/apartment buildings that dotted the landscape, but this one had been specifically chosen. Jam-packed into the cloistered area of east Amman, it was built next to a hill and was one story taller than the building next to it, so close that the concrete balcony was only five feet from the adjacent roof.

Unlike his frantic run earlier, this had been planned. He needed a way to enter his building, ensuring the clerk at the bottom saw him, then exit without being seen. He'd initiate the assault, letting his team do their deadly tango, then return without ever having exited the front. All the desk would know—and would provide the police, should that become necessary—was that he'd entered, then stayed in his room for the duration of the attack. Thus, he couldn't be complicit.

That, coupled with his stall shopping a moment ago, should be enough to escape scrutiny. The name he'd used in this building wasn't in a passport. All they knew was what he looked like, and the fact that he had entered, then never exited.

He walked inside the tiny anteroom, a thin piece of wood to the right making a counter, worn smooth by years of use. Behind it was the custodian. Ringo had no idea what he was paid for, because every request since he'd first rented the suite of rooms had fallen on deaf ears. He walked over and, speaking in Arabic, said, "Did you get the shower on the third floor to function?"

"No. Not yet. I'm working on it."

"And the sink?"

"No."

"And the toilet? Does it flush now?"

"No. No, no, no. I'm not a miracle worker."

Ringo smiled and said, "You're pretty much nothing at all, aren't you?"

The clerk, a gnarled older gentleman, stood up and said, "This isn't London, you little shit. I do what I can. If you don't like it, leave. Find another place with running water. If you can."

The man who'd met Ringo outside laughed at the slur against his English accent. Ringo bristled, and said, "Maybe I will. Maybe I will."

He walked away, aggravated, but confident the clerk would remember the conversation. Remember him walking up the stairs.

40

Jennifer watched Shoshana enter the broken-down brick structure and wondered if she was just going to start slaying. She didn't think so, but her opinion meant little in determining what the Israeli killer would do. Put bluntly, she was regretting her decision to allow the operation to continue. Regretting how she'd ceded control to Shoshana.

As soon as the men had entered the makeshift apartment building, Shoshana had said, "I'm going in. I'll provide early warning if they leave from another exit."

Jennifer had said, "No. You're not. We have the building. Jeez. Do you want to pin his location to a bathroom or something? This is enough."

"No, it's not. All we know is they've entered. We don't know if they'll stay. We don't know if this is the bed-down. Maybe they're just getting explosives or weapons here, and they might exit out of another door."

Shoshana had stood without another word, leaving Jennifer alone at the café table. And then Pike had called. He'd found her van, empty, and wasn't just a little aggravated.

"What the hell is going on?"

"We've got the site. I'm at a café outside. You have my location?"

"Yeah, I see it. We can't get there in a vehicle. We'll have to go on foot, depending on how accurate this sat photo is."

"It's good. Where are you?"

"Next to your van. Where you're supposed to fucking be."

She ignored that little jab. "Continue up the street through the markets. You'll see a narrow alley on the left. Really just a garbage lane. Bypass that one and take the next. It's bigger, with some outdoor cafés. Take that to the north and you'll get to me."

He said, "Got it. Don't move. You understand?"

"Yeah, yeah. I'm going nowhere. You have situational awareness of the Jordanians?"

"No. They should be rolling now, but I have no contact."

"How will you pass the location?"

"Showboat. He's talking to the Taskforce."

"And they'll feed it to the CIA, who will then feed it to the Jordanians? Seriously? That'll take forever."

She heard, "Best I can do. Don't let Shoshana convince you to do anything stupid. Or anything *more* stupid."

He hung up, and she waited, thinking of Hussein. Wondering if anyone would tell his father what had happened to him. Did the CIA do that sort of thing? Or would they let the Jordanians attempt to figure it out, not caring if they ever did?

Hussein's last conversation replayed in her head. The panic in his voice, then the despair. Ending with quiet resignation at his own death. It made her queasy. Outside of his father, he probably had no family. His mother was more than likely dead from AIDs in prison, and he'd given no indication about brothers and sisters.

The thought of siblings made a piece of the conversation snap into her head, about friends he did have. Ringo had called Hussein a name. An innocuous one on the surface, but hiding a much greater danger below.

Hussein was a Lost Boy.

The realization made her head swim. It held such gross implications, on so many levels, she had trouble acknowledging the impact.

They'd been told that Hussein had killed a CIA source reporting on an insider threat involving Americans. Unknown, non-Arabic Americans, planning an attack against the White House, called the Lost Boys. Hussein was a CIA source himself, recruited, vetted, and inserted into Syria, and he'd just been called a Lost Boy.

Beyond the CIA web of lies or incompetence, there was one concrete fact: Her team had used Hussein to stop this attack in Jordan, but in so doing, they'd given up their ability to penetrate an attack by American citizens against her very own seat of government. The one reason the Taskforce had been created. They'd killed the only lead they had.

She felt sick.

She saw movement on the third-floor balcony of the target building and recognized al-Britani standing with another man. The sight of him crystallized the death of Hussein, and another, critical realization.

He knew Hussein was a Lost Boy. Which means he knows who the others are. Knows what they're planning.

She saw al-Britani gazing across the rooftops to the north, pointing. She leaned forward, trying to determine what he was doing. She studied his building and saw that it was one story taller than the adjacent structure across from him. Only three stories tall, it was followed by two more buildings going up the side of the hill, each a story smaller than the one before, with the last one a single story in height and built right into the hillside. If al-Britani were to move across the roofs, he'd have an easy path to the hilltop. He'd be on foot, racing down the back side without ever having reached the street.

And she realized what he was going to do. How they were going to leave, but now she couldn't let that happen. Facilitating the Jordanians to stop the attack had become a secondary consideration. Capturing al-Britani took precedence.

Torn, knowing she was making a call based on intuition alone, she clicked her earpiece.

"Pike, Pike, this is Koko, I have a Prairie Fire here. I need you to call off the Jordanians."

Prairie Fire was the code word for a team about to be overrun. A call that would cease all operations to protect those who made it. She knew she was misusing the command, but also knew it would snap Pike into attention.

And it did. Pike came on immediately, "What's your status? What's going on? You have shots fired?"

She said, "No, no. I'm fine, but the mission has changed. You need to call off the Jords. We need to take down al-Britani. We need to conduct an Omega on him, and get him out like we were going to do with Hussein."

"Why?"

She saw al-Britani come out on the roof again, this time with three people. All were carrying duffel bags. They stacked them against the balcony railing, then went back inside.

Prepping to move.

She stood, looking up the street for Pike. She said, "I can't explain it now. I need you to trust me. What's your ETA?"

"We're five minutes out on clandestine foot. Two and a half to three minutes if you want me to break cover."

Meaning he would start running roughshod over anyone in his path with guns drawn.

She said, "No, no, don't break cover, but I do need you quickly. Target's about to move."

"Where's Shoshana?"

Jennifer studied the adjacent building, looking for entry. If she could get inside and go to a stairwell, she could access the roof. She could bottle them up right there. Sandwich them between their balcony and Pike coming in from below. She saw an iron gate.

She stood and jogged down the street toward the secondary housing structure. She said, "Shoshana's inside the target building. I'll have her go out into the street so you can link up. Pike, they're going to exit using the roof of another building. I need you here now."

"Jennifer, back off. Let the Jordanians handle this. The attack doesn't stand a chance. They can't reach the hotel and execute, even if they leave the building. Don't let Shoshana push you into something. Al-Britani is their target, not ours."

She reached the building, stopping at the wrought iron gate blocking the alcove to the main door. She tried to enter. It was locked from the inside.

She said, "Pike, he's our target now. He knows the Lost Boys."

41

Pike said, "The Lost Boys? What the hell do they have to do with this?"

Jennifer backed up, looking skyward at the side of the building. What she saw pleased her. Rough-hewn brick and balconies. She glanced back up the street, seeing the crowds and realizing there was no way she could do what she wanted out front.

Knowing Pike hadn't heard the final words between al-Britani and Hussein, she said, "Pike, I can't explain right now. I need you to trust me. Al-Britani knows who the Lost Boys are. He said so while you were assaulting. It didn't click before, but he said it. Get Showboat ready to receive. He was waiting on Hussein, so it shouldn't be any trouble."

She jogged around the brick to the alley separating the target building from hers. She entered, running swiftly, glancing upward. She saw a metal ladder being maneuvered above her, bridging the gap between the balcony of the target building and the roof of hers. She kept going, reaching the back of the building in a narrow, fetid alley.

She scanned for a matter of seconds, planning her route and repositioning her purse to her rear. She pulled her cell and dialed Shoshana's number, knowing Shoshana, not having a specially modified Taskforce phone, was unaware of what had transpired. She answered and Jennifer said, "Target's in the corner room, northeast, third floor. He's preparing to escape across the rooftops. Pike's on the way. I need you to meet him out front."

The suspicion leaking through the phone, Shoshana said, "Why?"

"We're going to take him down."

The suspicion evaporated. "Us? No Jordanians?"

"No. Listen, we aren't working with a lot of time. I have to get to the roof. We need al-Britani alive. You understand?"

When she didn't reply, Jennifer said, "Shoshana? Do you understand? Capture only."

Shoshana said, "I've already told you, that'll depend on him." Then she hung up.

Jennifer cursed under her breath, sliding the phone into her back pocket. She grasped the brick in her hands and pulled herself off the ground, feeling the clock ticking. Wondering if they weren't already too late.

She began climbing the rough cinder block, using the cracks, seams, and window ledges to go ever higher, having no more difficulty than a gecko on a plate of glass. She reached the top, cinched her hands on the small parapet, and raised herself slowly, peeking over the edge toward the balcony. She saw one of the men throwing a duffel bag across, and noticed that two other bags were already on the rooftop.

She looked for cover and saw the outbuilding that held the stairway to the floors below. She waited until the man returned to the apartment, then pulled herself over the side and scampered behind the cinder blocks.

She keyed her radio. "Pike, Pike, I'm on the roof and they're about to cross. Where are you?"

"Just met Shoshana. We're on the way up. Third floor, northeast corner, right?"

She slid her head around and saw one man walking across the metal ladder, hands outstretched for balance.

She whipped back around, getting out of sight and drawing her pistol. She said, "Shit, they're starting to cross over! What do I do?"

"Seriously? This is your damn plan. But if it were me, I'd get a barrel in their face before they're all on your side of the roof. Just passed the second floor. About ten seconds out."

She rolled away from the outbuilding, seeing two men had reached her side, with another on the bridge. One was digging in a duffel bag.

The other saw her and shouted. She stood up and sprinted straight at them, holding the pistol in a two-handed grip. She skidded to a crouch fifteen meters away and, feeling ridiculous, screamed, "Freeze! Stop right there!"

She heard gunfire inside the apartment and knew Pike had entered. The man on the ground whirled around, pulling an AK-47 from the bag. She placed two rounds into his head, controlling the recoil of her weapon even as the standing man charged her, unarmed. She saw the third man leap to her roof and a fourth jump on the bridge, firing into the apartment with a pistol.

The charging Arab was on her in an instant, leaping at her and screaming. She backpedaled, pulling her weapon into her chest and breaking the trigger three times. He landed on her, knocking her to the ground with literal dead weight. She rolled him off just as the third man reached her. From her back, she popped two rounds into his head and rolled out of the way of his falling body.

She heard a bullet gouge into the brick next to her, spraying her with slivers of masonry. She brought her weapon up, refocusing on the man on the bridge. She saw it was al-Britani. He fired again, missing, and she snapped two rounds past his head, knowing at least *he* spoke English and understood surrender. The shots caused him to duck and lose his balance. He began windmilling his arms, and she held her breath. He fell sideways, slapping his hands through the gaps in the metal ladder.

She cocked her ears to the apartment, hearing no further gunfire. She heard, "Koko, Pike. Status?"

She exhaled in relief, and said, "I'm okay. Three down out here."

"Yeah, you could have told me there were eight of them. We busted into a hornet's nest. But no jackpot. Doing site exploitation now. Got a laptop, but not much else."

"I have precious cargo out here."

"You got him? Alive?"

"Not yet. He's on the metal bridge. Hanging on for dear life."

She saw Shoshana come out onto the balcony. Jennifer smiled and walked to the parapet of the roof, weapon held high. She shouted, "Careful! He's still got a pistol."

Shoshana nodded, but kept walking forward. She reached the balcony railing and looked out at al-Britani. He saw her, but made no move, holding on to the metal ladder with a death grip.

She leaned forward and spoke to him. Jennifer heard Arabic and wondered what she was saying. She saw al-Britani's face go white. Shoshana spoke again, and he released one arm, trying to raise the pistol while still holding on.

Shoshana gave a wicked smile, and Jennifer saw the dark angel appear. She knew what was coming next. She shouted, "No!" just as Shoshana pushed the edge of the ladder off the railing. Al-Britani screamed all the way down, the noise cut abruptly as he hammered into the concrete four stories below.

She saw Pike come flying out of the apartment. He glanced down into the alley, then across at her. Jennifer was shocked, standing with her hands gripping the parapet until her knuckles were white.

He turned to Shoshana, glaring at her. Knowing what she'd done.

All innocent, the dark angel long gone, she said, "What? I told him to give up and he pointed his weapon at me. It was self-defense."

42

"Yes, it didn't end like we intended." Kurt inwardly winced at his own words. He was becoming more and more like the politicians he hated, now parsing his statements like the best of spin doctors. To his front were eight of the thirteen members of the Oversight Council, including President Warren. To his back was a damaging PowerPoint slide outlining the failed attempt to capture both Hussein and al-Britani.

"Didn't end like you intended? Seriously? It sounds to me like it ended on the opposite side of the universe from what you intended. That comment is like Noah saying, *We had a little rain.*"

This from the secretary of defense, usually an ally in Oversight Council meetings. If Kurt had lost him, he was in serious trouble.

Kurt said, "Sir, you know you can't predict what will happen in an operation. The enemy gets a vote. This time—"

Secretary of State Jonathan Billings said, "That's absolutely right. You can't predict where every operation will go, but you *can* predict which operations you'll do, because *we* give you that authority. You had none here. And I, for one, would never have given authority. You've just proven why this body exists, along with why Pike Logan can't be trusted. I knew bringing him back in was a mistake. We're looking at a major international incident."

Kurt said, "It wasn't Pike's call. It was Lieutenant Colonel Blaine Alexander's, the Omega ground force commander. And he made the call based on inherent in-extremis authority in our charter. We had strong indications of an imminent attack, and he decided to intervene. That's what we pay him to do. He was within his authority."

Alexander Palmer, the national security adviser, said, "The attack wasn't imminent *until* you intervened. And what the hell were you thinking by using the Israeli Mossad?"

Not wanting to derail his next steps with a debate on the Mossad, Kurt stuck with Pike's excuse. "Al-Britani was their target. It wasn't a question of using them. They were in the heart of the mission, and they were a known quantity." He turned to President Warren. "Sir, you personally gave both of them awards for their help in our operation in Brazil last year. We've worked with them before."

He'd deal with Pike's little team-building exercise later, but he wanted—needed—to get a favorable opinion on Aaron and Shoshana, because they were crucial to what he wanted to do next. To that end, he'd left out Pike's suspicions about Shoshana's culpability in the death of al-Britani, calling it self-defense.

President Warren said, "I have no issue with using those two, specifically, but I do have a concern with the Mossad. What's their stance? How was this left?"

"The team isn't working directly for the Mossad anymore. They're more freelancers now. Basically, they both 'retired' and now get hired through whatever shell companies and cutouts Mossad owns to do missions that are deniable. In this case, to operate in Jordan without the repercussions they've had in the past with active agents."

"Sounds familiar."

Kurt smiled and said, "Maybe on the surface, but there's a distinct difference. We use the Taskforce because it's offensively the best way to go about the mission, not defensively because we're afraid of using something else. Pike thinks it's simply a way for the Israeli government to cut them away if they get caught. Unlike the Taskforce."

Kurt wanted to ensure that nobody in the room confused the Taskforce's operational limits with the Israelis', and was gently reminding the Council that their teams weren't throwaway, no matter what happened with Mossad.

President Warren smiled at the mild rebuke. "Point noted, but you didn't answer the question. What's the damage with Israel? What do they know?"

"Nothing. They had a one-off contract, and the contract was fulfilled. Actually capturing al-Britani would have caused bigger issues with Israel than his death. Aaron and Shoshana reported success, and are off the leash. Mentioning us would have just caused complications they don't need. You know what happens when intel organizations get stray voltage. They start spinning, and that might have impacted payment to the team."

He glanced at Kerry Bostwick, the director of the CIA, and said, "No offense."

Kerry said, "None taken, as long as you don't hide similar things from me. What about the Jordanians? Nothing's spiked from my guys at the station. All they're reporting is a terrorist shootout with police and a roll-up of a bunch of thugs in Ma'an, apparently part of the Islamic State plot. What's Pike seeing from the ground?"

"The same. Your liaison connection was a little slow, but they conveniently arrived right after the shootout. The only thing it impacted was the site exploitation. We got a computer, but had to leave before fully exploiting the apartment. Anyway, we should be clean. No compromise."

Palmer said, "So where do we go from here? Anything that can help us with the Lost Boys?"

"We do have a new thread, but it's not from the Lost Boys. We are no longer confident they're a cohesive group."

President Warren said, "That contradicts the CIA assessment. What leads you to that conclusion?"

Kurt said, "Actually, Kerry and I have talked, and I'll defer to his judgment. He's leaning that way, and, at this point, I tend to agree. Kerry?"

Kerry put his elbows on the table and said, "Sir, nothing is a given, but all we had before was the brief report from BOBCAT. We never got to debrief him, and Hussein being called a Lost Boy contradicts the original assessment of a group of United States citizens with no ties to the Middle East being prepped for an attack. Hussein had ties to Jordan, and that's exactly what they used him for. If he was a member of a dedicated group, he doesn't fit the very profile we're afraid of. He was killed in Jordan, facilitating an attack with other Arabic men. This leads me to believe that it's just a term they use. Something they call a type of jihadist. Maybe it's for Westerners, or maybe just Americans, but at this time we don't assess it as from a specific, credible group targeting the United States."

Palmer said, "What about the White House comment on the beheading video?"

"It's just a comment. It could be something they use to engender support. He could have easily said 'for the crusaders' or something else. We can't use that to say they're targeting the White House."

President Warren said, "But the man in the video was a Caucasian."

Kurt said, "Yes, sir. Using BOBCAT's reporting, we now assess that there are several previously unknown Americans—without any Arabic heritage—now working for the Islamic State. It's still a threat, and something for the CIA to watch, but we don't assess they're working as a team, targeting outside the conflict in Syria and Iraq. They may still come home, and we need to identify them, but we don't assess it as a collective, deliberate targeting process."

Secretary of State Billings leaned back and said, "Thank heavens for that."

President Warren said, "That may be, but I don't want to be caught flat-footed, like we were on 9/11. We missed indicators then, and as far as I'm concerned, this is an indicator. Stick with it. Find out who they are."

Kerry said, "Yes, sir."

Warren turned back to Kurt and said, "You mentioned another thread? What did you find from this operation if it wasn't about the Lost Boys?"

"Believe it or not, a major target of the Khorasan group. You remember the alleged foreign fighter who had supposedly defected to al Qaida from French intelligence?"

"Yeah, but I thought he was a myth. He ended up being just a young French bomb-maker, and we killed him in an air strike."

"That was the conventional wisdom, but we scanned the computer al-Britani had with him. He was using Twitter to direct message with another man, and we believe this man is Rashid al-Jaza'iri, a Frenchman of Algerian descent who has had significant training with French intelligence. We know for a fact he's with the Khorasan group."

Alexander Palmer said, "That's pretty damn specific. Was there a folder called 'My Top Secret Jihadist Friends' on the computer? What leads you to this?"

"The Khorasan group connection is from the direct messages. Rashid was instructing al-Britani to do the attack, then claim credit in the name of Jabhat al-Nusra and Khorasan instead of the Islamic State. Apparently, there's not a lot of love between them, regardless of all the reports of reconciliation."

"And the name and background?"

Kurt shuffled his feet, thinking, *Here goes nothing.* . . .

He said, "The Israelis. While we were always wondering if he was a ghost or not, Mossad's been tracking him. Shoshana and Aaron recognized the Twitter handle as one he uses. It's never used for broadcast tweets. Only direct messages."

President Warren looked at Kerry. "And they've been keeping this from us?"

Kerry raised his hands and said, "Sir, we don't give them everything either."

President Warren shook his head, muttering something under his breath, clearly aggravated.

Billings said, "Why Twitter? Why not something more secure?"

"We don't know. Best assessment is that Rashid didn't have an email address for al-Britani. The British guy was all over Twitter bragging about his beheadings, so it may have been the only way for Rashid to find him. We do know that al-Britani was first fighting with Jabhat al-Nusra before switching allegiance to the Islamic State, so their paths may have crossed before. The rest is just speculation."

Palmer took over, asking Kurt, "So you want to do what, exactly?"

"I want to go get Rashid. The last ISP used is from an Internet café in Tirana, Albania. Give me Alpha authority to explore the issue, then on-call Omega to roll him up. It may not go anywhere, and I won't do anything unless I can confirm it's him, but when I do, I can't have a long debate. The Twitter ISPs have been all over the map, and he's probably not going to stay long. Let's do the debate now, ahead of time."

Billings said, "We're going backwards with this. In Nairobi, we got a report on the situation from the ground before granting Omega."

Kurt said, "*That* was going backwards. You severely restricted my ability to operate. I understand why, since we'd just conducted a separate Omega operation, but if we'd have let the Nigerian get arrested with everyone else, we wouldn't have gotten the intelligence that led to the elimination of the Islamic State emir."

The secretary of defense said, "How long will it take to spin up a team? If you're worried he's not staying, isn't this a moot point?"

"I'm using the same element from Jordan. We have a complete Omega package there, with a support team that was supposed to transport Hussein, Pike for assault, and Blaine's headquarters element as overarching control. It's only a two-and-a-half-hour flight from Jordan, and I've already got them prepping to leave. All I need is the go-ahead. You say no, and I'll turn them around."

He saw Billings's sour look and said, "I had to get them moving. All they're doing is flying. I didn't step on your authority."

Palmer said, "We're getting ahead of ourselves. How are you going to confirm that the target is correct? Surely he doesn't have his real picture on his Twitter profile."

"No, we don't have any pictures of him. The profile picture is the Twitter egg."

"Then how?"

Kurt considered his next words, the phrase *boom goes the dynamite* floating in his head. He ignored the rest of the room, focusing on President Warren. Needing his support.

"Sir, I . . . uh . . . have a couple of people with the team who know him on sight."

43

I said, "Yes, sir. WILCO," then hung up the cool, James Bond satellite phone affixed permanently to the small desk in front of me, thinking of the ramifications. I glanced at Jennifer, as usual in the window seat, watching the land of Jordan fall away as we rose into the air, her head pressed against the window like a child, the larger window facilitating a view that she'd never get on a commercial aircraft.

We were flying a Taskforce Gulfstream 650, which was conveniently leased to Grolier Recovery Services, the company Jennifer and I used for operations. While it was cool to zip around like a rock star, the plane actually had a few operational capabilities that were crucial. All of them built into an aircraft that rock stars used, and now available for us. As we say in the Taskforce, "money is no object."

Across from me, in another plush, full-size seat that faced my direction like one on a train, Knuckles said, "Well? Where are we landing?"

I glanced toward the back of the aircraft, where Shoshana and Aaron were sitting and said, "Looks like we're a go. How in the hell Kurt convinced the Oversight Council to let this continue is beyond me, but it was apparently a pretty good fight. Blaine says best behavior on this one."

"Did Kurt tell them about our strap-hangers?"

"He had to. They're the only ones who know what Rashid looks like. He couldn't get approval for Alpha without a lead, and having an anchor of an Internet café wasn't cutting it. At that point, apparently, things got ugly. Especially with that shithead Billings."

Knuckles laughed and glanced back, making sure we were outside of earshot. "Billings has had a hard-on for you since Brazil. I'm sure your Israeli love interest being both there and now here caused him to shit a brick. He's probably trying to figure out how you managed to get a Mossad team into Jordan to help your operation."

I bristled at that, saying, "She's not my damn love interest, and she purposely killed al-Britani. She has her own agenda, which concerns me."

He said, "Yeah, yeah, whatever. I may not be a spoon-bender like her, but I can see the connection."

I waited on Jennifer to defend me, and when she didn't, I said, "Are you going to let him say that shit?"

She said, "I'll correct him the minute he's wrong."

"I can't believe I'm even talking about this. The fact remains that she ignored orders and purposely killed our target. I get she's needed here, but I worry about what she'll do next."

Knuckles said, "I'm not going to second-guess what happened out there. The guy was a terrorist willing to give his life for the cause. He was apparently on a suicide run, and he held a pistol. He got what was coming."

I turned to Jennifer and said, "You were there. I got there late, but I saw that twisted thing in Shoshana. The one that comes out when she's killing. She looked like a damn demon. Tell me I'm wrong."

"I know. I saw it too. What Knuckles says is true, but there was no way he was getting off the bridge alive once she showed up."

I said, "And you let her go, when *you* broke orders."

She looked like I'd slapped her, the implications clear on who was responsible for the end result. Knuckles interrupted, "She made a bad call, but the guy beheaded four Americans—that we know of. I got no issues with what happened to him."

I said, "That shithead's death isn't the point. It's the manner in which he was killed. We have zero information from him because he cracked his head like a melon on the concrete. We might as well have used a drone."

Jennifer pursed her lips at my words but remained silent.

I said, "We have another mission, and this one is a capture to get to the heart of the Khorasan group. I don't know if she's capable of that. All she wants to do is kill."

Jennifer said, "Al-Britani was her target. She talked to me about it in the van, before we left. She'll listen to you. If she says she'll follow orders, she will."

"And how in the hell would you know that? Did you order her to eliminate al-Britani?"

"No! Of course not."

"Then what's changed? Are you psychic now too?"

She looked uncomfortable, saying nothing.

I said, "So it's women's intuition?"

I saw her eyes flash with anger and she said, "I lied about the bruises on my face. It wasn't from the fight across the bridge."

Taken aback, I went from her to Knuckles. He shrugged, unsure of where this was going.

She said, "Just get them up here. Give them the brief. She won't fight you. I've seen what her word means. If she says she won't do something, she won't. But get her to say it. Looking back, she never told me she wouldn't execute al-Britani. If she gives you her word, she'll honor it."

"You never trusted her before. What happened?"

"Let's just say that I found a connection. Okay? If she wants to talk, she can. It's her call."

What the hell? Jennifer was turning into an enigma. I used to be able to predict like clockwork what she'd say or where she'd stand on an issue, but lately, she seemed to be expanding her ability to deal with ambiguity. I wasn't sure if I liked it. That was my terrain, and I relied on her as a sounding board. It did no good to talk to a mirror for answers, and she was rapidly becoming my image in the mirror.

I said, "Get 'em up here. Just them at first. I want some words with Aaron with Shoshana present. Then we'll bring up the team."

Knuckles did so, giving up his seat and standing in the aisle. The team in the back looked on curiously, but knew they'd be read on soon enough. I'm sure they were spinning conspiracy theories about what was going on.

Directly across from me was Aaron, with Shoshana in the window seat across from Jennifer. With a smile, he said, "So? Are you willing to use our expertise? We are outside of a contract right now and are available."

I said, "First question, and this is from my higher command: Are you truly independent? Or is Mossad going to get a detailed operational summary of what occurs?"

"You mean, can I be trusted?"

"Yes, that's *exactly* what I mean."

Shoshana said, "That question was answered in Brazil. We never said a thing to Mossad about you. All they know is that we helped the United States. And got an award for doing so. They think it's CIA."

"How do I know that? Those are just words."

Aaron said, "Yes, it might be just words, but it's also irrelevant. If we were going to expose you, it would have already happened. But we didn't. And we have much less reason to do so now. Anyway, we don't even know who you work for."

I considered his answer for a moment, then said, "Okay, I'll believe you, but this is not for debate: I've got approval to *capture* Rashid. Take him down for follow-on intelligence. Is that going to be a problem?"

Confused, Aaron said, "No. Of course not. Why would we be against that?"

"Because your little assassin here wants to *kill* everything. *That's* why."

Shoshana bristled and started to say something. Aaron, his eyes still on mine, held out his hand and she stopped, amazing me that anyone could control her. He said, "Al-Britani was an enemy of the State of Israel. We were on a sanctioned mission. I cannot help that you interfered, but the mission comes first."

He didn't even question what had happened. Made no flimsy excuses. I said, "Just like the Russian in Istanbul."

He leaned back and said, "Yes. Just like Vlad the Impaler."

I said, "So what's the mission here? Lay it out. I'm getting sick of the surprises."

"Our mission now is that we work for you. I told you, I'm not under the constant employ of the State of Israel. I agreed to do this because you asked. Nothing more."

I glanced at Shoshana and she saw something in my eyes that she didn't like. She finally let out her feelings. "You Americans are always so superior. Always sure of your righteousness. You've never lived with the wolf at the door. Because of it, you put the mission second." She looked at Jennifer and said, "You're always willing to protect the men in your command at the expense of success."

I ignored the glance, knowing she was baiting me, and said, "Sometimes the mission *is* the men. You're so full of anger I can't believe you've lived this long. Sometimes you have to back the fuck off. Sacrificing your men on a suicide mission is what the enemy does."

She said, "Yes. And you fight fire *with* fire. The mission *always* comes first. Always. The enemy fears us precisely because of this."

I grunted and said, "Is that why your government traded over a thousand Palestinian terrorists for one Israeli soldier?"

She slammed back into her seat and refused to meet my eyes. She said, "That would not have been my call."

Looking at Aaron, I said, "Well, maybe they understand something you don't. Sometimes the mission you're given isn't the one you should conduct."

Aaron said, "We don't have that luxury. The mission always comes first. And your mission is ours. I promise."

I slowly nodded and said, "Okay. We're going to stake out the Internet café he's been using. We've got a team that's using al-Britani's Twitter account, saying the attack in Jordan was delayed and asking for guidance. He'll want to respond. When he does, we ID him—meaning one of you will do so—then get a pattern of life. From there, we take him down. Can you do that?"

I jerked a thumb at Shoshana. "Or will devil eyes here want to split his head open?"

44

Aaron smiled and said, "We can do that. Anyway, if you don't trust Shoshana, you can always pair her up with Jennifer. That'll solve the problem."

Aggravated again, I said, "Enough with the lesbian jibes. I'm serious here. I would think that you would be the last to disparage Jennifer or Shoshana's skills with a lame joke."

He scrunched his eyes and said, "Yes. I'm talking about her skill."

I looked at Jennifer, but she refused to meet my eyes, instead focused on Shoshana.

What am I missing?

Knuckles was as clueless as I was. Aaron said, "She didn't tell you? In my team, we know all, both the good and the bad."

Which really poked a sore spot. And made me wonder if Jennifer *was* complicit in the death of al-Britani. I looked at Jennifer and said, "No, apparently my team doesn't want to do that."

Jennifer closed her eyes and said, "It's not what you think. I told you that you could trust her. *I* trust her."

I saw Shoshana's eyes widen slightly in surprise. She turned to me. "I'll do the mission, just as you ask. I'm yours to do with as you see fit. Is that enough?"

Jennifer locked eyes with me, her glare telling me to back off. I held her stare for a moment, seeing some pain come out. Recognizing the moral compass I'd thought she'd lost. She was blaming herself for al-Britani because of my comment earlier.

I said, "Yes, it's enough."

Shoshana said, "Good, because your little lover there kicked my ass in the back of a van. I don't want to repeat that again."

I snapped my head to Shoshana, and she was grinning, reading me whether I wanted her to or not. She knew how much the revelation would mean, precisely because Jennifer had kept it from me.

She said, "You're a good man, Nephilim. Don't try to make me into less."

I turned to Jennifer, seeing embarrassment. And I understood it was true. Whatever had happened in the back of that van had been violent, and Jennifer had won. Which, because I'm a little bit of a Cro-Magnon, made me secretly slap the ground and cheer.

And Shoshana *knew* how I would react. She didn't give a rat's ass about her reputation. She was focused on the mission, and she was manipulating me to get it done.

I leaned back, acting like I was considering, but everyone understood it was for show. Shoshana could barely conceal her disdain for the act. Aaron waited patiently.

I said, "Okay, we're in play here. We've got to get you guys outfitted and cover some basic contingencies. We've got a support team in a separate bird, and they'll actually control our actions. We can't meet them—ever—except for the drop-off of the precious cargo. They're going into Albania under a completely different cover. We get Rashid, and that's the only time we'll meet. I'm sure you're used to operating that way."

Aaron said, "Yes, yes, we get the game. You made us leave our weapons and equipment. How will we do this?"

I said, "Knuckles, you want to show them the reason we fly with such incredible luxury?"

He said, "My pleasure. Follow me."

They moved to the aisle and I stood, feeling Jennifer's hand jerking my sleeve. I turned back to her and she said, "Pike . . . you know when we left the van, I didn't think she'd kill al-Britani. Right?"

I stopped, looked her in the eye, and said, "I know. I believe you." She glanced down at the floor and I took her hand. She looked at me again and I said, "I *know*."

She paused, wanting to say something else.

"What?"

And, because I'll never figure her out, Jennifer changed tack. "I think that whole report on the Lost Boys is crap. I don't believe it."

Like a guy seeing a car wreck, then trying to process it, I had to rewind her words to make sense. I said, "Jennifer, they've got the best minds in the world working on it. If they say it's just a nickname, it probably is."

"Maybe, but as far as the 'best minds' go, you rank right up with them. You've proven them wrong more times than they've been proven right. Half the time they're predicting sunshine in a snowstorm."

I moved down the aisle, saying, "Okay, okay. One mission at a time."

She said nothing else and we reached the back of the aircraft. Brett said, "I guess we're a go?"

Knuckles said, "Yeah, believe it or not. Let's show our guests what they've won."

Retro grinned and turned to the wall above the kitchen galley. He inserted a special tool into what looked like a straight plastic covering, firmly riveted in place. Magically, the entire panel fell away, exposing an interior full of armament where ordinarily the noise insulation would be. The entire aircraft was built as an infiltration platform, and housed everything from weapons to surveillance kits, all camouflaged to defeat host-nation customs and immigration.

Aaron said, "Very impressive. And we can choose what we want?"

Feeling superior, I glanced at the wall and did a double take. I saw a bunch of guns that shouldn't have been there.

I said, "What the hell is this? What are those?"

Confused, Knuckles said, "What do you mean?"

I stabbed my finger at a black rifle hanging on a hook. It looked like an M4 that had been chopped down, with a collapsible stock and a bulbous suppressor running off of a nine-inch barrel, the free-floating aluminum hand guard acting as a sleeve over both, with Picatinny rails sprouting all over. Something from a movie set.

"This, damn it. What is it?"

The weapon was nothing like the HK UMP we ordinarily used, a

.45-caliber sub-gun that could be suppressed without significant alteration of zero because the round was subsonic to begin with. Which is why we used it.

Sheepishly, Knuckles said, "We went away from the UMP. I thought, since you were a 'team leader' again, someone would have told you."

Aaron went back and forth between us, I'm sure wondering if we were clowns in a circus and whether he wanted to put on the four-foot shoes.

Since Panda was a pure intelligence collection mission, we hadn't needed a great deal of equipment in Kenya. We'd flown into Nairobi commercial, hiding our Glocks and surveillance kit the old-fashioned way: by breaking them apart in our checked luggage. When we'd redirected to Jordan for a capture mission, I'd asked for the deployment of the rock-star bird, complete with a package hidden inside. Due to cover concerns, it had arrived too late to be of any use, but would come in handy in Albania. Or so I thought. I hadn't realized my idea of a "package" was now old news.

I said, "Nobody told me shit. So you don't have my UMP here? The one zeroed for me."

"Uh . . . no. But we do have the ability to zero. With lasers. Right here in the plane."

Glancing at Aaron, and not wanting to make us look any worse, I said, "Okay, okay. What am I looking at?"

"Nothing more than an integrally suppressed AR, with some unique properties. Built by Primary Weapon Systems, it's got a proprietary long-stroke piston system, making it much more reliable than the old gas AR guns like the M4."

I said, "And that was worth the switch? Since when did we have issues with the UMP's reliability?"

"Reliability wasn't the problem. The caliber was. The PWS system is chambered in 300 Blackout. Much, much more knockdown power than the UMP's forty-five. The can is Gemtech. Believe it or not, it's shorter than the UMP suppressor, and it's built specifically for the Blackout round. In subsonic, it sounds like a pellet gun."

He saw my look and said, "You have to admit, we've been in some gunfights where the reach of the UMP was questionable. I know when we created the Taskforce we all talked about how the fighting would be within a room, but it hasn't worked out that way."

I said, "That's why we have the HK416. There are different tools for each job. I can't believe the Taskforce just switched complete weapon systems based on one idiot's recommendation. The damn UMP worked fine. It was concealable, and had serious knockdown power for close quarters. Now you want me to tote an AR?"

He gave me his *I'm going to act like I agree until I tell you you're wrong* look, something I'd seen for more years than I could count.

He said, "Yeah, okay, but let's do some counting. One, Bosnia. Outgunned from a distance. Two, Hungary. Outgunned from a distance. Three, Egypt. Outgunned from a distance. Four, Ireland. Not outgunned from a distance, because you gave Jennifer a 416. I could go on, but those are off the top of my head, in operations with *you*. I'm sick of that shit."

When I heard that, I knew arguing was going nowhere. Clearly, he was the man who'd done the testing, convincing the Taskforce to change, and I'd just insulted him with my comments.

He continued, ticking off statements on his fingers, "The 300 Blackout in supersonic has much greater knockdown power, and in subsonic it beats anything in its class. The HOLOsight has a Mil-Dot calibrated for both, so you don't have to worry about zero problems if you switch from sub to supersonic, and the Gemtech suppressor can handle both just fine. In fact, better than fine. It doesn't have the range of 5.56, but it works great for its purpose. A gap that needed to be closed. The PWS system will clear a room just like the UMP, but beyond that, it'll clear a block when shit gets bad. Unlike the UMP."

I grinned, and he backed off. I pulled one off the rack and said, "It's a little big."

He said, "Bullshit. It's a little heavier, but it's not big. What you're holding is a massive half inch longer than a suppressed UMP. Half inch. The only reason it's heavy is because it's made with actual metal instead of that plastic crap that kept breaking on the UMP."

I said, "But the UMP stock can fold over, making it a hell of a lot shorter."

He pushed a button right at the buffer spring, and I'll be damned if the buttstock didn't swing over, much like the UMP.

He said, "Only difference is you can't operate the weapon this way. It'll fire exactly once, but we never assault with a folded UMP anyway."

I grinned and said, "So, you don't have a vested interest in this experiment, do you?"

"Only because I've hated the bastard who brought the UMP into the Taskforce before I got there. Some asshole who always thought he knew best."

Which, of course, would be me. And he knew it.

I said, "Touché. Get them outfitted. I'm assuming the pistols are the same, unless you decided that we need to start using dart guns."

He grinned and said, "Nope. Same ol' Glocks."

Shoshana was gazing at the armament in lust, like a pothead entering a Colorado marijuana store for the first time. She stroked one of the systems and said, "May I?"

Happy at the interest, Knuckles said, "Sure."

Jennifer tugged my sleeve, saying, "Can I pull you away from the commando wet dream for a moment?"

I grinned and followed her. Out of earshot from the others, she said, "Did you hear what I said earlier? About the Lost Boys?"

"Yeah, yeah, I heard. What do you want me to do about it?"

"I want the reports. I want to see them for myself."

In the old days, when I really *was* a Cro-Magnon, I would have just told her to stow it, but Jennifer had shown a unique ability to solve problems others had missed. In this case, the problem set wasn't ours. We were after a different terrorist. I settled for logic to dissuade her.

I said, "Look, they did a complete scrub on Hussein. It all came up empty. He had no connections to anyone who went to Syria. Shit, even the school they found him in was closed down after he left."

"What for?"

"I didn't read the report, but apparently it was a pretty heinous place. Some kids killed a guard, and in the ensuing investigation to find them, they found out the school was hell on earth. Now the people running it are on trial. Apparently, they got what they deserved. Hussein is exactly what the name said. A fucking lost boy, looking for something to make his life worth a damn."

She looked out the window, thinking. I said, "What?"

"Can I get the reports? Please?"

"Why?"

"I don't know, I just can't shake the feeling that we're missing a piece. I just want to make sure there's nobody else looking for something to make his life worth a damn."

45

Walking across the famous Bridge of Sighs leading to the draconian prison at the Doge's Palace museum, Jacob finally saw a glimmer of hope. Watching the pious church leader pause at the far end, looking right and left through the crowds of tourists, Jacob saw a buxom woman appear and plant a sloppy kiss on his lips.

Jacob knew his target was married. Knew he was in Venice with his Catholic student group, ostensibly as a chaperone. His purpose was solely to ensure the safety of his charges. But clearly he had other things in mind, including a secret rendezvous with a mistress he'd probably flown in from the swamps of Florida while his wife stayed at home baking cookies.

Jacob gazed at the woman's breasts wiggling back and forth, covered in a low-cut top, with a modest scarf failing to hide their size.

Par for the course. Christian hypocrisy at its best.

The woman was the first indication that Jacob might have a lever to accomplish his mission. Something he had been having extreme doubts about since they'd landed at the Venice airport yesterday morning.

After the Lost Boys' experience in Syria, flying to Italy out of Istanbul had been surreal. Living on the ragged edge, their instincts trained to look for peril at every turn, trying to act like they were nothing more than tourists had been very, very hard. Every question directed their way was met with suspicion, and every action of the passengers viewed with a predisposition that they were attempting to obtain information.

At one point, Jacob had had to stop Carlos from getting into a fight over an overhead bin, the obese person bewildered at the rage Carlos held. When the flight attendant noticed the scuffle and began moving their way, Jacob had stood, squeezing his fist around Carlos's upper arm and saying, "Sit down. You are done."

The passengers around him had noticed the exchange, and he realized the risk of discovery was beyond some omnipotent intelligence agency finding out their mission.

It was held in themselves.

They had lost whatever civility had once coursed through their veins, and that had been slight to begin with. Before Syria, all they had known was the white house. Now, after having their humanity further eroded in actions supporting the nascent Islamic State, Jacob was leading a pack of wild dogs in a land of groomed Chihuahuas. If they wanted to succeed, they needed to be another Chihuahua. And Jacob wanted very much to succeed.

Maybe.

After the meeting in the hotel bar with Omar, Jacob had gone to sleep thinking about his future. Unlike his fellow Lost Boys, he hadn't fallen headfirst into the spell of the Islamic State. It was strange, even to him, given what he'd done in its name, but he didn't feel the fervor. Didn't yearn to slaughter people simply because they smoked a cigarette or were Christian. He only wanted to prove something to himself. To succeed just once, eradicating the failure that was his life.

He wanted to show the world that he wasn't just a bit of trash blowing on the side of the road. But, until the meeting in Istanbul, he'd never really believed it. He knew he was different from Carlos and Devon, in both capability and views, but hadn't realized how much different until fate had brought him to Omar.

That man was a creator. He was a force of nature that carved out what he wanted through willpower, intellect, and brutal skill. And he'd seen something in Jacob. Had recognized that Jacob wasn't like the other cattle flocking to the fight. It caused a conflict in Jacob's mind.

It brought questions. Things he couldn't answer now. The fact remained that Omar had entrusted him with success. Had bestowed on him the responsibility to win, because he believed in Jacob, and Jacob wouldn't forget it. Couldn't let him down.

That confidence had wilted once they'd arrived in Venice. Exiting the terminal, Jacob had had his first shock of the mission. Expecting to take a cab to Venice from the airport, he'd found that the only thing available was a water taxi. After thirty minutes of wasted effort, stumbling from one dock to another, they'd managed to make it to the small historic city-state, riding a boat that had no sympathy for their lack of knowledge.

He'd intended to check into the hotel room booked by Omar—a Best Western, which, by name alone, had given him an American image—and then spend the rest of the day hunting his prey. What had happened instead was he and his crew had dragged their luggage through a myriad of small alleys, walking on foot to find a hotel that apparently wanted to remain hidden.

The town itself was a labyrinth. An ancient city constructed out of the sea by brute force, whose locals had little sympathy for the influx of tourists.

They'd stomped around for forty-five minutes, crossing one canal after another without getting any closer to their hotel. They'd walked down an alley and ended up at a small dock next to the water, and nothing else. A dead end. Jacob had about lost it until a man had pulled up in a johnboat.

Jacob had asked a couple of questions, and the man was more than helpful, taking them in his boat and driving them to the closest point to their hotel, talking about his job and life as they passed multiple small docks, all with skiffs and johnboats. Jacob had realized two things: One, the quickest way around this place was on the water. And two, he could steal a boat.

Listening to the man describe life in Venice, Jacob began to understand how difficult the mission would be, even as Carlos and Devon marveled at the tourist attractions. The city was nothing more than footpaths, cut across in a chaotic way with canals, and separated from the mainland by a healthy bit of water.

Murdering four people here will be damn near out of the question.

Well, that wasn't exactly true. It would be easy to kill someone in Venice. There wasn't much police presence. Some outstations with *cabrini*, and some roving patrols, but all in all, if he wanted to take someone's life, then stake the body to a cross for all to see, he could do it, and he stood a fair chance of getting away.

His problem was much, much greater. He had to kill without anyone knowing. In Syria, such a thing would have been easy, leaving the carcass to rot next to the others in the desert. Even in his old world, he could make a single man disappear by burying him in the Everglades, letting the alligators have some lunch. Here, the terrain itself was formidable. There was no desert or swamp to transport the victims to, letting the sun and carrion eaters destroy the carcass before it was found.

On top of that, they had to kill *four* men. The chaperone and his three charges. They had only four nights to do it, and they had to accomplish the mission *here*, before the group traveled to Rome. Which brought up the final obstacle.

They had to do the murders in such a manner that nobody knew the victims were gone, because they intended to assume their identities.

Following the church leader, Jacob had begun to believe the mission was impossible. Right up until he saw the chaperone kiss the woman.

46

Jacob followed the couple through the remainder of the palace museum, stalking them through the myriad of palatial rooms and ignoring the history dripping from every corner. If asked later, he couldn't have described a single thing from the inside of the palace. Not one painting, one throne, or one sculpture. But he could have told you in minute detail what the man and woman did, because he photographed most of it, waiting on the money shot.

It didn't come. They never kissed again inside the museum. Jacob snapped plenty of shots of them close together, some where they were even rubbing against each other, but none that were inherently incriminating. Which was something Jacob needed to make his nascent plan work.

From the beginning, Jacob knew his target set was split in two: the chaperone and the kids. He instinctively understood that he had to divide in order to conquer. He simply had no idea how to do that. Outside of pure chance, there was no way to predict when the chaperone would be separated from the boys, and reacting to those occurrences—as he had today—was not a recipe for success. There needed to be some control. Some method to predict when the man would leave his charges or, better still, predict when and where he would be.

And now Jacob had it. If he could get the money shot.

The couple exited the marble courtyard of the palace, walking through the revolving gate into the Piazza San Marco, an expansive square flooded with visitors from all over the globe. Jacob gave the couple a second, then followed, temporarily losing them in the crowds.

He skipped past children playing with pigeons in the square, the filthy birds perched on shoulders and heads, parents taking photos and patently ignoring the prohibitions against engaging in such behavior.

He walked rapidly past the clock tower, swiveling his head toward the ornate San Marco Basilica. All he saw were lines of people waiting to enter both places. He went deeper, scanning for the purple scarf the woman wore. He caught it on the edge of the square, disappearing into an alley.

He sprinted to catch up.

He entered the alley, a small hallway carved out of stone, leading away from the square. He saw the couple ahead of him exiting, going left in front of a bridge across one of the ubiquitous canals. He began jogging, jostling people out of the way to catch up. He slowed at the bridge and turned the corner, now moving with the rhythm of the tourists.

He saw the chaperone and his busty date talking to a gondola coxswain. Debating a price.

One of the many small ports threaded throughout the city, it held multiple gondolas waiting for passengers, similar to a taxi stand in New York, only much, much more expensive. If the target was hiring a gondola, he had no destination in mind other than peeling the clothes off of the person he was riding with.

Looking like oversize canoes, the boats plied the canals all over Venice, some gondoliers singing, and some offering other amenities. Jacob remained where he was, knowing he was about to lose the chase. He raised his point-and-shoot camera and zoomed to the fullest extent of its cheap capability.

And got the money shot.

The man leaned over to the woman, surreptitiously cupped her breast, and kissed her full on the mouth. In eight-megapixel color.

He returned to the Best Western, finding Devon and Carlos sitting in the room going through the television channels as if repeated clicking would make one change over to English.

They glanced up at him, earnest faces surrounded by chocolate wrappers and potato chip bags from the minibar, the room a mess.

"Jesus Christ. What the hell have you guys been doing? Do you know how much this shit costs?"

Carlos said, "It don't cost nothing. It was all on top of the fridge. It came with the room."

Jacob shook his head, muttering under his breath. He kicked towels out of the way, stepping over the makeshift sleeping pallet on the floor that the other two men used. He noticed a prayer rug next to the pallet, an Islamic State–sanctioned prayer schedule next to it. He picked it up and said, "What the hell is this?"

As if Omar were in the room, Carlos said, "We can act like the infidel, but we will not become the infidel. We have to maintain our strength."

Livid, Jacob smacked him in the back of the head, shouting, "Are you fucking insane? You need to become Catholic. *Catholic!* What will happen if the maids see this? What the hell are you guys thinking?"

He stood, tearing the schedule in two. He turned in a circle, looking at the mess in the room, the two simpletons in it, and his own reflection in the mirror. He felt a clawing pressure. He saw the shock on Carlos's face from his outburst, and Devon cowering in a chair. He instinctively knew he was failing. Knew that leadership was needed here. Leadership such as Omar would have provided. The religion was nothing. He needed to rise above that and provide the leadership these men craved. As he had in the white house.

He sat on the bed and said, "Okay, okay. Tell me you knuckleheads did something today."

Like a light switch, Carlos turned from Islam and became the common criminal he had always been. He said, "I've walked all over the area here, and I've got four johnboats that I think I can steal. Two are on the Grand Canal, and two are on smaller feeder canals. If we need a boat, I'll get one. They don't pay a lot of attention to security. A rope and maybe a chain, and we're in."

Jacob didn't bother to ask any questions about operating the vessels. Coming from Florida, all three could operate a skiff and motor. Instead, he focused on the specifics. "How long before someone knows it's missing? Can we take it and get it back, or once we take it, the clock's ticking?"

"During the day, we're fucked. After about six, I think we're good. They won't notice the boat missing until the following morning."

Thinking, Jacob said, "And you can navigate the canals? If I gave you a spot?"

"Yeah. It's actually not that hard. I got a map. A water taxi map. I can figure it out."

Jacob nodded. "Good. Devon? Any luck?"

Devon was tasked with befriending the boys after the chaperone left.

"I followed them for a while, and they did what any tourist would do. Wandered around to all the attractions. When they reached the Rialto Market over on the other side of the canal they stopped for lunch. I approached them then. We struck up a conversation, and I asked if they wanted to party. They said no."

Jacob waited, then said, "And that's it? What, did you offer them cocaine or something? They're high school kids."

Devon smiled and said, "They said not today, but asked me if I was hanging around for a few days. They said they could maybe party later. Actually looked at one other as if they were breaking the law. I don't think they realize the drinking age here is, like, sixteen or something."

"So?"

"So they said their chaperone runs the show, but he's apparently here partially on business. They've got a sightseeing trip planned for tomorrow during the day, but tomorrow night they're free. The chaperone's going to be busy doing something, and the following day he'll be in business meetings. They're on their own. They asked if I knew of a place to go to after he left. I found a pub called the Devil's Forest. I told them to meet me there tomorrow night at nine."

Jacob smiled. *Business meetings. Right.* This might work after all.

"That's perfect. Devon, you meet them and get them liquored up. So drunk that they'll let you in their rooms. Figure out the lay of the land of their hotel. Get control of one of their keys. We only need one. Put them to bed but leave with a key."

He tapped his finger against his lip, thinking. He continued, "Do we know the specific room the chaperone is using?"

"Yeah. His is a floor above the kids. After you started following him, I found the room, but that hotel isn't good for a hit. It's a mess, with hallways and rooms spread out like a crazy aunt built it. I can follow the kids back and tuck them in, maybe even get a key, but we can't kill anyone there."

"I'm not going to. Carlos, I'm going to need that boat tomorrow around ten at night."

Carlos said, "For what? We can't kill them when they're out drunk with Devon."

"I'm not talking about the kids. We need the chaperone first. I'm taking him tomorrow night."

"How? All we know is that he won't be with the kids. You can't kill someone in this city like that."

"He'll be where I say, when I say. Does this hotel have a printer? A business center?"

"What does that have to do with anything?"

Jacob raised his camera. "I have to print some pictures."

47

Rashid read the direct message on Twitter and was astounded at al-Britani's lack of security. Didn't the man remember anything he was taught while working with Jabhat al-Nusra? Was the Islamic State so arrogant they no longer cared about operational compromise? How had Omar al-Khatami succeeded as long as he had with this example of leadership?

The message was succinct and to the point: *Attack delayed, possibly tomorrow or maybe the next day. Inside man's work schedule changed.*

Rashid put an email address from a service called ProtonMail into his direct message response. He ordered al-Britani to create his own account, encrypted end to end and anonymous, and send him a message tomorrow. He instructed al-Britani to set the encryption password for the body of the email the same as the subject line, which would come through unencrypted. It was a risk, as someone could conceivably crack the email with the hints given here, on Twitter, but they'd have to find the new account al-Britani created first, and ProtonMail—located in Switzerland—was outside the eyes of the prying NSA. Anyway, it was much better than talking over Twitter, and he would change the password after the first message.

He hit send, logged out of his Twitter account, then cleared the history of the browser. He stood and saw two police officers enter the café, sending a little shiver of adrenaline down his back. They went to the counter and bought time on a system, then walked behind him to a computer at the end of the row.

Rashid exhaled, realizing they were from the security of the US embassy next door, and more than likely just on a break.

Really need to find another Internet café.

He exited the dungeonlike shop, walking up the steps from the basement, leaving the gloom and entering the sunlight. He went down Rruga e Elbasanit, passing right in front of the United States embassy compound, threading through the local-national guards milling about. He kept his head down, and hid the smile on his face.

He took a left, going past the Tirana soccer stadium and leaving the embassy behind. Blending into the crowds, appearing more local than not, he continued on, looking for the small grocery/pharmacy his apartment was above. He saw the sign above the store and ruefully thought that at least the rejection of bringing his entire team had meant less rental space needed. Less coordination.

He'd convinced the leadership of Jabhat al-Nusra that his trip was to ensure the success of the Islamic State attack, but in so doing he'd cut off his ability to bring all the men he needed. After the crusader air strikes, he had five left who were fiercely loyal to him, and unquestionably lethal, but the al-Nusra emir had balked when he said he wanted all five.

Why? he'd asked. *Why do you need all of them to fly to Albania? If you're just making sure the transfer occurs successfully, from the outside? Two will be enough to protect the transfer.*

Yes, two would be enough to protect the transfer, but it made capturing Omar very, very hard. And there was no way he was leaving Tirana without Omar's scalp hanging from his belt. Quite possibly literally.

He entered the small hallway next to the market and tromped up the stairs. Not wanting a surprise, he knocked on the door, paused, then twisted the key. He found his two men sitting at the kitchen table, looking at him expectantly. He smiled.

"So how did your day go? Did you find me another Internet café? One away from the crusader embassy?"

The first nodded and said, "Yes. Actually, there's one about four blocks away."

Rashid scowled, saying, "And you sent me to the lion's den instead?"

The man recoiled, saying, "I . . . I didn't know. I've never been here. I did the best . . ."

Rashid waved a hand, saying, "You did fine. I just don't want to return there. How do we look for tomorrow? For the meeting?"

"We've both been into the garden. It will be hard. The meeting site is set back, in the glade, and there is no easy escape if we have to force a man to come with us."

Rashid said, "We won't take him there. We'll follow to a more suitable location." He saw the man had a further question, and said, "Yes?"

"Well . . . we were wondering . . ."

Rashid waited, but both were too respectful to talk. Rashid grew sick of the reticence. "What, Hashim? Damn it, don't act like a woman."

Hashim stiffened at the insult, then said, "Why aren't we talking to the Albanians? You know the meeting, and you could contact the men. Why are we doing this risky operation? Just get them to put a gun on him."

Rashid said, "That would seem to be easiest, but I don't trust the Albanians. They are working for money. Don't believe they have the faith, even if they're Muslim. They would just as likely tell Omar what we planned."

The second man said, "Why don't we just kill him? Why do we need to capture him? We could shoot him from a distance before the meeting, then get the Albanians to give us the weapons. After all, they're *our* weapons. They're just holding them."

"If all I wanted were the weapons, I wouldn't even bother killing Omar. I'd just get them back."

When neither man spoke, he continued, "The Albanians have no idea what Omar has planned. Only he knows that, which is why we will capture him. I want to know his plan, and, as I told our command, I want to facilitate its success. Only with our mantle. Our leadership. He will tell us what he's doing, and we will deliver the weapon to his team. And then we will claim credit, as we are about to do in Jordan. We will be the undisputed leaders, regardless of the propaganda from that blasphemous caliphate."

Hashim smiled at his words, nodding and looking at his partner. He said, "I thought so. I said as much to Kamal."

Kamal bowed his head to Rashid and said, "I'm sorry. I didn't mean to question. We have the weapons you requested. We can do what you say. Insha'Allah, it will be done."

Rashid said, "Look at me. Both of you."

They did.

"Are you prepared to find martyrdom tomorrow?"

The both nodded, with Hashim saying, "Of course. It would be our honor."

"Are you prepared to do so without accomplishing our mission? Do you want to meet Allah and tell him failure?"

Confused, they both slowly shook their heads.

Rashid stood, walking to the small kitchen and opening a bottle of water. He took a sip, reflecting, then said, "Allah will help us on our path, but make no mistake, He won't protect us from the Chechen demon. I've met that man once before, and it wasn't pleasant. Underestimate him, and you'll meet the afterlife sooner than you want."

48

Omar al-Khatami said, "Destroy the phone we're talking on as soon as we hang up. Use that email to communicate. Nothing else. Do you understand?"

He heard Jacob say, "Yes. It will be done. See you in four days."

Omar said, "As-salamu alaykum." *Peace be with you.* He clicked off the satellite phone he'd been given by Adnan, finding no irony in the farewell. He stared at the phone in his hand, considering. He had the meeting time and place, but this phone was the one link should anything change. It was the only way the Albanians knew to contact him—but now it was connected to al-Britani like a cancer, and Omar was sure, since he hadn't called back, that the British fighter was dead.

Al-Britani had called him in a panic, shouting into the phone that he had been tricked and was moving the assault up immediately, then had said he'd call back later. That had been twelve hours ago, and he'd heard neither from the Brit nor seen any news relating to a spectacular attack in Amman. He had to assume the worst: The attack in Jordan had failed—or, thinking with the glass half full, the planned diversion had succeeded—which meant someone could be tracking this phone right now based on the last call al-Britani had made.

And Omar had seen what happened when the hated crusaders found a phone. He glanced unconsciously out the window, as if he could hear the vapor trail from the Hellfire missile.

The vision made the decision for him. He separated the phone from the battery, dropped it on the floor, then smashed it with his boot. If the

Albanians changed the meeting time or place, he'd have to deal with it. Best case, when they couldn't contact him, someone would show up to tell him the change. Worst case, they would have to reassess their attack plan without the special explosives and detonators.

The explosives were really the least of his worries. They were critical, but he could get other means of attack and still use the Trojan horse Jacob was building right this minute, but such planning would fail if he couldn't trust Jacob. Al-Britani had said that Hussein was a traitor— and Hussein was a Lost Boy. In fact, he was the man who had recruited the entire team of Lost Boys now executing the mission in Venice.

That idiot Brit had killed Hussein in a rage, not even bothering to question him, so there was no way to know who Hussein was working for or what he had divulged. Maybe he'd simply been compromised by Jordanian authorities. After all, the entire purpose of the Jordan mission had been a diversionary attack designed to suck in the crusader's intelligence apparatus and camouflage the primary mission. Maybe that had happened, but Omar couldn't ignore the ramifications of the Lost Boys.

Carlos and Devon had embraced the strictures of the Islamic State much like the multitude of Western foreign fighters pouring into Syria, but Jacob was different. He'd shown commitment, but he had always been aloof. He'd sworn allegiance to the Islamic State, but had refused to change his name. He followed orders, but questioned them.

Omar thought about it, then decided such actions alone tended to show he wasn't a traitor. If he were truly sent as a spy, if he truly intended to destroy the very attack he was working, would he act in such a manner?

Omar couldn't see it, which made him turn back to Carlos and Devon. They acted as he would expect the traitor to act. Perfectly in accordance with the Islamic State. But they were also simpletons, showing no subterfuge or higher-order intelligence.

Jacob had sounded fine on the phone, asking about Hussein after he was told of the failed attack, but not overtly upset. He'd also detailed an elaborate plan to accomplish the mission, the pride at his work seeping through the phone. The target set had grown from just the group to some unknown female as well, a touch that sounded genuine.

But Jacob was smart. No doubt if he wanted to trick Omar, he would have woven a tapestry to cover his treachery. In fact, his nonallegiance to the Islamic State may be just that—a double-blind performance designed precisely to protect him from scrutiny, because nobody planning a traitorous operation would act that way.

Omar snorted at his own paranoia, rubbing his face in frustration. He was doing nothing but spinning himself into the ground, his theories sounding more like the rantings of a crazy man than a leader of all external operations for the Islamic State.

He wished he could travel to Venice to see just what Jacob was up to.

49

Chris Fulbright hustled about his small room, moving one suitcase to the bed to get him access to the minibar. Right on the water on the southern edge of the island city-state, the Hotel Savoia e Jolanda was pricey, but still adhered to the Venetian rules of lodging. The room was the size of a postage stamp. Not that he'd be doing anything but sleeping in here anyway. He'd laid out cash from a tax-deferred mutual fund for his love nest, two thousand dollars dropped into a pay-as-you-go credit card. He'd pay the penalty to the IRS, but his wife would never know.

He popped a beer, not caring that it was probably twelve dollars. He'd find some way to claim it. Fax from the business center, Internet usage, something. After all, he was chosen for this excursion precisely because his company did business in Italy. For the boys, this was the trip of a lifetime, but for him, it was work. Well, he'd call it work, anyway.

His company had aggressively attempted to gain an entry into the European continent, and through his efforts, they'd found a possible Italian contract for their services. While the Italian company was based in Rome, the key player of that endeavor lived in Venice. The perfect cover for his planned tryst. A little work, and a little head.

He thought again about the gondola ride, and took a swig of beer, wondering if the boys could see through his excuse for tonight. Tomorrow was taken care of. The boys knew he'd be working all day, but leaving each night was a risk. He was still crafting his story when he heard a small *snick* under the door.

He saw an envelope on the hardwood floor, as if he were checking out. He padded over to it in his socks, picked it up, seeing nothing on the outside. He opened it, unfolding cheap printer paper stained with poorly reproduced images.

He saw the first one and collapsed on the bed, feeling his world sucked into a black hole.

He flipped through them until he came to a grainy picture of him kissing Christine on the gondola, the most damning thing in the stack. He felt faint.

Chris returned to the photo and thought, *Why, why, why? Who would do this? Why did I do this? What was I thinking?*

Chris Fulbright was a comfortably happy forty-five-year-old man in charge of a small marketing department for a start-up company developing 3-D printers. Originally fighting tooth and nail for survival, they'd managed to cut a pretty good niche in the market, with foreign buyers wanting their services. Tax breaks in Florida had brought the company there, and he'd followed, believing in the inherent success about to be achieved. He'd worked hard, and had made a name for himself by landing the overseas accounts in Italy.

Now, all of that would mean nothing. He loved his wife. He loved his kids. He truly did . . . and then he'd met Christine, at, of all places, a Staples graphics center.

In a crunch for time, he'd needed to buy unforeseen posters for a launch of a product. His usual supplier had had no ability for a quick turnaround, and, in a panic, having run out of options, he'd walked into a Staples business store near his office. And seen Christine. Or, more correctly, had seen her breasts.

She was a community college dropout, fully fifteen years his junior, but she was vivacious and engaging. More to the point, she was interested in him.

They'd laughed at the similarities of their names, forming a connection that had led to a longer visit than his order took, and he'd then gone on his way, but he'd developed an itch. He'd found himself going back to that store more and more often. Eventually, he'd broached a date. Nothing but drinks, he'd promised. A little small talk, since it was closing time and all.

It had become a weekly habit, and he'd dared think about the next step. As a leader of the youth group in his church, he'd landed this sweet gig of chaperoning three altar boys over to Europe to meet the pope, and he'd hit upon a bold idea. A once-in-a-lifetime vacation for Christine, in a place where nobody knew either of them.

On their sixth "date," having done nothing but enrich the same bar, he'd broached the trip. Surprising him, she'd agreed. Nothing was said explicitly. There was no overt discussion of payback, but in her acceptance, he knew it was understood.

He had intended to close the deal tonight. Break his marriage vows forever by dropping into the abyss of Christine's lily-white breasts. Instead, he had a pack of pictures on his lap that would explode his world.

What the fuck had he been thinking?

He looked at the images again, and began focusing more clinically. Who would do this? They had a single competitor for their 3-D services on the European continent: a group out of Germany that had threatened them with all manner of European patent infringements. Because the technology was so new, it was open season, with the patents up for any number of attacks, and Chris had convinced the CEO that they were bluffing. But now it looked like they were playing hardball.

He crumpled the pictures on the bed, thinking of how he could extricate himself from the situation. Clearly, European operations were no longer in the equation. What he needed to do was ensure that the competition was willing to delete his transgressions. Permanently. A note accompanying the pictures gave instructions for a meeting, but nothing as to a demand. He'd have to determine that tonight.

He remembered Christine, but no longer felt any excitement. He only wanted to get her on the first plane back to the United States. At the end of the day, Chris was a married father of two. There was no way some copy girl from Staples could interfere with that.

He sent her a message saying he would have to delay their date tonight, and thought about just breaking up with her in the email, but he knew he couldn't. She'd have questions, and he'd need to meet in person to answer them. He realized she might not take it well, and was another possible leak. At that thought, he put his head into his hands.

He sat on the bed for the rest of the day, alternately squeezing his fists until his knuckles were white and unabashedly weeping.

50

The connecting door opened to my room, and Jennifer came in, followed by Knuckles. He said, "This is convenient. I figured you'd want a room that connects to the TOC, but I guess we all have our priorities."

Jennifer elbowed him in the gut, causing a *woof* of air. He backed up, rubbing his belly, saying, "Touchy, aren't we?"

She said, "This is serious. No joking around."

I saw her expression and knew she was about to make trouble. As if I didn't have enough to deal with. I was analyzing Google Maps, trying to figure out the best observation points to conduct surveillance of the Internet café, the only anchor we had, and I wasn't happy with the interruption. I preempted her, saying, "You guys finish with the plane? You got everything we need?"

While the Gulfstream was invaluable for infiltrating kit past customs, it was a pain in the ass to get said kit out of the aircraft and into our tactical operations center. A lot of back-and-forth, running "checklists" and doing "maintenance."

Knuckles said, "Retro's getting the last of the optics. We're good to go with weapons and commo. Believe it or not, the front desk helped bring it up."

Knuckles saw my glare and said, "I know, I know, but those guys won't take no for an answer. Me and Jennifer were toting damn near a hundred pounds of weaponry in three Gucci luggage bags. If we had waved off, they'd have become suspicious. They didn't seem to mind. Probably do that shit all the time for the Albanian mafia."

We were staying at the Sheraton Hotel, a five-star affair snuggled between the city and a giant green space, Tirana's version of Central Park. The hotel itself was probably the nicest property in the city, and it seemed the management knew it. They acted a little embarrassed to be working there, like the rich guy who brought home a normal date, now apologizing for the manservants and thousand-dollar espresso machines. It was annoying, but this was the only place we could find with high-speed Wi-Fi, and a lack of that was a nonstarter on this mission. Although having the management tote up our weapons was a bit much.

Jennifer said, "Hey, I've been going over the data from the Taskforce, and I think I'm on to something. I ran it past Knuckles, and he thinks so too."

I said, "Unless it involves a French terrorist of Algerian descent, I do not care. Do you realize what we're up against? The damn guy is using an Internet café right next to the US embassy. Like he's taunting us. Or planning an attack."

I stabbed my finger at the laptop screen and said, "He's using our own security to prevent us from snatching his ass. Maintaining eyes-on of that café is going to be damn near impossible. It's surrounded by police, all who work for the embassy, which we're not allowed to coordinate with."

Knuckles said, "Can't be that bad. It's a US embassy. We can get eyes-on from a distance. At least past the blast radius."

He was referring to a document called the Inman Report, produced after the 1983 bombing of our embassy in Beirut, which mandated certain standards for standoff and blast protection. Standards that grew more urgent after the 1998 bombings in Africa. It stipulated US embassies maintain at least a modicum of defensive capability, with standoff distances from vehicle-borne explosives and even glass construction specifications. Unfortunately, like a lot of quagmire in the US government, the design parameters apparently hadn't made it to Tirana, Albania.

The embassy was right in the heart of a neighborhood, with alleys snaking behind the back wall of the compound. It made me cringe wondering how easy it would be to obliterate, but my mission was in the

Internet café tucked next to the east wall, underneath a bar called, appropriately enough, the American Bar.

It was going to be hard keeping surveillance on Rashid, because the embassy had traded standoff distance for uniformed officers of Albania. They were everywhere.

But clearly, that wasn't why Jennifer had dragged Knuckles to my room. She had something more important in mind.

She said, "I went through the Taskforce reports."

I countered, "Are Shoshana and Aaron back yet? I need some input on bumper locations. And we need to develop a schedule. We're easy, but they're going to get smoked doing a fifty-fifty stakeout."

Jennifer crossed her arms and gave me the death stare, knowing I was trying to get her off whatever subject was coming. Knuckles said, "They haven't come back. I think you should hear Jennifer out. She's on to something."

Jennifer gave him a grateful nod, and, because he couldn't stand to back her up with me in the room, he said, "I mean, she appears to be thinking with something other than her dick." He glanced at the connecting door and said, "Unlike you. Although, after that last punch, I'm not so sure she isn't hiding a penis."

She whirled to him, shouting, "Do you constantly have to fight me because I'm female? Do I threaten you that much?"

The tone of her voice broke me away from my computer. Only half listening earlier, I was all ears now. It was beyond sharp. She'd always been good-natured about the ribbing before, but today, she was out for blood.

I saw Knuckles with a look of shock on his face, his hands in the air. He said, "Whoa, whoa . . . calm down. Jesus, Jennifer, what's up with you lately?"

She stopped and glared at him, but I could see the embarrassment coming through at her outburst.

I said, "Hey."

She flicked her eyes to me.

"What *is* up with you?"

She stomped away, getting a bottle of water from the small desk below the television. She unscrewed the cap, then sat down. She said, "You guys have been second-guessing me since al-Britani was killed. I had nothing to do with that. I am *not* Shoshana."

And I saw what was happening. It wasn't *us* second-guessing. It was her. Which made all the difference.

51

Nobody blamed Jennifer for what had happened. Every single one of us had been in her shoes at one time or another and made a decision that had ended badly. We'd dealt with it by talking to the team, and she felt she couldn't, because she believed she was unique. A female. She regretted the outcome of the mission in Jordan and was internalizing it.

I leaned forward, the team leader wanting to say something profound and uplifting, but before I could, Knuckles took a different tack.

He spit fire at her.

"Are you shitting me? Cut that crybaby crap. Is that why you've been acting like you're on your period? Fuck, girl, I was almost good to go with a female on the team. Now I have to deal with this hormonal bullshit?"

Her eyes flew open at his words. She leapt to her feet, fists clenched. He stood firm and said, "What? You want a piece of this? Bring it on. I'm sick of Pike protecting you all the time."

He looked at me, and I gave a slight nod, letting him know I was good with it. Showing him I understood where he was going.

He advanced on her and said, "You think you made a bad call, and you very well might have, but we all do. We *all* do. You want to talk about it, I'm all ears, but spare me the song and dance that I don't trust you anymore."

I saw confusion, then suspicion. She said, "You don't mean that."

He smiled, looked at me, and said, "You want to tell her about Sudan?"

I said, "No. I'd rather leave that fuckup in the classified dictionary of what not to do."

He returned to her and said, "That's *my* dictionary, by the way. You want to tell lover boy here what you found? Or just keep pining away because you don't actually have a penis?"

Her face grew red at the insults, stiffening her will to resist. I halfway stood, knowing what was about to happen, because she was one bull-headed woman . . . person . . . whatever.

Then I saw her reflect on what he'd said. Like in Nairobi, she realized he was actually patting her on the back and giving her an out.

She sat back into the chair and said, "I don't need to know what he screwed up. I see it on a daily basis."

Knuckles grinned and said, "Offer still stands. You want to talk about what happened in Jordan, I'm willing to listen. But I'd hate to waste Pike's time, since his attention span is so short. Show him what you have."

She opened her purse, withdrawing some computer printouts.

I said, "Okay, what the hell is the big deal? We have an operation starting tomorrow, and I have a couple of loony Israelis to deal with. Conspiracy theories are taking a backseat."

The next words out of her mouth made me second-guess who was loony.

"Pike, I read through all of the reports on Hussein, both open-source, and our own analysis. They missed something. The Lost Boys are real, and I think they're on the hunt."

I rolled my eyes and said, "We don't have time for this shit. We have a mission. Feed your suspicions into the system. We take orders. We don't make them."

She pursed her lips, glancing at Knuckles for backup. He said, "That's it? That's all you got?"

I returned to my computer, mapping out my surveillance strategy. Jennifer pushed the lid down, causing a spike of anger in me. She held a finger to my lips and said, "Hussein recruited the Lost Boys. I don't know why, but he did. Hear me out."

I started to bark at her and Knuckles leaned in. "For once, assume you're not the smartest in the room."

I gritted my teeth for a moment, then spit out, "Well?"

Jennifer said, "Remember the video? Of the guy saying he was doing it for the White House?"

I nodded. She placed a digital recorder on the table. "This is the last thing Hussein said before he died."

Hussein's disembodied voice floated in the room, chilling because we knew it was real. And he was dead.

"It's because of the white house. I never wanted to go there. Nobody wanted to go there. They did this. Ask Jacob. He'll tell you about the white house."

We sat in silence for a moment, then Jennifer said, "That's been pinging in my head for days, because it just didn't make any sense. His final words didn't match what the Taskforce assessed about the Lost Boys. So I asked you for the reports."

She laid an official Taskforce transcript in front of me.

"Hussein was incarcerated at a Christian reform school in Florida. The one that's now closed down. Remember you told me that? Well, the chief reason it was shuttered was because of horrific abuse, and that cruelty was primarily conducted in a building on the center of the campus. Called the 'white house.' They weren't talking about attacking America on that video. They were talking about something they'd all experienced. Together."

She let that sink in, then continued, "The murder of the guard that drew the attention to the place occurred during a breakout. Three men escaped. *Three.* They disappeared without a trace."

I went from her to Knuckles. "And?"

She slapped a cushion and said, "And they're the damn Lost Boys! The ones in the video. One of the boys who escaped is named Jacob, for God's sake. They're tied to Hussein. It isn't just a nickname given by the Islamic State. It's a group, and they're working together."

I said, "Even if they are, we have a mission here. What do you want me to do about it?"

"I want to get their names in the system. Get the Taskforce to check them out. We know who escaped, but the Taskforce hasn't looked at this thread."

I rubbed my face, not needing this distraction. "Fine, fine. I'll do that. Can we get back to our mission? We've got a killer here with intelligence training. I'm not too concerned about a bunch of escaped juvenile delinquents chopping off heads in Syria."

She said, "Because they're not holding a knife to your throat. But what if they're holding it to someone else's? Right this very minute."

52

Jacob leaned against the rough-hewn brick, trying to remain inconspicuous. It was a losing battle, and he knew it. He simply looked like he was up to no good. A single man, standing by himself in the gloom of night. He imagined he was representing exactly why the street had such a nefarious name.

Originally looking for an entrance to a canal, away from the gondoliers and tourists, he'd used Google Maps to find Rio Terrà Assassini. He'd walked it, a mere ten minutes from his hotel, and liked what he saw. No stores and only one bistro farther up the lane, it was narrow and off the beaten tourist path. The far end was nothing more than a set of concrete steps that dropped into the murky canal water, the walls of the alley just over ten feet across. A perfect spot to pull up a small boat, and, since it dead-ended into the canal, no tourists or locals would be using the alley as a thoroughfare.

Walking back to the hotel, he'd become intrigued by the name. He'd Googled it, and found that the alley had a little bit of a story behind it. *Assassini* referred to the assassinations and murders that had occurred in that small stretch of stone, with pickpockets and thieves preying on the wealthier class trying to sneak to the nearby brothels located in Calle della Mandola. The discovery surprised him, but it was fitting. Centuries could go by, but the killer instinct was drawn to the same locations.

He saw a group of Korean tourists leave the wine bar fifty meters away and turn toward him, clearly going the wrong way in the maze that was Venice. He tried to appear as if he had a purpose, kneeling down and pretending to work the rope anchored above the stairs. When he stood back up, he met the eyes of the lead tourist, and the man stopped dead in his tracks, seeing something he instinctively wanted to recoil from. He muttered something in Korean to his partners, then they all turned abruptly and began walking much faster back the way they'd come.

Jacob cursed and looked at his watch. Nine forty-five. *Where is Carlos?*

Their target was due here in fifteen minutes, and he wanted to get him immediately into the boat, while the man was still compliant and before he could alert any potential contingency he had planned.

He had a lot of information he needed to get from the target, and he wanted to do it out on the ocean, away from anyone who could hear him scream, should force become necessary.

First, they needed to find out where he'd stashed the lady. They had only two more nights, and didn't have the time to go searching. Second, they needed to know unequivocally if he'd talked to anyone. He knew the boys were clean, because he'd spoken to Devon. They were currently boozing it up in a pub a half mile away and had no idea what had transpired with their chaperone, but that didn't preclude the target from having alerted his mistress.

Those questions were significant, but the primary one was whether their target had planned to be gone for the duration of the day tomorrow. The boys indicated that they were on their own, and the target had stated he was doing business meetings, but Jacob wanted to know if that was true, or if he was planning on spending the day in bed with his lover.

Jacob wasn't too worried about a missed business meeting, as the mission would be done in a week. The worst they'd do was call the target's phone and leave a voice mail.

After the mission, he could care less what they found, but all of that was predicated on the target doing what he told the boys. If he was lying about the meeting and instead intended to get lathered in sweat with his honeypot tomorrow, it would be an issue, because the target was never leaving the boat alive tonight.

The thought brought back memories of the Kurd, reminding Jacob of what he was doing. The meat of it. The heart. He felt the filet knife hidden in his sleeve, knowing what it would taste in the next thirty minutes. An action that plenty of kids back in the school had blustered about, but never actually done—something Jacob could no longer say.

Jacob wondered if the act was worth the sacrifice. Once he did this killing, he was on an irreversible path. There would be no turning back. He would be a hunted man forever. The only place he could return was the cauldron of the Islamic State, forced to subjugate his newfound sense of worth for the rest of his life. Ironically, a sense of worth provided by Omar and the Islamic State.

But what was the alternative? Leaving now would mean abandoning his friends Carlos and Devon. They weren't smart enough to stay alive on their own. If he quit, fleeing to a new life, the mission would fail. Carlos and Devon would return to the Islamic State, convinced their faith would allow mercy. And they'd be tortured to death, ending up on a gruesome tape much like the very one they'd made earlier in Syria.

Hussein was already dead. Jacob felt some guilt at that. He could have gotten him out, but he had not, and he wouldn't do the same to Carlos and Devon. Everything he had been through, both in the white house and the Islamic State, told him that family was worth far more than anything else. When everything was boiled down, that was all that was left, and he now included Omar in that circle. The one man who'd ever shown him respect.

He thought about Omar and his skill. He could work for a man like that. He could do what Omar wanted, and he could achieve a bit of success. Maybe more than a bit. He'd recognized his skill, and felt a loyalty to Omar that he'd never experienced before.

He caught movement behind him, and saw a fifteen-foot aluminum-hulled boat float out of the gloom, a grinning Carlos working an outboard motor. He cut the engine and glided in. Jacob grabbed the bow and used the anchored rope to tie it fast.

Carlos said, "Sorry I'm late. Had a little trouble with the boat."

Jacob stood up and said, "You didn't have to hurt anyone, did you?"

"No, no. The owner was working late. I just waited for him to leave. I'd have called, but it worked out."

Jacob nodded and Carlos said, "Did he come?"

"Not yet. Should be here any minute."

"What if he doesn't?"

Jacob looked back up the alley, seeing a man break out of the crowds from the wine bar. Walking into the light, Jacob recognized the target.

"He's here. Get ready."

Chris Fulbright passed the bistro in the alley and slowed, straining his eyes. He saw two shadowy figures at the end, a canal behind them. He glanced back, as if there would be some help behind him, then continued on, much more slowly than before.

He came within the feeble light from a second-story window and saw that the men were mere boys, maybe twenty years old at the most, which raised a primordial instinct. He was unfamiliar with anything smacking of danger, but something deep in his gene pool registered a threat.

In his head, the odds were they'd been sent by the German conglomerate and were nothing more than hired messengers. But something about them was off. Feral.

Behind them was a small johnboat, with what looked like a load of rope and cinder blocks. He dismissed it as some local's conveyance.

He resolved to hear them out but give them nothing beyond what they had. He'd trade his enormous breakthrough into Europe, throw away five years of work because of a moment of infatuation with a set of tits, but he wouldn't give them leverage for anything else.

The taller of the two stepped forward and said, "Chris, my name is Jacob. Please step into the boat. We have some things to discuss."

53

Jacob saw the alarm on Chris's face and wondered if he shouldn't just tackle the man, flinging him into the boat. As quickly as the thought entered, he discarded it. They had to navigate up the small waterway to the major hub called the Grand Canal, and would be passing underneath several bridges to do so. They couldn't accomplish that with a writhing, screaming kidnap victim.

He said, "We only want to talk. Away from the crowds. On the water, where it's safer for us."

"Why? I don't have anyone with me. I promise."

"We mean you no harm. You agree, and you'll be on your way shortly." He held up a thumb drive. "You get this, and your wife will never know."

Jacob saw he wanted to believe, and knew it would be enough. Chris nodded and gingerly slid into the boat. Jacob untied the bow and Carlos started the motor. They began gliding down the canal, headed to the larger one.

Chris said, "What do you want? Why have you been following me?"

Jacob had known this question was coming, and had thought about his answer. He knew that Chris would have formulated the *why* already. He had no idea what that would be, but he knew it existed, and had decided to use Chris's beliefs against him. He said, "You know why."

Chris sagged back into the metal seat and said, "Okay, okay. Tell your boss he can have it. I'll leave Europe to him. I'll go to my meeting tomorrow and bow out, then tell my people it didn't work in our favor."

Jacob had no idea what he was talking about, but liked hearing about the meeting tomorrow. One question answered.

When he didn't speak, Chris said, "Is that not enough? Why are we still going anywhere?"

They passed under a stone bridge, Carlos waving at the tourists on top like a goofy local, then they entered the Grand Canal, an expanse of water seventy meters wide that threaded through the island city-state like a snake. Carlos turned to the north and opened the engine up, drowning out further talk.

They passed by water taxis and other boats, some big, some like theirs. They rode in silence, Jacob keeping his eyes on Chris. Going underneath the Rialto Bridge, one of the few that spanned the Grand Canal, Chris finally shouted something, and Jacob waved his hand, indicating he should wait.

He felt his weapon shift and clamped his other hand on the sleeve to stop its fall. He wasn't quick enough. The filet knife fell to the hull of the boat, clattering silently in the shadow of the engine.

Jacob looked at Chris and saw fear. The canal curved toward the west, the Rialto Bridge receding behind them. Chris tensed, and Jacob jumped toward the knife, instinctively thinking that was his goal.

Chris dove over the side.

Jacob screamed and Carlos cut the engine, the boat immediately slowing to a crawl. Carlos whipped his head to the rear, scanning the water and shouting, "What happened? Why'd he bail out?"

Jacob snatched the knife and glanced around, seeing no other boats. He heard Chris shout, churning about in the water, and jumped over the side.

He paused, getting a bearing on Chris, seeing him flailing toward the nearest bank, swimming in a modified dog paddle, hampered by his suit and lack of ability. Jacob, a much better swimmer, began stroking toward him.

Jacob came abreast of him and grabbed Chris's collar, saying, "Stop, stop. We aren't going to hurt you."

Chris screamed, "Help me! Someone help me!"

The shout seared Jacob with panic. He jammed the blade with an overhand strike, stabbing Chris in the chest. Chris let out a piercing shriek, and one thought exploded through Jacob's mind: *Silence him.*

He reached up and grabbed Chris's hair, pulling his head backward, dragging the man down below the surface, the scream becoming bubbles under the water. Chris began to fight in blind panic, and Jacob swam deeper, kicking his legs and pushing against Chris's body.

Jacob fended off the ineffectual thrashing of Chris's arms and felt the pressure in his ears. He knew he'd gone deep enough. He wrapped his legs around Chris's torso and cinched his hand deeper into the hair. He pulled the head back and jabbed the filet knife into his prey's neck, the water and darkness causing him to hit high, sinking the blade into Chris's jaw. He tried again, and found his target.

He missed the carotid artery, but caught the esophagus. He ripped out, feeling an explosion of bubbles. Chris's fight became feeble, then stopped altogether. Jacob held on until his lungs felt like they were about to burst, then swam upward, dragging the body with him.

He broke the surface with an explosion of air, treading water and cradling Chris's head as if he were a lifeguard. He scanned around and saw Carlos slowly circling in the boat. He waved, and Carlos increased speed toward him. Jacob looked toward shore, but saw nobody. They were across from the Rialto Market area, and at this hour, it was closed, the market nothing more than empty tables and stands, waiting for tomorrow's fruits, fish, and vegetables.

Carlos pulled up next to him and said, "You okay?"

"Yeah, yeah." Jacob looked down for the first time, seeing Chris's head bobbing in the water, blood leaking out from the massive tear in his neck, his hair floating about like a halo, his eyes open and wet.

Jacob said, "We didn't get any of our answers."

Carlos said, "We know he's having meetings tomorrow."

"Yeah, but he might be meeting the woman as well."

Jacob hoisted the torso toward the boat and said, "Hold his arms."

Carlos did so, awkwardly leaning over and tilting the hull with the weight of the body. Jacob went through the dead man's pockets, pulling out his wallet, passport, hotel keycard, and cell phone. He threw them into the boat, then began punching the blade into Chris's chest like he was using a fork on the plastic of a microwave dinner. Venting the body to allow water to enter the lungs.

He tossed the knife into the boat and said, "Tie him to the side. We need to drop him in the ocean, where we planned. We can't risk him being discovered."

Carlos dropped the rope into the water and Jacob began lashing, keeping the body below the waterline, Carlos helping where he could. A barge towing a bucket loader appeared around the bend and they stopped working, Jacob crouching below the gunwale.

It passed on without incident.

Carlos put in one final cinch of rope and said, "What are we going to do?"

Jacob pulled himself over the side of the skiff, water running off of his clothes.

"Continue on. What else is there?"

54

Opening his ProtonMail, Rashid was pleased to see a message. It was from someone called UnionJack7883 and the subject was "Timeline." He assumed it was from al-Britani, and used the word *Timeline* as his decryption password. It failed.

He tried again, this time in all lowercase, and the email opened, both pleasing and aggravating him. Al-Britani clearly had an issue with attention to detail.

The message was brief, saying the timeline had been pushed back a few days. The hotel had shifted the hours their inside man was working, going from days to nights. As the Gulf Cooperation Council conference ceased work at five, gaining access to the hotel after that hour wasn't conducive to an attack. Apparently, the inside man's schedule returned to a daytime shift in three days, and that was when al-Britani intended to attack.

All in all, not the message he was hoping for, but still a good sign. Al-Britani was communicating directly with him, and appeared to be committed to conducting the attack in the name of the Khorasan group.

Rashid typed a short message back, telling him to maintain the operational security, and included the new password for them to use for all future messages.

He hit send, satisfied with the Jordan side of things, but he was still unsure about his own mission. The real mission, not the one his masters in Jabhat al-Nusra believed he was conducting.

The thought made him realize he hadn't updated his leadership since he'd arrived, and they would want to know what was occurring. They might even go so far as to contact the Albanian cell that had been chosen to transfer the weapons, which would not be a good thing.

He pulled up another ProtonMail account in his saved contacts. One he'd used many, many times in the past two years. Before that, it was all Gmail. But even Gmail was better than Twitter direct messaging.

It had been an uphill climb convincing the leadership of just how enormously broad the collection capabilities of the crusaders were. He'd known it from his time spent with the DGSE—the French version of the CIA—but they had been convinced that nobody could find a needle in the haystack as large as Gmail. The vastness of the Internet was their protection, and it was just unfeasible that someone could track them in it. It took a spindly-armed, wispy-bearded man-child releasing a trove of secrets on the NSA before they believed.

They'd read the news reports the same day as Rashid, and he'd been brought in immediately, the leadership now asking him what they should do.

Initially, he'd given them Tor and PGP encryption, becoming the in-house expert on evading the crusader net. Later, he convinced them to switch to ProtonMail, which had been developed by kids at MIT and Switzerland specifically because of the man-child's revelations, and he'd thanked that American ever since, absolutely convinced that there would have been many, many more believers martyred without his childish vision of right and wrong. He remembered the initial leadership meeting well, after the man-child had fled to Russia. As a joke, he'd told the emir *they* should offer him asylum for his contributions.

He heard the bell above the door to the café tinkle and glanced reflexively toward it, seeing nothing but two Albanian teenagers. He returned to his email, typing a short message detailing a false account of what they'd been doing and saying he was happy with the professionalism of the Albanians. He was debating creating a lie about meeting Omar when his phone vibrated on the table.

He picked it up, seeing a text message from his team. Omar had been seen walking into Tirana Park. He felt a little stab of adrenaline. *So the meeting is going to occur on schedule. Good.*

He looked at his watch, feeling an inescapable desire to leave. He saw he still had close to an hour, though. Time enough to complete the message to his command. He resumed typing.

Sitting inside the American Bar, Shoshana and I drank Cokes and watched some random soccer game on the one wide-screen TV, surrounded by a group of die-hard loyalists for whatever European team was playing.

I turned my head to the street outside the window, seeing a stream of people walking back and forth, the Internet café right below us and out of sight. We'd been on the trigger team for the surveillance for close to two hours, all timed with the soccer game to give us a reason to be here. Unfortunately for Shoshana, between the two of us, she was the only one that knew what Rashid looked like, so I got to watch soccer, and she had to stare at the street.

I'd staged the rest of the team, minus Jennifer and Aaron, at potential avenues of escape to pick up surveillance once the target had been acquired. So far, they'd just sat.

"Aaron is due in for rotation with Jennifer in ten minutes. You want to go get a bite to eat?"

She looked at me and said, "You want to eat with a murderer?"

"Damn it, Shoshana, would you stop that? You have to admit, you screwed things up in Jordan. No telling what we could have gotten from al-Britani. Maybe we wouldn't even be doing this surveillance."

Eyes on the street, she said, "Mission comes first. Always."

I said, "It didn't in Brazil. Your mission was over. You could have walked away."

For the first time, I saw cracks in the ice princess. She said, "You could have too."

She'd volunteered to sacrifice her life to save hundreds of thousands of people in Brazil, and I'd decided that wasn't going to happen. We'd done something borderline stupid, but it had succeeded. Both of us working toward a greater good, regardless of our given mission. Which is why I knew, at her core, she wasn't just an assassin, killing men she disliked. At least I hoped so, because right now she disliked me.

She smiled, playing me a little, saying, "Okay, Nephilim. I'll go to lunch with you. I'll give you some deep introspection into Jennifer. Is that what you want?"

I said, "No, no. We're going to talk about *you*. Where you grew up, what you did as a child, that sort of thing. First-date stuff."

Her eyes narrowed, and she said, "Hmm . . . no games?"

"Nope."

"And I can ask the same of you?"

I hesitated for a moment, and she said, "If it's *really* a first date, I should be able to ask you whatever you ask me."

I said, "I thought you could read that *without* asking. That's what Aaron says."

I saw hurt flit across her face and wondered what I'd done. I said, "Okay, yes. You can ask whatever you want. I don't care."

She leaned forward, her eyes bright and clear. "I want to talk about something other than death. I want to talk about living. Like what you talk to Jennifer about."

Her gaze scored me like a laser, searching, and I felt pity. She was a creation of events beyond her control, manipulated by operations conducted before she even understood the cancer they would generate in her soul, and those actions had permanently twisted her. She had an ability few on Earth possessed, and her government had harnessed it, ignoring the toll it would take. And she was now trying to claw her way out of the abyss, to find a normalcy she'd seen between Jennifer and me.

I feared it was too late. After seeing what she'd done to al-Britani, I knew the abyss would swallow her, the undertow dragging her down no matter how hard she fought.

She leaned forward and took my hands, saying, "You were once like me. I feel it. How did you crawl out?"

The words caused me to recoil, pulling my hands away, afraid she could read my soul by touch. I'd felt it before with her, but it still scared the hell out of me.

She said, "What? Was it Jennifer? Is that it?" She reached out again and said, "I want to know. I want a life."

I kept my hands in my lap, saying, "You should look at Aaron. He's your Jennifer."

She scoffed and said, "Aaron. All he cares about is the mission." She saw the surprise on my face and said, "What?"

I said, "Really? You're some type of psychic spoon-bender and you can't read the man you've worked with forever? The guy's crazy over you. Regardless of your sexual orientation."

She looked back to the street, searching for our target. "He's my boss. All he cares about is success. The mission."

"I think you're selling him short. Is that why you left Mossad when he asked?"

Still looking out the window, she said, "Don't confuse trust with emotion. I trust him. He believed in me, and that was enough. I won't work for anyone else, ever again."

She returned to me and said, "You don't know my history. What I've done. What I was forced to do. Aaron isn't that way, but he's still Mossad. He'd sacrifice me in a heartbeat if it meant mission success."

I saw her eyes grow wet and she said, "I made fun of you in the aircraft because of your protection of Jennifer. I . . . wish . . . someone cared. . . ."

I felt such profound sadness at her words I didn't know what to say. She was convinced she was only a tool. Something to be discarded when the weapon was no longer useful.

I started to say something, and my earpiece clicked. "Pike, Pike, this is Retro. I've got Taskforce on the line, and Rashid's on a box, right now."

I leaned forward, eyes on Shoshana, saying, "We've been here the whole time, and he never entered."

She flicked her eyes to the street, looking for a ghost. Retro said, "Yeah, yeah, you're right. The Taskforce did a malware inject via email. Long story short, he's online right this second, and it ain't your café."

55

Omar trudged up the stone path into Tirana Park, eyes downcast and avoiding contact with anyone. Dressed like a local, with his red hair and blue eyes, he didn't look at all like a fanatical follower of Islam. The only indication would be the bulky left side of his coat, drooping low, as if he were carrying a bunch of lead weights in it. Had someone searched him, they would have found a Czech CZ 75 pistol in his coat pocket, chambered in 9mm. Definitely not useful for a late-afternoon stroll.

He passed a couple pushing a newborn in a carriage and smiled, then took a left on a footpath. Unmarked, nothing but dirt well worn through the grass, it led steadily uphill. He reached the top, hitting another flagstone path, this one much bigger. To the left was a monument for historical figures in the life of Albania. To the right was a restaurant. He went right, climbing again. He passed a man incongruously selling chances to shoot a small rifle at a target, the proprietor listlessly sitting next to the weapon and smoking a cigarette. Omar passed him, amazed. The man hadn't been here when he'd conducted reconnaissance the day before, and he found it incredible that someone could sell chances at shooting a target on top of a mountaintop full of parents and strollers. He wouldn't have allowed that even in Syria.

He crested the hill and saw the amphitheater to the left, the artificial lake of Tirana beyond, the area blanketed with families out enjoying the fading sunshine. He paused a beat, trying to spot his Georgian friends. He could not, but assumed they were near. He left the path, heading downhill toward the amphitheater.

Created when Albania was a member of the defunct Soviet empire, it was built to resemble a smaller version of one of the great coliseums from the Roman Empire. The difference was that instead of being carved from granite and limestone, it had been created on the cheap, poured from concrete, with cement chairs and a slab of a stage, all of which had seen the ravages of time much, much more than the ancient structures it supposedly represented.

Covered in graffiti, it looked a lot like a section of the burned-out city of Kobani, Syria. At the top, on squat cement blocks, was a square concrete building, used for lights or other artificial help for the stage below. A set of metal stairs led up to a single steel door, looking like the entrance to a prison cell.

The meeting site.

He walked up the steps, the rust flaking off the railing. He reached the landing and banged on the door. It was opened by a man with a prominent nose and a threadbare woolen blazer. He simply stared at Omar.

Omar said, "This place reminds me of Aleppo. Have you been there?"

The man smiled, showing rotting, gapped teeth, and said, "No, but I can help you get it back."

He swung the door open, and Omar entered, seeing a barren concrete room. Another man, standing in front of a table, moved forward and held out his hand.

"It is good to meet you. We've heard of your success, and support you."

Omar knew they were working for money alone, their only real contribution being the security they afforded as Muslims. That, and the enormous amount of cash they were being paid, money gathered by Islamic State kidnapping and extortion, something the men in the room understood very well. The difference was every penny of the Islamic State's income went to develop the caliphate, whereas their income went to their own satisfaction.

A fact Omar had no intention of forgetting. The meeting here was set up with the Islamic State, but it was facilitated by Jabhat al-Nusra. Men he'd tried to kill in the past. Men who were now in the upper echelons of power. A higher bidder, Muslim or otherwise, could cause his downfall.

He shook the man's hand and saw artifacts on the table. Strange cases the size of cigarette packs, and a smartphone.

Shoshana saw my face and knew something had gone terribly wrong. She said, "What? What happened?"

She'd heard my end of the conversation, but not what Retro had said. While we could outfit the Israelis with mechanical things like beacons and weapons, the classified capabilities of the Taskforce smartphone were something beyond what I was able to transfer, even if I wanted to. Each one was configured for the specific team using it before deployment, including biometrics for security to prevent unauthorized access, so it would have done no good to give her one. I had spares, but unless she could duplicate some seriously technical aspects of the team's biometric profile—voice recognition and fingerprint scans—the phone would simply shut down, reformatting itself.

Which meant Aaron and Shoshana were relegated to simple cell phone contact.

I ignored Shoshana, saying, "Retro, give me a grid. Break, break—"

He came back. "Already did. It's in a section called Blloku. About a quarter of a mile away."

I said again, "Great. BREAK, BREAK, nobody interrupt. Koko, you on?"

"Yeah, I got you. I heard. We're outside the soccer stadium. I got the location from Retro. What's the call?"

"Get to the target. Get Aaron inside. See if he can beacon the guy. Everyone else, box the area and stand by."

Knuckles said, "Moving."

Brett broke in. "Copy, copy. We don't know what the guy looks like. Get a picture."

I said, "I know, I know. Koko, you copy?"

She said, "Yeah, got it. We're two minutes out. Dropping Aaron as a Foxtrot. He won't have commo."

Foxtrot meant Aaron was going on foot. I stood up, nonchalantly throwing bills on the table. "I got it. I understand. Just get a fix. Give him instructions, and get a Dragontooth on the guy."

The Dragontooth was a Bluetooth beacon about the size of an SD card with a pretty cool adhesive on the back. It could be placed against all manner of material and persistently stick, which was the extent of its NASA capabilities. As far as beacon work went, all it did was throw out a signal that we could pick up if we were in range. Which was about seventy meters.

Like a lot of Taskforce equipment, the R&D section had scoured the commercial sector and had found a unique device designed to locate lost items. You placed the device, called Tile, on whatever was prone to being lost, and it linked to a smartphone via Bluetooth, allowing you to find it if you were in range. The cool thing was that *anyone* who used Tile became part of an ecosystem, so that their phone, working in the background, would register your device and alert *you*. Lose your keys in a bar? If someone else entered and had the app, it would tell you where they were. It was crowdfunded surveillance, and the Taskforce had taken notice.

The Dragontooth operated the same way, only the Taskforce had an app that was implanted through malware into a host nation's phone service, whereby our system was completely in the background. Basically, we hoped to turn the entire population—at least anyone with a smartphone—into unwitting surveillance drones. It was still in beta testing, but showed promise. Right now, the only devices with the app would be the Taskforce smartphones, but that was better than nothing.

The Tile system claimed a one-year shelf life, but it was operating on low-voltage Bluetooth. You had to be fairly close to the device before it registered. Ours was broadcasting a much more powerful signal, and that, coupled with the size restrictions, gave us a useful life of about forty-eight hours. That was it. Anything more would require a bigger battery, and that would require a bigger beacon. Unlike Hollywood, even the Taskforce couldn't break the laws of physics.

Jennifer said, "Roger. Got it. Moving."

Brett came on. "The Internet café is on a street with multiple avenues of approach. We can box it, but if he's leaving on foot, we can't cover all the alleys."

Walking down the stairs, I realized I didn't have a car to control the surveillance effort. I was supposed to take Jennifer's car when she entered. I said, "Knuckles, Knuckles, come get me."

He came on. "I can't. If I do, we lose the exit to the north. I'm already moving."

I looked at my phone, seeing the dots showing the team. I said, "Blood, swing right. Pick up Knuckles. Drop him off north of the café, then circle south. Knuckles, leave the keys in the ignition. We'll be there in five."

Knuckles said, "Pike, the streets are all one way. We do that, and we're going to lose him. Blood will have to do a loop, crossing the canal. He'll be tied up in traffic trying to get back and won't get in position. Stay Foxtrot. Catch up when you can."

The call countermanding me was uncharacteristic for Knuckles, and made me rethink my plan. If he said it was an issue, it probably was. But that didn't alter the fact that I couldn't control a surveillance effort walking on the sidewalk.

Jennifer came on. "Pike, Pike, this is Koko. I dropped off Aaron. I'm circling around. I'll be across the river and cut back down the avenue leading to the soccer stadium. I'll be there in five."

I said, "Roger all. Meet us there."

I heard the calls from the team, all trying to find a location that would prevent the escape of the target.

Shoshana, sick of being out of the loop, said, "What the hell is going on?"

I said, "Rashid went to a different Internet café. Your lover boy is in play. Hopefully, we get something."

Her face turned feral and she said, "We will. If Aaron's in with him, we'll get all we need."

I started jogging up the street, running past the host-nation police guarding our embassy, then paused at the crosswalk for the road leading to the stadium, Shoshana following without question.

Brett came on, saying, "I've got a reading from the Dragontooth, but no picture. Is it a false signal?"

I stopped, telling Shoshana, "Call Aaron. Find out his status."

She did. I waited at the intersection, seeing the soccer stadium in the distance. Jennifer came on. "I'm here. Where are you?"

I said, "Hang on. Stand by."

Shoshana hung up and said, "He got the beacon on, and got a photo. Coming out now."

My phone buzzed, and I saw a picture of a middle-aged swarthy man, could be Italian or Mexican. But I knew what he was. I said, "Everyone got it? Blood, you got it?"

He said, "Yeah, I got it, and I've got eyes on. Moving south towards the park. I'm on him. Gotta ditch the car, but if I do and he gets picked up, I'm done."

"Do it. Knuckles, pick up Aaron, then vector on Blood's signal."

We crossed the street, headed to the soccer stadium, and Shoshana said, "Are we doing anything for the surveillance, or just getting exercise?"

I realized she was still out of the loop because she wasn't on our communications net. I filled her in on everything I knew.

56

Rashid continued walking nonchalantly, not hurrying or doing any-thing that would spike the dozens of security cameras on the bars and stores he was passing. Blloku—or the Block—had been the heart of the Soviet empire in Albania, a section of the city that had housed the communist elite of the regime. Surrounded by vestiges of the old police state, with preserved pillboxes and sections of barbed-wire walls, Rashid understood that others believed the relics showed the death of the old guard, but he held no illusions that the surveillance state had gone with it.

He continued south, crossing streets and keeping a wary eye. He eventually reached a small restaurant outside the gates of Tirana Park, two policeman standing guard. He slowed, watching them as he pre-tended to wait on the traffic. Clearly bored, they spent more time look-ing at the women coming and going than for any potential threat.

He skipped across and threaded between them, drawing no atten-tion, but it reminded him to be careful on the return. When they were following Omar.

He walked about a hundred meters and saw two men leaning against a small wooden bridge spanning a creek. His men.

They saw him coming and stood. He took a left onto a footpath, walked uphill fifty meters until he came to a park bench, and sat down, waiting for them to catch up.

When they did, he wasted no time. "Where is he?"

"At the amphitheater. As predicted. He's inside right now."

Rashid nodded. "And he came up this path?"

"Yes."

"Can he leave without using this path?"

Hashim said, "Well, yes. Of course. This park has multiple exits with official stone walkways, and maybe forty more like the one we're on now. Just dirt paths leading back to the city."

Rashid nodded, thinking. He said, "Okay, so we have to get close. But not too close. We don't want to upset the meeting. Just follow him to where he's staying. I do not want to scare him. Let him do the mission, then follow. Understood?"

Both nodded their heads.

He said, "Can we see the theater from a distance?"

"Yes and no. It's in a bowl, leading to the lake. From the top, we can see the building he's in, but if he leaves through the amphitheater, going to the lake, we'll lose him. We need someone low and high."

"And you've been there? You know where you can spot the exit?"

"Yes. It's not difficult. There are people all over the area, most just sitting on benches or lying in the grass. It won't be an issue. The problem will be following him if he doesn't take the flagstone walkways. If he takes a footpath, we'll be behind him and he'll know. We can't follow him through the woods like that."

Rashid said, "One problem at a time. You both are armed?"

Hashim said yes, but looked alarmed. Rashid said, "Don't worry. I don't expect anything to happen, but I told you, this man is death. He has an instinct. Don't give him a reason to use it."

I saw Jennifer patiently waiting outside of the soccer stadium and sprinted to catch up, Shoshana right behind me. I slid into the passenger seat, hearing Shoshana slamming the back door. I looked at the icons on my phone and said, "Get to the front of the park. Stop short of the entrance."

She put the car in drive without a word and I started working the radio. "All elements, all elements, this is Pike. I'm mounted and headed to the university parking lot. I'll control from there. Status?"

Brett came on first. "This is Blood. I'm still the eye. He's inside the park, and he's meeting two other targets. He's got a team here, and something's going down. Stand by for photos."

Shit.

My phone blipped and I saw two more swarthy individuals. I said, "I want you to be clear: You think he's operational right now? As in an attack?"

I heard, "Stand by."

Then, "Meeting's breaking up. They're spreading out. Two UNSUBS and the target. All headed separate ways."

I thought about the ramifications. The park was full of kids and families. Why on earth would he do an attack here? What would it get him? Albania wasn't exactly on the list of crusader heathen states, being a majority Muslim country. I asked Brett again, putting a lot on his shoulders, "What's your read? Do we need to close for intervention? Is this a threat?"

The Taskforce charter in no way extended to hostile threats against foreign interests, but I wasn't about to sit back while that asshole conducted a Pakistan-schoolhouse-type attack, killing kids left and right just because he could.

After a pause, Brett said, "No. I don't think so. They may be armed, but it's pistols only, if they are. No backpacks and no long guns. I don't think it's an attack. They're doing something else."

Whew.

"Okay, okay. Knuckles, status?"

"Just pulled up to a B&B. Got Aaron and Retro."

"Roger. All elements flood the park. Blanket him, but loosely. No idea what he's doing, but I really don't care, unless he shows a threat. Ignore the UNSUBS. I don't give a shit about them unless they're going to compromise you. Keep tabs on them to prevent that, but if they choose to leave, let 'em go. Everyone have their pictures?"

I got a roger from all, then Shoshana said, "Stop the car. Let me out."

I said, "What for?"

"We're paralleling the park right now. I can see it through the woods right there. Let me out. I'll enter from here."

"You've got no comms."

"I've got a cell phone. This isn't hard. If he comes this way, call me. I'll pick him up. All of your guys are behind him. Put me ahead."

Jennifer had already pulled over, looking at me for a decision, the park right next to us, hidden by a string of forest as thick as Brer Rabbit's home. I said, "How are you going to get in? There isn't a path here."

She pointed, and I saw a gap through the woods, a trickle of water running off of a worn concrete sluice. The break was only about a foot across, but I knew the woods were thickest at the sunlight. She could crawl through, and I was sure it would open up. I just wasn't sure if I wanted to turn her loose.

I turned around in the seat, looking at her. She said, "You don't think I can get through the woods?"

I saw her eyes and knew she'd already read me in her creepy way. That wasn't what she was asking. I said, "I'm sure you can get through the trees, but I'm not so sure about getting out of the forest. The one in your head."

She leaned down and screwed a suppressor into the Glock we'd given her, saying, "I told you: This mission is yours. The mission comes first."

She sat back up and said, "I'll kill no one unless you tell me to. And I'll die if it's called for, without pulling a trigger. Is that what you want to hear?"

"No, damn it. That's exactly what I *do not* want to hear. Get up there and box him in, but don't do anything stupid. We've got the beacon, and worst case, we can always go back to the Internet café."

She opened the door and said, "Sounds good. I didn't want to miss my first date anyway."

She slid out, and Jennifer watched her slink into the culvert. She said, "That was a good call. She's really, really skilled."

I said, "Yeah, she's skilled all right. Skilled at mind control. I hope that wasn't a mistake."

Jennifer put the car into drive, heading toward the entrance to the park. She said, "It wasn't, but what was she talking about?"

She wove through the traffic, looking at me while trying to hide a grin. I said, "What do you mean?"

"What 'first date'?"

I spluttered for a moment, and Jennifer's grin broke out for real. "I can't wait to tell Knuckles he was right. She's smitten with you."

57

Sitting on a park bench, Rashid gave his men a couple of minutes, then trudged up the hill, just one more man enjoying the sunshine and green space. He reached the top, the chipped and crumbling asphalt path connecting to a wide lane made of white flagstone. He could just see the edge of the amphitheater down the hill, built into a bowl. He went away from it, heading along the flagstones deeper into the park, leaving the surveillance to his men.

Rashid had no doubt that he was branded into Omar's psyche, and one glimpse of him would immediately initiate a gunfight. Like a wild animal, Omar would recognize the threat Rashid represented, and would seek to eliminate it with overwhelming force. Just as Rashid would do if the roles were reversed. Or, more precisely, just as Rashid intended to do.

He reached a small alcove of granite set into a copse of evergreens, the flagstones ringed with monuments. In the center was a pedestal with three bronze busts from Albania's past, a raised step of granite leading to it. Rashid ignored the busts, sitting on the granite and watching a child and father kick a soccer ball back and forth.

He pretended to be engrossed, but kept his eye on the amphitheater. From this distance, due to the slope of the hill, he could make out only the top of the projection building, getting a small sliver of the steel door leading inside.

He sat, patient as a snake on a hot rock, flicking its tongue out, tasting the wind.

Waiting.

*　　*　　*

I passed the drive leading to our hotel, the Sheraton standing tall on the hill. I pulled in front of the university, looking for a place to park. To my right was a huge roundabout—really a football-size square of asphalt—probably used for parades back in the bad old days. I saw a couple of cabs parked on the outskirts, their drivers out and smoking cigarettes. I crossed the lanes of traffic and pulled in behind them, nose aimed toward the south. Toward the park. Driving a Ford minivan, I didn't really fit in, but I wasn't standing out that badly.

I could hear the chatter on the radio, the team working the problem. I broke in. "Knuckles, this is Pike. You with Aaron?"

"Yeah, I got him."

I explained on the net what Shoshana was doing, saying, "She's his baby. Make sure he can control her. You stick with him."

"Roger, but I was planning on running him down the hill. There's an amphitheater here and it's pretty large. With Shoshana to the east, I got that covered, but Blood's the only guy to the south, keeping tabs on one of the UNSUBS."

"I copy. Retro's still got eyes on?"

Retro cut in. "Roger. He's just sitting at a monument. Killing time. I'm okay for a longer spell. If he leaves, I'll trigger, but I can't pick up the follow."

Knuckles said, "Can you get Koko in here?"

I looked at Jennifer and said, "If I do, I'm the only one locking down the entrance. I was going to use her as contingency."

"If you want me to stay with Aaron as control for the Israeli team, I need her to the southwest. I'll pick up the follow when Retro triggers, but we've lost contact with the second UNSUB. He's to the southwest somewhere. Get Koko in here for that."

She was already digging out kit from a large pack in the back. I said, "Roger all. She's coming in east of the main entrance, on a footpath. Vector her in."

She glanced up, wondering what I was talking about, looking for clarification about her approach. Off the radio, I said, "See that café?" An indoor/outdoor sandwich shop about two hundred meters away from the primary entrance, it fronted the street with a small patio. She nodded, and I said, "Go farther up the hill. See those goats eating in that little pen?" She nodded again and then saw what I was talking about: a thin footpath that wound from the pen up through the scrub of the hillside, disappearing into the trees.

She opened the bag wider and said, "How many long guns do they have?"

"Brett took one, but everyone else is carrying Glocks." The weapon choice had happened before we thought there was a threat. Before Rashid had met a team.

She pulled out a harness, saying, "You still think there's a potential that Rashid is up to something? It's a little hot, but I can get away with a light jacket."

The harness was nothing more than a double loop that went over the shoulders, with a magazine holster on one side, the magazine itself positioned upside down for fast removal, and a quick-release clip on the other side that held the folded rifle at the buffer spring, both riding uncomfortably underneath the armpits of the person wearing it.

It was built for concealment, not speed, and worked fairly well when the weather was cold or rainy, when we could cover the bulk with coats, but sort of sucked in the summertime. Luckily, Albania was still a pretty formal place, with nobody wearing shorts and most men sporting leather coats or cheap woolen blazers. Brett was no monster in height, but he was built like a fireplug of solid muscle. Given his size, the harness worked for him. He could pull it off, but I wasn't sure Jennifer's jacket would cut the mustard.

I said, "Leave it. Rashid's definitely up to something, but I don't think it's an attack. Take a Glock. The last thing we need is you getting busted by some stranger because you've got a suppressor hanging out of your hem."

She slid a suppressed Glock 30 compact into a concealed sleeve on the side of the duffel bag she called a purse. It looked like someone had skinned a water buffalo to make it, and she packed it with all manner of feminine bullshit and Taskforce kit. I swear, I had no idea how she lugged it around everywhere.

She rearranged some things in the bag—probably making sure she could get to her lipstick—snapped it closed, then pecked me on the check. "See you soon."

"Get a radio check with Knuckles."

She nodded, slid out of the vehicle, and jogged across the road. She reached the fence next to the café and found a break the locals used. She scampered past the goat pen and I heard, "Knuckles, Knuckles, this is Koko, I'm about two minutes out."

58

After twenty minutes of instruction on the weird detonation devices, Omar was growing impatient. He wanted to test one.

He said, "Look, I don't care about what type of chemicals are in the vials or why they react the way they do when mixed together. I'm not going to be building my own, and I left school at the age of ten. All I care about is that it will set off explosives. Will it or not?"

The gap-toothed man said, "Yes, of course it will. I'm sorry. I was told to give you all the information that I was given."

He removed one of the detonators from the table and held it up. About the size of a pack of cigarettes, it had no metal that Omar could see, with a black rubber button that protruded on one side, a tiny lever on the other, and twin nozzles on the bottom that looked like they'd come from an aquarium pump.

He said, "The device is completely immune to any current metal or explosives detection capability known today. Everything is rubber, glass, or plastic, with the exception of a single piece of steel inside, much too small to alert anything."

He waved to his partner, who picked up the smartphone. "On the surface, this replicates an ordinary cell phone. You can swipe left and right and pull up applications. The difference is that the applications are only shells and the phone cannot call anything. It should pass a cursory inspection, but if someone spends more than a minute inspecting it, they'll know it's a fake."

Omar said, "What's it for?"

Gap-tooth stuck a toothpick into what appeared to be the headphone jack, then levered upward. The front of the shell rotated out, exposing wires, circuit boards, and the battery—five triple-A-size cylinders encased in a plastic sleeve, a double strand of wire running out of the end. He popped the sleeve, exposing two glass cylinders, two metal blasting caps, and a true battery. He said, "The phone holds the chemicals and blasting caps. It's padded for travel and protection, and will reflect like ordinary batteries on an X-ray scan."

He palmed it, showing the cylinders. They each held a colorless fluid inside. He set the phone on the table and returned to the plastic device. He popped off the top and leaned it forward, showing what looked like a receptacle for holding batteries in a television remote control, two parallel to each other.

He said, "Before you put them inside, you have to cock the device. That's the only drawback, really. Once they're in, the thing is armed, and it really hasn't been drop tested or anything. By cocking it, you're basically drawing back that little section of steel with rubber bands, which is held by a dual check."

He moved the lever on the side from top to bottom. He let go, and it flew back to the top. He shook his head and said, "That's what I mean. Sometimes it doesn't catch." He did it again, more forcefully, and the lever stayed down. "Be sure you lock it in."

He then slid the vials into the tube and closed the lid. Omar said, "Does it matter which one goes in what tube?"

"No. You're going to smash the tubes and mix up the chemicals. It doesn't matter the order."

He closed the lid and said, "Now it's armed. All you need to do is connect the nonelectric firing tubes to the bottom, then press this button. It will release the metal breaker, and the chemicals will mix."

"How soon? How long does it take?"

"It's not instant. Maybe a second before the chemicals react, but when they do, it's a miniature explosion, with the jet of flame directed down the valves at the bottom. The man holding it will lose his hand."

Omar said, "That's of no consequence. What about the explosives? And I was supposed to get three detonators."

"Yes, yes. First, there's one more thing you need to know. The button is a dead man's switch. You push it in, and the breaker releases from one catch, but is still held by another. That catch releases when the button is released."

Omar smiled, "Dead man's switch. So once it's pressed, the only thing keeping it from going off is the man holding the device. Killing him does no good."

Gap-tooth flashed his tobacco-stained molars in what passed for a smile and said, "Precisely."

"And the explosives?"

The other man came forward and handed Omar what looked like a luggage retrieval receipt. "All of it is packed and ready to go at the Tirana airport, in the lost luggage section. It's safeguarded, and the men watching it have been paid handsomely, don't worry. They have no idea what it is, but we've done business with them many, many times. You present this, along with your flight information, and the bags will be loaded with the appropriate luggage tags for your final destination."

Omar felt his phone vibrate in his pocket. Having purchased it this morning, only two people knew the number. The two he had for security outside.

He held up a finger and said, "I must take this."

He turned away from the men, jamming his hand into the pocket with the pistol. He said, "Yes?"

"Omar, there are people outside of the amphitheater. We've watched them for a while, and they're not acting like they're here for the sunshine. One, a woman, has passed back and forth three times."

He glanced at the men in the room and said, "You are positive?"

"Yes. She's not Albanian. She's foreign. Her dress is off, and she's constantly talking into a cell phone. What do you want to do?"

He withdrew the gun and pointed it at the men. They took a step back in shock, raising their hands. He said, "Take her out of play, but I want her alive. Get her to your place. Do not go to mine. I'll meet you there."

He hung up and said, "I was told to come here alone, as were you. Who is outside of this building? Who's the woman?"

As if he'd been in such situations many times, Gap-tooth calmly said, "Yes, you were told to come alone, and clearly you didn't. We have done the same. We only have some security. You must understand. But we have no women. It's not us."

There was a crack from outside. It could have been a car backfiring, or maybe some children playing with fireworks, but nobody in the room believed it.

The other man jammed his hand into his leather jacket, got a pistol halfway out, and Omar fired, catching him in the right cheek, the left half of his face exploding outward. He fell, and Omar dove at Gap-tooth, preventing him from drawing his own weapon. He slammed the man into the concrete, ripping the detonator from Gap-tooth's hand and twisting his arm ferociously. He felt the tendons snap, and the man screamed, his fetid dental work wide-open. Omar jammed the end of the detonator in his mouth and punched the button.

He held it and said, "I am not some criminal to be trifled with. I *am* the Islamic State. I will meet Allah. You will not."

Eyes rolling wild, Gap-tooth shook his head, trying to talk, drool running freely. Omar pushed the detonator deeper, breaking Gap-tooth's jaw and wedging it in the soft palate at the back of his throat. He let go of the button, then leapt up, backing toward the door. Gap-tooth frantically sat up, and even managed to get his hands on the device before there was a flash, then a *pop*, like a large firecracker had gone off. His lower jaw exploded downward, and a jet of molten flame severed his spinal cord at the neck.

59

Relaxing on the marble, watching the children play, and getting regular updates from his two men, Rashid heard the first gunshot and bolted upright. Everyone around him was looking left and right, just as confused as he was. He tried to identify where the shot had come from, but it was impossible. It reverberated off of the hills, confusing his ears. He knew it was close, though.

He stood, bringing his phone up and straining to hear something that would tell him what was happening. He dialed, getting Hashim. "What was that?"

"I don't know . . . I don't know. It wasn't here, at the amphitheater. It's farther away."

"What's going on at the amphitheater?"

"Nothing. Nothing at all. The meeting's still going on."

No sooner had the words left his mouth than another *crack* split the air. From the amphitheater.

Hashim shouted, "Shooting! Shooting from inside the building!"

Rashid whipped his head, but saw the door was still closed. Hashim said, "Two men just came forward. Both have pistols drawn. They're running toward the building."

Rashid started walking toward the theater, torn between fleeing and his need to kill Omar. He saw the door open, and Omar came spilling out, leaping down the stairs and disappearing from view because of the slope of the hill.

Then gunfire erupted: multiple *snap*s of noise from at least four shooters.

While the locals began running away, he sprinted toward the fire-fight, drawing his own weapon. He reached the top of the hill, the bowl of the amphitheater below him, full of children ducking and screaming. He saw Omar rapidly shooting, hitting two men within five feet of him. He scanned the stage area, and saw Hashim rise up from between the concrete seats, squeezing the trigger. He saw a child go down, blood spraying from his back, the mother screaming maniacally. Omar ducked, then returned fire.

Rashid knelt down, getting a bead along the sights of his pistol, Omar right below him, the blood lust raging, then a bullet smacked the concrete pillar next to his head, spraying him with spall. He fell flat, searching for the shooter, confused because he'd heard no sound. He saw a black man deeper in the bowl, behind the stage, and he held a rifle with a fat barrel, pointed right at him.

He saw the muzzle flash, then felt rounds driving around his head. He ducked down, panting. He heard Omar's pistol spit fire, then another burst of gunfire from multiple locations, sounding like firecrackers on a patio. He peeked over and saw Hashim shooting at Omar. The black man swung his weapon as if it were on rails, then surgically put two rounds into Hashim. He saw the light leave Hashim's eyes as he fell face-first into the concrete seats, his arms splayed forward as if he were trying to catch himself.

There was a flash of movement from the other side of the amphitheater, and Rashid heard a yell. Kamal leapt onto the stage, screaming and shooting. He took two steps before his body jerked, hit from bullets that made no noise. Rashid looked at the black man, but he wasn't firing. He was aiming his weapon dead center on him, without squeezing the trigger. Someone else was shooting. Someone with the same skill. The sight of Kamal sliding, lifeless, onto the concrete stage made up his mind for him. Omar would live another day. All that remained now was escape.

He snapped two hasty rounds toward the black man, getting nothing but a small duck in return. He saw Omar sprinting, running away from the amphitheater to the east, and rolled into a small hollow in the ground, preparing to do the same.

He heard stomping feet and turned, seeing Albanian police swarming down the flagstone path. He jammed his weapon into his waistband and lay flat, screaming for help.

They went past him without pause. He lay still for a split second more, then jumped up and began running the way he'd come, passing the monuments. He crested the hill, diving behind the concrete wall and trying to maintain his balance as he tumbled through the woods downhill.

My radio crackled. "Shots fired, shots fired," then nothing else. I rolled down my window, straining to hear and wanting like hell to break into the net, but not wanting to step on any of my team's radio transmissions. I waited for an eternity, which was really probably five seconds, then Knuckles came on.

"Pike, Pike, we have a situation. I don't know what it is, but I heard a shot at the amphitheater. Rashid's on the move that way. We've got him in sight."

An attack? Was I wrong?

Brett came on. "Pike, this is Blood. Two new guys to my west with pistols, running to a concrete blockhouse here at the amphitheater. UNSUB one still in sight, and he's got a pistol out as well."

"Is this an attack?"

"No, I say again, no. It looks like they're all confused. The place is full of kids, but the gunmen aren't shooting targets of opportunity."

"If you've got the UNSUB in sight, who're the guys with weapons?"

"Don't know. . . . A man just broke out of the building. He's firing on the run, and he's good. Just took out the two runners. UNSUB one is firing at him. What's the call?"

I needed more information. "Knuckles, what's the target doing?"

"He's headed towards the gunfight. He's got something to do with it, but when he left, he looked as confused as I am."

"You still got eyes on?"

"Yeah, well, no, he's below the crest, but I know where he is."

"Koko, Koko, what's the status with UNSUB two?"

"Break, break, Pike, this is Blood. We've got a shootout going on. Kids are everywhere. Someone's going to get hurt."

Shit.

"Break out. Leave the area. Break contact and return to the hotel. Knuckles, can you maintain eyes on?"

"I think so. He's out of sight now, but Blood's right. It sounds like Fallujah now."

Brett: "Pike, they just hit a kid. He's down. These guys can't shoot worth shit. They're spraying lead all over the place. I got eyes on Rashid. He's on the high ground, and he's got a weapon. He's going to start shooting too. Let me do something."

I paused, knowing what the right answer for the mission was. But, fuck, they were killing kids. I said, "Okay, okay. For the record, it's my call. Blood, discourage Rashid, but remove anyone else with a gun."

His voice grim, I heard, "Roger all."

60

I sat in the car with my fists clenched, wanting more than anything to be up on the hill, directing the fight. I waited, knowing the team would give me a call when they felt it necessary. Which didn't make it easier, I'll tell you that.

I pulled out a small set of binoculars and focused on the entrance to the park, seeing uniformed police running about, with many headed up the path.

Won't be long now. Clock's ticking.

Finally, Knuckles came on. "Target is fleeing. Back the way he came. He's avoiding the path and the police. He's coming down through the trees."

I said, "Straight north?"

"Yeah. Straight north."

He's going to hit Jennifer's path.

"Can you keep eyes on?"

"Not without compromise. And he's got a weapon."

The unspoken command being, *I'll have to kill him.* I said, "Let him go. I think he's going to end up right in front of me. All elements, all elements, give me an up."

I heard from Retro, Blood, and Knuckles. All had successfully avoided the police and were now working their way back. But no Jennifer. I called again, "Koko, Koko, status?"

At the crest of the hill, I saw a figure appear. Running down the hill. I put my glass on him and recognized Rashid. I said, "All elements, all elements, I've got eyes on. He's coming down the hill. My van is in the square across from the university. I'm going to leave the keys on the right front tire. Retro, you got the van. Stage until I call. Knuckles, Blood, you guys get down the hill and vector in on me. He's coming fast."

I got a roger from all, then said, "Koko, Koko, what is your status?"

I got nothing again, which gave me pause. A little tendril of dread. I saw the figure halfway down and knew I had to make a decision quickly. I said, "Knuckles, I'm now going Foxtrot. You are surveillance chief. Blood, redirect. I need you to find out what's up with Koko."

He knew the unspoken emotion behind that call. She was a teammate to all of them, but he knew she was something more to me. He said, "Roger. Headed back to the amphitheater. Don't worry. Probably just a bad mic."

Then, "This is Koko. This is Koko. I'm okay. I monitor all."

I wanted to explode at her, in between the relief I felt. I saw Rashid reach the goat pen.

I left the vehicle, locking the doors and surreptitiously putting the keys on the front tire. All clinical, I said, "Roger. What's your status?"

"Got caught up in the police response. I couldn't talk. I'm on the way."

Rashid passed through the fence, glanced left and right, then began walking at a hurried pace, headed north one road over from where I was. I said, "I got the eye. He's going into the Block."

Rashid went north, moving deeper into the area once reserved for communist royalty, but now full of bars and kitschy boutiques. I intersected his line of march at an angle, losing sight of him for a panicky two minutes, but finding him again soon enough. He kept glancing back, and was clearly shaken. His tradecraft earlier had been pretty good. Better than any of the usual goat herders I tracked—which, given his training with DGSE, was to be expected—but now he was moving as fast as he could without drawing attention by simply running. He was scared.

He went about a quarter mile, then hung a left, and I alerted the team. "Now on Abdyl Frashen Street, headed west. He's afraid, looking for the bad man. Get a team ahead of him; my heat state's getting bad."

Knuckles said, "Roger. Got Blood and Koko headed that way. Give me the pass when you have to." Meaning, give him a call when I had to pull off or get compromised.

He then said, "Pike, what's your feel? Is he going to run?"

I said, "Yeah, if I was going to call it now, he's running. Whatever happened back there was probably the reason he was here, and it clearly went to shit. Would you stay? He can't know what the police are going to find, and he sure as shit isn't going to wait to find out."

"Yeah, that's what I was thinking. Uhh . . . you think it's time to call Showboat?"

Which was something I'd chosen to forget. I'd kept LTC Alexander in the loop for the surveillance today—before the last bit of high adventure—and I wasn't sure where Knuckles was going. I didn't need his approval to continue surveillance, and I wasn't going to waste my time telling him about the gunfight because it would just lead to a giant list of questions I couldn't answer. I said, "For what?"

"For in-extremis assault. If he's going to flee, this is it. You find his bed-down, and the clock's ticking. We've probably got enough time for him to get on the Internet and buy plane tickets, then get to the airport. We can't take him down in a cab. We have to hit that site before he leaves."

Everything he said was true. I saw Rashid cross the street, running to a drugstore. He disappeared into a side door, and I caught a quick glimpse of stairs. This was it. I couldn't follow him inside, and he'd disappeared.

I said, "All elements, all elements, I'm at the bed-down. You got my location?"

Knuckles said, "Yeah. Signal's strong. We got you on the map. Moving now. Look for Blood and Jennifer. Find a place to stage with all of us, including the vehicle Retro's bringing."

I said, "Don't get ahead of yourself. Still got to make that call to higher."

I heard, "Yeah, yeah. Like that's ever stopped you."

I felt good that Knuckles was pushing the issue. I thought he was right, but if he believed this was critical, it meant a lot. You read books about the great leader making decisions that bucked the odds, or was proved right when "everyone" said it was wrong, but in my experience, it was never one guy. It was one guy in power backed by a small minority who felt as he did, giving encouragement from the background. Unfortunately, for every one guy who went down as the stalwart defender of freedom, there was another who went down as a goat.

But this wasn't a decision that would make me a goat. As long as forty-two thousand things didn't go wrong. I said, "Going off the net. Calling Showboat."

I dialed, waiting on the encryption to catch up. A commo guy answered and said, "Send it," as if I was going to give another sitrep. I said, "Put on Showboat."

He said, "He's engaged. Send it to me."

I snarled, "Put him on the line right now, or I'll rip your throat out. I don't care if he's taking a shit. I need to talk to him."

I heard some fumbling, then, "Jesus, Pike, what did you say to the guy? You know your reputation, and I don't need them afraid of you."

"Nothing. Just that I needed to talk."

And I gave it to him: the good, the bad, and the ugly.

He said, "Shit. I need to get to Kurt on that. I can't do an in-extremis without lives at stake. Keep eyes on." He did a calculation in his head and said, "It's lunchtime in DC. I'll have to track him down."

I said, "I'm good with that, but I need a call right now, in case I see indications he's leaving. I need to know my authorities. Something happened in that park, and it was important. I have no idea what it was, but Rashid does."

"Pike, you said he went into some dive apartment complex. You don't even have a room. You couldn't hit if you wanted to. Let me contact higher. Get some sanction."

What he said was true, with the exception of one thing. I said, "Sir, Aaron got a Dragontooth on him. I can find his room. The sun's going down right now. It'll be dark in thirty minutes. All I need is assault authority. I can do it. I have the team closing now."

"How will you exfil?"

"With my vehicle. It's a minivan. It's got windows, but I can keep him low. I can get him out."

He said, "Okay, okay. Build an assault plan, but you have no execute authority. After Nairobi, I need some backup. I can't go crazy just yet."

61

I knew where Blaine was coming from, and I appreciated the support. I said, "Roger all, but Rashid's going to flee, and sooner rather than later. Once he's on the pavement, he's in the wind. Tell them that. Let them know the urgency. We can do it clean right now. Later, it gets much, much messier."

I saw Brett and Jennifer walking up the street and heard, "I got it, I got it. I'm working it."

They reached me and I said, "We need to find a staging area for the van. That's you, Brett. Jennifer, I want you to penetrate the apartment. Get up the stairs and use the Dragontooth. Find the apartment he's in. Nothing fancy. Just get in and walk, then get out. Pay attention to atmospherics. Let me know where the stairs go and what we'll encounter if we try to drag a body out of there."

They both nodded, no questions, Brett surveying the street and Jennifer looking at the door next to the pharmacy. I said, "Where's Knuckles?"

Brett said, "He's coming. Right behind us. Aaron was controlling Shoshana, and he can't get her on the phone. Knuckles went with him to sort it out."

I took that in, not really worried. Shoshana could take care of herself better than about 99.9 percent of the human population. I clicked my earpiece, saying, "Retro, Retro, you got the van?"

"Got it. Headed your way. You got a place for me to stage?"

"Not yet. Circle the block. Blood's on it." I nodded at him, and he disappeared, walking toward an alley next to the building.

I looked at Jennifer and said, "Time to go."

She said, "What's up with Shoshana? All she was doing was locking down the eastern exit. She wasn't even near the gunfight."

"I don't know, but it's not a worry. She's not tied into our commo structure. For all we know, her battery is dead in her cell phone. You were a lot closer, and you didn't get in the fight. She's fine."

She looked at me and I saw something in her eyes. I said, "What?"

She glanced away, making sure Brett hadn't come back, and said, "I killed a man. One of the guys running with a pistol. I have no idea who he was. I heard the call you gave to Brett, saw the kid get hit, and went into autopilot. He stood up right in front of me. He had a gun out. . . ."

She was looking for absolution. She said, "What if he was a cop? What if they have security in the park? I just pulled the trigger. I didn't even think about it."

She was staring into me, not unlike Shoshana herself, reading me. Wanting to know if what she had done in the name of the United States was correct.

I said, "If he was there with a weapon, he was bad. You did the right thing. You can make up stories in your mind forever, second-guessing, but they don't have undercover police in that park."

I saw doubt and said, "Did he shout anything? Did he say, 'Police!' or anything? Try to mitigate the violence? Try to stop it?"

She reflected and said, "No, no. Nothing like that. He jumped on-stage and started shooting at that other guy. The one that got away."

"Then quit fucking thinking about it. Look, I don't have a single clue what went on there, or why it happened. What I do know is that if you'd let him go on, he probably would've killed three or four kids with the wild-ass spraying of rounds. You did good."

She nodded and I said, "Get inside the apartment. We're running out of time."

She nodded again, this time more firmly, then turned to go. I grabbed her arm and said, "Sorry about the slight on the gunfight. I didn't know you were in it, but I'm glad you were."

She said, "Shoshana would've been better."

"No, she wouldn't. She would never question. Which is why you're on my team."

She showed a flicker of a smile, then broke away, jogging across the street.

I watched her go, then Retro came on. "I'm coming back your way. Where do I park?"

I called Brett. "Blood, Blood, what do you have?"

He said, "Bring him right into the alley. The one you saw me go down. It's deserted. I've been to the end and back. There's one drunk homeless guy, but he's passed out. Stage in the entrance. I'm there now."

Which was perfect, because it was right next to the pharmacy and the door to the apartment. I jogged across the street to meet him, saying, "Nothing back there?"

"Nope. Some doors, but it's dead. Stinks like shit."

My phone rang, and it was Blaine. I said, "Tell me you got somewhere."

He said, "Okay, you got Omega, with some caveats."

I thought, *Of course.*

"You can assault tonight, but only if you determine you can exfil successfully."

I said, "That's it?"

I could almost hear the grin. "Yep. I know that's stupid. Kurt was pretty pleased."

Both Kurt and Blaine knew that I would *never* assault for a capture if I couldn't get out clean. But apparently the Oversight Council thought they'd better make that clear. Just like every level of command I'd ever had. Making statements of the obvious.

I said, "Okay, then. Get the support package ready. We're coming home with Jackpot."

He said, "WILCO. Nothing stupid, right?"

I said, "Not tonight. It's a good situation. I promise. Gotta go. My support team just showed up."

Retro pulled the van in, did a three-point turn until the nose was facing the street. He exited and said, "What's the story?"

"We're taking him tonight. Get the long guns ready. Jennifer's going—"

I was cut off by a call from Knuckles. "Pike, Pike, we're out of the park. We're in the Block but this phone isn't tight enough for a location. I got you on the street, but I got a fifty-meter gap with the circle. Where are you?"

The sun had dropped during all the planning, the twilight now bathed in a glow of sporadic neon signs. I said, "You see the traffic circle?"

"Yeah. Just to my right."

I strained my eyes, the circle about seventy meters away. I couldn't see him with all of the people on the sidewalk, mostly young, the men dressed in black jackets and wearing peculiar half Mohawks, stubble on the side but the hair long on top, and the women wearing skintight jeans. All going to the Block for party time.

"I'm in front of a pharmacy, on the south side of the street. There's a sign advertising drugs."

He said, "I see you. Be there in two."

Jennifer came out on the street. I saw her exit the door, look left, then right, and saunter our way. She said, "I got the apartment. 2A. Just up the stairs. The Dragontooth was booming right inside. You go up, take a right, and it's the first one. Atmospherics are good. No people that I saw. It's poor, and probably full of folks who don't open the door if they hear anything. There's a lot of noise from inside his place. He's packing and throwing things around. He's running."

I said, "All right. Good job. Jennifer, you're the driver. Stage here. Brett, you're lead man. Retro, you're number two. I'll be third, and Knuckles will take the rear. We enter and dominate. No gunfire. When I say that, I mean it. If he pulls a weapon, you'd better be quicker than him. I *do not* want him shot. Is that understood?"

In the gloom of the alley, away from the street, Brett was checking his long gun. Retro pulled a weapon and shined a light on it, seeing a piece of tape that marked it as mine. My brand-new 300 Blackout. He handed it to me. I have to admit, it felt better than a UMP. Reminding me of hundreds of assaults in the past, before the Taskforce. He pulled out his own and said, "Got it. No killing. Unless he's about to kill me."

Knuckles and Aaron arrived, breathless. I said, "Late for the game. He's here, we have Omega, and we're going in. Aaron, you're out here with Jennifer. I want you to lock down the entrance. Knuckles, you got tail-gunner."

Knuckles said, "We got a problem."

I said, "What?"

Aaron said, "Shoshana's missing. We searched for her, but all we found was her cell phone, smashed on the ground."

62

Omar fled the park like a demon was after him, running like a child afraid of the night. He avoided the main entrance and went deeper into the woods, thrashing through creeks and stands of brush until his hands were cut and his clothes torn. He slowed up after twenty minutes, listening. He could hear police sirens in the distance, and assumed they were in reaction to what had happened, but he couldn't be sure.

He continued on, the dropping sun making it hard to see his footing. He bumped into the back fence of the Sheraton Hotel and searched for a way out. He thrashed through the brush and heard someone shout on the other side, then ask another if he'd heard the noise. Omar moved higher, back into the woods, continuing east.

Eventually, he hit a makeshift game trail, one of the many in the park. He followed it and saw that it spilled out east of the soccer field.

He wedged open the small gap in the fence and dropped from the four-foot concrete wall, now on the street. Now safe.

He began walking north, uncertain of where he was but sure he could find his way once he hit the city square. He reflected on what he knew. What had happened.

There were many, many people with guns in that amphitheater. Some were from his contact, of that he was sure. What he was less sure about was whether he'd been wrong in killing them. Not in a moralistic way, but simply in a business way. He'd made the decision, then executed. It wasn't until he'd left the stairs and seen the myriad of men shooting that he'd had doubts. They weren't all shooting at him. In fact, they were shooting at one another. He'd seen a black man with a silenced rifle kill at least one, and two others shooting against themselves. Why? What the hell had happened up there?

He remembered Hussein. The Lost Boy. He wondered if it had something to do with him. Omar had the luggage ticket for the explosives, but even that was in danger. Should he use it, or would he be walking into a trap?

Omar had spent the better part of his life paranoid, first in Chechnya, then in Georgia, always looking for the traitor, but this was unlike anything he'd ever experienced. He wondered if he was being played. Was there a reason for the Islamic State to fight him? Were they the ones doing this? But Adnan had been killed. There was no way they'd kill the emir of Syria for a play. Adnan could have slit his throat on any number of occasions, just by giving the order.

He thought about that strike, and another chill went down his spine. Had the Lost Boys killed Adnan? Was it really the satellite phone, or had they told the crusaders where to launch the Hellfire?

But then, why continue on? If they had that capability, why had he lived to cross the border? Maybe it was simply because they were with him. He remembered the other strike against the convoy from the camp. The one where no Lost Boys were riding.

But that made no sense, in the end. The attack today was pathetic. A bunch of confused gunfire. If the Lost Boys had anything to do with it, why didn't they just assault the building? Why the strange confusion? It was like nobody on the ground understood what was going on, and all were just shooting because that's what they knew.

He quit speculating. The answer would be held with the woman his men had caught. She would tell them. And she would provide the distance he needed, if they brought her home.

He crossed the fetid canal that split the city, the concrete littered with cans and plastic bags, and checked a street sign for his bearings. He saw Rruga George W. Bush, and shook his head. He hoped that wasn't a sign of things to come.

He pulled out his worn tourist map given to him by Anzor, reading the Cyrillic Anzor had written on the edge detailing directions. He continued on, searching for a street called Toptani. Two blocks later, he found it, and took a left, walking down a pleasant pedestrian thorough-fare with various stops extolling Tirana history. He reached a wall of ancient stone, now grafted onto new edifices, and saw what he was looking for. A cheap hotel called Kalaja, built right into the old walls of a defunct castle. He passed through the archway and warily walked up the steps, avoiding the front desk.

He saw nothing to alarm him.

He went down a short, worn hallway and found the door he'd been given. He put his ear to it, hearing nothing beyond.

He pulled his pistol, keeping it low, and knocked. He heard move-ment, then the door opened. He recognized Anzor and broke into a smile. "I thought you had been killed."

Anzor scowled and said, "No, no. We weren't killed, but we do want to know what shit you've brought us."

Omar pushed the door open, saying, "Let me in, and I'll tell you."

He walked forward, seeing a cheap room not unlike a hostel. Chipped tile and a seedy shared bathroom connected to the adjacent room, the lights illuminating someone digging through a bag next door. There were two twin beds perpendicular to each other, and a small desk with a computer, but none of those details captured his attention. In the center, tied to a chair, was a woman with a gag in her mouth, one eye black and swollen, the other wide and fearful.

Anzor said, "We want no part of this. We will not get into an Islamic war. Whatever you're doing, you do. But we're done."

Omar tossed his backpack on the bed and said, "Then why did you bring her here?"

Levan, the one who'd spoken out earlier at their first meeting, came from the adjacent room and said, "We did what you asked, but that was before the damn killing at the amphitheater. Two children are dead. Two more wounded. The police will be ripping apart anyone with ties to crime. We are going to get raked because of it."

Omar said, "You did right. You have helped the caliphate."

Levan said, "Fuck the damn caliphate. I want no part of it. I *told* you that."

The third man, Davit, said, "I got the weapons because you said it was a business transaction. You said it was simple. This wasn't simple. It was a bloodbath."

He stood, facing Omar. "I appreciate our time in combat, and support your cause, but this is too much. While I support you, you do nothing but destroy me."

Omar held up his hands and said, "Okay, hear me out. I speak the truth. I had no idea that was going to happen. I thought it would be a simple exchange, but I feared it was something else. That's why I called you. I truly do not know what happened."

Anzor said, "You're fucking lying. You knew she was hunting you, and she probably has a team with her."

"Are you sure she was?"

"She had a gun. A silenced Glock. She almost killed me with it. If Levan hadn't been behind her, I'd be dead. She's quick as a snake, and she's killed before. I can tell."

Omar heard that and paused. This wasn't the Islamic State. One thing eliminated. He said, "What do you know of her?"

"She's Israeli. As if that is a surprise to you."

Israeli? That placed a whole different spin on things. No Lost Boys. No Islamic State. His paranoia kicked in full force, confirming his worst fears. *Of course.*

He said, "How do you know? She has an Israeli passport?"

"No. Her passport is Australian, but she sure as hell isn't. I spent some time in Gaza. She can deny it, but she reeks of Mossad. We had a checklist we followed whenever we suspected someone, and she's matching up. Australian passport, silenced pistol with the serial number acid-etched, European labels in her clothes, trained in martial arts. She's a Jew."

"Give me her phone. I want to call her contact. Give him a message. Let them know what will happen if they continue the hunt."

Anzor said, "She smashed it in the fight. She got off one round, and I knocked her down. She fought like a demon. She didn't stop until I got a gun in her face, and even then, she almost caused me to shoot Levan. She knocked it out of the way, and it went off. When it did, she pretended to submit, then smashed her phone."

Omar took that in, thinking. He looked at her and said, "Protecting your team. I appreciate that."

He walked to her and withdrew the gag. He said, "I want to know what your team knows. I want to know how you found me."

She said nothing, lowering her eyes.

He raised her chin and said, "You have heard of the Islamic State, yes?"

She simply glared. He said, "Do you know what we did with the Yazidi women? Sold them. Married them off. Raped them. And all they did was make the mistake of living. Do you know what I will do with you? A Jew?"

She spoke for the first time, and Omar saw the steel. "I have been fucked by better terrorists than you. And I killed them after."

In that instant, he knew that fear would never work with her, and he didn't have the time for pain. He needed relief from the hunt. Soon. He said, "You have a team here. I want them to stop. I have something special planned, and I can't have them searching for me. Give me the number of your team leader. I wish to talk to him. Man-to-man. You do it, and I'll make an accommodation that will be favorable to you."

She said, "No."

He said, "Your team leader is going to get the message. I can either do it on the phone, and you die with a bullet, or I can do it my way."

Her expression as flat as a stone in a river, she said, "It looks like it's your way."

He nodded, actually feeling a kinship with her courage. Keeping his eyes on her he said, "Anzor, in the rucksack on the bed is a GoPro video camera. Would you mind getting it?"

Anzor rummaged around in the bag and Omar said, "I need a knife. Preferably a large one."

63

I said, "What do you mean, you only found her cell phone?"

Knuckles said, "Just that. It's smashed like someone stomped on it."

"But that makes no sense. If someone were interested in what she was doing, smashing her cell phone would be the last thing they'd do. Are you sure it's hers?"

Aaron said, "Yes. That's exactly why it's smashed. Shoshana did it. To protect me. To protect us."

He tried to hide it, but the pain leaked out nonetheless. I could see his mantra of *the mission comes first* at the root of the ache. Shoshana had destroyed the only way we could find her in order to protect us. And now I was asking him to continue without knowing what had happened to his teammate.

I said, "Aaron, I've got authority to take down Rashid." He nodded, and I felt like an enormous hypocrite after my speech on the aircraft. I hated the words coming out of my mouth. I *hated* the mission. I did some math in my head, running the numbers I needed. I said, "You want to abort?"

His expression said, *Yes, of course I do.* His mouth said, "No. I won't sacrifice her actions. She did it to protect this mission."

I said, "I can spare Jennifer and Retro. Jennifer's good at finding solutions in the puzzle, and Retro's a computer geek. They might be able to figure something out from the phone. I need everyone else for this."

He thought about it, then said, "Thank you. I appreciate it, but no. This man may be the quickest link to her."

I was a little disappointed in his answer, thinking back on what Shoshana had told me in the café earlier, but maybe he was right. I said, "Okay, okay. You lock down the stairwell, we tuck this guy in, and in thirty minutes you get my whole team. We'll find her. I promise."

He nodded, the fear still on his face, but the professionalism of his chosen path dictating his actions. He said, "Yes. Mission first. Then Shoshana."

I despised the words. In my mind, it wasn't an order of priority. It was what I could do *right now*. At least that's what I told myself. I couldn't quell the feeling that my doing the one was causing the death of the other.

I shook it off, looking around the small circle of Operators in the alley. They were all reflecting on Shoshana, believing she was a teammate. Jennifer said, "Pike, she's our responsibility on this thing. Maybe we should . . ."

Her voice trailed off, but the implication was clear. I shut that down, saying, "Listen up. Forget about Shoshana for now. We've got about a thirty-minute window here. I need everyone's head in the game." I went eye to eye, stopping with Jennifer. *"Everyone."*

She squinted, telling me the call was bad. Telling me I wouldn't be doing this if it were her missing. I ignored the glare, projecting the calm leader, but truthfully, continuing with the mission made my stomach sour, because I wasn't sure she was wrong.

I reiterated the lineup for entry then said, "Get on him quick. Lock him down. Brett, Retro, you got SSE. Once he's down, search for media, computers, and documents. You've got three minutes. Knuckles, you and I will get him out. I want to walk him, but if he shows any signs that he's going to be trouble, hit him with the drugs. Aaron, all you need to do is provide early warning if something's going bad from the street. Jennifer, I call, you pull straight out, park right in front. Aaron gets the door, and he's in like a bag of dog food. Jennifer and I take him to the transfer site, everyone else disappears."

I got a nod from the team and said, "No mistakes on this. Are we good? I need to abort if we're not."

I focused my attention on Aaron, knowing that distractions in combat could end up exponentially bad. I needed to ensure he was focused.

Aaron said, "Don't worry about me. I'm good."

I wasn't so sure about that, probably because I'd been in his shoes before. He wasn't "good," but I was comfortable he could fight. I went eye to eye with everyone else, seeing we were ready. I said, "Okay, time to test out these new black rifles. Retro, you got knock-knock. I'm not fucking around. You make breach, and we're doing some damage."

Knock-knock referred to a small, very heavy battering ram. Retro nodded, reaching back into the van and flipping up the backseat. Underneath was what looked like a sixteen-inch chopped-off telephone pole, two folding handles on top. Made of steel.

Ordinarily, we'd surreptitiously pick the lock, then slink in, working in the shadows, the whole point being the man would disappear without our ever exposing we'd been there.

Here, the target was on edge and hyperalert. We could try to pick the door and potentially get gunfire through it if he heard. With Jennifer's report of the atmospherics, I was fairly sure that nobody would come to interfere, no matter what we did. I'd worked in some postdictator countries, and it was amazing how the old instincts came to the fore. *Someone breaking in a door? Pretend you're cooking. Not your problem.* I was also positive—if we got out in time—that the police would find nothing. He wasn't an Albanian citizen, and I was sure he'd checked in under a false name. It would be a mystery.

I glanced up and down the street, seeing people walking, but nobody close. *No time like the present.* I said, "Ready?"

Knuckles pulled his charging handle back a smidge, checking for the glint of a round. He let it forward and said, "Let's get some."

We walked past the pharmacy, just a group of guys headed to a bar in the Block, weapons held low in the gloom. Aaron opened the door, letting us flow in. I passed him and said, "Thirty minutes. That's all you've lost."

He said, "Just get the target."

We entered, Brett in the lead, rifle held at the low ready. I pulled out my phone and initiated the Dragontooth app. It showed a circle, with one sector pulsing. We entered the stairwell, and it jumped to two. By the time we reached the top, it was at four. Brett held up at the entrance to the hallway, looking back at me. I nodded. He moved forward, passing the door and pulling security down the hallway. Retro followed, holding the battering ram. Knuckles brought up the rear, locking down the stairwell.

I moved the phone toward the door and the sectors locked, all glowing green. *Jackpot.*

64

I nodded at Retro, and brought my weapon up, feeling the adrenaline spike. He positioned on the right side of the door, doing a left-handed slam to stay clear of the funnel of fire. He looked at me one more time, waiting. I whispered into my earpiece. "On my call . . . Five, four, three, two, one, execute, execute, execute."

Retro's arms went back at two, going forward at one. He split the doorjamb at the first *e* of *execute*, shattering the lock and flinging the door forward. Time slowed, like a *Matrix* movie, my brain cataloging every movement in hyperdetail. The door flying inward, the pieces of metal from the lock exploding all over like Christmas tinsel, Retro dropping the sledge, slamming backward into the wall, and raising his weapon, clearing the breach for the team.

I ran forward, seeing Brett rotating around, swinging his barrel up. I entered the doorway, weapon raised and ready, seeing nothing. The room empty.

I swung left, painting the sector with my rifle, but it was clear. I felt the rush of Brett closing right, locking down that section. I caught movement out of the corner of my eye and turned, seeing Rashid exit the bathroom, a toilet satchel in his hands. He threw it at Brett's head and dove to a table on the right, screaming. He closed his hands on the butt of a pistol, and Brett fired, the sound a muted spit.

Rashid hammered into the wall and wailed, grabbing his buttock. Brett took two steps and buttstroked him in the temple, knocking him out.

I cleared the rest of the small area, finding nothing in the bathroom.

I came back out, seeing Knuckles in the doorway, weapon at the ready, and Retro searching the room. Brett was bandaging up our target. I walked over to him and said, "Ass shot? Really? Tell me that was intentional."

He looked up at me and said, "I want Shoshana back. It took all I had not to raise my sights."

I smiled. "I can't say I'd have had the same control, but Aaron will appreciate it. Same as me."

I turned into the room and said, "Retro, status?"

"Got a computer and phone. Some tickets and other shit. I say we're done."

I looked back at Brett. "He stable?" A nod. "Hit him with the dope and let's get the fuck out of here." I keyed my earpiece. "Koko, Koko, Jackpot. We're exfilling now."

We'd been inside the room a total of three minutes. We bundled Rashid up and Retro looked out the door like we were on a panty raid in college. He called all clear. We carried him down the stairs, reaching the front door. It was Aaron's turn to make the call, with us kneeling inside until a group of drunks passed by. We hustled to the van like a group of Goodfellas in Brooklyn with a body in a carpet, which, I suppose, we were. We dumped Rashid in the back and I said, "Everyone starburst. Aaron, Knuckles, head back into the park. See if you can get a thread on Shoshana. Retro, get on the computer and check hospitals and police stations for an unknown. I'll get the interrogation going on Rashid. Meet back at the Sheraton in an hour and we'll assess where we are."

They nodded, and I jumped into the mom van, Jennifer hitting the gas. We drove for about fifteen minutes, headed toward the airport and the warehouse the Taskforce had rented. I made sure Rashid wasn't on the verge of cardiac arrest while Jennifer called Showboat.

We entered farmland, sporadic petrol stations and random blockhouses the only things around. Jennifer turned back to me and said, "Showboat's ready to receive. He said he's got some news."

I looked up from the finger blood-pressure monitor I'd placed on Rashid and said, "News about what?"

"He didn't say, but he didn't sound happy."

Two miles out from the airport, on a lonely stretch of asphalt, Jennifer turned right, pulling into a warehouse facility illuminated by vapor lights. She paused at the gate, flashed her headlights, and they opened, sliding left and right on metal rails.

We went forward, seeing a roll-up door slipping into the ceiling of the warehouse. It was going back down before we even shut the engine off. I saw Blaine coming down a set of metal stairs, a hard look on his face, and it made me sick to my stomach. I'd seen the same thing years ago. When he'd told me my family had been murdered.

I exited hesitantly, saying, "Good to go. There's going to be a police response, but they'll get nothing. Rashid's true name is nowhere in the database. They'll be searching for ghosts. We got out clean."

He nodded, and I said, "What's going on?"

He looked at Jennifer and said, "Her detective work paid off. The three boys from the school are real. They flew out from Miami to Istanbul four months ago. They disappeared—until a few days ago. They reappeared in Istanbul and flew to Venice, Italy. All three. Consensus is they're working on an attack."

Jennifer stepped down, her mouth open. She said, "Seriously?"

He said, "Yeah. Well, all except that consensus part. I think you're on to something, but the Council is split. They think they're bad, but aren't sure they're still working for the Islamic State. With the rash of guys fleeing the fighting and trying to get back home, some wonder if they're just juvenile delinquents. Nobody thinks they're saints helping with food relief, but not all are convinced it's our business. Either way, we have the order to explore. Kurt wants you to head to Venice and scope them out. Their check-in involved running their passports into a database. We have their hotel. You guys get over there and see if there's any smoke to the fire."

I said, "Okay . . . I'm game, but I've got a little cleanup here first." I jerked my finger to Rashid, his body being placed on a stretcher. "And it involves that asshole."

Blaine was watching the support crew take Rashid out, checking vitals and making sure he wasn't having a stroke. He wasn't listening to me.

I pushed a little bit, saying, "Sir, I'm missing one of the team. I didn't have time to tell you, but Shoshana never showed after the park. I'm not leaving until I find her. It may be nothing, but I'm staying until I prove it one way or the other. Get someone else into Venice."

I glanced at Jennifer, and she nodded. I went back to him. He said, "Pike, you've got orders to get to Venice. Don't push this."

I couldn't believe how nonchalantly he was taking what I'd just said. In fact, I *didn't* believe it. He'd known what I was going to say. The same dread I'd felt when I'd first seen him on the stairs dripped through my body, like a clammy fog. I said, "Sir, look at me."

He did.

"What's going on?"

"Pike, I've got orders. I've got to get you moving. You and the team. Aaron is no longer relevant. He stays here."

I saw Jennifer's eyes slit, her arms across her chest. I said, "Sir, did you hear what I just said?"

"Yes. It's an Israeli problem. Not ours. We have our mission."

I slowly shook my head. "No, sir. It's a team problem. And she's on my team. What the fuck is going on?"

He took a deep breath and let it out. He looked at me, and I could see the pull between orders he was given and loyalty to the team. He said, "Okay, okay."

Nothing else.

I said, "Talk to me."

He turned a small circle, debating with himself. He hit the wall with his fist and said, "I'll tell you, but you're getting on that plane, right?"

I said, "Maybe."

He shook his head and cursed. He said, "I've been ordered to keep this classified. To keep it from you. You, specifically. The Council wants the Lost Boys under surveillance. Right now."

I leaned back against the van, feeling sick. I asked, "What is it?"

"Intel spiked on a jihadist website. We have a YouTube video. It's not pretty."

65

Jacob sat within seventy meters of the spot in the alley where he'd met the chaperone. While Chris had had the courage to walk to his death, boarding the boat of his own volition, Jacob had no illusions that his big-titted mistress would do the same. He'd decided to meet her in the wine bar up Assassini lane.

He looked at his watch. It was now past midnight, and he knew in his heart she wasn't going to come. Whether it was a shot across the bow to Chris for the way he'd "treated" her, standing her up last night, or whether she was suspicious, he didn't know.

What he did know was that if she didn't show, he'd wasted this night. Because of it, he had only one more cycle of darkness to kill the three kids. She was going to get away. He'd planned tonight as a repeat of last night, convinced he could entrap her, but maybe that had been the lack of sleep talking.

After dumping Chris's body in the bay, blood leaking out and bubbles forming around the cinder blocks, they'd returned the boat and walked back to the hotel. He'd really wanted to sleep, but had waited for Devon to show up. He had, drunk, but with a key.

They'd discussed the alternatives, and Devon had said he could keep the boys in play for another day, plying them with liquor. He'd put Devon to bed and asked Carlos what they should do. They now controlled two of the three legs for success: one, Chris, at the bottom of the ocean; two, the boys, under Devon's sway; but the third—the woman—was outside of their control, and she was a wild card that could affect everything.

Jacob had planned on killing the boys tonight, then taking the train to Rome, a full two days in advance of when they were supposed to be there in their new personas. Enough time to survey the terrain before pretending to be something they weren't.

But the woman beckoned. Chris's dark secret was running loose, capable of forestalling all they hoped to accomplish. He'd discussed it with Carlos, Devon snoring five feet away, and they'd decided to attempt to kill her.

The next morning, they'd sent a bleary-eyed Devon back to the boys with a mission. He'd entered the room with the key he'd taken, and woken up the hungover teenager sleeping there. Devon had spent an interminable amount of time in the room, annoying the hell out of Jacob. Waiting in the lobby, his eyes gritty from the lack of sleep, watching people from all over the world eating the breakfast buffet, Jacob began thinking about just bashing the kid's head in to get the information he needed.

Jacob wanted to hack the chaperone's computer, using social engineering through Devon's newfound friends. Devon had learned the night before that the boys hadn't brought their own systems, and that they all got a minimum of five minutes every other day to send well-wishes to whomever they wanted, Chris leaning over their shoulders as they typed. All Jacob needed now was the password.

He'd started to ask for another glass of water, getting a stare from the waitress because of his lack of having ordered anything of monetary value, when he'd seen his partner come down the stairs. Devon smiled, looking like he was still a little drunk, and Jacob wondered if it was the liquor or the lifestyle. Devon sat down and handed him a slip of paper, saying, "I got it."

Jacob unfolded the slip, seeing a barely legible scribble, and said, "No spike? He didn't wonder why?"

"No. He's out. Probably the first time he's ever been drunk."

"And the rest of them?"

"Same way."

"You know you have to trap them all day. Keep them happy."

Devon smiled and rubbed his eyes. "That's not going to be an issue.

I'll get them drunk again. Last night they were talking about how today was their day. Time of their life and all that. I'll take 'em out. Hell, they won't get moving until at least one. Once I'm done with them, they'll sleep for the rest of the night."

Jacob had started to remind Devon of the stakes, of how Devon needed to keep his head about him, then remembered that Devon had been on cocaine benders that had lasted for days. Altar boys from an affluent high school stood no chance.

He'd said, "Get your passport picture before you become engaged again. It'll be your only chance."

Jacob had left him, going to the chaperone's room, praying the key still worked from the soaking last night. It had. He'd entered, seeing the clothes splayed about, as if the owner were coming home. It had given him pause. He'd gone into the bathroom and seen the toothbrush. It was . . . almost melancholy. He'd caused the death of a man, and was seeing the vestiges for the first time. The artifacts left behind. He'd thought again of his worth, strangely proud and wondering if he was wasting his talents in the service of the Islamic State.

He'd opened the laptop on the desk, typing the password Devon had gleaned. It had worked. He'd scanned all the emails until he'd found one from someone named "Poster Girl." He'd used a search function, then rummaged through past emails, finding photos she'd sent: her wearing a bikini, her holding a poster from Chris's company, selfies with major cleavage, lingerie with a Staples "easy" button on her crotch. They went on and on.

He felt like a voyeur, but couldn't quit clicking. He looked into her eyes, knowing he was going to kill her. He came to terms with the choice.

He created an email, asking her to meet "Chris" at the bistro on Assassini, and apologizing for missing their earlier date. Blaming business. Then he'd left and collected Carlos at their hotel, both getting their own passport pictures for the forging to come.

That had been twelve hours ago, and she still had not shown. Now he was contending with a waiter who'd run out of patience, just as he had in the hotel. The café was famous for wine, and he had done nothing but drink water. The man came out one more time and said, "Are you sure the lady is coming?"

Jacob said, "No. I'm not. I'm sorry."

He threw some money on the table and stood up, the waiter growing indignant. Putting his notebook into his apron, he started to say something—maybe a curse, maybe a slur—and Jacob caught his eye. It was enough. The man took the money and retreated.

Jacob walked to the end of the alley, finding Carlos sagging in the seat of the johnboat. Jacob tapped the aluminum, waking him up.

"She's not coming. Get the boat back. We'll need it tomorrow."

"What now?"

"We're out of time. We keep the boys tomorrow, and kill them tomorrow night."

"What about the girl?"

"Nothing I can do about that. For all I know, she's flying back to America. I contacted Omar, but he didn't reply. We don't have a lot of choices. We kill the kids and get to Rome. Tomorrow night."

"Maybe we should wait for guidance from Omar."

Carlos saw Jacob's aggravation and said, "You know, in case he has a change or something."

Jacob looked away and said, "I don't know why he didn't answer, but I'm not waiting on him for a decision. For all I know, he's dead."

66

I blinked my eyes, the lids feeling like sandpaper from staying awake for the last thirty-six hours. On the screen was a still image from the YouTube video, showing a clearly terrified Shoshana tied to an ornate wooden chair. Behind her stood a large man wearing a black hood with the eyeholes, nose, and mouth cut open haphazardly, as if it had been done in haste.

He had blue eyes and was holding what appeared to be a large serrated bread knife. Something that would do significant damage to the neck it was against, and not in a humane way. Staring at the screen, I felt impotent, wanting more than anything to be with her in that moment. I wished I could will myself to her location, teleport right into the middle of the room, then set about delivering justice to every one of the murdering psychopaths.

As much rage as I felt, it was a candle to Aaron's sun. He was quiet and showed no outward displays, but the heat coming off of him was palpable. He kept looking at me for a miracle, believing the US government had some magical way to resolve the situation, but I feared we were already too late. Rashid had given up nothing in an initial interrogation, either because he didn't know or was holding out. The Taskforce continued to work him, but our best intel was the video.

My watch had crawled past 2:00 P.M., and we'd had the footage for over sixteen hours. The Taskforce had done what they could with it, starting with the usual IP addresses and other computer linkages. It had produced nothing, the kidnappers masking their computer trail well, using temporary ISPs and the Tor network. Leaving the network associations behind, the Taskforce had looked at the image itself, and with what they'd found, we'd necked the location to five different hotels within a half-mile radius of the city center, but so far it hadn't been enough.

Retro and Knuckles were at one more hotel, the last on our target deck, and the one least likely to prove any use. It was a budget number that barely registered above a hostel. It didn't even have a website, so expecting it to have Internet was beyond the scope of wishing, but we were all holding our breath, waiting on Retro's call. The one good thing was that I didn't need to worry about Kurt Hale or Showboat calling instead, ordering me to leave.

Through voice analysis of his speech and accent, the Taskforce had concluded the captor was from the Caucasus—Georgia, Chechnya, Dagestan, or some other such place. Further, because of his stated affiliation to the Islamic State and his specific threats of beheading Shoshana, the analysts were speculating that he might be the mythical Chechen called Omar al-Khatami, the tactical genius behind the Islamic State's ability to roll up most of Iraq and Syria. If it was him, the analysts were flabbergasted that he'd left the protection of the Islamic State, and felt it was a huge spike of something serious. That had been enough to turn off the war drums for the team going immediately to Venice. Nobody was sure if it *was* Omar, but it was enough to tip the balance. They had sent every photo they had of the man, some crisp and others grainy, showing a large fighter with ice-blue eyes and a lumberjack's red beard, constantly adorned with grenades and weapons. Kurt had given me something better; another day to sort out whether he was here, in Tirana. After that, the Oversight Council figured Omar would be in the wind, and further searching would be a waste of time.

Left unsaid was the threat of Shoshana's neck being ripped out by a bread knife. I could give a crap about the Chechen, but it got me twenty-four hours to find Shoshana, time that I was rapidly burning through like a drunk dropping quarters into a slot machine.

Initially, the Taskforce had made great strides toward necking down her location, impressing the hell out of me and almost making it seem easy. After working such issues in the past, I should have known it wouldn't be. The American James Foley was testament to that. In 2014, US intelligence had identified what they thought was hard data on his location. Special Operations forces had launched a daring nighttime raid into the heart of the Islamic State in Syria, and found a dry hole. Foley was beheaded shortly thereafter.

In our case, the Taskforce, after the hyperventilating and jumping up and down over Omar, had dissected the video almost at the ones-and-zeros level, and they'd sent us a pretty impressive list of forty different points. Some speculation, some facts. Most were worthless, but three were critical.

1. They identified a noise in the background. After isolating it from all other sound, they determined it was a clock tower, and that it was tolling 9:00 P.M. Nine from the gongs, and P.M. because a cycle of darkness hadn't yet happened.
2. They used image extrapolation to identify an object in the shadows. It was the corner of a laptop, and it had an Ethernet cord coming out.
3. They'd seen the edge of a map coming out of the Chechen's pocket, and, after magnification, had identified Cyrillic writing along the top. They'd used digital manipulation and a proprietary predictive algorithm to create their best guess of what the writing said: *Justin's Place*.

We put the information to immediate use. Knowing that the firefight had happened right at dusk, it meant the Chechen had had less than an hour to take Shoshana and hole up somewhere, which indicated he was still inside Tirana.

Brett had identified the only clock tower in the city, a once-derelict brick structure that had been restored in 2010 and was now competing in stature with the minaret of a mosque next door. Using that as a focal point, we'd drawn a half-mile radius around it, then identified all hotels, motels, and hostels within that circle. We had about twenty. Way too many.

We'd immediately focused on those with any variation of the name

Justin in the title, and had come up completely empty. Truthfully, that piece had been a bit of a guess on the Taskforce's part, so I wasn't surprised, but Aaron—having expected more—had not taken it well.

Disgusted, he'd cursed under his breath and stomped to the bathroom, growing more and more impatient. I wasn't looking forward to what would happen when he reached the end. I could only imagine the pain he was feeling because he'd allowed his professional obligations to supersede his personal ones. At 9:00 last night, we were planning for the assault against Rashid. I wondered if he was second-guessing his decision, believing he'd placed too much faith in our ability to find Shoshana.

It hadn't helped things when the video showed the Chechen demanding *Israel* back off of the Islamic State. Somehow, they'd figured out Shoshana's nationality, and it might have just been the usual blustering, but if they *did* know, it didn't take much to imagine what they'd done for the information. I'd let Aaron go, returning to the list of forty points from the Taskforce.

Studying it, Retro had found the remark about the laptop with Ethernet, which had set up our next step. We refined the search, seeking out all potential hotels that had Internet. In Tirana, it wouldn't be a large list. We'd come up with four. A manageable number.

Between the Taskforce analysis and our own work, we had burned through most of the night. At 8:00 A.M. I'd sent Retro and Knuckles to the first hotel, dragging along a healthy hacking package. They'd gone in and, with the help of the Taskforce computer network operations center, had flayed open the system, looking for a computer with the telltale vestiges of the YouTube video. And had come up empty again.

They'd taken about five hours going from hotel to hotel, and had found nothing. They'd come back to the Sheraton bleary-eyed and aggravated, primarily because we weren't sure that they hadn't been to the right hotel, only to have the suspect computer air-gapped from the Internet when they probed, or turned off.

We were war-gaming a second line of attack when Jennifer had entered, interrupting us. Retro was banging away on Google Maps, Knuckles, Aaron, and I looking over his shoulder while Brett talked to the intel geeks in the rear. Jennifer said, "Pike, I think I've got something."

I held up a finger, still staring at the screen. She leaned past me and said, "Retro, search for any hotels near the Tirana castle. It's inside the envelope of the clock tower."

I started to snap at her, the lack of sleep shortening my temper. Aaron took one look at Jennifer and said, "Listen to her. Do it." He was searching for a miracle, wanting to see Shoshana's unique abilities in Jennifer. He would believe anything at this point, and I didn't have the courage to disagree. I nodded, and Retro began typing.

He found one hotel, called the Kalaja, built right into an old wall left from centuries ago, the last vestige of the castle that had once stood there. The hotel had some reviews on various travel sites—none very flattering—but didn't have a website of its own, which didn't leave much hope for them having Internet, a cut line given the information we had. I said, "Why are we wasting time on this?"

She said, "Something about the name *Justin* was sticking in my head."

Retro said, "But this hotel has nothing to do with the name *Justin*."

She said, "Yes, it does. I think it was a bad translation from the Taskforce. The Tirana Castle is really no longer a castle. It's just called that for the tourists. It's a single wall, and it's called the Justinian Wall by locals. That's what he wrote down. I'm sure of it. With the digital extrapolation, and then the translation from Cyrillic, I think they gave us a bad name."

Nobody moved, wanting to believe but fearing the consequences. Aaron broke the silence. And the fear.

He looked at her in amazement and said, "What on earth led you to that? How did you know the history?"

Knuckles patted Jennifer on the back and said, "Because she's a pencil-necked professor at heart, that's how. Retro, load up and let's get over there. Check it out."

Retro left the desk, starting to repack his hacking kit, and Knuckles looked at Jennifer. "Saved by your useless history trivia."

He shouldered his ruck and turned to the door, saying, "This pans out, and you can forget about that bad call in Jordan. You're back in hero land."

She grinned as if it was just a joke, but I could tell what Knuckles had said meant a great deal to her. I knew he meant it too, because, well, he was Knuckles. Make no mistake, he'd done the same with me a few times.

Aaron said, "It'll pan out. I can feel it. She's there."

That had been twenty minutes ago, and now we were all sitting around staring at the phone, waiting on it to ring. It did.

"Yeah, what do you have?"

"I got nothing yet, but when we checked in they said I had to pay if I wanted to use Internet. They don't have Wi-Fi—only Ethernet from, like, 1998. We're in the room, and Retro's getting set up." He paused, then said, "The chair Retro's sitting in is just like the one in the video." I could hear the excitement coming through the phone. "Pike, I think this is it."

I said, "Crack the system. Find the computer. Get me a room."

He acknowledged, and I gave out the good news. Everyone began hustling at that point, me giving instructions on what to pack, and Aaron asking how far we were willing to go. I said, "As far as it takes, I promise."

He gave me a grim smile, and the phone rang again. I snatched it up, expecting to hear more good news. It was Showboat, and it most definitely wasn't good.

"Pike, I've got an abort on your current mission profile. I'm sorry."

"What the hell are you talking about? What about Omar? You said the director of the CIA thought he was the find of the century."

"He did. Does. But we've got the further interrogation results from Rashid, and it's grim. The Lost Boys are on the warpath. They're real. Rashid says they're going to be passed specialized explosives through some other cell—things that can evade conventional detection. He's holding out on what the target is, or doesn't know it, but the Council is looking at a real threat. Omar isn't an Omega mission right now. The Lost Boys are."

Aaron had stopped moving, looking at me, knowing something bad was happening. I said, "Sir, we've found the bed-down. Give me tonight. Please."

"You have a pinpoint location?"

"No, not yet. But I will in another couple of hours. I'm sure of it."

"Pike, that's not good enough. Shoshana's an Israeli problem. She's not Taskforce. I can't do anything about it."

Jennifer and Brett had both stopped packing kit, warily watching me. I looked into the computer screen at the still video image, seeing Shoshana's eyes. Hearing her words in the American Bar.

I said, "I'm sorry, sir. I'm not leaving tonight. Tell Kurt this is a Prairie Fire. Shoshana may not be Taskforce, but she's on my team. My call."

Instead of indignation or anger, I actually heard relief, and knew why: According to our charter, a team leader making that call got absolute support, and Showboat didn't like leaving her either. Shoshana wasn't officially Taskforce, but it would be enough to buy me a night. He said, "You're calling Prairie Fire? For Shoshana?"

I said, "Yes. Relay that to Kurt. For tonight, I have control."

He said, "Get her back, Pike. It's the only thing that will mitigate delay on the Lost Boys."

I nodded at Aaron, and he slowly began packing again, eyes on me. I said, "Sir, don't worry about those juvenile delinquents. They'll keep. There's no way they're doing any attack in Venice."

67

Jacob watched the sun drop, absently drinking his beer as Devon and the three targets slowly went through the entire minibar. He caught Devon's eye, telling him to slow down. They had a lot of work in the next twelve hours, and, while Devon's primary role was babysitter, Jacob didn't want him so drunk he couldn't control the situation.

One of the kids—even though they were only a year or two younger than Jacob, he couldn't help but think of them that way—let rip a horrendous expulsion of flatulence, causing all of them to laugh. Jacob stood, saying, "I'm out."

He grabbed his phone, hearing the fart boy say, "What's his problem?"

He entered the hallway, not waiting for Devon's answer, thinking, *Fart Boy is first.*

He couldn't kill all three at the same time, especially since they had only knives, so he'd decided to take them one at a time.

After last night's failure with the woman, Carlos and Jacob had returned to the hotel, waiting on Devon. He'd been out with the boys all day long, calling intermittently, then had finally given them the answer they'd waited on: He was sleeping in his new friend's room.

Jacob and Carlos had gone to bed, woken up early, packed up their bags, and cleaned out their room. They had it for three more days, but that had been done intentionally.

They'd entered the Best Western hallway, dragging Devon's bag with them, when Jacob had stopped. Carlos had said, "What?"

Jacob had returned to the small minibar, saying, "Make sure the do not disturb sign is out." He opened the minibar, sweeping all of the small bottles, candy bars, and soft drinks into his carry-on. Carlos had stared and Jacob had said, "Let the Islamic State pay for it."

They'd left the hotel for the last time, walking out of the back door so the desk didn't see their bags. Making small talk, ignoring the mission and what they were about to do, they'd walked to the targets' hotel, where Devon was waiting.

They'd avoided the front desk and walked up the stairs to the chaperone's room, dumped the bags, then gone down to the room that Devon was in. Jacob had banged on the door, and Devon had finally awakened. They pushed in, shouting and yelling as if they were ready for some fun. The boy, eyes red-rimmed from two days of drinking, acted game, then had sprinted to his bathroom, throwing up.

Soon enough, they had all three targets in the room, talking about what they were going to do for the day, Devon introducing Jacob and Carlos as another youth group also free from their chaperone.

They'd gone to lunch, then had traipsed around Piazza San Marco, just another group of tourists annoying the locals. During that time, Jacob had planted the seed for the night, teasing the boys' sense of adventure. They'd returned to the room at four in the afternoon, with Carlos breaking free for his part of the mission.

During the entire day, there had been only two spikes, both from the nascent leader of the group—Fart Boy.

After lunch, he'd mentioned that they should let the chaperone know what they were doing, worried that they'd get in trouble. The other boys, under Devon's lead, had drowned him out, calling him a mama's boy. Later, once they were back in the room, he'd said he was going upstairs to send a message to his parents from the chaperone's computer. Once again, Devon had taken the lead, giving him a minibottle of wine and challenging him to drink it.

Nothing had become of it then, but Jacob had determined that he would be the first to go. He didn't want any trouble, and Fart Boy was the most likely to provide it if he were sitting by himself, the last target left alive.

In the hallway, hearing the drunken slobber from the room, Jacob called Carlos. "You good?"

"Not yet. I need ten minutes. Let it get full dark."

"Okay. I'm taking the first boy. By the time we get to the alley, it'll be night. You need to be there. Remember the story?"

"Yeah. We're going to a pirate's cave over by the airport."

"And why aren't we going all together?"

"Because the boat is rated for three. The Italian Carabinieri will pull us over with more."

Jacob had no idea if that was true, but neither would the boys. He said, "Did you get the cinder blocks?"

"Yeah. I found a construction site. I drop you off, then go load up, then return. No problem."

"I'll see you in twenty minutes. Be waiting."

Jacob returned to the room, smiling and saying, "Carlos is ready! Who's first? Come on, let's go check out the cave!"

On cue, Devon stood over Fart Boy and jerked him to his feet. "You go first, big guy." Fart Boy looked a little uneasy, the wine and beer flowing through him.

He said, "Maybe we should tell Chris what we're doing?"

Devon scoffed and said, "What? You think he'll let you go? Our chaperone thinks we're in our rooms. And we're not even in our hotel. Don't be a pussy. This is the last night."

Fart Boy stood, a little weakly, and Jacob dragged him by the arm. They exited down the stairwell, away from the elevator, and spilled out into the lobby. Jacob pushed Fart Boy to the side door that led to the alley, glancing into the small lobby to see if anyone was watching.

And saw Chris's mistress sitting in a chair, pretending to read a newspaper.

68

Knuckles opened the door, asking, "Did you spike at the desk?"

I said, "No. It was empty. But I don't know about any camera systems."

Knuckles stepped back and we flowed into the room, dragging three carry-on suitcases. He said, "Don't worry about that. I've already checked. There aren't any."

Retro was in the rear on a cheap desk, stroking the keys of a laptop. Aaron, Brett, and Jennifer started unpacking the kit, breaking out weapons, cameras, and other things. I said, "So, what's the status?"

"We got the room. Well, we got the room the computer's in. The hotel only has ten rooms total, six on the second floor with shared bathrooms and four on the first floor with their own bathrooms. We picked a room with its own bathroom figuring that's where he would be, but we were wrong. The computer's on the second floor."

"Access?"

"Outside stairwell right in front of the entrance and an inside one at the end of this hall. Straight linear target. The room is the second one in from the outside stairwell."

"Recommendation?"

"Inside stairwell. It's farthest from the door, but to get to the outside one you need to pass by the front desk."

"Assault plan?"

"Bang it hard, just like Rashid. Hit both rooms, the computer one and the one it connects to. The problem will be exfil. We get the Chechen, he's not going easy. We'll have to take him down, then exfil with the dead weight."

He lowered his voice, glancing at Aaron. "Even if we don't, we have to assume Shoshana's been hurt. Worst case, we're exfilling carrying two."

"We brought some litters, and Brett's prepared to do limited trauma care. Showboat's ready to receive with medical support. What's the story on the renters? How many and who are they?"

"Hotel database is shit. They don't run passports and work mostly on cash. When we signed in, they didn't even use a computer. They used a ledger from 1970. The Internet system is self-contained, like someone built it stand-alone in an attempt to modernize, then gave up." He pointed to the Ethernet cable and said, "Look at this thing. It's slow as shit and definitely an afterthought."

The plug for the cable was glued to the wall, with the line leading to it running on the exterior, as if it had been added as a temporary fix.

"So we don't know who's got the room, or who's on the other side?"

"No. All we have is the room the computer is in."

"What did we get from it?"

Retro looked up and said, "It's not Islamic State stuff. It all looks like organized crime shit. Mafia things. Business transactions hidden by steganography, a bunch of pimp lists, some porno, things like that."

I said, "Are we sure this is it?"

Retro nodded. "The raw file from the video is on this box. So is the YouTube upload trace. That video was sent from this computer."

I nodded, thinking. I went to the door, cracking it and looking at the lock. A cheap dead bolt worked with an old-fashioned key. Easy to pick, but no way would I waste my time manipulating a lock on a hostage rescue. Well, that's not exactly true. I'd pick it with the knock-knock, shattering the damn thing into a hundred pieces. Hostage rescue was all about speed, surprise, and violence, and we needed to ensure we had all three.

I said, "We need more intel. I want to know how many are in the room. I want to know who's next door. I want to know what weapons they have. I want to know—"

Retro interrupted. "I got someone on the box right now. Sending a chat request."

We all gathered behind him, and he said, "The chat's in Russian. Stand by." He manipulated the keys and another chat window came up from the Taskforce. He typed a command, and the man on the other end started work. Five seconds later we were looking at the person typing a floor above. A thin-faced, bald-headed man with brown eyes and a goatee. He looked nothing like the pictures Kurt had sent. Behind him was an empty room. No Shoshana.

"Who the hell is that?"

"No idea. Hang on. Taskforce is using a key logger. We'll get a read-out of what he's typing."

We waited, Aaron jostling for a better view. The chat window began spitting out words.

Sender: *The guy is crazy. He's going to kill her here, to-night.*

Receiver: *Get out. Don't get involved. It will damage every-thing.*

Sender: *I don't think I can. You don't know this man. We'll be back tomorrow one way or the other.*

Agitated, Aaron said, "She's alive. She's right above us. Come on, let's go."

My mind cranking through the information in the small chat, formulating an assault plan based on what we knew, I said, "Hang on." I pinched my chin, then started issuing orders. "Okay, he said 'we'll,' so we know there's at least three, which means we hit both rooms. Retro, you get the knock-knock on the computer room. I'll be behind you. Brett, you get the adjacent room with Knuckles. Aaron, Jennifer, you lock down the hallway for breach—Aaron in the front, Jennifer in the rear. Everyone, it's a hostile force rule of engagement. My call. You see a threat, you take it out. Capturing the Chechen is secondary to recovering Shoshana."

I held up one of the pictures of Omar Kurt had sent. "This is all we have, but remember, he might have ditched the beard, dyed his hair, or something else. Look for the size and his eyes. This is kill or capture. If you can incapacitate, do so, but don't work at it."

A noise came from the computer. Retro leaned in and said, "The mic's on, the mic's on. Shh."

Everyone grew quiet, waiting. The speech came in incoherent, and I realized it was in a foreign language. I hissed, "Get the Taskforce on it. What's he saying?"

He started typing, and I heard the words from the speaker slip into space, losing valuable intelligence while we waited. Eventually, they petered out, and the man in front of the computer stood up, leaving our view. I stomped in a circle, cursing, then Retro said, "The Taskforce got the tail end."

Aaron said, "And?"

"Translation coming in now."

We watched the screen, and what came out caused my blood to run cold.

Quote: *I'm coming. Calm down. The Internet is shit in this place.*

Quote: *Get the camera. Hold her still.*

End Quote.

*   *   *

Shoshana heard the man called Anzor coming back through the toilet and knew her time was close. He said, "Internet doesn't work any better in there than it did in here. I'm amazed you actually got the video to load in the first place."

Omar said, "Get her on top of the plastic. Pick up the whole chair. There will be a lot of blood."

Anzor said, "Omar, think about this. You want to kill her, fine, but doing it here, in a hotel room I've rented, is too much."

Omar looked at him, the death he represented flooding into the room, a power that had grown in the time the men had known him in Georgia. Anzor held up his hands and said, "Hey, Omar, I'm not fighting. I'm just talking sense."

Omar said, "Surely you didn't give them your real name?"

"No, of course not, but at least use the bathtub."

"No. I want the propaganda. Go get the vehicle ready. Pull it on the other side of Toptani."

Levan said, "We didn't sign up for some crazy Islamic killing."

"You signed up to help me, and that's what you're doing. You complete this, you take me to the airport, and you disappear, end of mission."

The three looked at one another, and Anzor slowly nodded, saying, "Okay, but this is it. Our debt will be paid in full. No more help."

Omar showed his teeth and said, "Of course. After this, all you need to do is take me to the airport. Nothing more."

Anzor left the room.

Shoshana watched Omar pick up the bread knife and walk toward her. He said, "Levan, hold the camera. I want them to feel the pain of her death."

Levan said, "Fuck you. Do it yourself."

Omar snarled, "It's no different from the punishment you've dealt out. Only you do it to prostitutes for not fucking enough people."

Levan remained defiant, and Omar slipped his hand into his coat pocket. "You're either with me or against me." He paused, going from one man to the other, then said, "And I'll kill everyone against me."

Davit glanced at Levan and said, "Hang on. I'll do it."

He picked up the camera, and Shoshana thrashed, the thought of being slaughtered on tape more than she could bear. She felt Omar's hands on her head, holding her tight. She stopped struggling.

He said, "Any last words for the camera? I'd prefer it if you denounced Israel, but I'm fairly sure that won't happen."

She looked into his eyes, and without even meaning to, she read him, her talent touching the depths of the abyss. She felt a blackness unlike any she'd experienced before, drenched in the blood of innocents.

She felt the pain of others long gone, saw the slaughter he'd caused, and recognized the truth, as she had in the past. She raised her head, looking him in the eye. She said, "You believe you're powerful, but only because you kill the helpless. You are nothing."

Bemused, Omar said, "And how would you know what I am?"

"You are no different from every terrorist that takes the lives of innocents. No different from the men I've tracked. You murder, then begin to believe you're better than the ones who are dead. You project yourself as a killer of men, living within the superiority of someone with absolute power. You think that gives you strength. That you're invulnerable. And your tribe reinforces the myth, kissing your ass and bowing to your control. But you make a mistake."

"What is that, Jew girl?"

"You aren't superior, no matter how many you kill. You are *human*. You live and breathe. You have blood that pumps through your veins. In God's eyes, you are no more powerful than the man you put under the knife. And someday, it will be you."

He scoffed. "That power is enough today."

She didn't say anything. He stared at her, and she saw a shadow of doubt flick across his face. A brief moment, but there nonetheless. More to himself than to her, he said, "I'm strong enough to kill you, am I not?"

She drilled into him with her eyes. "No. You're not. I have something you do not possess. I have salvation."

He took the words in, then raised the knife.

He said, "Only Allah has salvation. And He doesn't offer it to offal like you. But I can give you what you want, if you feel so strongly about it."

She closed her eyes and dropped her chin into her chest, wanting to make him battle for her soul. She thought about Aaron, and begged for the strength he possessed. She remembered her grandfather, fighting to save the athletes in Munich so long ago. She desperately wanted to focus on what was pure. What was right about her chosen path.

All she felt was fear.

Eyes closed, Aaron came to the fore again, and she was crushed at the pain he would feel upon seeing her death. He would need something to help. Something to show he'd done the right thing in bringing her here. She took a breath and decided to die looking the devil in the eye.

When she did, he was above her, holding the knife. He showed no animosity. Almost detached from what he was doing, he said, "You and I are not that different, but it will not save you. We both have a destiny. Mine is to secure the caliphate of Islam. Yours is to die."

He brought the blade down slowly. Almost reverently. She closed her eyes again, waiting on the bite. There was a gunshot in the hallway, then a slamming noise outside of the adjacent room. Omar jerked his head up, shouting at Levan to find out the cause, but she knew what it was.

Like looking into a soul, she *knew*.

69

The last chat still glowing on the screen, I said, "Everyone kitted up? Ready?" A group of nods. "We go right now, as briefed. Knuckles, where's the interior stairwell?"

He said, "Follow me," and slipped out the door. We reached it and spent a brief few seconds in the landing getting sorted for assault. We jogged up the stairs in stack order, Aaron leading the way, followed by Brett with the battering ram, then Knuckles. The second team was Retro, me, then Jennifer as tail-gunner. Aaron paused in the alcove on the second floor and peeked out. He nodded, looking at me. I pointed, and we entered the hallway at a jog.

The two rooms were the last ones on the left side, the outside stairwell just beyond the first door, an alcove on the right with a picture window showing starlight and the vague glow of a vapor lamp. Aaron had just passed my target room when the exterior stairwell door opened, a man appearing. A man I recognized.

Computer chat guy.

He took one look at the group, weapons bristling and radiating menace, and snapped back into the stairwell.

Aaron got off two rounds, the bullets hammering into the door as it slammed shut. I said, "Execute, execute, now, now, now."

I slid out of the way, giving Retro access to our door, and a weapon appeared at the stairwell. An MP-5, held only in a fist, the body behind cover, and it began firing on automatic.

Retro slammed the sledge, bullets ripping through the hallway, the first team firing from the prone, jammed on top of one another in the narrow space, all trying to dig their way through the carpet. The door exploded open and I entered on the run, rifle barrel high and finger on the trigger. I swept, seeing a man with a pistol coming out of the bathroom. I split him open with a double tap while still racing in, clearing the breach for the others.

I heard someone shout, then my earpiece came alive. "Retro's hit, Retro's hit."

I said, "Abandon second breach. Abandon second breach." I reached the door of the bathroom and held up, waiting on another assaulter. I felt a squeeze and didn't even look to see who it was, kicking in the door. We advanced to the far side and rounds split the air, puncturing the connecting bathroom door with both of us falling into the bathtub to get out of the fire. As soon as it raked past, I bounced up, moving forward to the breach. I kicked the door open, seeing Shoshana being dragged by the hair into the hallway, making her captor fight for every inch.

A man popped back inside, spraying high with a MAC 10, the recoil impossible to control with one hand. I squeezed the trigger, feeling someone fire from my right at the same time, multiple rounds puncturing the gunman's body. He dropped, and I ran to the breach, sliding forward on my knees, weapon up, far enough behind cover to catch only a sliver of the hall.

I saw the outside stairwell door, now propped open with a chair, and chat man just down the steps, covered by the slope. He raised his MP-5 and sprayed, splintering the jamb around my head. I pulled inside and said, "PC moving, outside stairwell. Need suppression on the door."

I looked to my right, and saw it was Aaron who'd entered with me. I wasn't surprised, but wished it were one of my men. Behind him was Brett, hugging the wall out of the line of fire. He said, "We need to move," and I knew he was right. Retro was hit, but there was no time to stop the assault to determine his status. All that mattered now was speed. And violence of action.

The MP-5 sprayed again, clipping the door, and I knew we had to box him in, catching him in a crossfire. Otherwise, he'd hold that stairwell for days, like the three hundred at Thermopylae. Still calm, I said again, "Knuckles, Knuckles, need that door suppressed."

My earpiece echoed, "On it. In two. One. Go."

I heard nothing but a clanking of bolts, then saw the stairwell door splinter like someone was working a chain saw. I slapped Aaron in the leg and said, "Let's go!" On my belly, I slithered across the hall into the alcove I'd seen earlier, Aaron right behind me. We pulled against the wall, now feet away from the stairwell door. The MP-5 came forward again, the barrel outside, but so close the fire from the rounds split the air right by us like a Roman candle.

I said, "Blood, Blood, get him looking your way," then heard Aaron shout, "Pike! He's on the run! We're losing Shoshana!" I leapt to the bay window he was peering out of and saw a sloping half roof just below the sill, and farther out a large man dragging Shoshana by the hair into the shadows, her arms bound behind her back. I recognized Omar al-Khatami.

Fuck the stairwell.

Without conscious thought, I grabbed a flower pot from the alcove table and shattered the window. I backed up three feet, then sprinted forward, crossing my arms and leaping up.

I smashed through the window feetfirst, landing on my butt on the stucco roof. I bounced once and went into free fall. I hit the ground on my feet and reflexively rolled as if I were landing under a parachute, only it wasn't nearly as soft. I slammed into a cheap fountain, hearing another body hit the concrete behind me.

Omar let go of Shoshana and raised a pistol. He fired, spanking the plaster of the fountain and ripping my head with spall. From my back, I squeezed off two rounds, missing, but causing him to duck. He shouted something and took off, running down the alley.

I let him go, pausing for a half second to assess the fact that I was still alive. I got that useless shit out of my system as Aaron jumped to the alley entrance. He locked it down, and I sprinted to the base of the stairs. I saw the MP-5 shooter crouched, spraying rounds into the hallway. He yelled in Russian, then glanced my way, looking for support. What he got was two rounds from my rifle, both hitting him in the head and breaking it open like a watermelon smashed with a mallet. The 300 Blackout round was definitely growing on me. He slumped down and everything grew quiet.

I looked at Aaron kneeling at the alley entrance, and he shook his head, telling me Omar was no longer a threat. Meaning he had escaped. I keyed my earpiece. "All clear. Jackpot. I say again, Jackpot. Give me a status."

I turned back to the courtyard, feeling the adrenaline start to subside like an ocean tide, exposing the bumps and bruises from my stupid stunt.

Aaron went to Shoshana, cutting her free. I could see she was a little bit dazed.

Brett said, "Retro is okay. Just nicked in the thigh. Everyone else is fine."

Looking at Shoshana, Aaron tending to her, I said, "Blood, get the vehicle. Stage on the south side of the courtyard, away from the city square. Knuckles, get back to the room. Pack it up and leave when you think it's natural. Give your weapons to Koko and act like you're pissed you took a room at a drug hideout. Get a read on the police response and potential compromise. Koko, get Retro down here. Get ready for exfil. I want to leave in less than four minutes."

I walked over to Shoshana and knelt down. She said, "What happened to the mission?"

Smiling, I said, "Don't even fucking go there. Don't do it."

Aaron finished removing her bonds, his relief so great it permeated the entire courtyard. Shoshana was looking me in the eye, and she was going deep. The bravado was gone, and I could see the cracks in her facade. Tears formed in her eyes, and she started shaking, coming to grips with the fact that she wasn't dead.

I leaned into her face, cupping her chin. "You okay?"

She said, "Pike . . . I . . . I . . ."

I said, "There is no *I* in *team*. Although there's apparently an *Aaron*."

She looked at him, and he leaned in, kissing her forehead, breaking a sacrosanct rule and finally showing her what she was worth. His very life. Left unsaid were all of the conversations earlier. Gone as if they'd never existed.

I saw the tears start to flow and said, "Jesus Christ. Get this blubbering woman out of here."

She laughed, but kept crying. Jennifer came down the outside stairwell, Retro right behind, holding a bandage on his thigh. He seemed okay. He said, "Was it Omar?"

"Yeah. It was Omar." I knew he was asking for more than identification. I said, "Fuck him. We need to get out of here. He gets to live another day."

70

Jacob walked through the lobby, his pants a little wet from the last trip, a product of having to clean off the blood. He scanned the chairs, but the mistress still had not returned.

He'd come back from killing Fart Boy—a ridiculously easy event, as it turned out—only to find her gone. He'd hoped that she would remain until after he was complete with all three, thereby giving him a shot at removing her as well, but it wasn't to be.

He went back up the stairs for the third and final time, thinking about the mistress. The fact that she'd shown up to the hotel meant she was more persistent than he'd given her credit for. It also meant she'd be back, sitting and waiting. Eventually, she'd grow tired of anonymous stalking and would start asking questions. That could potentially derail their entire plan.

It wasn't a given. The attack was close, and it would quite probably take her longer to even determine that something was wrong, then much longer to figure out what that was. Especially if the mistress had to wade through a foreign police department. It wasn't like she'd call the wife, demanding answers. Or would she?

Such a conversation would be the only thing that would cause an immediate collapse of the card house they'd built. The church would become involved, the emails to parents dissected, a brief moment of confusion at the conflict between the mistress's story and the mail, then the Vatican would be contacted with a demand to speak to Chris, the official chaperone on a once-in-a-lifetime visit to see the pope. If the

Lost Boys showed up in that firestorm, pretending to be the group, they'd be arrested immediately.

Something to think about.

He exited the stairwell and refocused on the immediate mission. He reached the room and knocked. Devon answered, looking more sober than the last time Jacob had left. He stood back from the doorway and said, "Last guy's fallen asleep. I let him. Got sick of keeping him happy."

Jacob handed him the first two passports and said, "Start working on these. You have the passport photos for myself and Carlos, right?"

"Yeah. You know these have electronic chips in them, right? This isn't like what I used to do on the block, ripping pictures for driver's licenses."

"I know, but we aren't crossing any borders. Won't matter. The only thing I'm worried about is the hologram. You used to be able to work through those on the DLs. It's no different here."

Devon shoved them in his pocket and said, "You want me to wake him up?"

"Not yet. He's the last connection we have. You sure you've got all of their email addresses? You know how often they talk to their parents?"

"Yeah, yeah, that's all good. They're set for today. Next contact is supposed to be tomorrow, after they get to Rome."

Jacob nodded and leaned over, slapping the foot of the last victim. "Hey, you ready to go? It's getting a little chilly outside. Everyone's waiting on you."

The boy sat up, confused for a moment, still a little tipsy, but nowhere near as drunk as he had been before, when he was cheering on Fart Boy.

He said, "I don't think I want to go. You guys head out without me. I'm going to bed."

He put his head back into the pillow and Jacob said, "No, no, no. It's all for one and one for all. You're going."

"No, I'm not."

Jacob jerked him off of the bed, one hand on his collar and another on the waist of his jeans. He slammed him into the wall and said, "Yes, you fucking are. Nobody's riding this one out. I came all the way back here to get you. You didn't want to go, you should have said so before I left last time."

The boy cringed in confusion and fear, his sleep-and-alcohol-addled brain trying to gain traction. He said, "Okay, okay. Sorry. Sorry. I want to go."

Jacob pushed him toward the door, nodding at Devon.

The boy opened it and said, "Isn't he coming?"

"No. He's tired."

"What?"

Jacob pushed him out the door without an answer. They walked down the stairs in silence, the boy out of fear, Jacob because he was reflecting on the mistress and missed opportunities.

Had he been paying more attention, he would have caught the signs. Seen the suspicion building in the chubby teenager in front of him, along with a latent dose of courage. But he was thinking of bigger problems.

They reached the lobby, the boy pushing open the door leading to the alley. Jacob turned back, looking one last time for the mistress, failing to see his target watching him. Waiting. He caught a flash of sharp movement and whipped back around. He saw the door swinging back, empty.

He darted forward, catching a glimpse of the teenager lumbering down the flagstones in the alley, then turning the corner. *Jesus Christ. I'm worrying about the mistress and that little shit is going to destroy everything.*

He broke open the door, sprinting to catch up and pulling out his cell phone. He hit speed dial, slipping on the stones as he rounded the corner. The boy was on a bridge, crossing a canal. Jacob took off again, running just to keep him in sight. Carlos answered, and, midstride, Jacob said, "Where are you? Have you docked?"

"No. I'm still coming in. What's wrong? Why are you out of breath?"

Shit.

Jacob hung up, the use of his phone having caused him to lose distance. He increased his pace, seeing the target dart to the left into another alley. Jacob kept pushing, driving his legs, getting into the zone, like he did when he ran from the police. A blackout feeling where nothing existed but the stride and the escape.

Back then, he knew they would eventually quit if he could only keep them running. The fear then had been the speed of radio, and now the roles were reversed. He had no one to radio, and the kid had every incentive not to get caught.

But he was chubby. Out of shape. A fat altar boy. He probably hadn't run more than a block in his life. Jacob could catch him.

Jacob rounded the corner and saw the boy leaning against a wall, gasping for air less than seventy meters away. The boy heard Jacob coming and began to run again, now a shambling trot. Jacob closed the distance to him just as he crossed another bridge, passing into a darkened square with a fountain in the center. For the first time, the kid remembered he had a voice. He stopped running and began shouting, screaming for help, the noise echoing off of the black stone. Jacob reached the far end of the bridge and saw a light flick on in an apartment overlooking the square.

The boy heard his footsteps, turned, and shrieked. Still running full-out, Jacob slammed him into the concrete of the fountain like a lineman sacking a quarterback. Stunned, the boy feebly fought for his life. Jacob saw another light come on and punched the boy in the face, then dragged him kicking into the shadows of the bridge. The boy kept struggling, releasing a keening wail over and over. Jacob wrapped his hands around the boy's neck and slammed his head into the concrete corner of the first step of the bridge.

The initial blow shut the boy up. The second and third caused his head to crack open, warm blood flowing over Jacob's hands and arms. The boy's legs twitched, then grew still.

Jacob saw steps leading down into the water below the bridge and dragged the body out of sight, hearing murmuring from the windows above. He sat still, listening. He heard something *clank*, wood on wood, then a fragment of a song. He caught a light on the canal, coming his way.

Gondola.

He put his cell phone in his mouth and slipped into the water, dragging the body under the bridge. He waited, one hand holding on to a spike coming out of the rough exterior of the bridge, the other holding the arm of the body.

The gondola glided by, the gondolier serenading a couple wrapped in an embrace, both completely unaware of the grisly scene they were passing. When they were out of earshot, Jacob swam back to the steps, remaining out of sight of the window. He called Carlos.

"We've had an issue. I had to kill the last kid here, on the island."

"You're shitting me. What happened?"

"Not worth talking about. I'm in a canal right now. I think east of you, but definitely north of our hotel. Where are you?"

"At the dock. What do you want me to do?"

"Fucking come get me. We need to dump this guy, and you and Devon need to pack up for the train."

"What do you mean? What about you?"

"There's one more thing here that needs to be taken care of."

71

Omar threaded through an outdoor eatery in a courtyard just east of the hotel, still within the pedestrian area of Toptani. He was sweating profusely and walking with his hand in his jacket pocket, drawing curious glances from the patrons.

He went through one café and entered another, the only demarcation being different-colored umbrellas and chairs. He wanted to stay within the population, keeping to areas that would prevent the Israelis from hunting. He was sure they would value operational secrecy over brute force, but he was in a dilemma. He needed to get to the airport, and to do so, he'd have to leave the safety of numbers, walking the street looking for a cab. He knew there was a stand east, on the canal road, but it was a canalized route. He'd have to walk straight down the road, the canal to his right and the road to his left. All it would take would be a simple van riding parallel to him, three seconds of chaos, and he'd be theirs, either dead in the street or tied up in the back.

He should know. He'd done the exact same thing to innumerable innocent victims in the lucrative trade of hostage ransoms in Syria. Germans, Turks, Swedes, rich Iraqis and Syrians—he'd taken many men. Some had lived, and others had died, but all had been captured with simple tactical procedures that he knew well. Procedures that were tailor-made for his walk to the taxi stand.

He considered returning to his hotel room. He could do so fairly easily, threading through the bar area of the Block, getting in and out, but he was sure it had already been targeted, which was why he hadn't gone there in the first place. Abandoning it wasn't that big of a deal. Just a loss of clothes.

Then he remembered the computer, and the messages on it. Jacob had emailed him from Venice. He hadn't responded, but the email was in the system nonetheless. The message was innocuous, stating Jacob was continuing on with the "project," but nobody who searched that computer would mistake it for an email from a friend. If the Israelis had known to find him at his Albanian contacts, they'd already have ripped through his hotel. They'd have the email from Jacob, something Omar needed to cauterize immediately.

He decided to ignore the taxi stand, taking the risk of entering the streets of the Block. He threaded his way past the bars and pedestrians until he found an Internet café. He surveyed the street, seeing nothing suspicious, then walked down the stairs to the basement.

He paid for thirty minutes and sent a single email telling Jacob to abandon this method of communication. He knew that whatever he put in the email would be compromised, so he simply said they would never use this email again, and he'd see Jacob soon. He hoped Jacob had enough sense to understand it meant destroying anything that had touched that email address.

He left the café, hovering outside the exit and studying the street above the stairwell, wondering if he'd see a van pull up and men spilling out.

After a moment, he jogged up the stairs and hit the street on the run, hoping to throw whatever surveillance was against him into disarray. He drew curious glances, but no action. Nobody matched his pace, which meant they were either really good, or not there. He saw a taxi idling outside a bar and raced to it, ordering the cabbie to take him to the airport. He sagged in the backseat and ignored all attempts at conversation.

Twenty minutes later, he entered the airport, going to a ticket counter for Alitalia and looking at the next departures. He saw one for Istanbul in an hour, then one for Rome in two. He decided the risk of delay was worth it, and purchased a ticket to Rome with cash. Such an exchange would have raised flags in any country in the European Union or in the

United States, but here in Tirana, they didn't care. When asked for luggage, he said he had a carry-on. When informed they needed to place a tag on the carry-on, he said it was outside and he'd bring it in shortly.

The signals he was sending were beyond strange, but nobody questioned him, Tirana still operating in the Cold War of the 1980s. He counted out a stack of Euros and took his ticket, then traversed the small airport to the baggage claim area.

He approached the lost luggage counter, surreptitiously looking at the two customs officers lounging next to a small tourist kiosk. They ignored him.

He had no name or other contact info. All he had was the ticket, and he was sure he was walking into a trap. Could Israel co-opt the Albanian government? Get them to stage a sting operation? He was so paranoid at this point, he would believe anything. But he also had no choice. He put one hand in his jacket, caressing the grip of his pistol, and presented the ticket with the other. A hatchet-faced man behind the counter took it, read the numbers, and disappeared in the back. He was gone for five minutes, time Omar spent wiping the sweat from his neck and stealing glances at the uniformed police.

The curtain parted, and another man appeared. Omar closed his palm around the butt, putting his finger on the trigger, then saw the man also glance at the police officers, a good sign. He said, "You have luggage that needs to go somewhere else?"

Omar said, "Yes. Rome." He showed his boarding pass. The man read it, looked at Omar, and said, "You have identification?"

"Not that you need to see."

The man squinted, debating, then nodded. He said, "Okay. You pick it up in Rome. You call Alex when you get to Rome and retrieve the bags. He'd better pay this time."

Omar said, "Of course. Alex is good for it."

The man went to a computer and printed out three luggage tags. He slid across the tracking bar codes and Omar glanced back at the police again, seeing them engrossed in conversation. He pulled out the pistol, slid it between the pages of a newspaper, and said, "Pack this in as well."

The man saw the pistol and showed alarm. Omar realized he had no idea what was in the luggage, probably thinking it was simply contra-band. He withdrew a wad of Euros and counted out three one-hundred notes. He laid them on the table and the man quickly hid the newspaper. His eyes slid to the uniformed police and he said, "Okay, okay, but leave now."

Omar did, walking back through the luggage area to the departure lounge. He got in line with everyone else waiting to pass through secu-rity, surprised at how easy his escape had been. His confidence grew. Maybe all the Israelis wanted was their bitch back.

Maybe nobody is tracking me after all.

72

Alexander Palmer said, "So you're confident it was Omar al-Khatami?"

"Yes. Pike said he had positive identification. With that and the information we're getting from Rashid, we've changed our assessment of the Lost Boys. Rashid hinted at a separate cell passing explosives, but under further interrogation, he's admitted that the cell was Omar himself. We now believe the Lost Boys are real, and are actively targeting Western interests."

"Yeah, well, we might have lost our only lead in Venice. Pike played a little fast and loose with the Prairie Fire alert on this one. The Israelis don't get the same protection as Taskforce members, regardless of what they were doing. I know it sucks, but we have a greater duty. We may have blown our only shot at the Lost Boys. If they aren't there . . . If they've left . . ."

His words drifted off, but his meaning was crystal clear. Kurt said, "Sir, you know where I stand on such things. If the man on the ground calls Prairie Fire, there's no way on earth I will ever second-guess it. You can blame me for any repercussions, but if I had to do it over again, I'd do the same damn thing."

The secretary of defense defused the charged atmosphere, asking, "Did the hit on Omar disrupt anything? Did they find explosives?"

"None on-site. If he had them, he'd already sent them on their way."

"Any granularity as to the Lost Boys' target?"

"No. Rashid's talking, but we assess he doesn't know the target.

From what we've learned, he was in Tirana to kill Omar. He's Jabhat al-Nusra, and he has no love for the Islamic State."

"Then why was al-Nusra transferring explosives? Why were they passing technology developed by the Khorasan group?"

"We don't know, but our assessment is that it's personal with Rashid. We think he was operating on his own, or it might have been a double cross with al-Nusra. Maybe he was attempting to co-opt the Lost Boys. Remember, the Khorasan group is his baby. He probably wasn't too thrilled to be giving away everything that he'd worked for, and the foot soldiers go back and forth between groups all the time."

President Warren said, "Are we sure he doesn't know the target, or is there a chance he's holding out?"

Kurt took a moment to form his words, then said, "There's always a chance he's holding out, especially if the attack is imminent. The time frame would represent a goal for him, but we don't assess that's what he's doing. He's been under . . . umm . . . significant pressure, and he's talking."

Easton Beau Clute said, "What exactly does that mean?" Fairly new to the Oversight Council, but an old hand with intelligence oversight—both the good and the bad—he looked at President Warren and said, "What are the rules of engagement for interrogation by Taskforce personnel? Why isn't he in CIA hands?"

Meaning, why isn't he in an organization that has to report to congress?

The D/CIA, Kerry Bostwick, said, "We're out of the detainee business, period. No way do I want to get involved in that snake pit again."

Secretary Billings said, "So who's in charge of this interrogation effort? Some underqualified pipe-swinger like the CIA used after 9/11? Are we talking torture here?"

Kurt said, "Ultimately, it's you people in this room, and no, we aren't torturing him. The interrogators are the best in the business, and are working within the protocols outlined in our charter. Long and short of it, we aren't using the enhanced interrogation techniques that you are familiar with."

President Warren said, "Let's stick to the business at hand. What *has* Rashid disclosed?"

"He's detailed the explosives that were passed, and it's pretty standard stuff with the exception of the detonation procedures. They're all nonmetallic, chemically activated, and very hard—if not impossible—to detect through normal means. An explosives detection capability would find the Semtex of the charge, but traditional scanners and metal detectors will not find that or the detonation method."

"So he can fly it into the United States? Without fear of being caught?"

"Well, TSA randomly checks for explosives residue, so there is some chance of compromise, but it's minimal considering the number of pieces of luggage that enter the United States. Especially if they launch the attack from a smaller airport overseas and get the bags into the system, which is why we think they're in Italy."

Billings said, "Why Venice? That seems so odd to me."

"We have no idea, honestly. There is nothing in that city that would be of benefit to the Islamic State or Jabhat al-Nusra, and they've put in a lot of effort into this attack. All we own at this point are the Florida law enforcement rap sheets for the Lost Boys, and their travel history. It ends in Venice."

President Warren said, "What about Omar?"

"He got away. We have no idea what name he was traveling under, and Pike had his hands full exfiltrating without compromise. The hotel room targeted was tied to a Georgian organized crime syndicate, which ended up being a good thing. The police are assuming criminal retaliation—drug deal gone bad, that sort of thing. All we have is the anchor in Venice."

"And?"

"And Pike's headed that way as we speak."

Alexander Palmer said, "Let's hope it's not too little, too late."

73

I leaned in closer to the plaque, intrigued by the write-up. I said,
"Jennifer, come here. Take a look at this: Venice had an Oversight
Council."

She turned from the ornate wooden throne she'd been studying and
walked over to see what I was reading, our inspection of the premises
just about over.

We'd come to the famed Doge's Palace in Venice to investigate why
the Lost Boy named Jacob Driscoll had toured it, but so far had come
up with nothing. The museum offered little beyond showcasing the old
rulers of Venice—known as the doges—and appeared to hold nothing
that would inspire an Islamic State attack.

Jennifer saw the plaque and smiled, saying, "Wait, you actually like
the history here? You're not bored out of your mind wandering around
this dusty palace?"

I said, "Not with stuff like this. They had a body called the Council
of Ten. It was formed after an attack on one of the doges, and was in
charge of state security. It was supposed to be temporary, and it operated in secret. Sound familiar?"

Jennifer said, "Let's hope not. The Council of Ten ended up pretty
much ruling the Republic of Venice, sticking their fingers into everything
from diplomacy to taxes."

I should have known she would have more historical knowledge
than the museum plaque. She possessed an encyclopedic mind for ancient stuff, constantly reading dull archeological magazines that made

National Geographic look as exciting as *Playboy*. And I don't mean that because of the half-naked pictures. The *National Geographic* ones, that is.

I said, "Yeah, well, it looks like it started the same way our own Oversight Council did. Protection of the state from an external threat, and operating in secret. Something to think about."

She said, "So you finally admit history has something to teach us about the future."

In mock surprise I said, "Of course I do. I love it when we go look at fossilized poop and pottery shards."

She gave me her disapproving-teacher glare and I said, "Let's head back to the hotel. See if the guys found anything from the surveillance cameras. We're getting nothing from this place in person, and I'd really like to know if Jacob's history here has anything to do with the future he's planning."

We'd hit the ground late last night and gone straight into action, trying to make up for the lost time we'd spent rescuing Shoshana. I didn't regret that decision at all, but it was a Solomon's choice, and Kurt had made it clear that the Oversight Council felt it was a mistake, especially if saving her had taken away our ability to stop an Islamic State attack.

Initially I didn't really worry about what they thought, because choices always had to be made in this line of work, and I had been convinced that the Lost Boys could wait. After our investigations last night, my confidence was starting to evaporate.

The Lost Boys were using their true passports, and the Taskforce had given us a hotel they were using, which had made necking down the room they were in child's play. Retro had repeated the actions he'd taken in Tirana, penetrating the hotel servers of a Best Western, and had identified a lone room. Aaron and Shoshana had done the breaking in.

Using them may have seemed counterintuitive, but a B&E wasn't risk-free, and I wanted a throwaway team in case they were burned and no longer useful for surveillance. They were exploiting Venice as nothing more than a clean break from Tirana, and would be gone tomorrow. I decided to keep my team fresh, with a heat state at zero.

Having them here at all had been a little bit of a fight. I'd had a debate with Kurt on their exfiltration, wanting them to fly with me instead of taking commercial transport, and, after much back-and-forth, he'd finally agreed. They needed to vacate Tirana as quickly as we did, and I didn't want them getting stopped by Albanian gestapo trying to board some broken-down aircraft in Tirana. The only other option had been going out with Showboat and the support crew, which—given they were transporting Rashid to Taskforce detainee operations—wasn't really an option. Kurt had said they could fly with me to Venice, but were to break free from there. He hadn't given me a time, so I figured using them for a final op was okay.

They'd done the B&E, first using a RadarScope—a motion detector that could see through walls—to determine the room was empty, then an ingenious device made of coiled wire and a metal rod that slipped under the door and manipulated the door handle from the inside. Since hotel room doors were designed to prevent someone from locking themselves in, they always opened when pulled from the inside, regardless of the locks in place. We could have hacked the key-card, but such access left a digital trail in the database at reception, something we wanted to avoid.

They'd spent less than five minutes in the room and had found three interesting things, the first two telling me my decision in Tirana may have caused mission failure on finding the Lost Boys in time.

One, the room had no luggage. It still had a DO NOT DISTURB sign on the door handle, and a sleeping pallet on the floor, along with a mussed bed and dirty towels, but no clothes, toothbrushes, or anything else.

Two, the minibar had been cleaned out, empty of all liquor and candy bars. It was something a juvenile would do if he were vacating early.

The Lost Boys still had another two days on their reservation, and the credit card used was valid, so put together, it told me they had moved somewhere else. The fact that their passport trail ended here, along with the two extra days on the hotel reservation, caused a disconcerting feeling, reminding me of a last covered and concealed location before an assault: a last clean staging area before going underground, and quite possibly the final spot before an attack. I prayed that wasn't the case.

The third thing they found was a ticket stub for the Doge's Palace museum with Jacob Driscoll's name on the tag. It was a really weak link, and may have been nothing more than a way for Jacob to waste some time, but it was all we had. I'd directed Retro to get with the Task-force and hack into the surveillance cameras while Jennifer and I went to check it out in person. That had proven of little value, other than the history lesson of the Council of Ten.

Exiting into Piazza San Marco, Jennifer could sense a little desperation leaking out. Worry that my decision on Shoshana may end up costing much more than saving a single life.

She took my arm and said, "Hey, you made the right call. No matter what happens. We can't always be the ones on the X. We do what we can, and in this case, we did right."

I said, "Tell that to whoever feels the wrath of the Lost Boys. I'll be willing to bet they'd disagree."

"Shoshana wouldn't."

I turned to her and said, "You sure? Because I'm afraid to ask that question."

She said nothing, knowing, like I did, that while Shoshana was certainly happy to be alive, she would never want to be the reason for a terrorist strike succeeding.

I'd made my decision, and could do nothing to alter the past. All I could do was my best to prevent a specific future. The one the Lost Boys had planned.

74

We wound our way through the alleys, reaching the small bed-and-breakfast we'd rented for our op center, situated right on a canal full of gondolas. Like that was anything fancy. Having a canal location in Venice was about as special as a Motel 6 next to a McDonald's in the States.

We'd rented rooms in several different hotels to disperse our footprint, and we'd decided on this one for a TOC due to its central location. That and the fact that it had a room that was bigger than a pizza box.

I entered and found Retro banging away on a keyboard, Knuckles behind him on a phone saying, "We need a name. Can't you guys figure that out?"

Aaron and Shoshana were off to a side, sitting patiently. Brett was nowhere to be found.

I closed the door and waited for Knuckles to hang up the phone. He did, looking at me with a question. I said, "Nothing. Not sure what I expected to find, but it's just a damn museum. No signs saying 'Secret Islamic State Mission' or anything like that."

He nodded and said, "Well, we've got something. It's a thread, but we can't find the end to pull it."

"What?"

Retro leaned back and said, "Take a look. Taskforce ran all the surveillance footage on the date stamp of the ticket through a facial recognition suite. They found the Lost Boy called Jacob."

Jennifer and I leaned over, seeing his laptop screen split into four sections, a different camera view in each. In one, the subject was turned, facing the camera head-on. It was grainy, but I could make out Jacob from his mug shot. Even with the pixilated image, he gave off an evil vibe. He just looked bad, reminding me of a pus-filled wound.

I said, "And? You've got his entire visit?"

"Yeah."

"So where's the secret dead drop? What was he doing there?"

"Nothing at the museum. That wasn't his focus. He was following someone."

"Who?"

Retro manipulated the screen, flipping through a dozen camera feeds until he found the recording he wanted. He hit play and a man and woman walked across the marble floor, arm in arm, jerking in grainy black and white. "These two. No idea why, but he sticks with them the entire time. At first we thought it might just be a coincidence—you know, one tourist following the path of another—but he took pictures. He used his camera probably fifteen times, and not once did he take a picture of something artsy-fartsy or old in a room. Every time, he took it of those two."

I leaned in closer to the screen, as if that would help me ascertain what was going on. Jennifer said, "Who are they?"

Knuckles said, "Don't know. We got nothing on the man. He's a dead end. He bought his ticket from the booth out front and showed no ID. The girl we have a slim lead on. She presented a ticket purchased from a package tourism site in a hotel, printed out from a computer. We have the hotel, but no names. Assuming one or both are staying there, we're working to neck it down now. Brett's at the hotel."

I said, "What is Jacob doing? Why the follow? I'm assuming they aren't important?"

"Not that we can see. I mean, they have no overt personal security, and appeared to be skulking around like secret lovers—which they might be. The man showed up *after* the woman, and they met inside. Also, like I said before, they bought their tickets from different locations. It was coordinated, but not enough to be what normal tourists would do. Why not meet outside and go in together? Why buy tickets from different places? It doesn't make any sense."

"To us. I promise it makes sense to Jacob. So what do we have on the woman?"

"Making some assumptions—the biggest one being she's staying in that hotel—we came up with four possible names."

Knuckles interjected, saying, "I told Retro to focus on single American women. I know that may be way off, but it's a start. Out of that four, Brett's checking with the hotel to see if we can get it down to one."

"With what?"

Knuckles sheepishly looked at Retro, then Jennifer. "Ahh . . . boob size."

Stupidly, I said, "What?"

Jennifer rolled her eyes and said, "Tell me the world's foremost counterterrorism team isn't really tracking someone by the size of their breasts."

Knuckles held up his hands and said, "It was Shoshana's idea. She watched the tapes. And she's right. The chick has really big tits. I'm not kidding. Retro, pull up that one—"

Jennifer cut him off, saying, "I don't need to see it. Shoshana?"

Shoshana was grinning, leaning forward with her hands under her chin, elbows on knees, thoroughly enjoying the conversation. Aaron seemed a little amused himself.

She said, "Jennifer, have you seen a female concierge here?"

"No."

"And what happened at your hotel? When you checked in?"

I saw where she was going, because I'd witnessed the jerk's actions at the concierge desk. I said, "He burned a hole in her ass."

Shoshana nodded, breaking into a smile. "Very good, little Jedi. Same thing happened to me."

I said, "It's 'young Jedi,' if you're going to use an American reference."

She ignored me and said, "Jennifer, did you look at the picture?"

Jennifer shook her head with disdain. "No. I don't need to see another woman's breasts."

"Hey, me either. At least that's what I tell Aaron. Take a look. No way will any concierge miss them. Trust me. This is the quickest way."

Everyone was grinning at that point, really enjoying the subject matter. Knuckles pulled up the picture in question, one where she was leaning over to offer her ticket, her scarf falling away, and I'll be damned if Shoshana wasn't right. She looked like she was schlepping around a couple of volleyballs, and she wasn't afraid of showing them off.

I said, "So we have a biometric identifier, and Brett's running it to ground."

Jennifer said, "Wow. Like we're tracking DNA."

Shoshana said, "Jennifer, it's just as real as a fingerprint. Want me to show you?"

Jennifer bristled, aggravated at the sexual harassment, but not knowing what to do with it, coming from a female. The guys felt it too, now uncomfortable themselves. The joke fell flat, as often happened with that little devil woman. I started to say something, and Shoshana stood up, speaking first.

She ignored all the men in the room, focusing on Jennifer. "I apologize. After your sacrifice, that was callous. I know why I'm walking the earth. I owe you my life, and I will never forget that. The Lost Boys will not succeed. I promise."

Now it was really awkward. I said, "Shoshana, stop that. We did what anyone would have done. Don't make this into something it's not. I don't need some death wish from you to repay a nonexistent favor."

She said, "I have seen the mission profile. I know my life has now put others in jeopardy. You have it whether you want it or not."

The comment made me realize where she was going. The chips she was stacking in my corner, waiting to be repaid. I didn't need that here. I said, "Shoshana, you and Aaron are out. Done. You can't continue on with me."

She simply smiled. I looked at Aaron and said, "Hey, man, you guys have to get out of here. Get back to the kibbutz or whatever else you guys do in Israel. No more with me. I'll get my ass kicked for using you here in the first place."

He said, "Pike, I know. We will leave. But Shoshana may make me go where you go."

"Screw that. Jesus. Go home. Or wherever you top secret Mossad types go. Scandinavia. Paris. I don't care."

Aaron said, "I need a vacation. Maybe we'll stay in Italy. Maybe Tuscany or Rome."

Aaron looked at Shoshana, and she nodded. I could smell the connection coming off of them. Weirdest thing in the world. A lesbian and a straight guy, both paid assassins in the employ of Israel. I couldn't make it up if I tried.

I said, "That's perfect. Get on the train to Rome."

The door to the room opened, and Brett entered, all triumphant. "Got her! Big tits and all!"

The witticism didn't work like he wanted. He saw the somber mood and said, "What's going on?"

I said, "Nothing. What do you have?"

"Her name is Christine Spalding, and she's done with Venice. I have no idea what she has to do with the Lost Boys, but it's definitely her."

"What do you mean she's done with Venice?"

"According to the front desk—who remembers her very well—she bought a train ticket. She's out of here."

"Where's she going?"

"Rome. And she's not 'going.' She left. An hour ago."

I glared at Shoshana, wondering how the hell she'd known what was going to happen. She took Aaron's hand in her own and squeezed it, then gave me her disembodied stare. He looked at me with pity.

She said, "I had no idea where this was leading, but I'm not changing my vacation destination. Someone is going to pay for me being alive. You know it and I know it. It will *not* be a stranger I've never met. And it will not be you, Nephilim Logan. It will never be you again."

75

From the back of the cabin, Jacob Driscoll watched the woman get on the train. Watched her load her luggage. Watched her fiddle around, getting comfortable, and wondered if she knew none of that mattered. She was dead.

He actually felt a little sorry for her. She hadn't done anything to deserve this. All she owned was a large set of breasts, and she'd plied them into a vacation in Venice. Unfortunately, those same assets she'd flashed at countless nightclubs, gaining nothing more than a free drink for a grope, were now going to cause her death.

He wished she'd taken a different path. All she had to do was go back to America, taking her lumps of rejection with her. The flight alone would have been long enough to ensure the success of his mission. Instead, she'd purchased a ticket to Rome.

He had no doubt she would attempt to make contact with Chris, and in so doing, she sealed her fate.

He'd spent the night in Chris's room, conducting online checkout and tidying up various email contacts through Chris's computer, informing the church and his family that he'd dropped his phone in a toilet and it no longer functioned. A partial truth.

Jacob had made sure that Carlos and Devon were on the first train leaving for Rome, using the forged passports and tickets from the boys, then spent the morning sitting in the lobby. Watching and waiting.

He'd decided that if she didn't show, he would leave tonight, assuming she'd given up. Just before noon, she'd approached the front desk, and he saw she wasn't the bimbo she appeared to be. She was both determined and smart, using guile, subterfuge, and an ample showing of cleavage to the concierge at Chris's hotel. Without disclosing why she was asking, camouflaging her important questions in the cloak of those less meaningful, she'd learned that Chris had "checked out," and had discovered the partner hotel in Rome where the church group had their next reservation. A reservation that would never be used.

He'd followed her from there, tracing her back to her hotel, where she'd purchased a ticket through her own concierge. To Rome.

She had no idea Chris was dead. And no idea that she was as well.

Sitting four seats behind her, Jacob wanted more than anything to kill her on the train, but he couldn't. He would have to wait for a better chance, and knew time wasn't on his side. He would have only a small window before she caused trouble.

He settled back into his seat and closed his eyes.

Omar knocked on the door and heard shuffling inside. He waited, letting Jacob use the peephole. The door opened, and he found himself looking at Carlos. Instantly suspicious, he said, "Where's Jacob?"

"Still in Venice." Carlos handed him a letter. "He told me to give you this."

Omar opened it, saying, "Get my bags. Careful with the last two."

Carlos shouted at Devon, then went into the hallway, lugging in a large, hard-sided suitcase. Devon followed with another. Omar pretended to read the note, but in reality assessed the pair of *shahid*. They showed no outward signs of deception, displaying fawning grins and gangly struggles with the bags. He turned to the note.

It was short and to the point. Jacob was tracking a woman connected to the identity of the man Omar was to assume. According to Jacob, she was a potential threat to the mission with a determination to find out what had happened to the church leader, and he was going to ensure she was eliminated. At the end of the note was a new cell phone number, purchased courtesy of the church leader's credit card. A clean one.

Omar crumpled the paper, wondering if it was real. Carlos came back to the door, bounced from one foot to the other, eyes downcast, then said, "We had no trouble getting in. The envelope was in the locker you said it would be."

Omar said, "And the guns? Were they here?"

"Yes. Two pistols and a sawed-off shotgun. Some bullets. Nothing more."

"That's fine. We shouldn't need them anyway. Those suitcases have the real weapons."

He pushed inside, getting off the cobblestone street and surveying his new home. Spartan, with a threadbare couch, a wooden kitchen table, one bedroom upstairs and one down. It would do.

Omar had coordinated for a contact in Georgia to rent an apartment from a service called AirBnB. Really just a clearinghouse on the web for people who wished to rent whatever space they had available, it listed everything from a tree house in Spain to a castle in Croatia. Anyone who wanted to list a room, no matter how small or strange, could do so. His contact had found a first-floor flat in the Trastevere area of Rome, south of Vatican City and just west of the Tiber River. He'd rented it for a month, placing the weapons in a closet and the keys to the flat in a locker in the train station. With no maid service or other bothersome intrusions, the apartment would work perfectly for the rehearsals they needed to conduct. But first, they had a more specific rehearsal.

Omar closed the door and said, "My identification? Do you have it?"

Devon appeared, holding an American passport. Omar opened it, seeing the name Chris Fulbright next to his picture. Looking closely, he could ascertain the damage to the passport, but it was slight. Something that might be noticed by a close examination, but he didn't expect that. The bigger issue was that the name wouldn't match his accent in any way whatsoever. He would have to hope for the blessed ignorance of the United States citizen, something he'd find out in the next thirty minutes.

Carlos said, "You want to clean up from your trip? We have hot water. It's not much, but it'll work for a single shower."

Omar said, "That can wait. We have to be at a rehearsal in twenty minutes. Are you two ready?"

They both nodded. Puppy dogs wanting to please the master. He said, "Put on a button-up shirt and slacks. It's time to start acting like altar boys."

Twenty minutes later they had taken a cab to Vatican City. They passed by the entrance to Piazza San Pietro, Saint Peter's Basilica off in the distance, and Omar saw the chairs being placed in the square. The preparations for the ceremony, and the Lost Boys' rendezvous with destiny. It made him smile.

The cab continued on, stopping in front of what looked like a small theater, the doors out front solid and large, but the paint old. A line of young men milled about in front.

Omar waited until the driver had pulled away before saying, "You know the church, correct? You can speak like a Catholic?"

Carlos said, "Yes, yes. We've memorized the mass. We know when to cross ourselves and when to kneel. We've memorized all of the canonical rites."

"Well, don't try to prove you're a genius at it. Just follow along. And whatever you do, let me speak. Don't try to outdo anybody. We're from a small parish in Florida. Act like that."

Devon said, "What about Jacob? What will we say?"

"He's at the hotel, sick. Let me handle that."

They crossed the street and Omar walked up to the first adult he could find, a priest with a clipboard shouting names. Omar introduced himself as Chris Fulbright, and the priest looked at his clipboard, confused. He went down it, then said, "Florida? Sacred Heart? That Chris Fulbright?"

"Yes. That's us."

The priest smiled, saying, "Sorry. You don't sound like you're from Florida."

Omar matched his grin, hoping it came out sincere. "I'm from Russia, but I'm an American citizen now."

"No worries. We weren't sure you guys were coming." He stuck out his hand, "Father Patrick Brimm, from New York. I'm the guy who's been put in charge of the American representatives for the ceremony, and we couldn't get you on the phone. You were supposed to check in yesterday. Almost scratched you. I've got twelve different parishes represented, and didn't have time to track you down."

Omar said, "I apologize. I dropped my cell phone into the water in Venice. I bought a new one, but didn't know I needed to pass the number. The schedule I had said today was the first day. We could have cut short our trip there if I'd have known."

Father Brimm waved his hand, dismissing the problem. "You aren't the only one. I'm still missing Alabama and Connecticut. They don't make this rehearsal, and their church paid for a trip to Italy for nothing."

Omar said, "So what do we need to do to catch up?"

"I need the passports for you and your boys. Need a photocopy of the page so Vatican security can run a background check."

"That's easy. There a copy machine around?"

"One inside."

Omar turned to go, then snapped his fingers. "Father, one of my boys is sick. He's in bed right now, at our hotel. I don't have his passport and didn't know you needed it."

"He's a no-go, then. Sorry. Security is an absolute. Crazies have threatened the Holy Father on a number of occasions. They won't bend the rules. This ceremony has people coming from all over the world, even members from the Archdiocese of Kirkuk in Iraq and parishes from Jordan and Lebanon. You can see why the security would be harsh."

Omar said, "You just need his information, right? You don't need an actual photocopy, do you? I can call him. I can get the information and give it to you with our photocopies. Please. He's traveled a long way. This is a special mission for him."

Father Brimm pursed his lips for a moment. He said, "If he's not here for the rehearsal, he can't go anyway. My rules. It wouldn't be fair to the others."

"We're here. How hard can it be? They conduct the ceremony, then we go single file up to the basilica, right? I could see if you had no one from the parish here, but we'll put him in between my other boys. Monkey see, monkey do."

Father Brimm relented, "Okay, okay. Stay for the rehearsal. If you get me the information before we leave today, I'll turn it in, but I can't promise they'll grant him approval. I don't know if the copy of the passport is a necessary requirement."

Omar let out his breath in relief. "Thank you. Venice was fun, but tomorrow's ceremony is the only reason he came."

Father Brimm smiled and said, "I don't suppose they'll be too afraid of an American from Florida. He hasn't been to Syria in the past six months, has he?"

Omar laughed and clapped the priest on the back. "Not that his passport shows."

76

"Sir, I don't know where they are. My gut tells me they've left Venice." The VPN connection on our laptop made Kurt Hale look a little like Max Headroom, with the small delay in the synchronization of the sound of his voice and the movement of his mouth adding to the effect. Behind him, I could see George Wolffe pacing back and forth. He was the deputy commander of the Taskforce, and an old CIA hand. It took a lot to ruffle his feathers, which wasn't a good sign.

Drily, Kurt said, "Your gut is not exactly something I can take back to the Council. Tell me you've got some thread to follow. Airline tickets, cell phone trace, something."

"I've got the woman. What's her story?"

"Christine Spalding. A copy girl at a Staples in a one-light town in Florida. That's it."

"Florida? Just like the Lost Boys?"

"Yeah, we thought the same thing, but there's no connection. She's East Coast, they're West Coast, up near the panhandle. We dug through her life six ways to Sunday. There is absolutely nothing connecting them other than being from the same state. I have a complete packet for you. Driver's license, credit reports, past residences, mother, father, the works. The only unique thing is she applied for the passport she's using less than six months ago. Before that, she'd never left the country."

"Same as the Lost Boys. That's an indicator. Anything on the man she was with?"

"No. We got nothing on him. We ran his surveillance picture through every database we have, and it didn't trigger. The credit card used for Christine's room was a pay-as-you-go. Nothing we can trace back; all we know is it's holding about a thousand dollars. Might be his, might be hers."

"She's got something to do with the Lost Boys. We're just missing the connection. If I leave right now, I can beat her train to Rome."

"Pike, we have a full-court press on them. Their passports are in every port of call and police station in Europe, and they haven't triggered. They're still within the scope of your team, and our assessment is that Venice is the endgame. I need you to stay in Venice, at least until the reservation runs out on the room. I need you to find them."

"Sir, we've been on it since we got here. I'm telling you they've left. They don't need to show a passport to travel throughout the EU by train."

"They came to Venice for a reason, and it wasn't to shop. We know that Omar al-Khatami was facilitating their attack, and we assess he intends to conduct a linkup in Venice."

"Sir, that makes no sense. Have you seen this place? I couldn't pick a worse location to pass explosives. You'd have to transfer them about forty times from plane, train, and boat, and then do the reverse to get back out. Why not meet in the countryside?"

George Wolffe leaned in, saying, "Tell him what we're hearing. Let him know the assessment."

That caused me to sit up. "Boss?"

Kurt said, "Pike, we've got intercepts from Syria. ISIS is talking about an attack in the next two days. One that will cause 'unimaginable harm to the heart of the infidel.' If the timeline's correct, they don't have the space to get to America and set up an attack. They're going to do it there, on the Continent, and it's going to be close to Venice. You've got the only anchor. Their hotel room."

I sat back, reflecting on what he'd said. In my heart, I believed that waiting in Venice was a waste of time, but I didn't *know*. If I was wrong, and the Lost Boys did meet Omar here, I'd be responsible for their killing spree.

The easy answer would be to just sit back and follow orders. Rotate the team through the hotel and run random patrols around the area, hoping to hit the jackpot. If the attack succeeded, I would have followed orders like a good soldier and it wouldn't be my fault.

At least that's what I told myself. Right up until Shoshana came into my mind's eye, with her saying someone would pay for her being alive, and *I* was responsible for that, when I'd chosen her over the Lost Boys. She was determined that it wouldn't be an innocent civilian, and she was headed to Rome. It wasn't much on the logic train, but it felt right, and it was enough to snap me out of my cowardly desire to just sit back and follow orders.

"Sir, I think they've already made linkup. I think I missed them with the Prairie Fire call for Shoshana. I let Omar get away, and at the same time let the Lost Boys slip through."

He said, "Pike, that's bullshit. We didn't know what Omar was up to until *after* your hit. We didn't know he was involved with the Lost Boys. Don't put that on yourself."

"The Lost Boys were still in Venice. I could have stopped them."

"And Shoshana would be dead. You made the call, and I stand by it. Shit, you're not the only game in town. I could have pulled Johnny's team out of Istanbul, but I didn't because I felt the same way you did. I didn't think the timing was critical, and pulling Johnny would have destroyed the mission he's executing. In hindsight, I should have, because his pissant target is just a financier—like Panda in Nairobi—but I didn't."

I appreciated the sentiment, but it didn't alter the facts, or my culpability in them. I said, "Let me go to Rome. I can beat the woman's train. She's connected. She's a thread to the target. We have two days, and the Lost Boys aren't here."

I saw him slowly shaking his head and pressed forward. "Sir, you saw the tapes. Jacob was following her. If she's in Rome, maybe he is too. Maybe that man with her is the contact for Omar. Maybe that's why they came to Venice."

He looked behind him and said, "George?"

I waited. George leaned into the screen, saying, "I don't know. Pike, how will you even find her? All we have is a name."

"She's no terrorist mastermind. Whatever she's doing, she's an unwitting linkage target. She'll pay with the same credit card. You can track that and tell me the hotel. Best case, she's there with the man in the picture. Even better, she's there with the Lost Boys."

He said, "Why don't you leave a footprint in Venice? If all you're going to do is interview the female?"

"I need my team. It's all or nothing. If I split forces, I won't be able to conduct an operation at either location. If I find something in Rome, I won't be able to action it. Yeah, I'm just interviewing a woman, but I have to be prepared to find Jackpot."

I saw him rub his face and knew I was losing the argument. I back-pedaled, remembering I had a team I could call on if I needed it, and they were already headed to Rome. "Okay, okay. I'll leave a two-man element here with eyes on the hotel. If I find something in Rome, I'll pull them in. If they trigger in Venice, I'll haul ass back here. Will that work?"

George said, "Can you execute with that timeline?"

I gave him the truth. "Probably not. You're asking me to split my forces until neither is capable."

He took that in, then said, "You feel strongly about this? Rome is the thread?"

"Yes."

He looked at Kurt and said, "Let him go." He returned to the screen, saying, "Billings hates his ass, which probably means he's right. We could use a little Pike magic on this. We're getting too close to the flame."

Kurt said, "Okay. Get in the air. I'll shoot you the credit card report as soon as I can."

I said, "Yes, sir," and reached my hand up to shut off the VPN, but Kurt cut me short.

He said, "Pike, if this decision is wrong, and we miss an attack because you're in Rome, we're done. There will be no justification."

I paused, my hand over the disconnect button for the call. I said, "Sir, there *never* is. Shoshana told me someone would pay for my time spent rescuing her. She knew the implications, just like we do. If it's any consolation, she said it wouldn't be me."

I saw his eyes narrow, and he said, "Shoshana? What do you mean it won't be you? What the hell does she have to do with this?"

"Nothing. And everything. She's hell-bent on preventing the Lost Boys from killing anyone. She feels it will be on her head. And she's in Rome."

"Rome? Doing what?"

"Making sure the payment for her rescue is given in terrorist blood."

77

Christine Spalding dropped her carry-on suitcase and flopped on the bed, exhausted from trying to find her way in a foreign country. The farthest she'd ever traveled was to Washington, DC, as a child, and the adventurous excitement of flying to Venice had fallen away, leaving the grimy smear of trying to work her way through train stops and foreigners who wanted nothing more than to pick her pocket. Or worse.

The decision to purchase a train ticket to Rome had been a monumental one, fraught with unknowns, not the least of which were Chris's actions to begin with. She had a paid ticket to the United States, courtesy of him, and would have used it, if only he'd bothered to say goodbye. She knew what she was, and had no illusions about her role in Chris's life—even as she fantasized otherwise—but his dropping her cold before any consummation of the relationship just seemed weird. Downright odd.

She'd decided to follow him. She knew it would be against his wishes, but, Lord, she'd flown all the way to Italy because he'd asked. The least she was owed was an explanation. She didn't care if the excuse was the wife, the church, or a simple illness, as the email stated. She just wanted some closure. After the enormous effort she'd put into getting here—vacation time off from work, buying clothes, the emotional distress of figuring out a foreign country—she deserved to know.

She lay on the bed, pondering her next move. She knew the hotel he was using, and could call it directly. If she could figure out how to make a damn call in Italy. Truthfully, she didn't have the energy to sort through the dialing procedures, talking to people who didn't speak English, and even if she had, she wanted to make the call from his lobby. Where he couldn't say no. Where he'd have to at least face her. She knew he had the ceremony tomorrow, and would probably be busy, but she was at least owed a face-to-face from the coward.

She'd already mapped the hotel, and it was only about a half mile away, across the Tiber River near Vatican City. She'd found herself a cheap boutique hotel right near the Spanish Steps and the best shopping in Rome. Proud of her use of the Internet, learning how to operate in a country foreign to everything she'd known, she was gaining confidence.

She decided to walk to his hotel, going through the shopping district on the way. It was late in the afternoon, but the stores would be open. It would give her time to decide on what she was going to say. How she was going to take the rejection, which she knew was coming.

She sat up and popped the top on a bottle of water, knowing she'd end up paying for it. This hotel was on her dime—her credit card—but she didn't mind. She was seeing the world, with or without Chris.

She stood up, looking at herself in the mirror and wondering if it was something she'd done, when her hotel phone rang, startling her.

She answered.

"Yes, this is room service. We've been to your door twice, and nobody answers. Do you wish the dinner you ordered?"

"I didn't order any food. I just got here."

"Is this room three forty-two? Gustavos Bittering?"

"No. I'm in room four nineteen. It wasn't me."

"So sorry, madame. Forgive the intrusion."

She hung up the phone, happy that the man on the other end at least spoke English with an accent she could understand. She stood up, putting on her scarf.

Jacob disconnected his cell and said, "Room four nineteen. We should go right now. Take her in the hotel."

Omar leaned back and said, "I'm not sure. What can she do before the ceremony? I'm thinking we let her run amok. Trying to kill her now may be more trouble than it's worth."

"That's a mistake. She's determined, and she's not an idiot. I think she smells something wrong. If she confirms it, she's going to raise an alarm, and we'll show up tomorrow to an arrest."

Omar said, "But that would be better than being a *shahid*, no?"

Jacob smiled at the insult from their earlier conversation and said, "Same as you. Same as you."

On the train, an hour out of Rome, Jacob's new phone had rung, and Omar had demanded he provide the passport information from Fart Boy, the kid he'd killed and assumed the identity of. He'd given it, then provided Omar the rundown of his fears with the woman. Jacob heard the suspicion in Omar's voice, but had no time for it. He agreed to call when he arrived, and hung up. He spent the rest of the train ride alternately thinking of his future and the mission. Deciding what he would demand from Omar.

After they'd arrived in Rome, he'd exited the train rapidly, before the woman could identify him, and waited. She'd finally appeared, clearly lost. He'd followed her back and forth, aimlessly wandering about looking for an exit, then eventually out of the train station, getting into the cab line right behind her. When his cabby had asked, "Where to?" he'd actually uttered the most trite thing imaginable. "Follow that cab."

He'd identified where she was staying, then had the cab drop him off in Trastevere. Not wanting anyone to be able to reconstruct his movements, he exited four blocks away from the safe house, paying the cab with Chris Fulbright's credit card. He'd found a pub called the Mate Bar just outside of the American John Cabot University and called Omar.

Omar had arrived with a small duffel bag and a large amount of hostility. Jacob had explained where they stood. The risk of the woman, but more than that, he told Omar the thoughts that had been plaguing his mind. Where his dedication lay. What he wanted.

Omar had opened up the duffel and showed the hilt of a sawed-off shotgun. He'd said, "Remember what we talked about in Istanbul. The attack is tomorrow. You are with the Islamic State, or not. Are you with me?"

Jacob had said, "I am with you. With *you*. I will not be a *shahid*. My life is worth more than that. Just as yours is. You can send Devon and Carlos to their deaths, and they'll do it willingly. I will not."

Omar had leaned back, saying, "What does that mean, *with* me?"

"It means I'm better than the others. I'm not cannon fodder. You know it. You told me that very thing. I want to work for you. I want to be your second in command. We'll do the mission tomorrow, and we'll succeed, but I won't be the man killing the target. I'll control it, and I'll get out, just like you. From there, we'll take the fight to whomever you want."

He'd seen Omar's face cloud, and wondered if he'd pushed too far. But he didn't really care. He'd made his decision. He was better than a *shahid*, and all that mattered was whether Omar agreed. If he didn't, they'd wrestle for the shotgun. If he did, they'd move forward.

He'd waited. Omar had tapped his fingers on the table, his cobalt eyes on Jacob. Finally, he'd said, "You wish to move into leadership of the Islamic State? You, who have never shown any allegiance to Islam?"

"No. I wish to work under you, and you alone. If it supports the Islamic State, so be it. Religion means little to me. It's just a method for people to justify their actions, which is why I have no trouble killing the Christian tomorrow. I've seen what he causes."

Omar had studied him, then said, "We'll take this one step at a time. You won't have to martyr yourself tomorrow, but it's not for the reasons you state. I can't guarantee you can get in, so I've already thought about altering the plan. Devon and Carlos have confirmed seats, and are rehearsing with the explosives right now, but because we didn't have your passport, because you were on this chase after the female, we may not get you cleared for security. We'll find out tomorrow."

"If I hadn't, the only thing promised to Devon and Carlos would be handcuffs when they show up. She needs to be killed."

"But we lose the propaganda. Carlos and Devon were going to eliminate his personal security, giving you space for your speech prior to the final explosion. Now it'll have to be quick, and the speech will be done on the Internet, after the fact, competing with others wanting credit."

"It can't be helped. I didn't make the woman up. And there are ways to ensure they know who did the attack. Evidence we can leave. You and I."

"Do you even know her room?"

Jacob had picked up his cell phone, saying, "I will shortly."

78

Sitting with Jennifer and Brett outside of the hotel, I waited for the cell to connect. After three rings, I heard Shoshana say, "Well, that didn't take too long. Did you miss me?"

She sounded nonchalant, but I knew she'd been waiting. She'd probably been sitting in a hotel room staring at her phone, begging it to ring.

I said, "I've had a little downsizing to my team. I had to leave Knuckles and Retro in Venice, and I could use some additional muscle here in Rome."

"That sounds interesting. Does it involve the busty woman?"

I laughed. "Exactly. I have her room, and I could use a female touch. Meet me at the outdoor café on Via Veneto. Right outside the Hotel Imperiale."

She said she was five minutes away, and hung up. I turned to Jennifer, "I want you and Shoshana to talk to her. Be nice—you know, girl talk. I don't think she's involved in whatever the Lost Boys are up to, but she's tied somehow. There's way too much smoke around her."

We'd landed a little over an hour ago, and, because we were leaving a huge trail flying all over the place without a whole lot of justification for Grolier Recovery Services, I'd asked Kurt for the use of a safe house instead of checking into another hotel.

We had them in every major city, rented from about four hundred different cutouts, but we rarely occupied them. A safe house was supposed to be just that: safe. If you used it every two weeks, you tended to draw attention to it, and risked compromise. In this case, I deemed our heat state from flying all over the world a justifiable reason not to splash our names into yet another hotel registry.

He'd agreed, and gave us a sweet two-story flat located in the north of the city in Municipio III, about two miles north of the old Urbe airport, a general aviation facility that made it pretty convenient for the rock-star bird. Even better, the house came with a dented four-door Fiat clown car in a roll-up garage.

No sooner had we moved our luggage in than Kurt had called, saying that Christine had used her credit card to check into the Hotel Imperiale. The strange thing was she'd used *her* card. Not the pay-as-you-go card. Stranger still, the pay-as-you-go card had *also* been used, once at a store in Venice, and today at a cab company—in Rome. Kurt was running down what the other purchase was for, but the Rome connection was enough smoke to get everyone's blood pumping. Now I hoped Jennifer and Shoshana could find the fire.

Jennifer said, "What if she doesn't want to talk?"

"If she stonewalls, go good cop/bad cop on her. Shoshana will have no trouble being the bad cop. If she really clams up, give us a shout. Brett and I will be right here for some extra intimidation. Either way, we're getting something out of her."

Brett said, "I see the little killer coming."

The café we were in was a literal glass house built right on the sidewalk, allowing anyone to stop and stare as you ate your food. I don't know who thought that was a great idea, but it allowed me to turn around and see Aaron and Shoshana walking past the metro station to the south, headed our way. They came abreast and I tapped on the glass, letting them see us.

They came inside, with Aaron saying, "Shoshana told me on the train you'd call. I didn't believe her."

"Well, I hadn't planned on it, but circumstances with my higher command forced me to make a choice, and I figured Shoshana here would want a crack at the target. Get her off Jennifer."

I glanced at her, proud of my jab, only to find her ignoring me, staring intently out the window instead.

I heard Jennifer say, "Pike, the target just walked out of the hotel. She's headed north."

I whipped my head around and saw Christine strolling up the street, carrying a large purse and looking like every other tourist out for an evening walk.

"Shit. Okay, okay, we follow her to see what she's up to. If she's just wandering around, seeing the sights, Jennifer and Shoshana will interdict on her line of march."

Jennifer nodded, and I looked at Shoshana for confirmation. She was still staring out the window, and I saw the dark angel appear. In the span of an instant she went from smiling to radiating so much violence it was like feeling heat from a bonfire.

I followed her gaze, confused as to why Christine would provoke such a response, and then saw the engine driving her rage. Omar al-Khatami and the Lost Boy Jacob were on the street. And they were following Christine.

Walking up the avenue, tourist map in hand, Christine ran through her head what she was going to say to Chris on the phone, trying to develop an answer for every conceivable way he could try to avoid coming to the hotel lobby. She wasn't leaving until she had her face-to-face. She was owed that, even if his answer was a blunt *Go away*.

She'd even considered threatening him with exposure, but she quickly discarded that idea. It wasn't in her to be vindictive, and she knew she was just as culpable as he was. There was no way she could bring herself to expose their illicit relationship—especially since it had never been officially consummated.

And that was the ugly elephant in the room. Chris had paid for her to fly all the way to Italy, and she'd known all along there was a price. She was willing to pay it, in fact was looking forward to it, and then Chris had disappeared with nothing more than an email. It wasn't like him, and, as much as she was afraid of rejection, she was secretly petrified that something was terribly wrong.

She reached the top of the famed Spanish Steps, the dying sunlight illuminating a mass of people in the square below, vendors scurrying among the crowd hawking flowers and chances to use a selfie stick. She paused, taking in the scene and wishing she had a camera.

She looked at her map, planning her route to Chris's hotel through the shopping district beyond the square. She pinpointed her location, then went down the steps, trying to ignore the aggressive sales techniques. She reached the bottom and was literally cornered by two young men trying to sell her flowers, or maybe trying to get something else.

Mildly alarmed, she stuck her hand in her purse, saying, "No, no, no," while she fished for her small bottle of pepper spray. She eventually convinced them, and they let her go on her way, but she kept her hand in her purse.

She walked down the first street she found, lined with high-end stores selling things she could never afford, but that wouldn't stop her from looking.

79

Shoshana stood and I clamped my hand on her wrist, saying, "Don't." She snarled something unintelligible and tried to pull her hand free. I feared she was going to run out of the café and launch herself onto Omar's back. I torqued her wrist, bringing her back into her chair.

She fought me, leaning over the table in an effort to break free, knocking a glass of water to the floor. I said, "Shoshana, no. Not here. Not now. You can't do anything on the streets of Rome."

The dark angel glared back, wanting to hurt me. The twisted thing was greater than I'd ever seen, and I had no doubt she'd kill me if she could. Aaron reached over and touched her shoulder, then whispered something in Hebrew into her ear. Like a wave receding, the potential violence dissipated and Shoshana appeared. I let go of her wrist just as the waitress came over.

Speaking to the waitress, but keeping my eye on Shoshana, I said, "Sorry for the mess. Can we get the check?"

The waitress glanced at both of us, then dropped a towel on the floor. Brett said, "I got it. Please, the check."

She left and I said, "Shoshana, you brought us here, now let me finish it."

She bored into me, reading my intent in her peculiar way, then slowly nodded. Still looking at her, I said, "Brett, Jennifer, hit the street. Eyes on, loose follow."

They stood and Shoshana said, "I go with them."

I said, "No, you don't. If there's anyone who's burned, it's you. Brett and Jennifer are clean. He never saw them in the assault. Aaron and me, less so. We can probably get away with a limited action. You, on the other hand, are completely useless here."

"I'm not going to sit here while that fuck walks the earth."

Jennifer began configuring her phone and putting in her earpiece. Brett said, "What's the end state?"

"Find a bed-down. Find the nest of vipers."

"You providing backup?"

"Yeah, it'll be me and Aaron. We'll be on the street right behind you. First, I've got to get Knuckles and Retro's asses down here, and to do that I need to get the rock-star bird to Venice. I just hope the pilot isn't out boozing."

Brett nodded in his calm way and turned to go. I touched his arm. "Don't lose them. This is it."

He said, "Have some faith. At least you don't have Jennifer wearing a Rastaman wig."

I smiled and said, "Keep an eye on her. When shit gets bad, she has a tendency to climb things like a cat running up a tree."

He grinned at her and said, "She'll only do that if I'm running away." He returned to me. "And I'm not running away. We clear on the rules of engagement? He's DOA, right?"

He was referring to a small rule the Taskforce had, called Dead or Alive, meaning the target was such a significant threat we were authorized to kill him instead of capture him. It wasn't my call to make, and required a sanction from the Oversight Council. I was kicking myself for not setting that up beforehand, in the long discussions with Kurt. I made the decision anyway.

"Yeah. He's DOA. He poses a threat to the team, you take him out, but *only* if you have to. I want that bed-down. Killing them might not stop the attack, and the other Lost Boys are out there."

They turned to go and I caught Jennifer's arm. "You heard that discussion, right?"

She nodded. I said, "No mercy. They pose a threat to you, don't think about the mission. Don't think about finding the other Lost Boys like you did in Jordan. You plant those fuckers. You understand?"

She glanced at Shoshana and said, "I got it."

They turned to go and Shoshana said, "So I'm supposed to sit here doing nothing while your lover kills that scum?"

I said, "No, you get to drive our vehicle. Track us. It's a really cool Fiat. You'll like it."

She glared at me and I tossed her the keys, saying, "It's about a block back, crammed into a spot the size of a loaf of bread. Bring it up here and stand by."

She stormed off and Aaron said, "I don't think antagonizing her right now is the smartest course of action."

I said, "I've got a lot of phone calls to make. Why don't you ensure she doesn't run anyone over?"

He left, and I began dialing, going through a million operational what-ifs in my head.

80

Jennifer kept eyes on Jacob, tracing behind him as he and Omar went down the Spanish Steps and into the shopping district, following Christine Spalding. Twenty minutes had passed, and the sun was rapidly setting. With the close confines of the buildings, they'd be in the dark soon, and she was now having questions.

She'd seen their mannerisms, and they clearly had something nefarious in store for Christine Spalding, and yet she'd failed to ask Pike about Christine's status. The key was the bed-down, but would they allow the terrorists to capture Christine—if that's what they planned—and then follow all of them, or would they interdict to prevent it? Or worse, if they attacked Christine, would they allow that to continue in order to locate the viper's nest?

She turned to Brett, who was pretending to look at a rack of expensive watches in a window. "Hey, she's on the street again, and they're still behind."

He glanced their way and said, "Man, she really likes to shop. This must be your dream follow."

She smiled and he began walking, keeping pedestrians between him and the target. She matched his pace and said, "Brett, hey, what are we going to do if they try to interdict her? Are we going to stop it, or just watch?"

He continued walking, the dusk setting in at a rapid pace, but the crowds on the street getting bigger. The pedestrian-only lane made keeping tabs on the terrorists both easy and hard. Easy because they could blend in. Hard because it allowed them to do the same.

Brett said, "We don't need to worry about that. Unless she does something stupid, there's no way they'll attempt anything in this atmosphere."

And then she did something stupid. She left the main thoroughfare, entering a smaller cobblestone street. The area wasn't nearly as crowded as the original avenue, but there were still groups of pedestrians shopping for discounts off the beaten path.

She walked about a hundred meters, then paused in front of a store, using the light from a window to read her map. She looked up at the street sign embedded in the brick, then right, down a narrow alley.

Brett said, "Don't do it. Don't do it."

She turned the corner, leaving the pedestrians behind for a shadow lane barely lit with tepid incandescent bulbs.

"Shit." Brett keyed his radio. "Pike, Pike, this is Blood. Busty's moved into an alley, cutting across the main streets. She's on a destination, but she's put herself at risk. What's the ROE for this? You still want a follow if we're not threatened?"

Jennifer let Omar and Jacob penetrate, then moved to the entrance of the alley, seeing Christine walking, oblivious to the wolves behind her, the lighting looking like something out of *The Exorcist*. She heard Pike answer through her earpiece, "What's the status? I need more information." She lost sight of the two terrorists in the shadows, but saw Christine appear in a light further down, stopping in the pool of illumination to look at her map.

She cut in, saying, "Pike, this is Koko. She's all by herself, and she's like a goat staked to a tree. She's going to get hurt."

"Keep up the follow. I've got you on my phone. I'm on the way right now."

She saw a shadow appear in the light, the two men having circled around the web of illumination, one on one side and one on the other. She said, "Brett! They're on her!"

She pulled her weapon from her purse and sprinted down the alley, hearing Brett on the radio say, "Shit. Pike, we're committed. Get your ass here."

She made it about fifty meters before she saw Jacob slam Christine into the wall, Omar pulling a knife. Jennifer shouted, and they both froze at the noise, looking her way. Christine dropped her purse, then brought something up, spraying Jacob in the face. He screamed and fell back onto the ground. Omar turned to the noise of Jennifer running and she saw a flash. *Gun.*

She jumped right, into the shadows of a building, hearing the snap of rounds. She took a knee and raised her own Glock. She saw Jacob roll upright, pulling a short-barreled weapon from a bag. Much larger than a pistol.

She heard the mechanical *snick* of suppressed rounds and felt Brett sliding to her left, pumping bullets down the alley. Her earpiece came alive with Pike shouting for information. She saw Jacob rise and thought of nothing but the front sight of her weapon. She squeezed the trigger. Jacob's weapon spit fire at the same time and she saw Christine thrown against the wall, then Jacob drop to the ground from her shots, screaming.

Omar fired again, then rolled backward, grabbing Jacob by the shirt and dragging him down the alley. She saw Jacob stand and begin hobbling, then both disappeared into the darkness.

She rose and sprinted forward, feeling more than seeing Brett on her left. She reached the splash of light and saw the carnage. Christine splayed out like a broken mannequin, her legs folded, one shoe off next to a can of pepper spray, her upper body against a roll-up metal door. And her right side pumping blood from a close-range shotgun blast.

She knelt down, putting her hand over the wound, hearing Brett running forward. He slid into the light on his knees, conducting triage of the rest of her body and talking softly to her. He nodded at Jennifer and she stood, letting him get to work with his medical skills. She stared down the alley and caught a glimpse of movement. She took off, talking into her earpiece.

"Pike, this is Koko, Christine's been shot. Brett's conducting trauma management, but she's hit bad. I'm moving south down the alley. I've lost lock-on of the targets."

Brett came on, "Pike, she's been hit with a shotgun. Looks like small shot, maybe nine-shot. Maybe bigger, but it was close-range. No arterial bleeding, but she's losing fluids. Need exfil immediately."

Bouncing from shadow to shadow, Jennifer heard Pike's voice come on. The calm one. He said, "Standby. Working exfil with Shoshana. Stabilize and prepare for movement. Who's on the target now?"

Jennifer said, "Me. Koko. But I can't see them. I've lost them. I'm just following down the alley."

"I see your position on my phone. Hold what you got. Hold up. Looking now, and there are about five ways they can get out. Or ambush you."

"Pike, they're going to get away."

"Got it. They'll still get away after they put a bullet in you. Stand by. Break, break—Brett, I can't get Shoshana to you down that alley. She's on the road you left to get in it. You see headlights to the east? Should be flashing."

"Yeah. I see 'em."

"That's your exfil. Can you CASEVAC to that location?"

"Yeah, yeah. I can do it. She ain't that heavy."

"Do so. Break—break—Koko, pull back to Brett. Exfil with the casualty. Give him a hand. Aaron and I are circling on foot. We'll try to interdict. Be on call for linkup."

Leaning against a wall, hidden in the shadows, Jennifer started to object, then realized he was right. She was asking to get killed hunting blindly in the dark.

She sprinted back to the pool of light, seeing Brett ripping strips of Christine's jacket and shoving them into the wound. She saw the blood coming out, Christine's eyes rolled back into her head, and felt sick.

81

Out of the line of fire, Omar dragged Jacob down yet another alley, thinking of nothing but getting away. He'd made multiple lefts and rights to confuse whoever was after them, but in doing so he had become hopelessly lost. They reached a main thoroughfare and he realized he was still openly carrying his pistol. He shoved it into his waistband, then pushed a struggling Jacob into a stairwell, sitting him down.

"Where are you hit?"

Curling into a ball, his eyes and nose running freely from the pepper spray, Jacob said, "My groin. My groin. Shit, it hurts."

Omar pulled Jacob's hands away, looking for the wound. He saw torn clothing and a smattering of blood, but no significant trauma. He unbuttoned Jacob's pants and pulled them aside.

The hipbone was swollen and red, surrounded by small lacerations and bits of metal, but no hole, and no gout of blood that should have been there. Omar reached into Jacob's right front pocket and pulled out a mass of broken metal and plastic. Jacob's cell phone.

He laughed for the first time. "Young lion, you may not believe in Allah, but He believes in you."

"How bad? How bad is it?"

Omar held the cell phone in the light. "You'll have a massive bruise, but the bullet ricocheted off of your phone. It didn't penetrate."

Jacob wiped his nose and eyes, incredulous. Omar grabbed his arm, saying, "Get up. We're still being hunted."

Omar helped him out of the stairwell, then leaned him against the wall of rough brick, saying, "Wait here." He walked to the mouth of the alley and surveyed the street, his head on a swivel attempting to spot his pursuers. He came back, saying, "There's a taxi stand fifty meters to the south. Walk as normally as possible. Lean on me, but make it look like you're drunk instead of injured."

Forty minutes later, they crossed the Tiber River and exited once again in front of the Mate Bar.

Omar said, "Can you walk from here?"

"Yeah. If the house isn't too far away."

"Just a few blocks."

They set out, once again going through narrow cobblestone alleys, moving in silence. Eventually, Jacob said, "What do you think?"

"I don't know, honestly. On the one hand, I'd say the Israelis are still after me, but the attack in the alley makes no sense. How would they know we were going there? *I* didn't even know it until you arrived."

Jacob said, "It's the girl. They were following the girl. That's the only thing that makes sense."

"But how would the Israelis know her? And if they did, why not interdict her in Venice?"

Jacob shook his head, remaining quiet.

Omar said, "Did you kill her?"

"I think so. I was close, and it was a shotgun, but I was hit right after. I dropped the gun and didn't get off another shot."

Omar said, "Doesn't matter. She's definitely wounded, and I doubt the Israelis even remained behind to help. I wouldn't have, given the complication of taking her to a hospital. She'll spend the rest of the night fighting for her life. If the police get to question her, it will be about the shooting. Not about what she's doing in Italy."

Jacob said, "So you think continuing with the attack is smart? Seriously? After that shootout?"

"Yes, I do. Think about it: If they knew the target, why try to interdict us in the street? Why not just wait until tomorrow? The crusaders are famous for sting operations, not random shootouts."

"Maybe. Or maybe they planned on getting us tomorrow, but we caused them to jump the gun."

"That doesn't explain why they were following the girl. If they knew everything about us, they would have just swept in. No, they were following her because they know we exist, but not what we intend to do."

They reached Via del Moro and Omar held up. Jacob said, "What?"

"The house is right down the street. No reason to walk into a trap."

"But you just said you thought we were still safe."

"I believe it, right up until it proves untrue. Wait here."

Omar left him and went quietly down the street, searching for a hidden enemy. He saw nothing. He circled down the small alley behind the apartment, moving past rubbish bins and stabbing the barrel of his pistol into every shadow. He reached the back of the flat and saw the flicker of a television, then Carlos move in front of it. He hid his pistol and retreated back to Jacob.

"We're good."

They walked straight up to the front door, Omar first knocking before using a key. The door swung open and Devon was standing in the foyer, his face white.

Omar immediately withdrew his pistol, whispering, "What is it?"

Devon closed the door and said, "Our pictures are all over the news. Me, Jacob, Hussein, and Carlos. Old mug shots from Florida."

82

The doctor came out of the bedroom and said, "She's stable, but sedated. She'll be out for a while."

I said, "Doc, I really need to talk to her. She's the key to a terrorist attack, maybe within the next twenty-four hours."

"Mr. Logan, I don't know what to tell you. Get some sleep. It looks like you could use it."

"Fuck that. I can sleep when I'm dead. She's getting sent to the US on a medical bird in the next six hours. That's all the time I've got."

"She's going nowhere. That's my call as a doctor. I'll stay here until she's able to fly, but I'll never help your organization again if she leaves before I say."

I admired his conviction, given that he had no idea who we were. I'd figured he was just in it for the retainer, and he'd do his job but not quibble if he was told to stop.

As soon as we'd loaded Christine into our Fiat, Shoshana driving and Brett providing medical aid, I'd had a choice to make: Either take her to a hospital and lose any chance to learn what she knew, or take her to the safe house. To do the latter, I needed to trigger a deep asset reserved for helping Taskforce members working undercover.

The Taskforce was big, with tendrils all over the world, but most of the activities were benign, with unwitting personnel servicing safe houses or operating cover companies. They were trusted individuals who knew they were doing something for the United States government, but were not read on to Project Prometheus.

Early on, we'd determined that we might need medical help after a fight somewhere, and driving to the local hospital with a gunshot wound wasn't going to work. Kurt Hale had set out to recruit doctors in select regions of the world.

The idea was simple: Find military MDs on the verge of separating from service and ask if they'd like to get government assistance moving to an overseas retirement location, then a major monthly stipend for simply being on call—a call that may never come. This doctor—Colonel Shepard Linkletter—was an emergency room surgeon who'd seen multiple tours in Iraq during the hell of the surge. He'd already put in his retirement paperwork while serving at Aviano Air Base, Italy, when he was approached. He'd planned to stay in Italy anyway, and had snapped up the chance to have Uncle Sugar pay for it. As far as I know, he'd only been used once, when another Taskforce team had gotten into a scrape across the Adriatic Sea in Croatia.

I knew he existed because I'd heard the stories from the team he'd helped, but now I needed Kurt's permission to activate him for someone who wasn't on the Taskforce roster, not to mention that, in so doing, I'd contaminate the safe house for good. A lot of work went into procuring these clandestine operational houses, including stocking them with medical and other supplies, but once the doctor saw it, not to mention Christine, it could never be used again.

Kurt had been surprisingly amenable, going so far as to initiate a casualty evacuation plan with another Taskforce aircraft flying from Germany to get Christine to a trauma center, and by the time I'd arrived back at the safe house, Dr. Linkletter was calling for directions. He'd shown up twenty minutes later with his wife in tow. She turned out to be a former civilian DOD nurse, so the team was a twofer.

He'd immediately begun working on Christine while his wife turned one of the bedrooms into a mini-ICU. After an hour and a half, with me just sitting on my hands, he'd come back out, telling me she wasn't going anywhere.

I said, "Okay, Doc, how long until she's conscious and lucid? Best guess?"

Before he could answer, the doorbell rang. I put a finger to my lips and nodded at Jennifer. She looked through the peephole, then opened the door. Knuckles and Retro came in, lugging suitcases. Knuckles took one look at me and said, "So my rush down here was for nothing?"

"So far. You and Retro got the room on the left upstairs. Retro, how's your leg?"

"A little stiff. Stitches itch like hell, but it's okay."

"Can you run?"

"If I had to, sure."

"I mean, can you run without leaving a blood trail?"

"Questionable."

I said, "Okay, everyone get some sleep. We've got no lead right now, and can't talk to our source until . . . Doc? You never answered my question."

"Best guess, seven to nine hours. Who do you want me to wake if it's sooner?"

"Me. I'll be in the bedroom right next door."

Knuckles said, "You get your own room? What's up with that? How come I'm sharing?"

Retro picked up his suitcase and snickered. I said, "I'm sharing, just like everyone else."

"With who? Brett? Aaron?"

He saw me scowl and grinned, really enjoying punching my buttons. "Come on. You gotta say it."

"Shut up, Knuckles." I walked off to my room, a bewildered doctor looking on. He saw Jennifer follow behind me, and broke into a knowing smile. I said, "You shut up too."

I opened my suitcase, pulling out a T-shirt as Jennifer closed the door. She said, "You really shouldn't let him get to you like that."

I changed into the T-shirt, saying, "Really? You're the one who was sneaking out of our hotel room in Nairobi. Anyway, I'm getting a little sick of his jokes. He needs to get over it."

She put on a pair of sweats and slid into the miniature European queen bed. She patted the pillow next to her and said, "He *is* over it. You're the only one it aggravates now."

I said, "You're going to sleep in sweats?"

"Well, yeah. I'm not having that doctor come in here to wake you up while I'm wearing my panties and a T-shirt."

"So I get the ribbing without any of the benefits? What's up with that?"

I got the disapproving-teacher glare, and she changed the subject. "Christine's going to live, right?"

"Yeah, she'll live."

"We should have been quicker. I knew that bastard was going to harm her. It happened so fast."

"Actually, that was my question to you. Do you think you took Jacob out of the fight?"

"I honestly don't know. I hit him. I know that, but he got away under his own power. Omar wasn't carrying him. What did you and Aaron find?"

"Nothing. No blood trail, no Lost Boys. They managed to get out, and I couldn't find any evidence he'd been hit in a bad way."

She rolled over, turning out the light. "I've got a bad feeling about this. We've never done a chase where we've been completely behind the ball at every step of the way. You should have seen Omar. That man is a demon. He's going to kill a lot of people."

"I know. Get some sleep. At least Kurt's got the Lost Boys in the system. I saw them on TV tonight. Jacob didn't look anything like the Jacob I saw, but at least they're out there."

She rolled back over and said, "We should let Shoshana go. She wants to, and she's got a weird thing with Omar. I don't want to sound crazy, but she's got some inner bloodhound that can find him."

"She won't care who gets hurt if I let her off the chain. She's crazy. I can't control her. All she wants is him dead."

"You can, Pike. If you get her to say it. Tell her to find him and call. She'll do that. If she says so."

I lay in bed, feeling the incredible pressure to stop an attack, and an absolute helplessness that I would fail. I said, "Maybe I will. Let's see what happens tomorrow."

Tomorrow came a hell of a lot earlier than I thought it would. Around dawn, I was awakened by my cell phone. I fought through the fog and answered. It was an intel analyst from the Taskforce. He said, "Pike Logan?"

I sat up, rubbing my eyes and saying, "Yeah. Who is this?"

His next words woke me up completely.

"Kurt Hale gave me an order to contact you as soon as we identified a credit card purchase in Venice. We did. The pay-as-you-go card was used to buy a cell phone. We have the number. Do you need it?"

83

Omar shook Jacob's leg, saying, "Get up. It's time to get ready."

Jacob groaned, gingerly feeling his groin, his eyes still puffy from the pepper spray. He peeled down his pants and saw an ugly purple bruise on his hip. He said, "What time is it?"

"Seven in the morning. You have to be in position at nine. We need to get Carlos and Devon dressed."

Jacob sat up, scratching his head. "Have you thought more about the attack? You still want to go?"

"Yes. I'm convinced that they don't know what our target is. If they did, they wouldn't have put your faces all over the screen. They're trying to scare you away because they can't predict where it will be. They don't know, but they're looking. Which is why I'm changing the plan."

"How?"

"As we discussed, you won't be the martyr. I'm taking the final martyr vest with me. I'll create a diversion. A strike that will draw the police and deflate their fear. They'll think the attack has occurred."

"You're going to be a *shahid*?"

"No, young lion. I'm going to kill infidels. We'll still meet as we discussed. Take the ferry to Tunis. I'll be waiting."

"But how will we get inside? Even if they don't know our attack plans, the Lost Boys' faces are all over the news. Surely they'll stop us."

"I don't believe so. Have some faith. Remember when we discussed the attack? The threat of the security?"

"Yes."

"Vatican City is not Italy. Yes, they talk, but the target is not an Italian citizen. You are all over the news in Italy, but that means little for the Vatican. I studied it extensively, and the Vatican coordinates with the Italian police, but does not fall under them. Maybe they have the bulletin, but they might not."

"*Maybe* isn't a way to plan for success."

"Look at it this way: Those pictures are over six years old. You don't even look like them, and your passport information isn't for the Lost Boys."

"How will we get in without you? You're Chris Fulbright."

"Wake up Carlos and Devon. Let's get them ready. While they shave and shower, I'll call my contact. I told him you were sick before. I'll tell him I'm now the one who's ill. I'll get a feel for him and tell him it wouldn't be in the best interests of the rest of the church groups for me to come contagious." He smiled. "A sacrifice on my part."

Jacob went to the other sleeping pallets, shaking the legs of Carlos and Devon. They woke up and Omar stood above them, projecting the aura of the first time Jacob had met him, his power absolute.

"It's time. Prepare yourself for martyrdom. Cleanse your body and clear your mind. Your greatest triumph lies ahead."

84

I got one more negative contact from Knuckles and began to wonder if the phone was turned on. I said, "You sure you've got the right IMSI in the box?"

Piqued, he came back, "I got what you gave me. Maybe you'd better ask the Taskforce asshole who sent the information."

I looked at my watch, feeling the time slip away. It was now past seven thirty, and our opportunity to find the bed-down site with the phone information was growing smaller and smaller. Soon, it would be on the move, and we would lose the chance to hit them together, at a place of our choosing. I feared the next hit would be the one of their choosing.

The Taskforce intel analyst had given me the information on the handset purchased in Venice, a so-called drop phone bought at a train station kiosk. They'd gone into high gear and hacked the database of the phone vendor, learning the serial number and—more importantly—the international mobile subscriber number, or IMSI, attached to the phone. This was the unique identifier the phone would use to communicate with the network, and something that could be tracked.

We'd done the large-scope search, and seen the phone had only been used a few times. Some of the calls had been placed in Venice, one had been in between Venice and Rome, but the latest were in Rome itself, telling me the phone purchased with the suspected credit card was now running around the capital. All I had to do was find it, which I most definitely had the capability to do.

We had the general location of where the phone had been due to its constant talking to cell towers, but that wasn't enough of a refinement for a surgical assault. It *did* show me a pattern that proved hunting the IMSI was worth the effort, because the phone's last tower contact had been in the vicinity of our gunfight the night before.

I'd awakened the pilots and Knuckles, telling them what I had and getting them moving to the rock-star bird.

In addition to transporting my team around in style and hiding our equipment, the Gulfstream had a suite of surveillance capabilities nestled among all of the electronic gear that allowed the aircraft to fly. One was the ability to geolocate a cell phone down to a ten-digit grid. Basically acting as a flying cell tower, the aircraft would suck in and reject thousands of cell phones, searching for the correct IMSI. Once that was found, the phone would be locked and we'd trace the signal straight-line to a location, taking three readings and finding where they intersected.

Knuckles came back on, the connection from the aircraft to my computer making him sound like he had a head cold. "We've lapped Trastevere twice, with no joy. I'm recommending a grid pattern search."

The Trastevere area had the longest stay of the phone, according to the cell tower data, and I was hoping it was the bed-down location, but nothing had registered. The cell was either off or already on the move to a different location.

The IMSI grabber in the aircraft was limited in range—it couldn't suck in every phone in Rome—and thus had to be targeted at a specific area. Knuckles was asking to start flying over Rome like he was mowing the lawn, but that posed its own problems—namely the air traffic control over the airspace of Rome. They'd want to know why we wished to fly willy-nilly across the city.

I said, "What's the pilot's take?"

I waited, then heard, "He's saying he can do it, but it'll be short. He thinks he can convince them that we're sightseeing, flying over the Colosseum and the Vatican before we get on our way. We won't get the city."

I thought about it, knowing it would be the last thing we did. I was about to give them the go-ahead when Jennifer came into the room, holding my Taskforce phone. "Analyst on the line. He's got a lead."

Into the computer I said, "Stand by. I got the Taskforce on the phone. Head out of the city and loiter."

I took the cell from Jennifer, put my hand over the mic, and said, "Christine?"

Jennifer said, "Nothing yet. Doctor says she's still out from the sedatives and the trauma. Her vitals are good, so he thinks she'll come around soon."

Not what I wanted to hear. Well, I mean I was glad her vitals were good, but, Jesus, couldn't she wake the hell up already? I put the phone to my ear and said, "What do you have?"

I'd given the analyst the mission to identify all the calls our target cell had made, and I was hoping they had something I could use to broaden my search.

"We think we have the bed-down location. One of the contacts made by the handset was to the Hotel Imperiale. It's the only hotel they've called, and the same one of your linkage target. Our evaluation is they're staying at it. We recommend penetrating through cyber and getting a guest readout. We can analyze for anomalies if they're using an alias."

Not a bad bit of analysis, but unfortunately way off. This analyst was dedicated to finding linkages through electronic tethers, and not an all-source guy who could provide predictive intelligence based on multiple inputs. He had no idea what had transpired last night, but at least he was trying.

I said, "Thanks for the information. Who else has that phone called? Do you have the other IMSIs?"

I could hear the deflation over the phone. "Yes. There are a few other numbers, most mundane. We've got one other pay-as-you-go cell, bought in Rome. But I really think you should focus on the hotel."

I said, "I might. Give me the IMSI."

He did and I relayed it to Knuckles, telling him to put it in the system, re-attack Trastevere, and if that was a bust, to conduct his limited grid search. It was all I could do.

Jennifer said, "It's now past eight."

"Thank you for that reminder."

She took my sarcasm in stride, waiting. I said, "What?"

"Shoshana. She says she can find Omar. I think we should let her try."

"Jennifer, that is fucking crazy. I may not have a lot of leads, but I'll be damned if I'm resorting to calling the psychic network for answers. We let her loose and she's just as likely to burn the operation as facilitate it."

"Pike, talk to her. Give her your mission parameters and she'll execute. I'll go with her. I'll keep her in check."

I thought about it. Kurt's conversation with me last night had driven home that a slaughter was coming. All indicators were putting the attack as imminent, and the Islamic State had shown a barbarity unlike anything seen since the Middle Ages. They'd put enormous effort into this plan, and the end result would be commensurate. Something more horrible than the burning of the Jordanian pilot.

Kurt had inserted the Lost Boys into the Italian system, and the United States was blaring from all classified agencies to every liaison in Europe, but hoping some cop stumbled across them was not a means for success. It was like 9/11 all over again, with everyone warning of the punch, but nobody knowing how it was coming.

But waiting on Christine to wake up was doing little as well. In truth, I hated sitting on my hands. I wanted to be proactive. To be *doing* something.

I said, "Go get her. But you're going with her."

Jennifer smiled and raced out of the room. She came back in almost immediately, making me wonder if Shoshana had been waiting right outside.

Shoshana said, "I appreciate your trust." No witty sarcasm. No playful banter. She was all business, but the dark angel was hidden.

I said, "Don't appreciate anything just yet. I *don't* trust you. I have some parameters. First, Jennifer goes with you. Is that an issue?"

Without hesitation, she said, "No." And I knew they'd been conspiring.

"Second, you pinpoint him, you call. No direct action, period."

She glanced at Jennifer, then said, "Pike, that will depend on him."

I went to Jennifer as well, almost calling it off. She gave a slight nod. I said, "No. I want your word. No unilateral action."

She clenched her jaw, staring at me. Finally, she said, "Okay. You have my word."

I saw Jennifer relax at her statement, then my computer came alive.

"Pike, Pike, this is Knuckles. I got a hit on that second phone. It's in a two-story flat in Trastevere. Looking at it through optics. Photos coming."

85

Jacob watched Omar check the placement of the explosive vest. After he was satisfied, Omar said, "How does it feel?"

Carlos said, "Same as it always does. It's actually a little lighter with the Kevlar ball bearings instead of the steel ones we practiced with in Syria."

"You need to look natural at all times. People will be studying everyone who arrives. Anything that sets off an alarm in someone's mind could result in a physical search."

Carlos nodded, saying, "It's no different from stealing from a store. They always have people wandering around looking for suspicious characters."

Omar slapped him lightly on the cheek. "Listen up, both of you. You aren't taking a candy bar without paying. You're killing the most revered Christian on Earth. They will be looking, and you need to be flawless."

Jacob said, "I'll be there. Don't worry. Yeah, it's a killing, but we've done things like this before. Devon once walked out of a store with a complete car stereo, and when he was stopped, he convinced the security guard he'd already paid. Trust me, they can remain calm."

Omar said, "Devon, how does yours feel?"

"Same."

"Put on your shirts and jackets. Thread the detonating tube down your sleeve, but wait on the neckties until we do final adjustments."

They did so and Omar had them turn in a circle. He nodded his head in approval. "You can't even tell they're in place."

Devon and Carlos smiled at the praise. Omar said, "Okay, where do you put the detonator?"

In unison, both said, "Right front jacket pocket."

"And your cell phones?"

"In our hands at all times."

"And you can remove the blasting caps and initiation chemicals from the phones? You should be able to do that blindfolded by now."

Carlos said, "Yes, we worked with the real cell phone yesterday. It's not the same as the blocks of wood we used in Syria, but not that much different."

"They are charged? Look real?"

They nodded in unison. Omar said, "Remember, you have to make sure that lever on the side locks up. And to both press *and* release the button. Don't forget the dead man's switch. I don't want to see a picture of you on the news running forward, waiting on it to go off, only to be shot."

Jacob said, "Our time is running short. We have to meet Father Brimm in less than forty-five minutes."

Omar said, "First, the videos. The evidence supporting the Islamic State."

Jacob said, "Omar, we should have done that earlier. You're going to make a video that most likely won't even be found."

Omar said, "They'll find it. Eventually, they'll figure out everything we did and they'll come to this house. Even if they don't, you and I can speed things up by telling them where it's hidden. Unless you'd rather make the speech inside the basilica. Be the martyr."

Omar had called Father Brimm earlier, giving him his fabrication of being sick. He'd asked for the Father's help with his boys, and Brimm had agreed, telling him that all three were cleared. Which meant Jacob could be back in play with the original plan. Outside of earshot of Devon and Carlos, Jacob had reiterated what he wanted, refusing to take the martyr's role and stressing the value of the planned diversion. Omar hadn't fought him then, and Jacob wasn't going to start the argument all over again now.

Jacob said, "Let's get it over with."

Time *was* running short, but truthfully Jacob didn't want to watch his friends make a martyr tape. Didn't want to participate in the macabre ceremony. Even given what he was about to do, seeing his two best friends bragging about killing themselves seemed obscene.

Omar set up the same GoPro camera he'd used in Tirana, Devon and Carlos against a wall, grisly smiles on their faces. The scene reminding Jacob of the forced Christmas photos he'd taken at the school. The ones sent out as postcards for donations, proving the "good" the Christian evangelists did for the downtrodden and misguided.

Standing together, both Carlos and Devon read from a prepared speech, highlighting their detonators and their original, true-name passports. After an enthusiastic denunciation of infidels and the proclamation of infallibility of the Islamic State, it was done. Carlos and Devon's conversion complete.

Omar left the camera in plain view on the kitchen table and said, "You know where to meet Father Brimm?"

Jacob said, "Yes. Left colonnade outside of Saint Peter's Square at the first aid station. I looked on Google Earth."

"And the restroom?"

"Just past security, right side at the facade to the basilica."

"Remember, don't ask to use it until you're through final security. If you do it before, they'll direct you to one outside of security. And that would do no good."

"I got it, I got it. We need to go."

Omar picked up a small duffel bag, the canvas cloaking the final vest. He drew himself up to his full height, his eyes showing fire. Jacob expected him to make a speech, but all he did was shake the hands of both Carlos and Devon.

He said, "Time to make history."

86

Crammed into the Fiat with four other people, I really did feel somewhat like a clown. I would have driven, or at least called shotgun, but I had way too much coordinating to do. Jennifer was behind the wheel, with Shoshana in the passenger seat acting as navigator. Shoehorned into the bench seat in back with me were Brett and Aaron, all working through the assault.

Knuckles was still in the aircraft overhead, with orders to loiter until I called him again. Retro, with his leg wound, had been given the unenviable task of acting as the headquarters element, doing LTC Alexander's job with Kurt Hale and the Taskforce.

He'd bitched, of course, but given the stakes of the attack, I needed someone switched-on talking to the Taskforce. I told him he shouldn't have been a bullet magnet.

I'd thought long and hard about going unilateral on this mission instead of alerting host-nation security forces, and decided it was the only way to solve the problem. I knew I could have passed the target information to Kurt, and he'd in turn get it to the Italians, but the time lag was just too great. In my mind, all I could think about was duplicating the *Charlie Hebdo* massacre in Paris, with a bunch of Italian police blundering in without the right information, then Omar and Jacob escaping and slaughtering everyone they met on a bid to flee.

I knew the target and the threat they posed. And my team was one of the best on Earth.

I decided to act.

In the middle, Brett held a tablet with the photos taken from our eye in the sky. Knuckles had given a 360 to the target, with multiple digital images showing the building, as well as the roads around it.

Brett said, "It's a stand-alone, thank God. We won't have to bust into a hundred different apartments looking."

The phone lock was good, but not pinpoint precise. If the target had been four stories tall and a block long, that would have left a lot of real estate to cover. Brett was happy it was a small two-story, meaning it probably didn't have any sublets, and whoever was using it was all bad.

I said, "How many breaches?"

"Not counting windows, looks like two. One in front, and one in back, near the alley with the trash cans." He handed the tablet to me, showing me the roof of what looked like a slice of pizza, the crust end butting up into the refuse alley, but the front getting narrower and narrower as it was hemmed in on two sides with cobblestone streets.

Brett pointed to the right side of the building, "That's Via del Moro, the road with the main entrance. The other road just runs down brick, then the alley cuts in between both of them."

I said, "How can you see a back breach? It's hidden by the buildings. Are you guessing?"

He leaned over and ran his finger over the screen, flipping through twenty pictures, trying to find the one he wanted. Eventually, he did, a long-axis shot of the alley from above. You couldn't see exactly what was down it, but you could see a light fixture and a row of garbage cans. Which meant a breach. Nobody puts a light fixture on the back side of an alley wall unless there's some reason for a person to use it.

I privately thanked my lucky stars I'd made Knuckles get in the plane. He knew what we needed, and hadn't quit taking photos until he had it.

I studied the image a little more, building a plan. Knowing what I thought we should do, but wanting input, I said, "What's your call?"

Brett said, "Low-vis entry, back door. No knock-knock on this one. Stealth. Get on them before they realize we're there. Koko and Carrie lock down the front if we screw up."

Which is *exactly* what I thought. I said, "Aaron?"

Before he could answer, Shoshana said, "Who the hell is Carrie? What am I doing?"

Brett grinned at me and said, "Uhh . . . it's your callsign for this mission. For on the radio, you know, when we have to talk in the clear."

She said, "I don't get it. Why Carrie? Is this some joke, like calling Jennifer a talking gorilla?"

I cut above the fray, speaking sharply. "Enough of this shit!" Everyone got quiet and I said, "Aaron, what are your thoughts?"

He said, "Brett's plan is sound. As long as we don't get into a gunfight on the street out front."

"I'm good with that. Carrie and Koko should be able to lock them inside as long as we give them a heads-up we're compromised. If we push them out, and they choose to fight, it's their bad luck."

Piqued again, Shoshana rotated around and said, "What is Carrie? Why am I that?"

Aggravated, I said, "It's just a callsign, but it fits. You scare the shit out of me *and* my team. You *are* Carrie. She's a character in a book that slaughtered half a town with her mind. Killing everyone because she was slighted, using her brain alone."

She took that in, then said, "So no talking monkey."

I looked at her, incredulous. "It's a *bad* callsign. It means you're a telekinetic psychopath."

She turned back around, happy, saying, "Koko and I can lock down the front."

Aaron was grinning, and Brett looked like he'd just created a monster. We crossed the Tiber River, entering Trastevere, and Jennifer said, "About two minutes out."

I said, "Okay, Jennifer, do a drive-by of the front of the house, on Via del Moro. We'll take a quick look, then roll out at the alley. You park, then provide squirter control on the front breach. You and Carrie position close on the door if we call. Any questions?"

I got none, and the pizza house came into view. Jennifer rolled around the point, us staring at the front door like it would tell us something. It showed nothing. Just another Roman house on a street full of them.

She left Via del Moro, turning onto the other leg of the triangle, and I cracked the door. She reached the alley, and we rolled out, scurrying into the small, rat-infested lane. I unhooked my PWS, flipping out the buttstock and whispering, "Brett. Your door."

He and Aaron did the same with their weapons, and we advanced, making sure not to kick cans or other refuse. He reached it, and Aaron pulled security on the far side while I took the near. Brett knelt down, pulled out an old-fashioned pick kit, and set to work, going very, very slowly.

He felt the lock release and turned to me. I raised my weapon, caught eyes with Aaron, then nodded. He swung the door open, and I flowed in, rifle high.

I entered a small anteroom, a stove visible through another door. I went in enough to allow space for the rest of the team, then took a knee, listening. Brett slowly allowed the door to close and we all paused, straining our ears. I heard nothing. I glanced at Brett, letting him know I was moving, then took a position on the door that allowed me to pie off the room. I saw nothing. Brett came up behind me and squeezed my arm. I entered the room, going left, feeling him go right, both of us still moving gingerly.

The room was empty.

We continued through the small house, but it was deserted. Nothing.

I called in Jennifer and Shoshana, and ordered site exploitation. While that was going on, I called Knuckles, saying, "We got a dry hole. Need another lock for the phone. Get overhead."

I got acknowledgment from him, then Brett brought up a GoPro camera, saying, "You have to see this."

He turned it on, and I watched the other two Lost Boys chanting a bunch of crazy shit, exposing suicide vests.

A martyr tape. And they were gone.

"Fuck! Give me something from this place. Right now."

Aaron came up with a hand-drawn diagram of some sort of ceremony. Nothing identified where it was, but it was big. A lot of people. It had sketches showing where to target and who to kill, confusing marks that had been erased and redrawn, as if whoever had made it had been in a discussion with others, changing the plan.

I said, "Any idea where that is?"

"None. Brett's still looking. Their luggage is here, so this is the end-game. They aren't coming back."

Knuckles came on my earpiece, saying, "I got the phone. It's on an island in the middle of the Tiber, close to Trastevere, headed north. Whoever's got it is on foot. It's moving slow."

I said, "What's north? What's the target?"

I got nothing for a minute, then, "The Colosseum. That's the biggest thing around."

I looked at Brett. "What time does that place open? Find out."

Jennifer came back downstairs, Shoshana behind her. I said, "They're on the move. It might be the Colosseum; it might be something else."

Brett said, "It opened at eight thirty. It's open right now. According to this, worst crowds are between nine and ten."

"That's it. Pack up. We need to go."

I called Retro, relaying what I had and telling him to contact Kurt. It was time to get the Italians involved. Let them know the threat. We might be able to stop it, but I couldn't live with myself if we failed and hadn't given some notice.

Retro tried to interrupt me several times, until I told him to shut up and start taking notes. He did so. When I was done, I said, "Get that out right now. Tell Kurt we're on the move, but we may be too late."

He said, "Roger all. Pike . . . Christine's awake. She's talking. I got her information."

I was on the verge of hanging up the phone when what he said penetrated. "What did she say? What does she know?"

"Nothing, really. She was screwing some guy from America. She's a mistress, but she was here with a man hosting a church group. The man hasn't been seen in days. It's why she came down to Rome, to find him. I've run his name, and he's from Florida. He was here leading three boys on a Catholic church group trip."

"So? What the fuck does that have to do with anything?"

"The three were in Venice last week. Same as the Lost Boys. And today, they're having a personal audience with the pope at a ceremony. But they never checked into their hotel here in Rome. Their trail ends in Venice."

His words hit me like a lightning bolt.

Jesus Christ. They're going to assassinate the pope.

87

Jacob rode in the front seat of the cab, with Devon and Carl in the back, sitting stiffly. Paralleling the Tiber River, the driver kept pulling him away from his thoughts, aggravating Jacob with his broken English.

"You are going to the canonization ceremony, yes?"

"We are. We can't wait."

"It is a glorious day for it! Who would have thought the Holy Father would bestow sainthood on an Arab? Strange times."

Arab? An Arab Catholic?

Jacob had painstakingly learned the entire laborious process for beautification and canonization by the papal authorities, but had never bothered to discover whom today's ceremony was for.

The cabby continued, "I've driven more Arabs this week than I have in my entire life. I never even knew they had Christianity. It was strange."

They made the turn onto Via Paolo VI, and Saint Peter's Square came into view, thousands of people milling about, waiting on the ceremony. Jacob was taken aback at its size. He'd studied it and the basilica relentlessly with Google Earth, virtual tours, and plain old tourist brochures, but none did the site justice. It was breathtaking.

How will we find Father Brimm? There appeared to be over five thousand people in the square, with more spilling in every second.

The driver said, "Here? Is this good? I can't get any closer because of the ceremony."

Jacob got his bearings, seeing the left colonnade on the other side of the square, where Father Brimm was supposedly located, and the facade of Saint Peter's Basilica in the distance, the dome rising into the blue sky.

He said, "This is fine."

They exited, Jacob paying the fare with the Fulbright credit card, the last time he would do so. He held the back door open, his two friends walking stiffly up to the barricade on the square. Jacob waited until the cab left before saying, "You two are acting like you have a fucking bomb strapped to you. Loosen up."

Carlos grinned and said, "Sorry. I'm afraid of setting it off."

"You couldn't cause it to explode with a hammer right now. It's not even primed. Come on. Let's find the first aid station."

They pushed their way past the crowds, going to the first of two security checkpoints. Jacob showed his ticket, then walked through a metal detector exactly like at an airport. The Vatican policeman waved him on. He stood on the other side and held his breath. Carlos showed his ticket, handed his cell phone to a policeman, and came to the far side. The machine did not beep. Jacob let out a breath as Devon followed. Jacob said, "Thank God for small miracles. Looks like we're going to make it."

Now inside the square, he turned to find the aid station, flabbergasted that so many people would show up for a ceremony involving someone who'd died centuries ago. The square looked like someone had cracked open a rock concert and dropped it into Vatican City.

Jacob kept his eyes open, scanning for undercover security, but only seeing a large, overt police presence. He saw a sign for the first aid station, and a priest with a clipboard in front of it, checking his watch. He said, "Is that him?"

"Yep. That's him."

Jacob walked rapidly up, bumping people out of the way, and the priest turned, recognizing Carlos and Devon. He said, "About time. You guys are almost too late."

Jacob said, "Father Brimm, I'm sorry. Mr. Fulbright said to be here at this time, way before the ceremony."

"Way before? Yeah, it's way before the ceremony, but it's the time for you to be inside! Not trying to get through security. We're meeting the pope *before* the ceremony. You were supposed to be here an hour ago."

Jacob immediately thought about Omar's diversion. It was supposed to happen before the papal visit, to draw off the police before they conducted their attack, but now he was operating on a different timeline. Father Brimm said, "You have your passports, right?"

All three nodded and the priest took off across the square toward the other colonnade, Jacob struggling to keep up with his bruised hip. Father Brimm turned as he walked and said, "They told you what's going to happen, right? You missed the rehearsal."

"Yes, sir. It doesn't seem that difficult. We're meeting the Holy Father before the canonization."

"You stand in line, you kiss his ring, you move on. Once you're through the receiving line, you leave the basilica to the square and take your seat with everyone else."

"How many are going through the receiving line?"

"I don't know about who else is attending, but from the United States I have thirty-two. Thirty-five with you."

They reached the inner ring of security, the one leading to the entrance of Saint Peter's Basilica, and it was much, much more formal than the outer one. The men manning the gate wore civilian clothes, suits, ties, and mirrored sunglasses, and each had an earpiece coming from one ear. Father Brimm showed a badge and said, "Sorry we're so late. These are the last three."

The first man, working a tablet, said, "Passports, please." Jacob collected all three and handed them to him, wondering how hard he would check for a forgery. He didn't at all. He fiddled for a little bit, tapping the tablet, going through various things Jacob couldn't see, then handed them back with a smile. "Enjoy the ceremony. Not many get to actually meet His Holiness."

Jacob said, "Have you?"

The man laughed, saying, "Yes, of course. I protect him."

Jacob smiled back, thinking, *Not today.*

88

Jennifer saw my face and said, "What's Retro got? What did he figure out?"

I didn't even want to voice it, because doing so would make it real. But it *was* real. "The Lost Boys are going to try to kill the pope."

Aaron said, "What? That's crazy."

I said, "Brett, get online and check the Vatican calendar. Jennifer, call Retro, find out what the schedule was for the church group."

I paced in a circle and Shoshana said, "The phone going away is Omar. Not the Lost Boys."

I waved my hand and said, "I don't need the psychic shit now. I need to think."

I had some tough choices to make, and not a lot of time to make them. The Vatican was hell and gone from the Colosseum, but I had a target phone headed that way. Which to choose?

Shoshana said, "It's logic, not 'psychic shit.' The first phone you were tracking came from Venice. Meaning Lost Boys. The second phone called from here. Both phones ended up in this place. The first one was Jacob. The second—the one on the move—is Omar. He's going to kill someone too. A dual attack."

Shit. She was right, and I'd stepped into the biggest mess I had ever imagined. For the first time, I felt it was out of my control. I could stop one, but not both.

Brett looked up and said, "Canonization ceremony right now. The pope's there."

Damn it. I'd halfway hoped the thing was tomorrow. I said, "Jennifer, what's up with Retro?"

She pulled the phone from her ear and covered the handset. "Chris Fulbright was leading some boys from a Catholic parish for a personal visit with the pope. Outside of Christine, nobody's registered them missing."

Which means "they" were at the ceremony. But how? How on earth could they assume the identities of a complete church group? Didn't any of them ever call home? Email?

I said, "Tell Retro I need Kurt on the line right fucking now. Call my cell or give me a number to call him secure. Tell him to get ready to mobilize whatever assets we have in Italy. Everyone else, pack your shit. We're leaving for the Vatican in thirty seconds."

Shoshana said, "Omar's getting away. He's going to kill a great many people. Let me go. I'm no use at the Vatican."

I looked at her and saw a flicker of the dark angel. Jennifer said, "Kurt's calling in two minutes. He's up to speed."

Shoshana said, "Let. Me. Go."

I said, "Brett, call Knuckles. See if he still has the phone."

He got on the radio and I said, "I let you go, you just identify, like last time. You call me and we'll sort it out."

She shook her head and said, "No, this isn't like last time. You won't be able to respond."

Brett said, "He's still got the phone. It's still moving north. Moving slowly."

"How far?"

"Off of the island and into Rome proper. Maybe twenty minutes to the Colosseum. Knuckles says that was their last pass. Air traffic control is telling them to get out of Rome's airspace."

My phone rang and Kurt was on it. He said, "Please tell me this is just a bad rumor. I've got the Council shitting bricks. I told them about a possible assassination attempt of the pope, and now I can't give them enough information."

"It's not a rumor. I believe the Lost Boys have infiltrated a ceremony and are now going to kill the pope. I need massive assistance. I need you to tell them to shut the ceremony down, and I need someone to facilitate my entry."

I heard him start shouting orders, then he said, "I'm getting the word to them right now, but there's no way they'll shut down the ceremony based on a threat. This is like the State of the Union for them. We'd never pull the president because of a threat."

"Then get me in! The ceremony is locked down, and I can't get access waving guns. It's in the heart of Vatican City."

"We have no assets in Vatican City. We're going to have to rely on liaison. We'll get the word to them, but that's the best we can do. We have the names of the church group, and we know the plan."

"Bullshit. Get me in. Those mug shots are worthless. We're the only people that know what the Lost Boys look like, and it'll take forever to sort through the BS to get an alert to his personal security. You only send a bulletin over the wire, and the pope is dead."

"Pike, I know the risk, but I can't magic you inside."

"Don't we have an embassy there? The US ambassador for the Vatican will be at that ceremony. Get the president to get his ass on the line. Tell him to meet me at Saint Peter's Square."

He said, "Okay, okay, yeah, that might work. I'll start making calls." Someone in the background said something and he turned from the phone. When he came back he said, "The damn ceremony's being live-streamed. The pope's about to get murdered on global Internet. Get going. I'll call with the linkup."

I hung up and said, "Get ready to load up. Jennifer, go get the vehicle."

Shoshana said, "What about Omar?"

"He's a secondary consideration. I can't do both."

"Yes, you can."

"We don't even know if he's doing something bad. He may just be escaping the city since he's set his plan in motion."

Jennifer said, "I'll go with her. We'll take Omar; you guys head to the Vatican."

I paused, and Aaron looked at Shoshana. He said, "Let her go."

I relented. "Okay. You two identify Omar, then call." I looked squarely at Shoshana and said, "Track him only."

The angel flickered in the background. She said, "That'll depend on him."

I felt Jennifer waiting on me like last night. Waiting on me to force Shoshana to say the words. To commit to no killing. Shoshana was boring into me like she had in the past. I felt the connection, the same yearning I held to kill the evil in the world, and it was enough.

I nodded. "So be it."

Jennifer's mouth fell open, and I saw the darkness blossom in Shoshana until it consumed her. What her country had recognized early in her youth, and what she now abhorred, she was yet again. A perfect killing machine.

She smiled, showing teeth but no joy, and said, "Don't worry. I'll wash my hands before our date, Nephilim."

And she slipped out the door without looking back.

Jennifer looked at me in shock, saying, "You know what she's going to do, right?"

I said, "Yeah. Go help her."

89

After the passport check the Lost Boys went to another metal detector, where another robotic man wearing sunglasses said, "Do you have a cell phone, camera, or digital device? iPod?"

Jacob said no, but Carlos and Devon handed their phones over. He punched the home key of each, then flicked the screen left and right, spending about five seconds with them before putting the phones on the belt of an X-ray machine.

He waved Jacob forward, and they proceeded once again through another metal detector. Jacob struggled to keep his face neutral, feeling the itch to run. He kept his eyes on the man running the X-ray machine, waiting to see if he leaned forward or ran the belt back again. He did not.

Carlos and Devon passed through the detector unscathed. As they waited on the phones, Jacob asked Father Brimm, "Who are those guys?"

"Swiss Guards. They've protected the Holy Father for centuries."

"You mean the guys who wear the old-timey uniforms we saw in the front?"

Father Brimm smiled and said, "Yes, the same organization, but these guys are definitely not a ceremonial function. They're everywhere in here, along with the Gendarmeria, ever since someone tried to kill His Holiness in the eighties."

Jacob knew as much as a civilian could on the pope's protective detail, having studied it for hours on the Internet in Istanbul. He knew the

Swiss Guards protected the right of the Holy Father and the Vatican police—the Gendarmeria—his left. He knew the counterterrorist abilities, the explosives expertise, and had studied every single attack a sitting Pope had experienced in the twentieth century. He knew what he was about to face, but he feigned innocence.

"Why would someone try to kill the pope?"

For the first time, Father Brimm said something profound. "Some on this earth care only about destruction. It makes them what they are, and they can elevate themselves only by destroying what others see as good."

Jacob studied Father Brimm, seeing that he truly believed it. He wondered how naïve the man could be, but remembered the priest had never witnessed the white house. Had never experienced what someone he called "good," cloaked behind the mantle of a Christian school, could do.

But that didn't explain the massive crowd of people, all here to celebrate the canonization by the Holy Father. Plenty were Arabic, and they'd suffered mightily because of their religion in the land they lived within, and yet all were peaceful. No slogans of death, no demanding slaughter for the injustice.

No circle of men on their knees.

He realized he'd never seen an Islamic State ceremony that didn't involve death. He shook the thought from his head. The crowds celebrating here were no better than the ones in the Islamic State. The difference was men like Omar told you up front what was expected, and then delivered the punishment in public. They didn't hide it under a cloak, lying about why it was your turn to go to the white house. And yet Father Brimm's words held a power, if only because of his conviction.

The phones came through, Carlos and Devon snatching them up, and, as planned, Devon said, "How long is the ceremony?"

Turning to lead them in, Father Brimm said, "Probably thirty minutes. Not long, because he has to do the entire canonization ceremony on the square."

"I need to use the bathroom. Really bad."

Exasperated, Father Brimm said, "You should have gone outside! There's no bathroom in the basilica."

Jacob said, "There's one right over there. Near the bag-check station."

Father Brimm looked, seeing no sign. He said, "How do you know?"

Jacob said, "Tour book. Let him go. It'll only take a second."

Father Brimm shook his head, clearly aggravated, then said, "Hurry up. We're late as it is. Your Mr. Fulbright is really taking liberties with this."

Carlos said, "I need to go too."

Father Brimm threw his hands in the air and said, "What on earth! Go, go."

They scampered away, and Father Brimm said, "Come on. I'll go back and get them. I need to get you to your seat before we're locked out."

They passed through another phalanx of civilian-clothed protectors, and entered the basilica. Jacob saw the expanse of space and was once again taken aback. It was huge. Well, that didn't adequately explain the assault on his eyes. It was more than that. A warehouse is huge. This was much greater than an expanse of steel and Plexiglas. It was the most exquisitely crafted thing he had ever entered. Unlike any church he'd ever imagined.

Stretching for multiple football fields in all directions, every inch was handcrafted marble and painted art. He'd seen the space in pictures and virtual tours, planning exactly how they would attack, learning all he could about the papal altar and the seating arrangements from past ceremonies, but the reality was more than he'd imagined.

Father Brimm pulled his sleeve, saying, "Come on, come on. Time later to sightsee."

In front of the papal altar were about one hundred chairs, all in a row, and all currently occupied. Father Brimm led him down the right side, past monuments and chapels, waving his badge in the air to various security men. They reached a spot midway up, four seats empty in the middle. He pushed Jacob forward, saying, "I'll bring your friends. If they don't show, it's because it's too late."

Jacob nodded, squeezing past the other boys, all dressed in suits. All looking at him in disdain. He didn't care.

He sat, feeling his anxiety grow, waiting on his friends. There was a stirring from the left side of the basilica, and an entrance of prelates, moving in solemn stride. He began to think it was too late, when he saw movement to his right. Carlos and Devon shuffling through the line of people to their seats. Father Brimm stood on the outside, sternly looking on.

They sat next to him, both of their right hands hidden. He merely glanced at them, and they nodded, eyes soulful but their courage resolute.

So they'd managed to do it. Managed to emplace the blasting caps in the sockets and connect the detonators to the tubing running down their sleeves. They were now walking bombs.

He exhaled and a stir began in the audience. The Holy Father came forward, walking with an easy grace and smiling. Far back, almost hidden, Jacob saw the security men. Keeping their distance because of the solemnity of the ceremony, but there nonetheless. Swiss Guards on the right, and Vatican police on the left.

The Holy Father mounted the papal altar, then stood for a moment, surveying the audience. He said a few words, but Jacob was too far back to hear. Everyone bowed their heads and he realized it was a prayer. He copied, hearing the audience murmur a liturgy. They raised their heads, and the Holy Father said a few more words, then came down from the alter, taking a seat in the center chair of a row placed in front of the confessional at the base of the altar. The first line of boys stood, walking up to him one by one, each kissing his ring and moving aside.

Like a snake uncoiling, the line moved forward. Quicker than he'd imagined, their row stood up. Jacob looked at Carlos and Devon.

"It's time."

90

Omar crossed the bridge for Tiber Island, moving at a leisurely pace. He checked his watch, seeing he still had at least forty minutes before he would attack. He knew the Israelis were on to them, knew they understood an event was imminent, but also fully believed they had no idea where.

He honestly didn't care if he killed a single soul, but knew he would have to in order to convince the authorities the attack had occurred. An explosion on an empty street wouldn't do it. No, someone would have to die. Probably a great many someones.

The pope's ceremony was set for 10:00 A.M., which meant the receiving line would be around nine thirty. All he had to do was set the explosives off before that time, and he could think of no better place than in the line of cattle trying to enter the Roman Colosseum. A hundred people or more, all waiting to feel the sting of his vest.

Omar walked past the obese, slovenly infidels, some taking pictures and others just sitting on benches because they were sick of dragging their bellies through the street. He couldn't wait to make them taste fire. He foresaw a glorious future. The Islamic State was on the rise, and he intended to be a leader of it.

Passing across the island, he realized he couldn't cut straight to the Colosseum, but instead would have to bypass the massive Roman Forum, adding time to his journey. He took a left on Via del Teatro di Marcello, picking up his pace.

*   *   *

Racing down the road in our little Fiat clown car, bouncing back and forth from Brett's attempts at avoiding traffic, I was having a hard time holding the phone to my ear, but at least I was in the shotgun seat instead of crammed in the back. Not that it would have been a big deal now, since only Aaron was back there.

I said, "So you got someone to meet us? Someone who can get us in?"

Kurt said, "Yeah, I think so. You have to remember, this is going through cutouts. They think you're Department of State, so don't go Neanderthal on them. We still have the cover to think about."

"Sir, really. We're toting weapons, and we're going to storm the shit out of that place. Can this guy coordinate with their security?"

"Yeah, yeah, they think you're from the diplomatic security service for the ambassador. You can have the guns, but you don't get the asshole attitude."

I didn't say what I was thinking. Only, "That's fine. Where are we meeting him?"

"Right on Saint Peter's Square. He'll be standing by with an American flag on a stick."

"You're shitting me."

"No. Best we could do. There are about ten thousand people in that square."

"We're coming around the circle now. Did you get the word to the Vatican?"

"Yeah, we did, but it was slow. The ambassador is supposed to have a Vatican representative with him, but I'm not sure how much got through. They know there's a threat, but that's all I'll promise."

"Great."

I saw a policeman waving us over and said, "We're here. Gotta go."

I hung up, telling Brett to pull over. I boiled out of the car and said, "I'm with the Department of State Bureau of Diplomatic Security. Looking for the US ambassador, because we've had a threat against our embassy."

In no way did I want to mention a threat against the pope. That would guarantee I went nowhere. The cop's eyes went wide, and he said, "I donno, I donno."

On the outskirts of the square, outside of the barriers, I saw someone waving a US flag. I said, "That's my contact. You can follow me, but I'm going there."

Brett and Aaron exited, and we started walking, the cop talking into his radio. I saw he was Italian police, which meant he wasn't part of the Vatican.

I reached the flag-waver, a young guy of about thirty. He said, "You Nephilim Logan? DSS?"

I said, "Yes. That's me. Where's the ambassador?"

"He's inside. What's the trouble?"

"I need to get into the ceremony, right now. I don't have time to explain. Do you have identification or a badge that can do that?"

"Well, yeah, but I need to know why."

I started to tell him why—namely that it would save him from an ass-kicking—when two distinct *thumps* came from the basilica.

And then the people started screaming.

91

Jacob got in line behind Carlos and Devon, the Holy Father less than thirty meters away. The Lost Boys began shuffling forward like a row of condemned men walking to their final resting place.

He watched the Father, ignoring the men around him. Watched him smile, small glasses on his face, joy in his manner. He wondered if the man could feel death coming. Wondered if he knew it and yet did nothing because of his stature. He'd read about previous attacks, with each pope declaring divine intervention that they lived, with one saying, "My defense is my cross." Did they really believe that? Did they honestly think that they were above death?

They crept closer and Jacob whispered into the ear of Carlos, "Remember the delay of the detonator. You must time it. Two seconds after release."

Carlos nodded.

The Holy Father continued to meet the line, and Jacob saw real happiness. Not make-believe political posturing because he had to be there. He felt a twinge of guilt and reflexively looked for Father Brimm. He was nowhere to be found.

They were now twenty people back, and one of the suited men with an earpiece came forward, whispering into the Holy Father's ear. He nodded, but didn't break his connection with the boys visiting. Another came forward, whispering to a prelate on the side. Then a third. Then a man with an earpiece came toward the line. Searching.

We've been discovered.

He said, "Carlos, this is it. Go now. You first, to kill the line of defense, then Devon, to kill the pope."

The kid behind him poked him in the back, saying, "Quiet. You're not supposed to be talking." Never even hearing the words.

Carlos and Devon separated from the line and began walking forward in a rapid manner. Jacob caught movement from the security, but knew it would be too late to do anything. They were too close.

Carlos saw the protective detail closing in and darted forward, screaming, "*Allahu Akbar!*" The security men coalesced like flies to sugar, beating him to the ground. He waited until all were on him, then detonated.

A huge explosion rent the air, and body parts were flung throughout the cathedral, the noise stunning everyone. Devon began running straight at the Holy Father, his hand held high, shouting the same Arabic phrase.

The remaining security men leapt on the Holy Father, three pulling him to the ground and two standing in front, shooting small submachine guns they'd produced from under their jackets. Devon took a staggering amount of rounds, but remained on his feet, still moving forward. His device detonated fifteen feet away, disintegrating his body and shredding the men surrounding the target.

On the ground with everyone else, Jacob realized instantly what had happened. Devon had mistimed the chemicals, expecting to reach the pope on the run. The bullets had slowed him enough to cause it to fire early. Among the screaming and crying, he stared at the mass of flesh of his friend, split neatly in half, his upper torso remarkably intact, his head looking back at Jacob, eyes open.

Jacob stood, preparing to run screaming out of the basilica with everyone else. He took one last look at the altar, surveying the carnage.

And saw the Holy Father move.

Shoshana was running flat-out, retracing the path that Omar had taken out of Trastevere. Jennifer matched her stride for stride, two steps back.

They ran down the sidewalk next to the Tiber River, reaching the bridge for the island and sprinting forward, keeping a pace that made Jennifer's lungs burn.

Moving across the spit of land, drawing stares from the tourists mingling about, Jennifer held up on the north side of the river, seeing a highway paralleling it, but nothing going into the interior.

Shoshana said, "Why are we stopping? Get us to the Colosseum."

Jennifer manipulated her phone, saying, "Trying to find a shortcut. Last contact was at Via dei Fori Imperiali, the road leading to the Colosseum. He's gone the long way around the Forum and is now headed east. We follow and we'll never reach him in time."

Exasperated, Shoshana said, "We'll never reach him sitting here. He's walking. We're running."

Jennifer put away her phone and said, "Yeah, you're right. He took the long way because there is no short way. The Forum stretches through this area. No roads. Let's go."

Shoshana said, "Wait, he's walking around the Forum because there's no road through it? And if we find a way, we can beat him?"

"Yes, but I just told you, there isn't a road that does that."

"There isn't one for someone carrying a bomb. Plenty of ways for people who run like deer. Show me the phone."

Jennifer did, and Shoshana said, "Satellite. Like you did before."

Jennifer manipulated the application, waiting on the resolution to come through. When it did, Shoshana said, "Right through there. We go straight up into that neighborhood. The road ends, which means it butts up into the Forum. We get into that area, it's wide-open. We start running, and we can cut him off."

Jennifer said, "It'll be fenced off. Protected."

Shoshana said, "Are you kidding me? You don't think we can get over?"

Jennifer said, "Well, yeah, I can climb it, but we don't have a ticket. . . ." Her voice trailed off as she realized how stupid that sounded.

Shoshana grinned at her. "We'll buy a ticket later, to make you feel better. Let's go."

They took off, loping forward at the same pace, chewing up the ground, running south, away from the path of Omar. They passed a park and cut east, now running directly toward the Forum, the Colosseum beyond. They eventually hit the outskirts and found it wasn't a simple fence. It was a brick wall reaching ten feet, covered in vines.

Shoshana ran down it for a hundred meters, then darted into a piazza, seeing benches and families enjoying the sunshine, a church on the end.

She stopped, hands on her hips, breathing heavily. "Shit. We can't get over that. Can't your phone tell us when we're stupid?" She paced a bit, then said, "We're committed now. We keep going deeper. Find a gap."

Jennifer looked at the wall and said, "I can get you over that."

"You mean you hoist me, leaving you here?"

Jennifer smiled. "No, Carrie. I mean I'll follow after I hoist you up."

"What the hell are you talking about? No way can you climb that."

Jennifer looked left and right, seeing a couple of pedestrians, but no cops. She moved to the wall and knelt down, lacing her hands together. "Let's go."

Shoshana shook her head, then sprinted to the wall, planting her foot in Jennifer's hands and leaping up. Jennifer exploded off the ground, throwing her higher, bearing the brunt of Shoshana's weight. She felt it lighten and watched Shoshana pull herself over the top and flip to the other side.

A teenager to the left, eyes wide, said, "What are you doing?"

Jennifer darted away from the wall, then faced it, coiling her legs, her arms swinging back and forth with an unconscious count.

She took two breaths and said, "I'm saving the world."

She sprinted as fast as she could, hitting the wall full-on, catching the rough brick with the ball of her foot and toe-kipping higher. She snagged the vines draping from the top, pulling herself up until she could muscle her way over. She paused on the apex, catching her breath, and saw the teenager below giving her a thumbs-up, beaming.

She rolled over to the other side and dropped. With an amazed expression, Shoshana said, "So that's why they call you Koko?"

Jennifer said, "There's always a little truth in a callsign, Carrie."

Shoshana grinned and took off running. Now inside the fabled Roman Forum, they had unimpeded access to reach the Colosseum. Beating the merchant of death to his destination.

92

Jacob stood, his ears ringing, the blood coating the teenagers in front of him and the screams filling the chamber. He shook his head and focused on the altar. The few unwounded Vatican prelates were slowly getting their wits about them. The security was in disarray, one staggering about, his face a bloody mess. Another was leaning over the Holy Father, pulling him to his feet. Alive.

Shocked, Jacob was momentarily immobilized at the sight. Devon and Carlos were split apart, their blood and body parts dripping down the marble pillars, and the pope *lived*. His two friends had sacrificed themselves for *nothing*. He couldn't believe the injustice. *No, no, no.* A bloodlust rage filled him, blotting out everything but the desire to slaughter the target. His mission came into focus. He was to be the *shahid*.

He pushed a kid out of the way, staggering toward the altar. He slipped in Devon's blood, but didn't even register the fact. He gathered steam, charging toward the confusion.

He crossed a torn body wearing a suit, the man's earpiece now askew, his eyes looking skyward, unseeing. He pulled the submachine gun from his grasp and kept going. He reached the Holy Father and put the barrel against the security man trying to help him to his feet. He pulled the trigger. The man's head exploded, and he dropped, collapsing on the floor like his skeleton had turned to Jell-O.

Jacob stared into the eyes of the pope and said, "Time to pay the piper."

The Holy Father did nothing but look back at him, showing absolutely no fear.

Jacob heard a pounding of feet and saw an avalanche of security running toward him, all with weapons drawn. He reached the moment of decision. Kill the pope right now. Do the mission. Take the pain, just as he had in the past, when the Christian monsters had tortured him in the white house.

The lead man saw the situation and screamed at the others to halt. They did, in a ragged line, all weapons aimed at him. Jacob held the gun to the Holy Father's head. He felt the tension in the trigger.

He pulled the Father's head up, and all that he'd done and seen went through his mind. All that he wanted to be, and all that had been taken from him.

The Kurd he'd killed burst forth. His neck. The knife. Cutting through the tendons. The blood. The twitching. The absolute control over life and death.

Ringo had been right. That killing was different. It had been his introduction to hell, and now he was on an inexorable path to eat the brimstone. All because of his commitment to the Islamic State.

It was too late to stop the slide.

Remember Devon. Remember Carlos. Pull the trigger.

His life was decided. He started to squeeze, then paused.

Enough.

Devon and Carlos had chosen their path, but he didn't have to follow. No way would he be a *shahid*. He wasn't dying for the Islamic State. He wasn't sacrificing himself for some sick bastards who burned people alive.

Fuck them.

He wasn't dying at all. He jerked the Holy Father to his feet, snarling, "Tell them to back off."

They stood, the security detail surrounding them watching in shock. The Holy Father was in disarray, his head now shorn of the famous papal attire, the blood from the men that protected him coating his official robes, but he was calm. He said, "Lower your weapons."

The men did. Jacob jabbed the submachine gun against the pope's back and said, "Walk."

His Holiness looked at Jacob and said, "Where? Where are we to go?

You can't escape from in here. Look at the men. Look at the weapons. Give up."

Jacob snarled, "Start moving."

He hid behind the pope's body and shouted, "Back the fuck up!"

The security men stumbled backward. At that moment, Jacob knew nobody was in charge. He was looking at a phalanx of individuals, all afraid to make a decision.

He pushed the Holy Father forward and turned in a circle, searching for what he'd seen on the Internet. The statue of Saint Longinus. The man who'd put the spear into Jesus Christ as he'd hung nailed to the cross.

He didn't reflect on the irony of his search, only that the sculpture of Saint Longinus, carved into the pillar holding the dome aloft in Saint Peter's Basilica, held the stairwell to the grottoes below. A means of escape.

He found it and said, "Get moving, old man. We're leaving now."

Walking at a brisk pace down Via dei Fori Imperiali, Omar saw the Colosseum ahead, the skyline it presented unmistakable. He checked his watch, and knew he was late. Doing the attack after the one in the Vatican would accomplish nothing. He began skipping forward, almost running, the duffel bag slapping his leg.

As he got closer, paralleling the Forum, he was accosted every step of the way by bloodsuckers looking to sell him tours. He brushed them off and kept moving. He saw the chaos around the road surrounding the Colosseum and began searching for the entrance. Looking for the means to kill the largest number possible.

He jogged forward, crossing the street, the ancient columns from the past towering above him, a creation he knew the Islamic State could never replicate.

They adhered to the same brutality the Roman Empire showcased in this very Colosseum, but that is where the similarities ended. There would be no grand architecture from the Islamic State. The duality of that thought caused him no angst. Creation of something profound wasn't in his makeup. The caliph alone was all that mattered.

He walked toward the entrance, the duffel bag against his leg. He saw the line, behind a fence. He approached the gate, and found he could enter. The checkpoint processing tickets was deeper in. He passed by a uniformed guard that paid him no mind. He kept walking, the lines getting more robust, the target getting better.

He paused, not wanting to get too far in without a means of escape. He turned around, making sure he could still make it out after initiating the chemicals, and saw someone running toward him.

The woman he'd held under his knife.

93

I heard the screams start and knew we were either too late, or about to be the heroes. I hoped it was the latter. The man from the State Department seemed incapacitated, the explosions and shouting causing his mouth to open and close like a fish out of water. I grabbed him by the collar and said, "How do we get into the basilica without fighting the crowds? How do we get in?"

His eyes rolled left and right, looking for a way out of the disaster, following the people fleeing. I slapped him on the cheek. "Wake the fuck up! Get me in. Right now."

He said, "The grotto. That will bypass everyone. It'll put you into the heart of the basilica."

I said, "Lead the way, but do it on the run."

We took off, fighting through the throng in Saint Peter's Square, most having no idea what had happened, but a few recognizing something was terribly wrong, causing panic in the others.

We went to the right of the facade and hit a security checkpoint, the guard manning it unsure of what was going on, but damn sure that nobody was getting past. My guide waved his badge, and was rebuffed. I pulled my weapon and said, "Let my team in. Someone's trying to kill the pope."

His eyes popped open like he'd touched an electrical socket, and he started shouting, reaching for his pistol in a holster, thinking I was a threat. I hammered him with the suppressor on the end of my weapon, dropping him to the flagstone.

The aide looked at me in absolute fear. I said, "Show me the way. Right fucking now."

He nodded and turned toward a courtyard to the right of the facade, moving slowly. I slapped the back of his head and said, "Quicker, damn it."

We started running, going through the courtyard and entering a hallway that turned into a catacomb. We wound through marbled corridors full of tombs, side cutouts housing the corporal history of the Catholic Church. I heard noise to our front and jerked our guide behind me. He fell to the floor and started whimpering, crawling toward an alcove.

We were at a turn in the corridor, the grotto splitting left and right, the noise coming from the left. I crouched, waving Brett forward. He came abreast, kneeling next to a rope barricade protecting a casket.

Aaron came to my right, saying, "This isn't going to play well in the press."

I said, "Because you're a Jew?"

"No. Because you're a walking disaster."

Jennifer and Shoshana reached the square of the Colosseum, seeing a massive amount of people milling about, some waiting to enter, others just buying souvenirs. They had nothing other than the last known location of Omar, indicating a movement toward this location, and Jennifer was beginning to believe that thought was incorrect.

Now outside of radio range, she tried to call Pike on her cell, and got no answer, which didn't surprise her. She called Knuckles, asking for another lock-on for the phone, but he was on final approach to the airfield, forced to land. They were out of options.

She said, "We've got no help from the Taskforce. I don't know what else to do."

Shoshana said, "He's here."

Jennifer looked at her and saw the weird glow. She said, "Shoshana, where? Why do you think that?"

"Because he's going to kill a lot of people. I can feel it."

There were about two hundred souls in the square, but Shoshana began walking to the entrance with a destination in mind. Jennifer said, "Where are you going?"

"To him. He's inside."

"What? How do you know? Shoshana, this is crazy."

Shoshana said nothing, entering the small alley that led to the ticket booth.

They moved forward together, Shoshana bumping people out of the way and drawing sharp comments. Jennifer apologized for her, then tried to get her to stop. She reached forward to tap her on the shoulder, and saw Omar at the same time Shoshana did. He was deep inside the line for the Colosseum, carrying a small duffel bag.

She hissed, but Shoshana was already moving, the dark angel blossoming out like tendrils of black oil dropped in water.

Jennifer grabbed her arm, saying, "Wait," and Shoshana broke free, running flat-out through the line of people. Jennifer saw Omar turn around, saw his eyes grow wide, then him reach into the duffel bag.

She pulled her weapon, the people around her starting to react, shouting and running away. Omar held up something that looked like an Apple MagSafe adapter and pressed a button, yelling at Shoshana to stop. She did, panting, in front of him.

He said, "You take one more step, and we all die."

Jennifer closed the distance and took a knee, aiming at his head. He said, "This is a dead man's switch. You kill me, and it goes off."

The crowds running away and screaming, the chaos absolute, Shoshana looked him in the eye and said, "So what now? You walk away?"

Omar smiled and said, "Yes. Exactly. I walk away carrying this bomb."

Jennifer kept her barrel on his head and said, "No way. There will be enough police here shortly. You're going nowhere."

Omar looked at Shoshana and said, "She doesn't understand the commitment. You do." He raised the plastic device in his hand and shouted, "Tell her I *will* let go. Nobody needs to die."

Shoshana said, "I warned you about your path. Someday, someone would be holding the knife on your neck. And now it's me."

Jennifer saw a flicker of confusion, then Omar said, "Tell her I'll set this thing off. Tell her I'm not afraid to die. I *am* the Islamic State."

Shoshana said, "Yes, I know. And I'm the one who will kill you."

Jennifer watched Shoshana launch herself at him, wrapping his body up and forcing it on top of the duffel bag. She wrestled for the device in Omar's hands, and Jennifer thought it was for control. It wasn't.

Staring into Omar's eyes, a wicked grin on her face, Shoshana pried his hand loose from the detonator.

Jennifer screamed, "No!" then dove backward, holding her hands over her head. A second later it went off, with a *crack* that reverberated through the ancient hall. Omar was split apart. Shoshana was launched into the air, flying across the hall and slamming into stone. She crumpled in a heap.

94

Jacob dragged the pope down the stairs, into the grotto where the Catholic saints of the past were laid to rest. He knew it exited outside the basilica, knew exactly where it went from the massive research he'd done.

He wanted to live. That's what permeated his soul. The Islamic State had long since faded to the background. Now all that remained was escape, and he had the means to do so.

The Holy Father.

The man offered no resistance, walking forward without a fight. They passed the tombs of all the popes before, and the Holy Father spoke.

"Why do you do this? What can you get from it?"

Jacob said, "You of all people know why. You do nothing but profess goodness, and yet you perpetuate cruelty. I should kill you right now."

"But you do not. Why is that?"

Jacob said nothing. They reached a turn in the catacombs, the light from outside spilling in, and he saw three men with weapons. He snapped back, dragging the Holy Father, the adrenaline ricocheting through him.

On his knees, the Father said, "My son, I don't know what you have done with your life, but you will be forgiven. This isn't the end."

Jacob grabbed him by the neck and said, "Don't beg for your life, old man. Don't do that. I'll kill you right now."

The Holy Father looked at him, and Jacob saw nothing but pity. No fear. No pain. He said, "Kill me if you wish. It will do no good for your soul."

Jacob said, "My soul is my own. You don't own it, and neither does Islam."

The Father said, "I understand. More than you know."

Jacob gave a giddy laugh and said, "Get up. We're moving out of here. You get your wish. You're my salvation."

He turned the corner and saw a man with ice-blue eyes like Omar. And the same conviction.

I saw the two come around the corner and wondered about my luck. How on earth could this jackass from State have led me right into the fight?

I put my sights on Jacob's head and said the usual. "Put down your gun. This doesn't have to end in a bad way."

I heard "Fuck you. Let me out. I'm going right down this hall."

Looking at Brett, I mouthed, *Any ideas?*

He shook his head.

Every hostage situation comes about because of one of two reasons: either they took the hostage because they intended to, for a specific purpose, or they took the hostage because something had fallen apart, like a bank robbery or liquor store holdup gone bad. I was now dealing with a hybrid. Clearly, they had intended to kill the pope, but now this guy was running with him after the fact. Like he was trying to escape. I decided I'd just wait it out. Sooner or later, the Vatican police would come charging down the catacombs.

I realized that might get the pope killed.

I turned to the State guy, still curled in the fetal position. "Get your ass out of here and get some tactical guys. No standard police. Get someone who can shoot and knows when to pull the trigger."

He left and I turned back to Jacob, peeping out from behind the bend in the corridor. I saw his eyes, and recognized that he was serious, but not crazy. He held no fear. No hesitation. He was here to live or kill.

I said, "Jacob, I know who you are. I know what you went through. What I don't know is why you're doing this."

He waved the weapon, and I saw it was an HK MP-7, telling me he'd taken it off of someone dead above. Which meant there was some carnage, and he knew he was lost because of it.

He said, "I'm not a monster. I didn't want to kill that guy in Syria. I was forced to. I want nothing more to do with the Islamic State."

Every word was a revelation, every syllable something that a trained negotiator could use. Unfortunately, I wasn't a trained negotiator. I was a gunslinger.

"Jacob, the only way to prove you're not a monster is to walk away. Right now."

I heard the Holy Father speak, and worried he would only make the situation worse. Then I wasn't so sure.

Jacob soaked in the words, appearing to hear them. I had hope. He returned to me and said, "I will kill this man. I will."

I said, "I know you will. I believe you. I just don't want you to."

He said, "Then back the fuck off! Let me out."

I looked into his eyes and said, "You know where this is going. Sooner or later there's going to be someone who shows up to negotiate. Someone who'll blow smoke up your ass. I'm not that guy. Leave him alone. Or die."

Jacob cursed and pulled back behind the corridor. The Holy Father said, "He's right, you know. They *will* kill you."

Jacob said, "Does it look like I care about that?"

"I don't know what you care about. I can tell you I care what happens to you."

Jacob whirled on him and said, "You don't give a shit what happens to me. You're only worried about dying. And I might make that a reality."

The Holy Father held out his sleeve, showing the blood, and said, "I've seen the evil you do. And I still care."

Jacob said, "Why? Why would you give a damn what happens to me?"

"I care because I'm human. Are you not?"

"Yeah, I'm human. And I don't need the holy mumbo jumbo. If I had a soul, it was burned long ago."

"We're all born of sin, yet we can all be forgiven. Yesterday is done, but your soul is pure tomorrow."

Jacob snarled, "You haven't seen the 'pureness' I have. You haven't witnessed what was done to me in the name of Christ, or what I've done in the name of Islam. It is not pure, I promise."

The Holy Father stared deep into his eyes and said, "Don't confuse the fallibility of man with the grace of God."

The Holy Father's gaze was steady, and Jacob saw it was true. Saw the depravity of the Islamic State through the kindness in the eyes of the man he was supposed to kill. The waste of his life seeped through, the totality of how he had been cheated. He had one thing left to give, and it wouldn't be for them. He wouldn't destroy what was good with a hand bathed in evil.

His eyes watering, his face contorted in pain, he said, "Father, where were you?"

Before an answer could be given, he grabbed the pope's collar and dragged him out into the corridor. Jacob placed the weapon against the pope's head and shouted, "Time's up! Do it now."

He saw the muzzle flash a millisecond before the subsonic round split his head open.

95

The room was as quiet as a tomb, the heartbeat monitor the only noise. A couple of blips a second, dinging over and over until it really began to annoy me.

I know it was callous, but Jesus, couldn't they turn the damn beeps off? It was bad enough I had to see Shoshana wrapped up in bandages like a character in a bad soap opera. I looked at her sleeping form, the thought bringing an incongruous bit of humor. *She'll probably wake up and say she is an evil twin. Or she has amnesia.*

Then I remembered she might not wake up at all.

I heard the door open, and Aaron returned, looking haggard, a three-day growth of beard on his face. I said, "She's still beeping. Can't be all bad."

He smiled, a cracked thing without any real joy, and said, "She's always made me wait. Why should this be any different?"

I said, "She'll wake up. You know it and I know it."

He said, "I don't know it. I wish I did, but I don't."

I looked at her bandaged face and said, "I do. She *will*."

He said, "Thanks for the spell. I needed to get some food. Get out of here."

"I can stay. This wasn't a chore."

He said, "I know. I appreciate it."

He sat down and rubbed his face, his eyes squeezed shut. I could tell he was blaming himself for letting her go. He knew what was driving her forward. He'd let her walk out of that house with Jennifer knowing she was going to kill Omar, but he'd never thought she would sacrifice herself to do it.

And neither had I.

I'd be lying if I said I didn't feel guilt, in more ways than one.

We'd left Saint Peter's Basilica as the heroes of the world, having saved the Holy Father from certain death. Anonymous, but heroes nonetheless. The Vatican's version of a counterassault team arrived right after Jacob had been killed, and in the ensuing chaos, we vanished. They were taking credit for eliminating Jacob, and that was fine with me.

I'd been the one to pull the trigger, splitting Jacob's head apart with a 300 Blackout round, hitting him right above the nose. But I knew I hadn't saved anyone.

Jacob had searched the marble corridor with his eyes, and then had locked on me. He'd shouted his command, and placed his hand on the trigger, staring at me the whole time. I knew who had really spared the pope.

It was a difficult choice, and one I understood had to be made, but it left a confusing mishmash of emotions. The man had used me to kill himself, and I'd done it.

Initially, I'd had no issues with the shot. It was just one more, like the man I'd eliminated on the steps in Tirana. Later on, deep in the night, when the bad man came calling, I did. In the safe house, I'd woken up in a sweat, thrashing about, Jacob's eyes condemning me.

Jennifer had felt the motion and had woken up as well. She said, "What is it? What's wrong?"

I said, "Nothing. Nothing at all."

She'd sagged back into the mattress, not believing me. She said, "Talk to me."

"Don't have anything to say."

She remained silent for a moment, then turned to me. She said, "I do."

"What?"

Her eyes soulful, she said, "I think I killed Christine, and now Shoshana. I don't think I want to do this anymore."

I snapped fully awake. "What the hell are you talking about? Christine's doing fine. She's not going to die. And Shoshana made her own decision. Right?"

Her eyes now on the ceiling, she said, "Either way, I could have prevented both, and I didn't. Same as Ringo. Same as Hussein. I don't like this responsibility. I don't want it."

I said, "I know. I don't either."

She'd leaned up on an elbow, searching to see if I was just placating her. I was not.

I said, "We live in a violent world, with evil people who have no compunction about slaughtering innocents. Someone has to stop them. Nobody wants the responsibility over life and death, but someone has to take it. And that *someone* is us."

She said, "What happened in the grotto?"

I turned my head away and said, "I killed him. Period. Nothing else."

In a soft tone she said, "Nothing else. But everything to him."

I looked at her and said, "Yes. I caused a human being to cease to exist. I took his life, because he wanted me to. He made me kill him, and I don't like it. But liking's got nothing to do with the fact that he deserved to die."

She said, "Maybe we need a break from this. I don't want to become Shoshana. I don't want to crave a killing."

I sat up and turned on the lamp next to our bed. "Don't ever say that. Ever. Shoshana doesn't crave killing, any more than I do. She's just good at her job. Same as me. Same as you. Wishing evil won't come doesn't make it so. We did good today. Omar would have killed a hundred people. *You* stopped that. Saving Christine allowed us to alert the Vatican. It's what made the plan fail. *You* did that. Together, we prevented the biggest propaganda coup the Islamic State would ever achieve, which in turn will prevent more radicalization. Prevent more death."

I saw her eyes water at the statement. She said, "Shoshana is going to die. Because of me. I should have fired the bullet. I should have stayed to help her."

I said, "No, she's not. She won't. She has the best medical care in Italy. If you'd have fired, the vest would have gone off in the open air instead of with Omar lying on top of it."

Unlike when Christine was shot, the explosion at the Colosseum had triggered a massive response, with ambulances and first responders flooding the area. Shoshana had been immediately whisked away in an ambulance, and was now being treated as a hero, an innocent civilian who'd managed to stop an attack. Or at least mitigate its effects.

Jennifer had fled, hiding her weapon and running from the scene to protect our cover. She was a coward in her mind, and now she was being eaten alive by it.

Jennifer said, "If she dies, I'm done. Forever."

I'd said, "She's not going to die. She's waiting on a date from me."

Jennifer had laughed, but there was little pleasure in it.

Inside the hospital room, looking at Shoshana's broken form, I wasn't so sure I was right.

Staring at her, Aaron said, "I've got to find a different line of work."

The remark reminded me of Jennifer. Of leaving the fighting to someone else. I said, "Do you think you could do that?"

He said, "No. I don't know anything else. Not a lot of jobs for Israeli assassins in the world."

An idea grew, building steam in my head, but it was absolutely insane. I worked for the United States government, conducting operations solely on behalf of my countrymen, and the Israeli's motivations would always be questioned. But Aaron and Shoshana were some of the best I'd ever seen.

I said, "What's your real relationship with Israel? Do you honestly not work for the Mossad?"

He caught my tone and paused before answering. He said, "It's what I told you. I didn't lie. I'm independent now. They hire me for a contract, I work, but when that one's done, no more money. No more swapping secrets. Honesty, I don't think I can do this as a business. Not enough work to eat, and I'm definitely not getting paid for the risk. Why do you ask?"

I said, "How would you like to work for an archeological company? On a retainer basis? Give you a little cushion in between jobs. But our retainer would supersede Israel's interests."

He chuckled and said, "I'd like that, but I need to talk to my partner first."

He thought I was kidding, but I wasn't. I said, "And when she says yes, you'll give me a call?"

"What makes you think she will?"

"Because she's sweet on me. No offense."

He laughed for real, the first time he'd done so since Shoshana had been admitted. He started to retort, and Shoshana's arm moved. We saw the movement, holding our breath. It twitched again, and her eyes opened.

We both leapt up, Aaron shouting, "Nurse, nurse!"

I leaned over her bed, staring into her eyes, disappointed to see them unfocused, with a pale reflection, like a wax figure looking back. She blinked, and I saw her conscious mind coalescing.

She blinked again, the recognition gathering, her brain starting to engage. I said, "I told you to only follow him. I can't ever trust you."

A ghost of a smile flitted across her face. She glanced down the length of her broken body, seeing the tubes running out and the bandages. She said, "I didn't get to wash my hands. But you still owe me a date."

ACKNOWLEDGMENTS

Before getting to the kind folks who helped me write this novel, I'd like to acknowledge the most important person of all. That would be you, the reader. Without you, Pike Logan would have been banished to the trash bin of history long ago. This is my eighth novel—a feat I would have said was ridiculous a mere four years ago—and it is a direct result of you. Some writers will tell you that they craft their work solely for the art, regardless of the enjoyment of the reader, but that is not me. Having someone enjoy my work is the sole reason I write, and without you, I would go back to security work without a second glance, which would aggravate the hell out of my wife. Truthfully, I still don't consider myself a writer, even with eight novels under my belt. Describing myself as such seems arrogant, and I always fumble my words when I'm asked what I do for a living. I still can't believe it's true, and I have a single person to thank for it. You.

The Insider Threat has been one of the hardest novels I've ever tackled, precisely because it deals with a threat that is very real and very current. Predicting the twists and turns in the Middle East is almost guaranteeing failure, and predicting the fight against ISIS is even worse. Hell, by the time this goes to press, ISIS may no longer even exist, but I don't think that will happen. I decided to stick with it, focusing on what I knew about its aspirations and what I believed would be the worst threat—namely, jihadists with no background or profile coming home. At one point, near the end, I was at a complete loss as to what to do. I knew how the last page was going to read, but I had no idea how to get there. Every action seemed too easy, too coincidental, or too convoluted, and I'd painted myself into a corner with respect to the timeline of various events. Luckily for me, I know a James Island redneck named Beau. He invited me over to his house—my wife was more than glad to get rid of my complaining for a night—and after a case of beer and about eight hours around a fire pit, him bouncing ideas off me and me doing the same in return, I had my ending.

I do a lot of Internet/book research before I travel to an area, and invariably, that research is upended by on-the-ground information from a local. In Albania, it was a bartender at the Sheraton Hotel in Tirana. After about thirty minutes of talking to him, I threw out the guidebooks and started taking notes on Blloku and Tirana Park. Venice and Rome were a little easier, although my guide in the Vatican grew curious as to why I couldn't care less about the Sistine Chapel and only wanted to know about the pope's activities inside Saint Peter's Basilica. I finished that bit of research, and then when it came time to write, I couldn't, for the life of me, remember where the entrance was to the grotto below Saint Peter's. All I had was a picture of the stairwell, which did no good. Internet research was horrible, with most responses saying, "It's hard to find—but well worth the trip! And it's FREE!" Which made me feel like an idiot, because I'd done the walk and now couldn't find the stairwell. I was saved by another author. After begging anyone for help, author Meg Gardiner—who writes a pretty mean thriller, by the way—actually had a map from a 1960 Michelin guide. And she scanned it and sent it to me, saving the day. Physical accuracy is important, but technical aspects are even more so. A special thanks to Kurt, an agent on the president's protective detail of the Secret Service, for pointing me in the right direction with respect to the pope's security apparatus. While I would never want to compromise anything, I did want to get that right.

Combat technology continues its march forward, and with the US military's continuing quest for a new primary weapon, I figured it was time for a change in the Taskforce, both in weapon system and choice of caliber. The "black rifle" is chambered in just about any round imaginable, but I finally settled on the 300 Blackout round for reasons expressed in the book, and that was an easy choice. The weapon was a different story. There are literally hundreds of excellent builders of AR-type rifles, and I got to see plenty of them while doing research at SHOT Show in Las Vegas. I eventually settled on the Primary Weapon System MK109 because of its unique piston system, combining the reliability aspects of the AK-47 into an AR platform. Thanks to Bill at PWS for walking me through it. Believe it or not, suppressors are just as complex, some good and some better. GEMTECH suppressors are at the top of the pyramid, and I'm indebted to Casey for showing me the ins and outs of how his GMT-300BLK tames the noise of the Blackout round in both super and subsonic. I liked the setup so much, I'm building my own PWS/GEMTECH weapon system. Chambered in 300 Blackout, of course.

I'm not Catholic, and I'm indebted to Mike—a retired sergeant major and wayward, lapsed Catholic—for helping me craft the final scene with the pope. I was walking a fine line between cardboard, cartoonish characterization on one side and creating something unbelievable to anyone who understood Catholicism on the other. We worked through that small bit of dialogue over and over, and I appreciate the help. Any hate mail can go to him. . . .

As always, a huge thank-you to my agent, John Talbot, and the entire Dutton Taskforce crew. Ben, Jess, and Liza—Pike Logan would be working a spatula in the food service industry without your incredible efforts.

ABOUT THE AUTHOR

Brad Taylor, Lieutenant Colonel (ret.), is a twenty-one-year veteran of the U.S. Army Infantry and Special Forces, including eight years with the 1st Special Forces Operational Detachment—Delta, popularly known as the Delta Force. Taylor retired in 2010 after serving more than two decades and participating in Operation Enduring Freedom and Operation Iraqi Freedom, as well as classified operations around the globe. His final military post was as Assistant Professor of Military Science at the Citadel. His first seven Pike Logan thrillers were *New York Times* bestsellers. He lives in Charleston, South Carolina.